A CHARLIE SALTER OMNIBUS

ERIC WRIGHT

A CHARLIE SALTER OMNIBUS

THE NIGHT THE GODS SMILED

SMOKE DETECTOR

DEATH IN THE OLD COUNTRY

Castle Street Mysteries

THE DUNDURN GROUP
TORONTO

Printer: Webcom

National Library of Canada Cataloguing in Publication Data

Wright, Eric
    A Charlie Salter omnibus / Eric Wright.

(A Castle Street mystery)
Contents: The night the gods smiled — Smoke detector — Death in the old country
ISBN 1-55002-475-2

I. Title. II. Title: Death in the old country. III. Title: Night the gods smiled. IV. Title: Smoke detector. V. Series: Castle Street mystery.

PS8595.R58C42 2003   C813'.54   C2003-905003-3

1   2   3   4   5   07   06   05   04   03

THE CANADA COUNCIL | LE CONSEIL DES ARTS
FOR THE ARTS | DU CANADA
SINCE 1957 | DEPUIS 1957

ONTARIO ARTS COUNCIL
CONSEIL DES ARTS DE L'ONTARIO

We acknowledge the support of the Canada Council for the Arts and the Ontario Arts Council for our publishing program. We also acknowledge the financial support of the Government of Canada through the Book Publishing Industry Development Program and The Association for the Export of Canadian Books, and the Government of Ontario through the Ontario Book Publishers Tax Credit program, and the Ontario Media Development Corporation's Ontario Book Initiative.

Printed and bound in Canada.⊕
Printed on recycled paper.
www.dundurn.com

Dundurn Press
8 Market Street
Suite 200
Toronto, Ontario, Canada
M5E 1M6

Dundurn Press
2250 Military Road
Tonawanda NY
U.S.A. 14150

CONTENTS

THE NIGHT
THE GODS SMILED

For Valerie

Douglas College is an imaginary college in a real city. The characters, too, are fictitious, and any resemblance to real persons is entirely coincidental.

CHAPTER 1

Charlie Salter usually woke up badly these days. The worst mornings were those after nightmares when it took him whole minutes to realize that he was awake in his own bed, that he had not killed anyone or committed any other desolating or irretrievable act. There were other bad ways of waking, including times like this one when he lay waiting for the memories of all his failures to fade into the daylight. His first failures at school ('as soon as anything gets hard, you want to drop it'), his aborted university career ('you never finish anything'), his first, foolish marriage which collapsed within a year, and finally, his failure at his job. Salter was a police inspector; he had been an inspector for five years and he would almost certainly remain one for another fifteen years until he retired, a long way short of his early estimate of himself. It was this last failure which burned at the centre of his waking world, illuminating the others as they emerged from the base of his skull.

His eyes opened and he set about making the world liveable again. Beside him, Annie slept on, and Salter shoved his hand under her nightdress (one of his favourites, a thick cotton one she had inherited from her great-aunt, more erotic in the act of being lifted than any negligée) and stroked her, casually at first and then methodically, until she opened her eyes. He continued to caress her, waiting for her to pull out of reach or offer herself to him. She did neither, simply lay there under his hand, awake now, but with her eyes closed. He stopped, and she said, 'You are going to be late.'

He gave her one last squeeze, then pushed her on her back and rolled on to her, kissing her hard, grinding himself against her. This was all he needed. As his desire awoke (no failure here, yet) the ghosts of his other failures crept back underground for another day. Salter locked himself around her in a last playful hug, just for good measure, and sat up. The day could begin.

Downstairs, the door slammed. Seth, the younger of their two sons, had returned from his paper route. Seth was always back by seven o'clock. His fourteen-year-old brother, Angus, worked a double route and would arrive in another fifteen minutes. Salter swung his legs out of bed and stood up. 'You want some juice?' he asked. His wife turned away and pulled the covers up to her chin. 'Yes, please.'

In the kitchen, Seth was already eating the granary-floor sweepings that were traditional in the family, a mixture of grains and nuts that Annie compounded from ingredients bought at the St Lawrence market, inedible to Salter, but preferred by the boys to anything else. Salter grunted at his son and poured some orange juice. He filled the kettle from the hot-water tap to make some coffee, and took the juice up to his wife.

She was half asleep again, and he stood watching her come to life. As everyone reminded him repeatedly, she was an astonishing forty-year-old, with the same absolutely flawless, fresh complexion, the same short, thick brown hair with no trace of grey, and most astonishing of all, the same brilliantly white teeth as she had when she was fourteen. She was not a beauty, but she was as perpetually radiant as an advertisement for her own cereal. As she sat up now and took her juice, the door slammed downstairs once again as Angus returned.

'Big day?' she asked.

'No big days now,' he said as he moved into the bathroom. 'As far as I know, all I have to do is show some New York cops around the office.' He lathered his face and tried to guess which of the seven disposable razors on the edge of the bathtub was the sharpest.

'It's nice,' she said. 'You are always home on time.'

'So you've said.' Salter found a razor with an edge and began stroking off the stubble. Behind him, he heard her get out of bed and go downstairs. He finished shaving and put on his plain-clothes uniform: clean shorts and socks, yesterday's shirt, blue tweed jacket, grey pants, dark blue tie with red geese, and black shoes. After a tour of the second floor in which he switched off six lights and one running tap, he went downstairs, switching off two more lights on the way, and opened the front door to let in the cat which was howling on the doorstep. The two boys were eating their cereal watching a cartoon on television, and Salter switched that off, too. The day had proceeded normally so far, from despair to irritation; there was only boredom still to come.

'Duncan called,' Annie said, when he was seated with the paper and his coffee. 'He wants to confirm we'll be down for July 1st.'

'I wouldn't mind doing something else this year. We have a month. I wouldn't mind a change,' Salter said.

There was an uproar. Seth pleaded, in a whine, 'O -come - on - Dad - let's - go - to - the - Island, - please -Dad - please,' and so on. Angus said, 'Uncle Duncan said I could crew for him this year in the regatta.'

'Did he?' Salter responded to this last. 'Well, maybe you two could go, and your mother and I will take a trip.'

Annie looked concerned, and seeing this, Salter became further irritated. 'I'd like to see something other than the bloody Island while I still have a few teeth left,' he said, shaking out his paper. 'We've been to the Island for four years in a row, and most years before that, too.'

Annie said, 'Dad's had a bad winter. He isn't very well.'

'All right, all right. Could we talk about it tonight?' He glared at the boys who were waiting for him to concede.

The Island was Prince Edward Island, Annie's

birthplace and for generations the home of her family, the Montagus, a family that was prominent, ancient, and soaked in Island tradition. Two of her brothers were lawyers, her uncle was a judge, and her father a doctor who had given up medicine to devote himself to his real estate interests. He owned two gas stations, a street of houses in Charlottetown, a small lumber-mill, a fish-canning plant, and a resort hotel, one of the oldest in the Maritimes. It was in this hotel that Salter had met Annie one summer as he passed through on the run from the wreckage of his first marriage. Annie was helping to manage the hotel in an undefined but concerned capacity; she had registered him, taken his order for dinner, chatted to him on the hotel porch after dinner, walked with him along the beach at sunset, and, after three days, refused to join him in bed, but made it clear that there were other places, and other times. He felt himself blessed that the Island princess had fallen for him, and persuaded her, after the season was over, to move to Toronto to be near him.

In Annie's family there was a tradition that the girls spend a year away from the Island before they settled down, rather like a year of finishing school—in Toronto or Montreal, or even London. Before they left the Island for this last, safe fling, the girls usually got engaged to apprentice lawyers or doctors, often their childhood sweethearts, and they returned, on time, when the internship or the articling period was up, to set up house and cottage. Annie shook her family by not making any arrangements for her return, and appalled them by wanting to marry a Toronto police sergeant, but they were full of goodwill, and when Annie brought Salter home to the family church the following spring, they welcomed him and made him an honorary member of the clan.

Each year after that the Salter family made the trip to

the Island for the vacation. Sometimes they drove, though it took three days; more often they went by train and were met by Annie's brother with one of the cars that the family lent them for the holiday, along with the keys to the family guest cottage.

Salter had married a tradition, a tradition that Annie guarded with the resolution of a Colonial among the natives. They used some of the family silver on Sundays (old Great-grandmother Montagu having apparently had place-settings for about three hundred, a collection that was broken up when she died), and about their Toronto house were a number of pieces of dark, polished furniture that Annie had inherited from the family homes (there were no harvest tables or other pine pieces, for such peasant artifacts had not formed part of the Montagu world for the last century and a half). Annie ritualized their lives slightly, too. Once a week, on Saturday, she made the porridge she ate as a child, although no one liked it much. She cooked fish chowders a lot and baked her own bread, but since the Island has no cuisine except salt cod and potatoes, their meals, except for one or two dishes which she had borrowed from the other maritime provinces, were otherwise the same as if she had been born in Calgary.

Annie's family were well-bred, tactful, and keen to include Annie's choice in the clan. They absorbed Salter's family into their world of fishing, sailing, riding and perpetual lobster suppers as if he had paid dues. Most of the time Salter was happy to enjoy their world. Occasionally, impatient and constricted by it, he felt like the lone Christian in-law in a family of Jews, conscious of his uncircumcised state, his slightly albino look, and of the determination of his relatives never to let him feel like an outsider.

'We have to let Duncan know soon if we aren't coming,' Annie said, as Salter rose from the table. The guest cottage was free to them whenever they liked, but it was much in demand during the season.

Salter felt himself on the brink of going too far. Clearly his words had upset everybody slightly. That was enough.

'Tell him we'll come,' he said. 'But entertain the possibility that you and I might take off for a week, would you? We could have a mad fling in Moncton.'

'You'll be late,' she said. 'Don't work too hard.'

'Didn't I tell you?'

'Yes, I know Charles, but couldn't we talk about that soon, too?'

'About quitting? Go to work for brother Duncan? I'm a policeman.' He cut off any reply by walking out of the door.

Salter's household was in an Anglo-Saxon ghetto off Oriole Parkway in an area that not so long ago had been North Toronto. But with the expansion of the city after the war, accompanied more recently by the building of the subway to the perimeter, his neighbourhood found itself at the heart of the city. When they first moved to the area, Salter had driven to work like everybody else; now he left his car at home for Annie and took the subway. Once, for a month, he had tried cycling to work long before it became fashionable, but the city sloped the wrong way for him, so that while the ride to work was easy, the sweating uphill return came at the end of a long day.

This morning the train was crowded as usual, but he managed to get the connecting door at the end of the car to lean against, a desirable spot because it let him read the paper with both hands. As usual, there were far more young girls on the train than any other single group—the roads to downtown were still packed with automobiles occupied by lone males—and when the car filled up, Salter found himself agreeably wedged between a tiny,

pretty, Japanese girl who smiled at him to show she saw
no danger in him, and, on the other side, an equally
small Caucasian girl with a clean-smelling, frizzy head
that came to just below his nose. He put down his paper
to avoid mussing either of the heads beneath him and
concentrated on looking fatherly. As the train arrived at
his station he looked down to make sure he didn't crunch
any little feet as he shuffled forward. Both girls looked up
and smiled at him. The English are right, he thought.
They *are* birds.

He arrived at the headquarters building, and was
greeted, as he was every morning, by Sergeant Frank
Gatenby, The Oldest Sergeant on the Force. Gatenby was
not really that; there were a number of sergeants older
than he, but he had earned the title by his white hair and
avuncular manner, which he had acquired before he was
forty. For a long time he had been The Oldest Constable
on the Force, then someone in a burst of sentimentality
recommended his promotion, and he had been given to
Salter as an assistant.

'Quite a lot on your plate this morning, sir,' he said.
'You'll be quite the busy boy today, all right.' He smiled
like a butler addressing the young master.

Salter took his mail: arrangements to be made for the
tidying up of Yonge Street for a visit by the Mayor of
Amsterdam (I'll put a tart in an armchair in all the shop
windows, he thought; that'll make his worship feel at
home); report requested on the value of police horses in
suburban plaza patrols; an inspection of gunshops to
make sure they weren't selling machine-guns to minors; a
committee to be formed to investigate complaints about
the police cafeteria; a request for information from the
Montreal police. A typical pile of rubbish.

For Salter had been put out to pasture. In one year he
had gone from being a power in the internal structure of

the Force to the status of a non-person, simply because he had backed the wrong man for Deputy Chief too enthusiastically and without regard for the consequences. Too young to retire, as his mentor had done, he was too old to shift careers. His future had been with the Force; now he had no future.

Salter looked at the last item. 'What's this, Frank? What information do they want in Montreal?'

'Who can say, sir?' Gatenby said. 'Who—can—say?' he repeated, pronouncing each word slowly as if at the conclusion of an intense metaphysical speculation that had occupied him all morning. 'They phoned before you came in. I'd only just arrived myself. A man was found dead in Montreal last weekend. One of ours. I mean a Toronto man, not one of our boys. There's a sergeant coming in on the Rapido after lunch, so Chiefie is putting him on to you.' 'Chiefie' in Gatenby baby talk was the Superintendent. The Deputy Chief of Police was called 'Deecee'. 'There's a lot going on today, sir, and I suppose they couldn't spare anyone else.' The sergeant smiled like a host of a children's TV show.

'When's he coming?'

'Two o'clock.'

'All right. Tell "Chiefie" I'll do it. You never know. It might be a real job.'

'Chiefie's up with the Commission, sir. I think he just thought you would.'

Salter always went out to lunch. He didn't enjoy the food or the horseplay in the canteen, which was probably, he thought, why he had been put on the committee to investigate complaints. On this day he walked through to Yonge Street to a store that sold out-of-town newspapers, bought the latest edition of the *Montreal Gazette* and took it into a coffee shop that specialized in corned beef sandwiches. He found what he wanted on page three, a small item to the effect that one David Summers, of Toronto, had been found with his skull fractured in a Montreal hotel room. Police were investigating. Nice, old-fashioned murder. Sex, money or what? Why did the Montreal boys need help already? He paid for his food and worked his way back across a number of parking lots to his office.

Gatenby met him at the door. 'He's here,' he whispered, pointing elaborately over his shoulder into the office. Salter, resisting the temptation to put his finger in his mouth and roll his eyes in wonder, contented himself with walking past the sergeant into his office and holding out his hand. Gatenby trotted behind. 'This is Inspector Salter, Sergeant,' he said from under Salter's elbow. 'Cup of tea, anyone? Coffee? No? I'll leave you alone, then, to have your chat.'

When the door closed, both men sat down.

'Someone got clobbered, I hear,' Salter offered. 'How can we help?'

'My name is O'Brien, Inspector. Henri O'Brien.'

'Sorry. Yes. Charlie Salter.'

O'Brien took some papers out of a large envelope he was carrying. 'What we would like is some help with the questioning.' He was a small, trim man, a few years younger than Salter, with close-cropped hair and a weatherbeaten look like a lumberjack or a sailor. He handed Salter one set of papers and kept a similar set for himself.

'Let's go over it first, Sergeant. I know nothing about it. Start at the top.'

O'Brien started to read in slightly accented English. 'David Arthur Summers. Age 47. Married. One daughter. Professor at Douglas College. Found dead in the Plaza del Oro Hotel on Saturday, May 18, at 11 a.m. by the maid. Cause of death—fractured skull, probably caused by a whisky bottle found on the floor. Victim naked except for a dressing-gown. Room contained the clothes he had been wearing in a pile on the floor, his suitcase, still unpacked, the whisky bottle, nearly empty, two glasses, one with lipstick. No sign of a struggle. Time of death, about twelve hours previously.'

Salter wasn't listening. He was watching O'Brien read from a typescript in French and translate it simultaneously into English. Was there anyone here who could do that, he wondered? His own copy was in English.

O'Brien stopped reading, and there was a long pause.

'All right,' Salter said. 'What do you know about him?'

'His wife came to Montreal for the identification,' O'Brien said. 'She told us Summers was in town for an academic conference. It began on Friday and was to last until Wednesday. She said Summers and his colleagues went to this conference every year at this time, when the term was over. It is held in a different place each year so they get to see the country. A little 'oliday before they go off for the big 'oliday in the summer.'

The two detectives, who each got five weeks' paid leave a year, smiled at each other.

O'Brien continued. 'I have a statement from her here. She was not a great deal of help. She didn't know any reason why anyone should kill her husband. We couldn't question her too hard, of course, because she was very upset. We'd like you to talk to her again, also.'

'All right. He picked up a whore who rolled him, right? The badger game. What's that in French?'

'The badger game, Inspector. But his wallet was still in his jacket, with over a hundred dollars in cash.'

'They got disturbed,' Salter offered.

'We know most of the hookers in the city, except the teenagers. We are checking. We don't know any killers among them.'

'Someone he knew, then. Some woman. An affair de cur.'

'What?'

'You know. An affair of the heart. Sounds, silly in English. The lipstick looks pretty obvious.'

'The blows were heavy. The doctor said it was someone quite strong.'

'They all study martial arts these days, Sergeant. My wife can lift her end of a railway tie.'

'Yes? But do English professors get into fights with their lovers?'

'What difference does it make what he teaches?'

'I meant English-Canadian professors, Inspector. Though, as a matter of fact, he did teach English.'

'I see.' Salter paused. O'Brien had introduced East/West relations into the discussion. You Anglos are a mystery to us Québécois. 'I guess professors are the same everywhere, Sergeant. Give them three drinks and they smash each other's heads in.' Screw you, froggie, he thought.

'Yes. Sorry. But your sergeant said something about he had heard we had a "crime de passion" we needed help with. He said he thought that was allowed in Quebec. I thought he was making jokes. Maybe you and he together.'

'Frank is an asshole, O'Brien. That's why he makes the coffee. But he's harmless. We don't make fun of foreigners, even Canadian ones.'

'And you, Inspector? You are in the homicide department?'

'No. I'm not. I am what we call General Duties.'

'I see.' O'Brien looked around the room that Salter shared with Gatenby, at Salter's nearly bare desk, at the uncarpeted floor, at the room's single decoration—a photograph from a newspaper of Gatenby saluting with one hand while he held open the door of some royal duke's limousine with the other.

Salter thought: He thinks he's been fobbed off with me

and Frank. So he has. He said, loudly, 'You asked for help with the questioning. What else can we do? Check up on Summers? I'll put Frank on to it.'

'A bit more than that, Inspector. Some of our separatists are making noises. We have our hands full.'

'But they just lost a referendum!'

'Yes. It's made them angry. Like English soccer fans when their team loses. In England, I mean.'

Here we go again. 'Or like French hockey fans when Maurice Richard is suspended.'

'That's right, Inspector. I remember that, too. Well, what with the separatists and one or two other things we have had no leave for a month, so we do not have much time for cases like this.'

'Besides, it's just unlucky that he was killed in Montreal, right?'

'Right. What I am concerned with is screwing up at the beginning. Look. Like this. This man, at a conference with his colleagues, is hit by an enemy, or a lover, or, maybe, a whore. But if it is someone he knew, then a stupid investigator might talk to the person right away and not know it. He might miss the signs. There it is. I am busy and I am French. You see what I mean?'

'Yes. You haven't got the experience to watch out for English liars. So you want me to do it.'

'Yes. If you can.' O'Brien grinned. 'All Anglos sound like liars to me,' he risked.

Salter laughed. 'That's exactly what my wife said the other day about the French MP's you see on TV. Especially the cabinet ministers.'

'Tell her she's right, will you? You can't trust any Frenchman in Ottawa.'

They sat there, grinning at each other.

Salter said, 'Let's get down to it, Onree. What you are asking me to do is take over the investigation from here and give it back when I've got something for you.'

'If you have the time and the men.'

'I've got me, and Frank, and all the time I need. Now, what else? The suitcase. Anything unusual in it?'

'Nothing. Underwear, shirts, socks, two books. What you could expect.'

'The wallet?'

O'Brien read from the list. 'One hundred and six dollars. Two credit cards. Two library cards. Driving licence. Some lottery tickets. Membership of a squash club. A dirty piece of paper with some numbers on it — they look like telephone numbers — some charge slips. Here.' He dug into the envelope again and produced the wallet. 'You'd better take it. Show it to the wife when you talk to her.'

Salter took the wallet and dropped it into a drawer. 'That's it then. Coffee now?'

'Tea, if you don't mind.'

'Frank!' Salter gave the order and waited until the door closed. 'Anything I can do for you here in town, Onree? You know Toronto?'

'Not much. I thought I would spend a few hours here. I have a reservation on the overnight train, so my evening is free. But you weren't expecting me, so just point me in the right direction and I'll leave you to solve my case.'

'Which direction is that?' Sherlock Holmes would have known. The tan, the windswept haircut — what did they point to? The harbour for a quick sail around the islands?

'Greenwood racetrack. I've never been to the races in Toronto.'

Of course. 'I've never been either. Would you like some company? I wonder what time they start.'

'Seven-thirty.'

'Ah. Well, then, we could go and have some dinner, and go out to the track afterwards.'

'Fine, Inspector.'

'Charlie.'

'Fine, Charlie. But why don't I come back at, say, five-thirty, and then we could go out and have dinner at the track.'

'I don't know if they have a restaurant, Onree.'

O'Brien looked knowing. 'They all have restaurants. I will be back at five-thirty.' He put his envelope back in his briefcase and shook hands with Salter.

When the door closed, Salter phoned his wife. 'I won't be home for dinner,' he said. 'I think I may have a real job.'

Annie said, 'Fraud, arson, robbery with violence?'

'Murder.'

'And they gave it to you!'

'It's not on our turf so "DeeCee" and "Chiefie" don't give a pinch. But it's just like a real job to me.'

'Now we start skipping dinner again? Working all night?'

'Not yet. But you never know. It might come to that. I hope so. Don't wait up. First, I'm going to the races. 'Bye, dear.' He hung up, agreeably mysterious.

Annie was waiting up for him when he got home.

'You look pleased with yourself,' she said. 'Did you win?'

'I didn't lose,' he said smugly, and waited to be asked again.

'How much?' she asked.

'A "C-note",' Salter said, out of the corner of his mouth like a regular gambler.

'Enjoy yourself?'

'Bloody marvellous. Want to hear about it?'

'Of course. I'll make some tea.'

What's going on with her? Salter wondered. She's acting strange.

'What's the matter?' he asked truculently. 'You jealous of my night out?'

'Don't be silly, Charlie. Just tell me about it. What happened?'

Salter gave a mental shrug and resumed his euphoric mood. 'The thing is,' he began. 'It's harness racing—you know—chariots.'

She nodded, a little girl hearing about Daddy's day.

'They have two kinds of horses—trotters and pacers—you know about this? The trotters move differently from the pacers.'

'They trot?'

'Yes.' What the hell was going on? 'They move diagonally, but the pacers move one side at a time—or is it the other way round? I couldn't really see the difference, even when I knew. Anyway, it's quite a sight when the lights go up and there they go.'

'Did you bet on every race?'

'Yes. Onree explained it to me . . .'

'Onree?'

'This Frenchman whose case I'm on. I picked out my own horses, though. I chose ones with names I liked, although the trouble was, half of them seemed to have similar names like Armbro or Hanover or something. Anyway, to make the story short, I won on seven races and picked up a hundred and twenty dollars. Onree lost fifty, betting on form. Ha, ha, ha. It was terrific. I would have won on eight but my horse stopped running properly—they had a name for what it did wrong.'

'Broke stride.'

'What?'

'It's called breaking stride.'

'How do you know?'

'They use the same term on the Island.'

Salter was dumbfounded. 'You mean those races in Charlottetown are the same as these?'

'That's right, Charlie. The races we've been trying to get you to come to for the last fifteen years. The trots, we

call them. Daddy used to *own* a standardbred—that's
what the horses are called. You have refused to have
anything to do with them all this time and now some
Montreal policeman comes to town and *you* come home
to tell the world about this new thing you've discovered.
Charlie, you are the bloody limit.' She walked past him
up to bed.

After a while Salter had found enough justification to
stop feeling horrible. Surely no one had mentioned horses
around the Montagu home for years? (Right, but only out
of politeness to him.) Certainly no one had taken the
trouble to explain the sport to him lately. (No, not in the
face of his "I-don't-want-to-know" attitude.) The truth
was that harness-racing was only one, if the most
outrageous, example of Salter's attitude to the whole
Montagu world when he was there. From the beginning,
he had defended himself against feeling like the poor
cousin by refusing to get involved in activities such as
sailing, playing bridge, tennis, trout-fishing with flies,
and constructing bonfires suitable for baking clams.
Apart from the skills involved, he was sure he would get
the costume wrong, and appear in sandals for some
activity that required hiking boots or bare feet. So when
he was on the Island he played golf, a game he had been
introduced to by some police pals; he swam; and he
watched the other activities from a distance, or ignored
them altogether. Over the years his bloody-mindedness
and their consideration for his feelings had created two
worlds, one which involved him, and the other one which
they talked about and enjoyed among themselves. It was
an arrangement that suited him, preserved his
independence, as he put it to himself, and he took the
same attitude in Toronto to his wife's interest in and
understanding of art, horticulture, and science fiction.
Salter came by his attitudes honestly enough; his father
had tried no new foods, at home or in restaurants, for

thirty years, on the grounds that it was all foreign muck and you couldn't tell what you were eating. The truth was that the old man was afraid he would make a fool of himself by not knowing how to eat it.

Salter's attitude had its dangers, and the chief one was just being demonstrated to him. He could never be sure, when he did entertain a new enthusiasm, that his wife hadn't tried to interest him in it ten years before. Science fiction was forbidden to him because she had been recommending it for so long that he had no idea who were her favourite authors. He once knew that science fiction would bore him, and now that he was not so sure, it was too late.

But harness-racing. Jesus Christ! Gradually Salter recalled bits and pieces of things he had seen or heard and ignored over the years until he became fairly sure of the truth: that harness-racing was the major maritime pastime, and that the Montagus figured prominently in the sport. Oh shit, he thought. For another half an hour he swung between justification and guilt, until he went to bed in a mood of truculent misery.

CHAPTER 2

The following morning Salter phoned the chairman of the English Department at Douglas College and arranged for some interviews. He had often seen the college as he walked downtown from his office, and he had a vague impression of two or three converted warehouses, several shiny glass buildings, and a fountain. He established that the English Department was in one of the glass boxes, and set off from his office with plenty of time to walk. He wanted to have a look at the sleazy section of Yonge Street (his favourite stretch) to see what might be 'cleaned up'

for the visiting Mayor of Amsterdam. What am I
supposed to do, he wondered, as he viewed the morning
sprinkling of bums, homeless adolescents and strained-
looking gays who called this strip home. Should I get a
couple of hundred off-duty cops to walk their wives up
and down, like good Toronto burghers? What the hell
does 'clean up' mean? It would be easy enough to avoid
the issue and drive the Mayor round the Yorkville area
where, he had read in the paper, Toronto's beautiful
people gathered to be looked at, but the Mayor had
specifically asked to see Yonge Street because it was the
only street he had heard of. Salter made a mental note to
recommend that the Mayor be taken through at the
lunch-hour when the street would be crowded with office
workers.

The buildings of Douglas College appeared earlier than
he had expected, now that he was looking for them, and
Salter became aware that the College was much larger
than he had thought. It was a quiet time of the academic
year, between examinations and convocation, and there
was only a handful of students about. The first three he
asked had no idea where the English Department was,
but finally he stopped one who directed him to the right
building. Salter struggled through a pair of glass doors
apparently designed to guard the entrance to a tomb, and
found himself in the typical lobby of an academic
building at the end of term. Every wall was covered with
posters advertising last week's concerts, lectures, dances
and the monthly meetings of the Tae Kwon Do club. It
looked like the day after the Boxing Day sale.

At one side of the lobby a security guard was talking to
a small plastic box held up to his mouth. Salter had to
wait for him to finish his chat, evidently with a colleague
at another desk somewhere, about the need to make sure
someone called Wong did his share of the work. 'I said to
Teperman last week, how come Wong's always on days,

and me and Eddie do nights? He said, Wong's wife is up
the spout, he said. He's gotta stay home nights. I said,
How do you know my old lady ain't up the spout, too? Or
Eddie's. You know what he said? He said, You ain't
married, he said. I said, You don't have to be married,
not to get someone up the spout, I said. It's all right to
live common-law these days. He said, Are' you? I said, No,
but I could be couldn't I? You never asked me, but you
believe anything that fucking Wong tells you. He does,
Eddie. Sure. Anything Wong wants, and there's you and
me left sucking the hind tit. You know?' Listening to this,
Salter wondered again at the thousands of security guards
that had sprung up in Toronto in the last ten years. Was
there a job for him in the business if he ever got totally fed
up with errand work? Eventually the guard noticed him,
and broke off from Eddie long enough to direct him to an
elevator. He rode up to the fourth floor and stepped out
into an empty corridor. More notice-boards, but this time
most of the announcements were about literary events
and plays that had taken place during the term. One
small typed notice advertised a 'complete set of texts for
English 022 for sale, never been opened'. Another huge
poster, printed black on a grey background said, without
explanation, 'THE DEADLINE HAS BEEN CHANGED. IT IS
NOW THE 28TH.' Underneath, in pencil, someone had
written, 'Somehow, I still feel uneasy.'

Salter looked along the corridors which led away from
the elevator at right-angles, one to the left and one
straight ahead, wondering which route to take. Both
looked as though they had been trashed during the night.
Piles of dirty paper lay everywhere, concentrated in heaps
around the office doors, but strewn along the walls as
well. Some of it had been roughly gathered into
cardboard boxes stacked side by side, evidently a first
attempt at a clean-up. Salter's eyes cleared, and he
recognized the papers as English essays, waiting to be

picked up by the students, but his initial impression, that he had stumbled into an alleyway where the department threw its garbage, remained.

He chose the corridor to the left, and walked along it reading the names on the doors. As he turned the corner he almost stumbled over a girl seated at a desk, typing, and he asked directions to the chairman's office. She pointed to a corner office, the only one Salter had seen so far with the door open. There a secretary led him to the door of an inner office which opened as they approached it, and a large smiling man waved him in.

Hector Browne, the chairman of the English Department at Douglas College, was a fat dandy. Salter guessed his weight at two hundred and ten pounds, but there was nothing of the slob about him. His blue suede jacket, grey flannel trousers, and brilliant dark loafers were immaculate, and the toffee-coloured shirt made of some kind of thick linen, worn open at the neck, completed the impression of a carefully planned appearance. Salter found the total effect very pleasant, like stepping into a well-kept drawing-room. Because the building was new, Browne's office was the usual concrete and glass cube, but Browne had done his best to warm it up with some blown-up photographs of portraits that looked slightly familiar.

The chairman led him to a settee and sat down with him. 'It's about Summers, of course, Inspector?' he offered.

'Yes. Just some enquiries about what he was doing in Montreal, and who was with him.'

'It's shaken us up here, I can tell you. I wasn't close to David myself, but no man is an island, is he? Interesting how the clichés come into their own on the big occasions, isn't it?'

'Yes,' Salter said, 'If you weren't close to him—

Professor? . . . Mister? . . . What should I call you . . . Chairman?'

'No, no, not "Chairman". It sounds like the head of the party, doesn't it? "Mister" is fine. I *am* a professor, but so is everyone else around here, so we don't use the title much except on passports and that sort of thing. It's a great help in getting through the Luxembourg Customs. For hotel reservations, though, "Doctor" is better, if you *are* a doctor, as Stephen Leacock pointed out. Ideally, of course, one should have an arresting name—like Rockefeller.'

'Summers was a professor?'

'We all are, as I said. Do you know anything about Douglas College, Inspector?'

'Nothing, sir. Perhaps you could fill me in.'

Browne leaned back and put the tips of his fingers together, parodying the gesture. He began in a lecturing style, with enough exaggeration to show he was not to be taken too seriously. As he talked, though, it was evident that, rehearsed as he was, he believed what he was saying.

'Douglas College,' he said, 'was set up in the 'sixties in response to the explosion in the demand for higher education, a demand which the voters, as the politicians read them, wanted satisfied. For a brief period, unique in Ontario history—in my time, anyway—education was politically fashionable. It was a period when Ontario politicians anxious for higher office sought the Education portfolio as having a very high profile, one of the largest budgets and plenty of opportunity for headlines. During this time the curriculum of the secondary schools was entirely remade—destroyed, some would say—as the trendy word went out that schools should no longer teach subjects, but students. Schools became people-oriented. Do you have children, Inspector?'

'I have two boys, Mr Browne, but they go to a private school.'

'A cop-out, if I may make a play on words, Inspector. You've never had to deal with the system. However, let me go on. All the subjects were revamped: in English, Creative Writing replaced the study of grammar; in the universities, the explosion in the student population coincided with the activist movement and the students demanded the right to study what they liked. This was instantly granted, as were all other student demands. But back to numbers. To satisfy the hordes of potential voters demanding access to higher education, or *further* education as it was more and more called, dozens of new colleges and quasi-colleges were created, granting new kinds of degrees, diplomas and certificates in a variety of new 'disciplines', such as Photographic Arts, Horsemanship, and Gardening. The older universities welcomed these new institutions at first. As one professor at our rival across the street—' Browne pointed an elaborate finger in the direction he meant '—said to me at the time I took this job, "We are hoping you will take all the students we don't want." But inevitably the baby boom died down and all of the institutions of further education, new and old, started scrambling for students. The older institutions got frightened, for many of the students of the next generation actually chose us even though they would have been welcome across the street. The establishment rushed to protect itself. First, they lowered their entrance standards, though they will deny this violently, then they organized to prevent the upstarts from offering any further competition with their own programmes. But it was too late. In the struggle that followed some of the new institutions did suffer, but most survived and a few prospered. Their enrolment increased, against the trend, and in some areas they became established as the equal of their older sister institutions. They became, in a word, respectable.

'Douglas College—to come to my subject—is an

outstanding example. We were among the first of the new colleges, and we were blessed by an ambitious president, a downtown location, and enough time to get our feet under the table before anyone noticed. We now have ten thousand students, some programmes which take only one of four qualified applicants, our own degrees, a faculty club, and an alumni association. And we have professors with tenure, of whom David Summers was one.'

Browne was finished. Salter felt like clapping, but he had work to do. 'Thank you,' he said. 'Now about Professor Summers. If you weren't close to him, who was?'

Browne threw all his limbs into the air and arranged himself in thought. 'Good question. Pollock, of course. After that, two of the people he was in Montreal with—Carrier and Usher, and, oh yes, Marika, Marika Tils. They were all together the evening before.'

'And his enemies?'

'No one who would *kill* him, Inspector, Just academic squabbles.'

'I didn't expect you to give me the name of the killer, Professor—sorry, Mister—Browne. But an enemy might tell me something a friend would not see.'

'You can tell a man by his friends, but his enemies can save you the trouble, eh, Inspector? There are a few people who resented David. I didn't *warm* to him myself, although lately he's been more relaxed, more fun to be with.'

'Does anyone *detest* him?'

'This conversation is entirely confidential? Then Dunkley is your man. He was in Montreal, too. They couldn't *bear* each other. There was an *ancient coolness* between them, so that you would never put them on the same committee. They got on each others tits.' Browne leaned forward, smiling roundly, as he descended into argot.

'This *ancient coolness*. What was it about?'

'It started before my time. I've been here ten years, but Summers and Dunkley and several others go back twenty. Back then, those two were on opposite sides of the fence on some issue and they never forgave each other. I've heard it talked of often enough but I've never got to the bottom of it. I doubt if anyone could tell you now what happened, if anything did. It's like a neighbour thing that turns into a feud. So we kept them apart and the two of them never mentioned each other, even to their cronies. It was as if they knew some dreadful secret that kept them apart while it linked them in silent bondage, if you know what I mean. Like a theme for a Conrad story.' Browne pointed to one of the huge portraits, that of a bearded, middle-aged man.

'Conrad?'

'Joseph Conrad, the novelist, Inspector. That's his picture.'

'I know who Joseph Conrad is, Mr Browne. I meant *which* Conrad story. I've read some.' One, anyway, about someone on a boat.

'Have you? Not too many, I hope. They have a very bad effect. No. I meant it was *like* a Conrad story. One thought of Marlow and Kurtz, or "The Secret Sharer"—one of those "he - and - I - shared - a - knowledge - that - was - never - to - be - divulged - between - us" themes.'

'I see. A story Conrad never wrote.'

'No, no. The one he wrote *interminably*. Please don't take me too literally. I doubt the presence of a ghastly secret. One just thinks in these ways after years of trying to find useful analogies for first-year students.'

The phone rang and Browne answered it. 'Yes, my dear. I hadn't forgotten. Yes, my dear. I'll buy one at the Cakemaster.' He put the phone down. 'My wife,' he said. 'Reminding me that it is my daughter's birthday. I have to buy the cake. You thought I was a bachelor? I *wallow* in uxorious delight, Inspector. I have six daughters, one better than Mr Bennet. You assumed I was a bachelor because I still polish my shoes? It is possible to maintain one's standards within the nuptial bonds, you know. Conrad taught me that.' Browne was having a wonderful time.

Salter said, 'Nothing surprises me any more, Mr Browne. See? Another cliché. Now, where can I find these people? Carrier or Usher first, I think.'

'They are waiting for you. I've arranged interviews with everyone who was with David in Montreal. They are upset, but you are used to that I expect. Marika is in *misery*.'

'And his buddy, — Hillock?'

'Pollock. He's here, too.' Browne stood up with a little jump and started to bustle. 'Now I can't ask you for lunch because I always bring my own.'

'Diet, sir?' Salter asked rudely, curious to know what kept this shining beauty in trim.

'Wrong again. I like myself the way I am. So does my wife. See?' He opened the brown paper bag. Inside were four jelly doughnuts and a pint of chocolate milk. 'I pick them up on the way to work and I look forward to them all morning. I'm in my office all the time if you need me.'

'Will you be at the funeral?'

'Yes. Will you be there?'

'I expect so, sir. The killer always turns up, doesn't he? I read that somewhere.'

'Ha, ha, ha. I get it. Another cliché.'

'Would you keep our conversation confidential, sir? And try to stop any speculation around the office.'

'Mum's the word, Inspector. Good luck.' He looked forlorn for a moment. 'I hope it turns out to be a passing thug and not someone we know.' His voice was quavering slightly. Through the sparkle, Browne was keeping the horror at bay.

'It usually does, sir,' Salter said, resisting a mild impulse to give Browne a pat. 'Goodbye.'

Carrier was next. He sat behind his desk without speaking as Salter sat down in a chair opposite him. A tidy man in his early forties with fair, thinning hair, he was wearing a neat checked sports shirt and khaki trousers. He had his own teapot and cup beside him on a little table, and a packet of Peek Frean's biscuits. On the wall, three posters under glass gave the appearance of a matched set, although their subjects didn't seem connected as far as Salter could see. One was a portrait of a delicate young man with lace around his wrists, probably Shelley or someone; the second was a reproduction of a lot of writing—a page from the oldest book in the world? The third picture looked familiar, being an advertisement of an art gallery exhibit with a reproduction of a picture of a red checked tablecloth. What luck, Salter thought, as he recognized the only Canadian painting he had ever looked at closely. The original belonged to some cultured friends of his wife, and Salter had frequently studied it and failed to find any reason for its artistic and (huge) monetary worth. He introduced himself and pointed to the poster.

'Have you followed de Niverville's career, Dr Carrier?' he asked, one connoisseur to another.

'Yes,' Carrier said.

'Interesting painter,' Salter said, trying to remember a single fact about him.

'Yes,' Carrier said.

So much for art, the key that opens all doors, thought Salter. 'Now, sir,' he said, 'I want to ask you a few questions about Professor Summers. First, I'd like you to tell me what happened when you were all together on Thursday. You were with Professor Summers for dinner, I think. Who else was there?'

'Usher, Dunkley, Marika Tils and I. That's all. Nothing happened. We just had dinner.'

'Wasn't it unusual, Professor, for Summers and Dunkley to be having dinner together?'

'Yes.'

There was a long pause.

'Well?' Salter asked.

'Yes, it was unusual.'

'Then why were they together?'

'We all were.'

'So you say. But normally Dunkley and Summers avoided each other.'

'Yes.'

'But not this time.'

'No.'

Jesus Christ. 'Mr Carrier. I'm trying to find out who killed a man. I'd be glad of any help. Could you tell me, please, why, on this particular night these two old enemies were together?'

'Summers invited him along with the rest of us.'

'Ah. Why?' Could you perhaps offer an interpretation? Rack your trained, scholarly brain, Salter thought.

'He said that tonight was his night. He said the gods were smiling on him. So he insisted we all go out to dinner. Including Dunkley.'

'What did he mean by "The gods were smiling"?'

'I don't know.'

'He never said?'

'No. He just seemed very happy.'

'I see. He just said, "The gods are smiling; this is on me"?'

'I don't remember exactly what he said. We were all having a drink in a bar after the last paper.'

'All of you, including Dunkley?'

'Yes. He had just read a paper.'

'Read a paper?'

'Yes. On favourite epithets in John Clare's poetry.'

'I see. Read it to other people, you mean. Lectured, like.'

'Yes.'

'And then Summers issued his invitation.'

'Yes.'

'And no one asked what it was all about?'

'Oh yes. We all asked him. But he wouldn't tell us. He said he would tell us later.'

'A good dinner?' Salter knew the answer but was curious to know how long it would take him to get this bugger to tell it.

'I beg your pardon?'

'Did he give you a good dinner?' That seem clear, sir?

'Yes. We went to the Maison Victor Hugo. I can't remember what I had but it was very good.'

'Did you notice the bill?'

'Yes.'

In a minute, thought Salter, I am going to take this loquacious bastard back to the office and stick the Oldest Sergeant on the Force on to him. Gatenby would enjoy asking him the four hundred niggling questions he calls interrogation, and with this one it might work. Aloud he said, 'How much was it?'

'I don't know exactly.'

'Roughly. Give me a round figure.'

'About a hundred and thirty dollars. Plus the tip, of course.'

'Cash or card?' asked Salter, who had already seen the charge slip.

'He used a Visa card.'

'And then what?'

'After a while we went back to our rooms.'

'Where did you go first?'

'Marika went back to her hotel right away. About nine o'clock. Then we walked about a bit. Then Summers left.

Then the three of us went for one more drink. Then we walked to the hotel.'

'You were all staying at the same hotel?'

'Yes. The Hotel Esmeralda.'

'But Summers was staying at the Hotel Plaza del Oro or some such name?'

'Yes. But the rest of us were at the Esmeralda.'

'And you all went back to bed.'

'Yes.'

'And you didn't see or hear anything of each other, until breakfast the next morning?'

'I saw Dunkley, of course.'

'Why, "of course"?'

'We shared a room.'

'I see. That's wonderful. You two have alibis.'

'I think that is a ridiculous and extremely unpleasant remark, Inspector,' Carrier said, flaring up in a temper.

'True, though, isn't it? And Usher?'

'He shared a room with a friend of his from another university.'

'And Miss Tils?'

'She was on her own.'

'I see. Well, that seems to be everything you know, doesn't it? One or two more points. Were you all drunk?'

'Drunk?'

'Smashed. Loaded. Pissed. I don't know the academic term.'

'We had a lot of wine. But I wasn't drunk.' Carrier was still simmering.

'Who was?'

'Summers drank a lot more than the rest of us. He was stumbling a little.'

'Finally, then, you know of no reason why Summers should have been celebrating?'

'I had the impression that more than one thing was contributing to his state. "Everything's coming up roses" was what he said once.'

'Might there have been a woman involved?'

'What do you mean?'

'Could he have been in love, say?'

'I don't see why that should have made him buy us all dinner.'

Salter sighed. 'Nor do I. But middle-aged men, men of our age, Professor, do funny things, I hear. Thank you. Don't go out of town without telling me, will you? And don't talk about this case to anyone, especially the people you were with on Friday night.'

'Am I under suspicion, Inspector?'

'At this stage, Professor, we try to keep an open mind.

Salter walked down the corridor until he found Usher's office, wondering if all the interviewees would be as tight-arsed. His initial sight of Usher cheered him up. The door was opened by a swarthy little man so covered in hair that only his forehead and nose showed through.

'Come in, come in, Inspector. Here we go. Sit down here. Cup of tea? If this was Oxford we could have sherry, but here we have to make do.'

Usher was a shouter. His voice was as noisy as a television set tuned for the deaf. His accent was English working class, not quite cockney, for all his aitches were stressed heavily, but otherwise it was classically what the English call 'common'. As he made Salter comfortable, he moved about the office in giant loping strides that kept him close to the ground; he put a chair in place, settled an ashtray, cleared a space for Salter to write on, and finally seated himself behind his desk, all the while shouting and smiling through his beard, an enormous crescent of yellow teeth splitting his face like a half-moon.

'You all right now, Inspector? That sun bother you? Move your chair a bit over there. Go on. That's it. You want something to write on? Take my statement? Har,

har. No. You all right, really? Off we go, then.'

When he had subsided, Salter asked, 'Professor Usher?'

'Yes, that's right. The name's on the door. Smoke? Don't mind me. I don't. My kids won't let me. Har, har. Terrible'n't? I don't mind if you do, though. It won't come this way. No. I suppose you chaps are givin' it up like everybody else. Funny how it's changed. I used to smoke forty a day once.'

Usher did a comic cough, and Salter shot through the tiny gap. 'I wonder if you would corroborate your colleagues' story of the events of Friday night.'

'Glad to. Glad to. We met in the bar about half past five, had a drink and left about a quarter past six. P'raps twenty past. No. I'm tellin' a lie. It was *half* past six 'cause they were closing the bar up, you see.'

'I've got the main story, I think,' Salter shouted. 'Just one or two details. First of all, would you say Summers was drunk?'

'Drunk as a fart, Inspector. I've seen some people lap it up, but *him*! I thought we'd have to put him to bed. You think that's what did it? Someone saw him, followed him home? Seems likely, doesn't it? Rotten, really. He was having such a good time, too. I must say . . .'

Salter attacked again. 'Why?' he bellowed. 'Why was he having such a good time. Did he say?'

'No. He went on all night about the gods smilin', but he never told us why.'

'After he left you, you and Dunkley and Carrier stayed in the area for a while and had a few more drinks, right?'

'Old Carrier tell you that? You could call it that. Not quite true, though. He's a bit shy, is Carrier. No, we went back to *one* place and had a nightcap, if you like. More of an eye-opener, really.' Usher imitated a man looking through binoculars, and waited to be asked what he was up to. Salter waited in turn. Usher continued.

'Place called "Les Jardins du Paradis" — French place.

More like the Black Hole.'

'A bar?'

'Yerss. A bar. With gels. Strippers. Continuous live performance. Take it off, take it off, all the customers cried, and they did, right on the table.' Usher roared with laughter.

'You went *back* to this place. You had already gone there with Summers.'

'Yerss. Soon as Marika went home, old Dave started talking about finding the action. So he asked a policeman—that's what you do in Montreal—and he told us about these two bars. One of them wasn't much, but this second one, the Jardins place, was full of lovely crumpet. We had a real basinful.'

'A basinful wasn't enough, though. After Summers left, you went back.'

'That's right. Soldiers on leave, we were.'

'Then you all went back to the hotel. Did you stay in your room that night? I have to ask that.'

' 'Course you do. No. I didn't sneak out and do in old Dave. You can check up with my mate from New Brunswick, if you like. He was in the room when I got back and we were up half the night, talking.'

'You stayed with a friend from New Brunswick?'

'That's right, Inspector. That's the nice thing about these conferences. You get a chance to meet old pals.'

'Is that the main purpose, Professor?'

'Now, now, now, Inspector. Don't *you* start. A little conference once a year is the only perks we get. No. It's not the *main* purpose. The main purpose is to refresh us academically.' Usher gave a low-comedy wink. 'But it's one of the nice things about them. We all move around a bit in this game, first in graduate school, then usually a couple of jobs while we're finishing the thesis, and these conferences bring together everybody you've met. Actually it *is* a little outing for us. You see a different

place every year. Last year we all went to
Moncton—smashing lobsters there—and the year before
that was Saskatoon. Only a couple of us went there.'
Usher roared with laughter. 'Saskatoon, Saskatchewan,'
he said derisively. 'The year before that it was Edmonton.
That turned out all right because of the Hot Springs at
Jasper. Lovely, they are. Next year we go to Halifax.
There will be a line-up for that one, I can tell you. The
maritimes conferences are always popular. Except
Newfoundland.'

'Kind of a convention, is it? Like the Kiwanis?'

'Now you're being a bit sarcastic, I can tell. Still, fair's
fair. We do some work, of course, but the main thing is
getting away in a gang.'

'And is that how you go? All of you, in a gang?'

'If we can. Of course, we're not all as thick as thieves
when we are at home, but at the conferences we do stick
together, yes.'

'You travel down and back together?'

'We did this time. Marika and John Carrier and me.
We went down in my car. Dunkley always goes on his
own.'

'Why?'

'Who knows? He just does. But so did old Dave. He
always went on his own, too.'

'Why?'

'Search me. There was room in my car, but he went
down by train. Did the same thing last year. And he
always stays in a different hotel from the rest of us. I used
to think it was just chance, but I watched him this year,
out of curiosity. Sure enough, he dawdled about when we
were trying to make our arrangements, putting us off
when we were trying to double up in rooms, to cut down
the cost; then, when we'd all booked, he reserved at
another hotel. I realized then that he always does that. I
still don't think there's anything in it, though. I'll tell you

why. When we were in Moncton last year, he always
turned up late at the parties they have in the evenings. A
bit mysterious, you'd think? So would I. But you know
where he'd been? At the races. They have harness-racing
at Moncton, and he snuck off every night to play the gee-
gees. Someone saw him there. Sly bugger. But I think he
was just shy about telling us. Not very academic, is it?'

Usher had quietened down slightly as he grew
reflective, and showed signs of stopping altogether. Salter
thought he would never have a chance to hear about
Summers from someone with as little bias as Usher, and
he prodded him on.

'So you don't think it was unusual for Summers to be in
a room to himself in another hotel from the rest of you?'

'As I say, I did once. But he always stayed on his own,
didn't he? Every year.'

'So. At night he went to the races. What about during
the day?'

'He heard a few papers, like the rest of us. Not all day,
of course, and not the same ones.'

'There are different discussions going on at the same
time?'

'Oh yes. There were four sessions a day, and five or six
different papers at each session. In different rooms, of
course. There are always a couple of important sessions,
given by the big-wigs, and everyone goes to them, but
generally, for the small ones, we all go to different ones
and meet afterwards.'

'Did you see Summers at any of the papers?'

'There was only time for one session, wasn't there, and
Dunkley was giving one of the papers. I didn't go to it,
and I don't think anyone else did, either. Even David
didn't go, and it was in his field.'

'What field is that?'

'Romantic poetry. Wordsworth was all David cared
about.'

'He should have gone, then, to Dunkley's paper?'

Usher looked unhappy at seeming to criticize a colleague. 'Yes, he should have,' he agreed.

'Dunkley and Summers both taught Romantic poetry, did they?'

'No. That was the trouble.' Usher looked even more miserable. He consulted his watch. 'Here. Inspector. What about a bite. Let's go and have a sandwich and a bowl of suds and I will fill you in. It's all bullshit, really, but you might as well know it.'

Salter agreed, and Usher loped around the room, collecting his jacket and tidying his papers. 'I'll take you to the Faculty Club,' he said. 'Give you an insight into life at Douglas College.' Usher roared with laughter again.

'You know the college, Inspector?' he asked as they were descending in the elevator.

'I've walked past it dozens of times and your chairman told me the history. Why?'

They left the building and paused on the steps. 'We are now in the Arts Building,' Usher began. 'Over there is the Administration Building, the great big shiny one. That there is the library, and all those old houses contain the other departments. This is called the quad.' Usher pointed to the square of grass in front of them. 'We are going over there.' He started off across the grass in an outdoor version of the giant steps he used in the office. Salter was hard put to keep up without trotting as they raced across the tiny quadrangle.

'Here we are, then,' Usher said, leading Salter into the front door of a renovated old brick house. 'The Faculty Club — among other things.'

Inside a little hallway they hung their coats on a peg and moved into the dining-room, a pleasant, sunny little room furnished like a superior hotel coffee-shop.

'Mr Usher!' the waiter shouted, as soon as they were inside. 'How did I do, sir?'

'Bombed, laddie, bombed. Absolutely buggered,' Usher shouted back, grinning at the student. 'Good thing you've got a job here, but judging by your English exam, you must have trouble reading the menu. I have never come across such a load of unadulterated, illiterate twaddle in all my born days. And what did you use for a pen? Your handwriting, laddie, looks like the death-throes of a mad chicken who's just run through a puddle of ink.'

The waiter accepted all this with a grin, and asked again, 'How did I do?'

'You passed, laddie, you passed. Now get us two draught and I'll give you an "A".'

To Salter's relief, the horseplay now seemed at an end, and the waiter led them to a table. Usher looked round the room, waved at a couple of people, called greetings to another, and the beer arrived. Salter was beginning to be sorry he had accepted Usher's invitation. How was he going to question the man with a dozen people listening? He hoped his host had a confidential voice, but as soon as they were settled Usher picked up the story again in the same penetrating tones. Most of the conversation in the dining-room stopped as the other diners listened.

'The thing you've got to understand, Inspector,' Usher said, causing Salter to hope the others would take him for an inspector of drains, 'is that we all have a field. What we specialize in. My field is Lawrence. D.H. I come from Nottingham — did you realize I'm English? — and my grandfather knew Lawrence, or said he did, like most of the old codgers in Nottingham.' Usher broke off again for a sustained maniacal laugh at the lies Nottingham codgers told about Lawrence. 'Anyway, he had a lot of stories about Bert, so when I went into English, Lawrence seemed a natural to specialize in. Our chairman is a Conrad man, Carrier is working on Tennyson, and Dunkley and old Dave are Romantics. That's the trouble.

You see, we don't have many students, only about twenty in Honours English, and we don't have enough of any kind of students for two sections of anything—do you follow me?—and Dave taught our only Romantics course. He had seniority, and until he went on sabbatical, Dunkley wouldn't get a look-in.'

'When would that be? Summers's sabbatical?' Salter spoke so quietly that he could feel the other diners straining to hear.

'Year after next, I think.'

'I see. So, in a sense, Summers had Dunkley's course, until then.'

'I suppose so. But talking about "your" course or "my" course just leads to a lot of bad feeling, and there was enough of that.'

Their sandwiches arrived, and Salter took the opportunity to change the subject. He asked Usher questions about how hard he worked, how much professors were paid, and what the pressures were on a teacher of English at Douglas College, all designed to look like part of his investigation into the causes of Summers's death, and he got for his pains a lengthy speech on the teacher's life as Usher saw it, which ended with the information that Usher, personally, was delighted to be paid well for doing something he enjoyed and would do for much less if he had to.

'But not everyone feels like you do, eh?' Salter asked.

'There are just as many teachers who shouldn't be doing it as there are policemen, I expect,' Usher said. And then, 'Not us, though, by God. Not you and me, Inspector,' and he roared with glee again.

They walked back to the Arts Building together. When they reached the door, Usher put out his hand. 'I've got some errands to do, Inspector. I might see you later. I wasn't all that pally with David. Didn't know him well at all, but I was one of the last to see him alive.' Usher for the first time was speaking quietly. 'It's like the Venerable Bede said—in one window and out the other—that's life.' He turned away and walked off down the street.

Back in the English Department, Salter had plenty of time before he was scheduled to meet Dunkley, the next on his list, and he got the secretary to let him into Summers's office, which had been locked since his death.

A small room, furnished with two chairs and a desk, like all the others. On the wall, four or five mounted but unframed photographs, more artistic than realistic to Salter's eye (one of them was so out of focus it must have been intentional). Four shelves of books: on one shelf the books were interleaved with notes; all the other books looked like old texts or publishers' free samples. Salter opened a desk drawer; it was full of rubbish—overshoes, a coffee-pot, and a clock with a broken face. He opened the other drawers, and found a few personal-looking letters which he began to read. The door opened and a young man poked his head round it.

'Dave in?' he asked.

Salter shook his head.

'Know when he'll be back?'

Salter shrugged, dodging. 'Why? Who wants him?'

'I do. He's got my essay.'

'You a student?'

'That's right. Theatre Arts. Dave teaches us Modern Drama. Oh well.' The head disappeared.

Dave? A palsy-walsy teacher? Or was that standard these days? Salter continued reading the dead man's mail without much interest. A letter from a friend in England. Two others from former students.

The door opened again and another student stood in the doorway.

'Professor Summers?' he asked.

'No.'

'You're not Professor Summers?'

'No. What do you want him for?'

'I was told to see him. By my chairman. Professor Summers is my English teacher.'

'And you don't know what he looks like?'

'I'm in Journalism. We're pretty busy. Not too much time for English. I haven't had a chance to check out what's going on this term. Oh well. I'll come back later.' He disappeared.

Salter finished turning over Summers's desk and leafed through his desk diary—looking for what? Before he could answer that to himself, the secretary appeared to tell him that Dunkley was waiting in his office.

'I didn't like Summers, as you have no doubt been told.' Dunkley sat behind his desk, being interviewed. A handsome man; tall, thick fair hair to his shoulders, slightly balding in front. A still upright carriage. He was wearing army surplus clothing which he seemed to invest with its original military purpose. His office was lined with notices of meetings concerning aid to various refugee groups. Like most of his colleagues that Salter had seen, Dunkley was about forty.

'I've heard as much. But no one has told me why.'

'Because they don't know. It has nothing to do with them. Or you, either.'

'It might, you know. You've been feuding for ten years, I hear. Might be reason enough to kill him.'

'You are not paid to joke with suspects, are you, Inspector?'

'Perhaps you could fill me in on what I am paid for, Professor?'

'Persecution, mainly, of people who can't defend themselves, as far as I can tell.'

'Fascist pigs, are we?'

'Could you come to the point?'

'All right. Why were you feuding?'

'There was no feud.'

'Just you hating him and him hating you, for ten years.'

'We disliked each other. Can we get on, please? I am extremely busy.' The diction was precise, but underneath the vowels were flat.

'You are Australian, Mr Dunkley?'

'I was born in New Zealand. My family was German, originally. They changed their name from Dunkel in 1939 for patriotic reasons. I am married but separated from my wife, whom I still support. What else?'

'It's Summers I want to find out about. What did you have against him?'

'I detested him. In my opinion, he should not have been teaching here.'

'Why? Did he fuck the students?'

'Probably. I was more concerned with his academic standards.'

'Poor, were they, in your opinion?'

'Non-existent.'

'Bad teacher, was he?'

'In my opinion.'

'What about the students?'

'Some of them enjoyed the kind of thing he did, no doubt.'

'Did you ever see him teach?'

'No.'

'But you heard?'

'Yes.'

'From the students.'

'Yes.'

'They complained to you, did they?'

'They rarely knew enough to complain, but from what I heard I knew what was going on.'

'I see. Were his politics very different from yours?'

'He had no politics. He was an opportunist in that area, too.'

'I see. Well, well. He sounds pretty bad. Could we get back to the Friday night in Montreal? You got over your distaste for him enough to accept his hospitality. He bought you a dinner, I believe.'

'Yes, he did. I don't know where he got the money.'

'Why did you accept his hospitality?'

'He asked me in front of the others. They knew I had no plans. So I took the easy way out.'

'For a change.'

'What?'

'You took the easier path for a change. In spite of your preference for the hard one.'

'What are you talking about, Inspector?'

'I'm not sure.' Which was true. Salter had forgotten himself in his dislike for the man he was talking to. 'So you went along,' he continued. 'When did Miss Tils leave the group?'

'After dinner. About nine.'

'Then what?'

'Then Summers took us to a striptease show.'

'Then what?'

'Summers went back to his hotel.'

'Was he drunk?'

'Sodden. At least I thought so at the time.'

'What time did he leave you?'

'About ten o'clock.'

'Why do you say "you thought so"?'

'I think he may have been play-acting.'

'Why?'

'I think he may have gone off to get a whore.'

'What makes you think that?'

'He talked about it during the show.'

'But *you* were just watching the show to keep him company?'

'I saw it differently. Those girls were being paid to cater to the likes of Summers.'

'Exploitation of minority group?'

'Yes. As a matter of fact.'

'What happened after Summers went home?'

'We had another drink and walked about a bit. Then we went back ourselves. Carrier and I went to our room. I presume Usher did, too, although I can't confirm that.'

'That's all right, Professor. I can. But this last drink. Where did you go for it?'

Now Dunkley's face went darker. 'Back to the bar,' he said. 'As you obviously know.'

'I have to confirm everything, Professor. You tell me. The same show?'

'Yes.'

'Why?'

'I don't talk behind my colleagues' backs. Ask *them*.'

'I have. They wanted to see some more tits. What was your idea? To organize a protest?'

Dunkley said nothing. Salter pressed on. 'The striptease show didn't have the same effect on you, Professor? There was no thought of you finding a girl?'

'We went home to bed.'

'What time was that?'

'I couldn't tell you. About half past ten.'

'That's a bit early, isn't it?'

'I don't have to explain my sleeping habits to you, I think.'

'It was your regular time, then, was it? Ten-thirty?'

'Yes. And I had had a hard day.'

'Right. You read a paper that day. Get a big audience?'

'The room was half full.'

'But none of your colleagues here came.'

'None of my colleagues knew anything about my subject.'

'Summers did, didn't he? His field was the same as yours, wasn't it?'

Dunkley was silent.

'Wasn't it?'

'Summers didn't have a field.'

'I see. He thought he did, though, didn't he? Wordsworth, Keats, and such-like.'

'So I believe.'

'But you and he never discussed your fields?'

'Very few people around here talk about literature. Mostly they talk about mortgages and wine-making.'

'Sounds like our canteen. Could we get back to the night you went to bed at ten-thirty, your normal time. What time do you normally get up?'

'At six, as a matter of fact. I usually get a couple of hours' work in before breakfast.'

'So you got up at six,' Salter said, writing laboriously in his notebook. 'Carrier, too?'

'No. I *didn't* get up at six that morning. I had a very restless night, and I didn't get to sleep until the small hours. We didn't get up until after eight.'

Why is he lying, Salter wondered. Surely he and Carrier didn't do a Burke and Hare on Summers?

'I see,' he said. 'You won't mind signing a statement to that effect will you, sir?'

'Of course not.'

'Thank you, Mr Dunkley. And I'll tell you what. If you ever feel like telling me what you had against Summers, here's my number. I'll ask everybody else, anyway.'

Dunkley allowed the card to lie on his desk. He said nothing.

'Don't get up,' Salter said, rising from his chair, 'And don't leave town.'

'I am a suspect?'

'Everyone is, Professor, until we find the killer.'

Marika Tils spoke English with a thick, north European accent. What was *she* doing in an English Department?

'I am Dutch, Inspector. I learned my English as a

second language, although I have an M.A. from the
University of Toronto, which is the one they all bow down
to here. I compared *Paradise Lost* with a Dutch poem of
the same kind. Here I teach English to foreign students,
mostly Chinese from Hong Kong, although we are getting
them from everywhere.' The syntax was impeccable, but
the accent was so thick it sounded affected. Salter was
reminded of a story he had heard once about a similar
situation, and he tried to joke.

'Isn't there a danger of turning out a lot of Chinese
students with Dutch accents, Miss Tils?'

She smiled. 'Not much. But if the grammar were all
right, it wouldn't matter much, would it? Just an
interesting problem for the local Professor Higgins.'

Good. A nice relief from Dunkley. She was a woman in
her late thirties, just beginning to wrinkle slightly.
Straight blonde hair, nice, slightly lumpy features and a
good, if large, body. Graceful, feminine, she looked like
an athlete, a swimmer or an equestrian. In the right
dress, (or naked in the sun, thought Salter) she was
probably breath-taking. Her one disturbing feature was
that in colouring and in her carriage she seemed distantly
related to Dunkley. Her complexion was splotchy, and
her eyes looked sore. Someone, at last, was grieving for
Summers.

'I'll come to the point, Miss Tils. Would you call
yourself a friend of David Summers?'

'Oh yes. I liked him very much.'

What did that mean, translated from the Dutch?

'Does that mean you were lovers?'

'Oh no. Not in that way. But I wish we had been, now.
He was happily married, and I am also not free. No, I
mean I liked him. He was wonderful.'

'In what way?'

She shrugged. 'I could talk to him. I could trust him.
He liked me. What else?'

'He doesn't seem to have affected everybody that way.'

'Of course not. He was *my* friend, very special to me, but I don't mean he was Jesus Christ. Lots of people didn't like him.'

'But you weren't lovers?'

'I told you, no. But that was by the way. We didn't lie down together, but I might have.' She was annoyed at Salter's interest.

'Could I ask you about the Friday evening? First, do you know why he was so happy?'

'No. But it wasn't just a mood. Something had happened, but he never got a chance to tell me in front of the others. You know about him and Dunkley?'

'I know something. What was the trouble between them?'

'I don't know. They were involved in a way that made them hate each other. Like old accomplices who were ashamed of the old days. If you want to know what I think, I think it was something stupid, like they bumped into each other in a body-rub parlour or something. Dunkley is a fanatic, of course, and he would hate anyone who caught him doing something wrong. Maybe it was politics. I don't know. You can be sure it was something not very interesting.'

'Your chairman said they were like two people in a Conrad story.'

'Yes. I've heard him say that. But Conrad was another one who made mountains out of molehills.'

'From what you and others have said, Dunkley and Summers were very different people.'

'As chalk from cheese, Inspector.'

'Does that mean you don't like Dunkley?'

'This is very—unorthodox, isn't it?'

'Yes, I suppose it is. But I'm trying to find out what kind of man Summers was, and something about the people around him. You don't have to tell me.'

'All right. No, it doesn't mean that, of course, but in answer to your real question, I don't like Dunkley, but not for any reason connected with David.'

'What then?'

'Oh, for God's sake. I don't like the way he eats. His breath is bad. I don't know. Why don't you like people? I just don't like him.'

'Sorry. Now, after dinner you went back to the hotel. Did you spend the rest of the night by yourself in your room?'

She blushed deeply. Embarrassment or anger?'

'What does that question mean?'

'I'm sorry. I put it badly. Did you leave your room for any purpose after you returned to the hotel.'

'No. Oh, I see. You mean did I kill David.' Her tone was disgusted. 'No I did not leave my room and go to David's hotel and kill him.'

'That wasn't what I meant, although you are strong enough, and you might have a motive I don't know about. We found a glass with lipstick on it in his room.'

'Ah, you think I might have gone to make love with him?' She relaxed and shook her head. 'I wish I had. He might be alive now.'

'Somebody visited him, Miss Tils. A woman.'

'Apparently, Inspector, but not me. I haven't worn lipstick in ten years.' She looked interested in spite of herself, 'I wonder who David had tucked away in Montreal?'

'I'll find out. Miss Tils, as a friend of Professor Summers, do you know anything about his private life that might lead to someone killing him? Women, debts, anything like that?'

She shook her head. 'It must be something like that, I know. But I don't know of anyone. Certainly no one here, not even Dunkley.'

'How can you be so sure?'

'He's got an alibi, hasn't he? But call it my intuition. I

know Dunkley. He wouldn't do anything like that.'

Once again the hair prickled on Salter's scalp as he felt her withholding something. What's going on, he wondered.

On an impulse, instead of meeting his last appointment immediately, he returned to Carrier's office and walked in without waiting for an invitation. As he appeared, Dunkley rose from his chair and walked past him, ignoring him. Carrier sat still, saying nothing, and Salter took the vacant chair.

'Mr Carrier. I forgot to ask you about a statement. Since you and Professor Dunkley roomed together, you will be able to confirm each other's story, won't you? I'll need a statement signed. May I just check the facts again?' Salter consulted his notebook and pretended to read back to Carrier what he had said. He continued, 'A couple more details then. What time did you and Professor Dunkley get to your room?'

'About ten-thirty.'

'And you stayed all night in your room?'

'Yes.'

'What time did you leave it in the morning?'

'I don't remember. After eight.'

'You must have been tired out. A bit drunk?'

Carrier said nothing.

'Well, that checks, doesn't it?' Salter said with a smile. 'If you can think of anything that might help me, anything at all, anything Summers said or did, for example, you'll let me know won't you? I'll check all this with the hotel staff, of course, but I don't expect they will have noticed anything, will they?'

Why are you looking so frightened, Salter wondered. Probably because you went back for a last trip to the stripjoint. Or a whorehouse. Were they legal in Montreal?

Salter stared hard at the professor, wishing he knew more about interrogation techniques.

Last came Pollock. The name sounded familiar to Salter, but the man was a stranger to him. He was the first one Salter had met who looked like a proper professor. Dark suit, large bow tie, and black, old-fashioned boots which he placed at right-angles to each other as he bowed (or seemed to) his visitor through the door. Smallish and dapper, he affected a curly pipe with a lid, held in his mouth with one hand. When Salter was inside, he turned, placed his boots at right-angles again and waited for Salter to speak.

He's trying to twinkle, Salter thought, but he's a bit young for it. About thirty-five.

Eventually, after a long puff at his pipe, Pollock went around his desk and sat down, crossing his legs sideways to the desk and propping the elbow supporting the pipe on the desk with his head facing Salter.

He's going to say, 'What can I do for you, Inspector?' thought Salter.

Pollock removed the pipe, looked at it, put it back, puffed on it, removed it again, and said, 'What can I do for you, Inspector?'

'I need a motive, Mr Pollock, and I might find it in Summers's background. I am told you were his oldest friend here. First, do you know of any women in his life, apart from his wife?' Salter felt as if he was on stage, playing 'the policeman' to Pollock's 'professor'.

Pollock considered. 'No,' he said decisively. 'There have been. But not for years.'

'You are sure of that?'

'Certain. David never had long affairs. Over the years he fell in love once or twice; I always knew, because he told me. And his wife. That's why they didn't last long.'

'His wife put a stop to them?'

'No. Just the fact that she knew.'

'But he was not "in love" at the moment?'

'No.'

'You are certain?'

'Yes.'

'There could have been no brief fling in Montreal with one of his colleagues, perhaps?' I don't usually talk like this, thought Salter wonderingly.

'No.'

'You are certain?'

'Yes.'

Now it was in danger of becoming one of those nightmares on stage where a bit of dialogue keeps returning to its departure point because of a wrong cue. Salter shook himself.

'Do you mind telling me how you are so sure of yourself?'

Pollock puffed four times and delivered his line. 'Because he only has one female colleague, Marika Tils, and he did not have a brief fling with her.'

'How do you know?'

'Because I asked her.'

'I see. And she is to be believed, is she?'

'Absolutely.' Puff, pause, puff. 'You see, Inspector,' puff, 'Marika and I are lovers.' Puff, puff, puff.

Jesus Christ, thought Salter. What a world these people live in. He pulled a scrap of paper from his pocket. 'These conversations are entirely confidential, Professor, and I think I can trust you. This message was found in his mailbox in the hotel.' He read it: 'See you later. Wait for me. Jane.'

Pollock looked confused.

Gotcha, thought Salter.

Then: 'Ah yes,' Pollock said. 'I knew all about Jane, of course. But she didn't seem to be covered by your question. Jane is Jane Homer, Dean of Women at

Wollstonecraft Hall. They were just old friends.'

'I see.' Salter made a note. 'Now, Professor, I wonder if you would mind telling me everything about Summers that might help me to understand him. If I can get an idea of what kind of man he was it might help a great deal.'

Pollock began a seminar on his dead friend. Salter pretended to take notes to give Pollock's words their proper value.

'He was, I think, a good teacher, a very fair critic, a poor scholar, and a very poor student. He worked hard at his job here—too hard, probably; he had something interesting to say about what he was teaching, but he didn't keep up with his field and he didn't produce anything. His friends thought he failed to apply his talents, and his enemies accused him of having a butterfly mind. I think myself he had reached the age when it is now fashionable to change careers. The symptoms were that he had become involved in a whole host of activities in the last year or two that one could only see as distractions.'

'Like?'

'Like squash, Inspector. He took up squash last year, and played it four or five times a week. It was the high point of his day.'

'Was he good?'

'No. I played him after he had been playing for a year. He was no good at all. But among the people he played down at that club of his, he was able to find keen competition.'

'What else?'

'Making money. Obviously, he had decided to try and make his fortune. He was always a bit of a gambler—poker, the races—that sort of thing—he bought every lottery ticket going—and lately he was dabbling in commodities.

'Did he break out in any other ways?'

'You want to know if he was having a "mid-life crisis"? I think that's the jargon. Perhaps. He didn't start to dress like a gypsy, though, or wear a wig, or any of the other symptoms I've heard about. No, if I understand the mid-life crisis, it is an attempt to have a few more years of boyhood in middle age, at least that's how it manifests itself around here. Well, perhaps that's what he was doing, but in his case the symptoms were a sudden renewed interest in games and in taking risks.'

'Who were his friends, Professor?'

'Me, of course, and Marika. One or two others in the department enjoyed his company. Otherwise the people he and his wife socialized with. He didn't have many friends, the way people use that term nowadays, but he tended to keep them.'

'His enemies?'

'A lot of people were wary of him. He had a bad habit of looking for the funny side of any situation, and sometimes he was witty at the expense of others. He teased people and they took offence. And teasing *is* a form of cruelty, isn't it?'

'I'm trying to understand the relationship between him and Dunkley,' Salter said, coming to the point. 'Can you help me there?'

'Yes. I thought we'd come to that. You've heard Browne's theory, no doubt, of a Conradian link?'

'Yes. You think it makes sense?'

'Oh, it makes sense, Inspector, but it would be more impressive if someone else had put it forward. Coming from Browne, it doesn't carry much weight. Browne did his thesis on Conrad. That is the only author he knows.'

'You don't think much of it, then.'

'Not really. I think they just struck sparks off each other.'

'Summers never confided in you—about his feelings for

Dunkley, and the reasons?'

'No, he didn't. That's why I don't think there's any mystery. He would certainly have said something to me. We were very close.' And then, quite unexpectedly, Pollock stopped acting, and his eyes filled with tears. He put his pipe down, and blew his nose.

Salter gave him a few moments by pretending to scribble. Then he said, gently enough, 'It does seem strange, though, that he never discussed such a well-known feud with you, sir, his closest friend?'

But Pollock was now too upset to speculate with him. He shrugged and fiddled with the relighting of his pipe.

Salter put his notebook away and stood up. 'If anything occurs to you that you think I might find helpful, you can find me at the Headquarters building. Thank you very much, sir.' He left the professor still blinking at his pipe.

As he walked down the corridor he heard someone behind him, and he slowed down enough at the corner to see Marika Tils go into Pollock's office.

CHAPTER 3

'What would make two guys not speak to each other for ten years?' Salter asked. They were sitting at the back of their house on a concrete slab, looking at the grass. Their neighbours would have called it having coffee on the patio in the garden, but from motives of inverted snobbery, though different in each case, Salter and Annie referred to the area as 'the yard'. Salter had been raised in Cabbagetown, and 'the yard' was the proper term for the place where Canadians cooled off in the summer; 'garden' was an affected, English term. In Annie's case, the half-acre of lawn surrounding her family home on Prince Edward Island was still called 'the yard', and she found the term 'garden' Upper Canadian, and effete.

'Don't their friends know?' she asked.

'No. Bloody mystery. Probably nothing to it, but the guy who didn't speak to Salter is my chief suspect at the moment.'

'Why?'

'No reason. I just don't like the bugger.'

'Maybe there was a woman?'

'Nobody has said anything about it if there was.'

'Politics, then. What about you and Albert Prine?'

'What about it? I caught him listening to my phone calls.' Salter was immediately irritated. What did this have to do with anything?'

'But you couldn't prove it.'

'No, but the bugger *knows* I caught him. If I had accused him they would have called me paranoid.'

'He *was* listening, though. And you've never told anyone.'

'If I did, he'd soon hear about it and I would have to prove it, or get clobbered.'

'So you haven't talked to him for a year. You don't even mention his name around here any more.'

'No, because sometimes I think you think I imagined it.'

'Oh, I believe you, Charlie. You see what I mean, though.'

'All right.' Salter swallowed his irritation. 'So you're saying these two sort of had something on each other. I don't think it could be politics, though.'

'Money?'

'I don't see how.'

'Sex, then?'

'One of Summers's pals suggested they probably met one night in a body-rub parlour. From what I saw of Dunkley, something like that would bother him, all right. But Summers, I gather, would have been one to make a joke of it, once he got over his embarrassment. He wasn't shy about suggesting they all go to a girlie show in Montreal, but Dunkley was.'

'You mean all these middle-aged professors get away from their wives and they act . . .'

'Just like everyone else. Especially at that age.'

She accepted the tease. 'Charlie, would you go to a show like that, if you were on holiday away from me?'

'No, dear. Only on business.'

But she was concerned now. 'From what you've told me, half these people are having affairs their wives don't know about.'

'Just one, dear: Pollock. And I don't know if he's married.'

'Of course he is.'

Now they were off on a familiar misery, entitled, 'Why Do Married Men Play Around?' with the inevitable sub-theme, 'Do You?' Fortunately Salter was saved by the arrival of Angus around the corner of the house carrying a cricket bat. One of the traditions of Annie's family was that the men went to Upper Canada College, and she had used her trust fund, set up by her grandmother, to keep the tradition going for Seth and Angus. It would have been piggish to object, but their fancy ways made him uncomfortable, and he kept a firm, ironic distance from the goings-on of the quality his sons mixed with, and occasionally brought home.

'Did you win?' he asked now. 'How many bounders did you hit?'

'Boundaries, Dad. None. I was stumped first ball.'

'That sounds bad, son.'

'It is. It means I was out before I even hit one.'

Salter tutted. 'Did you pitch today?' he asked wide-eyed.

'Bowl,' Angus said. 'Bowl, bowl, bowl, bowl. NO!'

'That's enough,' said Annie. 'I'll get you some supper,'

another word she preserved in the face of Upper Canada's
'dinner'.

'Angus won't want any supper,' Salter said. 'He'll have
had tea. In the pavilion. Won't you, son?'

The other two ignored him, and his wife moved into
the house while his son took her chair, indicating a desire
for a chat with his father. This was rare enough for Salter
to stop his fooling and take an interest. Angus came to the
point immediately.

'Dad, the Civics teacher wants parents to come and give
us a talk on what they do. I said I'd ask you.'

Salter was thrown into confusion. While the subject of
his career did not crop up much around the house, he
had the impression that the boys, once over their 'cops
and robbers' phase, were slightly ashamed of him,
especially among their moneyed friends. Now here was
Angus suggesting he display himself in public. His first
instinct was an immediate and derisive refusal, but he was
slightly touched, so he played for time.

'Who have you had so far, son?' he asked.

'Pillsbury's father, who's a stockbroker, a chartered
accountant, two lawyers, and a big deal surgeon who
transplants hearts or something.'

Salter returned to his first instinct. 'No, thanks, son.
Too glamorous for me. I'll tell you what. I'll get my
sergeant to come over. He used to go round the schools in
Safety Week, teaching them to "Stop, Look, and Listen".
The kids loved it.'

Angus got up. 'I know. I heard him. I'll tell Mr Secord
"no", then.'

'That's right. Tell him all my work is highly
confidential.'

Annie returned from getting Angus his supper. '*I*
suggested that,' she said. 'He asked me and I said I
thought you might. Why don't you?'

'Because I'd feel a horse's arse, that's why,' Salter said

noisily, and picked up his notebook to cut off the discussion. 'Now tell me, where have I heard of Pollock?'

'I don't know. Perhaps, like everyone else, you've heard of him as a famous artist.' Annie was hostile, po-faced.

Never mind. She'd get over it. 'Right, thanks. What does uxorious mean? U, X . . .'

'I know the word. It means dotingly fond of one's wife. Why?'

'Guy called himself that today. Now tell me this . . .'

But Annie had left.

Late that night, in bed, she asked him, 'Charlie, have you had any other women lately?'

He grabbed her in a mock-brutal gesture. 'I haven't had *any* women lately.'

She took his hand away. 'I'm not surprised if that's how you go about it.' She sat up and took off her nightdress. 'Try a little tenderness,' she said.

Afterwards she asked, 'Well, have you?'

'What?' he asked. 'What? Oh, for Christ's sake, go to sleep.'

On Wednesday morning Salter phoned Montreal. He found O'Brien in the office. 'Hello, Onree. Charlie Salter here. I've done the rounds and it looks to me as if the guy we're looking for is in Montreal. Apparently Summers was celebrating something and throwing his money about. He was drunk, too, even before he got into the whisky. I think someone followed him back to the hotel and clobbered him for his money. Then they panicked.'

'You have interviewed all the people he was with?'

'Yes. An unlikely lot. One possibility, but my guess is still a whore and a pimp.'

'Did he spend the night, what do you call it, pub-crawling?'

'More or less. But they only went to three places. Here they are: Maison Victor Hugo, The Iron Horse, and Les

Jardins du Paradis. How's my accent?'

'Bad, Charlie, but I know these places. OK. I'll put a couple of men on it. You think any of them is the most likely?'

'Les Jardins du Paradis. They were in there between nine and ten, and my guess is that the killer was, too.'

'OK. You have seen everybody?'

'No, no. The funeral is this afternoon. I'll go to that. And I want to go down to this squash club where he spent so much time. Then there's the wife, who I'll see tomorrow. Oh yes, I found out who Jane is—you remember the note in his box? She's an old pal of his, apparently, so I don't expect to find anything there.'

'What about those phone numbers on the little sheet of paper in his wallet?'

'Not yet. I'll do that today. But I still think you will be looking for the villain in Montreal.'

'OK, Charlie.. This is taking up a lot of your time.'

'Time's what I've got a lot of, Onree. Talk to you later.' Salter hung up and turned to Sergeant Gatenby.

'Frank, would you let "Chiefie" know that this Montreal case is continuing, and I am assuming he wants me to stay with it. And here—' He picked up the IN tray on his desk, piled high with little errands. 'Send these back where they came from and tell them I'm all tied up. And don't take any more.'

'At all? They've got quite used to us doing their extra jobs.'

'Well, they'll have to get unused to it. They can figure out how to dispose of the surplus horse-shit from Central Stables all by themselves. I'm busy.'

'Being busy is being happy,' Gatenby said. He was fond of this kind of 'old country' patter. This time he was right.

The funeral was conducted from a parlour on Yonge Street, between an English Fishe and Chippe Shoppe and a tavern. When Salter arrived there were a dozen people sitting silently facing the closed coffin. He identified the widow and daughter, pale without weeping, dressed quietly but not in black. Pollock was there with Marika Tils; all the people Salter had interviewed plus several others, presumably from the English Department, sat in a group. One other man sat alone, several rows behind this group, and a girl of about twenty sat in the back row. The funeral was private, so only the most determined had come. The service was Anglican, without a eulogy, and was soon done. When the small crowd straggled out, Salter caught the stranger on the sidewalk and introduced himself. 'You were a friend of Professor Summers, sir?' he asked. The man was making no effort to speak to the widow, unlike the others.

'Not really. I used to play squash with him, that's all. Have to find another partner, now.' A summer-weight business suit and a dark tie; hair slightly shorter than the fashion; a completely typical and nearly faceless Bay Street type, although the shirt was cheap and the shoes too old. Now he acted as if he just wanted to get away, as if the funeral had been a duty of the worst kind.

Salter asked him, 'Who am I talking to, sir?'

The other man stopped walking away from him backwards, and contented himself with continually looking around him as if waiting for a car to pick him up. 'Bailey,' he said. 'Arthur Bailey. I'm called Bill, because of the song.'

'And you were his squash partner?'

'That's right. He played some other people, though. Me, mostly, I guess.'

Bailey was in an agony to be gone, and out of the corner of his eye, Salter noticed the young girl in the back row, saying goodbye to Pollock and Marika Tils. He said, 'This is a difficult time, Mr Bailey. Perhaps I could come and find you tomorrow.'

'I don't know anything about him, Inspector. I don't even know what his wife looks like. I just played squash with him.'

'In a situation like this, it helps to know as much as possible about the victim. Perhaps you can tell me why he was suddenly addicted to squash, Mr Bailey. Where can I find you?'

The man looked wretched. 'At the squash club, at four, before my game?' he suggested. 'I may be late. I have to go to our plant at Oakville tomorrow.'

The girl seemed to be saying goodbye. 'Perfect,' Salter said. 'I wanted to get a look at the club. Where shall I wait for you?'

'In the lounge.' Bailey was now moving backwards again.

'Thank you, sir. I'll be there.' Salter turned and swooped down on the girl just as she was starting away. 'Excuse me, miss, could I have a word?'

Professor Pollock crossed the sidewalk and introduced them. 'Molly Tripp, one of Summers's students, Inspector Salter.'

Thank you very much, Salter thought. Now bugger off.

Pollock did a bit of pipe-puffing before he realized that Salter was waiting for him to go. Eventually he made the best of it by inviting the girl to drop by for coffee at any time, and left them alone.

She had shed some tears, but was in control of herself. 'What do you want me for, Inspector?'

'I'm trying to find out all about Professor Summers, miss. You are the first student I've been able to find. What about some coffee?'

'I need something.' She looked at the tavern. 'I'd sooner have a beer.'

Salter led the way in.

'You must have felt pretty strongly about Professor Summers,' Salter began when the beer came.

The girl unbuttoned her raincoat and pulled her arms free. Underneath she was wearing a grey sweater and a dark skirt. Her hair was curly and seemed uncombed. 'I will miss him,' she said. 'He showed me things, and he liked me.'

'A great teacher?'

'No. Some of the students didn't like him. I did,. though, and some others.'

'Why?'

'I liked the way he got excited over poetry, especially Romantic poetry. It was from him I realized that poetry is written in a different language, not just prose with rhymes. A lot of people already knew that, I guess, but I didn't.'

Romantic poetry? 'You mean love poems?' he asked innocently.

'No, no. The Romantic period. Wordsworth and Keats, mainly, for him.'

'Why didn't the others like him?'

'They said they didn't get proper notes. They wanted more history. He wasn't very formal in class. And some of the stuff he was talking about he hadn't figured out himself. But he *told* us he hadn't,' she ended, more to herself, apparently echoing an old argument.

'I want to know what kind of person he was. Did you know him—yourself?'

'Personally?'

'Yes.'

'A little bit. I used to go up to his office once in a while and talk to him. As I said, he liked me and we had a nice time talking about stuff.'

'He took an interest in you?'

'He thought I might be able to write a real essay, as he called it. I tried. He told me a couple of weeks ago that the first page of my last essay was the best first page he had had all year. Still only got a B + though!'

While she was talking, Salter ordered two more beers. He could see why Summers liked Molly Tripp. He had very little to ask her himself, but a very great desire to sit with her for a while longer and watch her talk. She was nice.

'What made the essay so good? The first page, I mean.'

'I read it this afternoon. It sounded like him talking, you know?' She smiled as if she and Salter were talking about a mutual friend.

'And that was it? You were a good student?'

'Yeah, I guess so. Oh, shit, I see what you're getting at. He didn't try to get my pants off. He wasn't a groper.'

That is what I wanted to know, thought Salter, but I may have screwed this up. He acted puzzled. 'Huh?' he said.

'We talked about poetry, is all. We talked some personal stuff sometimes, but not very much.'

Salter thought of a way to cover his interest, to make it official.

'Professor Summers was not in the habit of seducing his students, then?' There. How did that sound? Nice and pompous?

'Hell, no. Oh, there was something there when I was in his office, Inspector. Isn't there always between any man and woman?'

Salter tested this against several ladies he knew, and thought, No. He nodded in agreement.

'The other kids said he spent half the time in class with his eye on me, but I think I was his litmus test. He watched me to see if what he was saying was making sense. I did like him, too. I kissed him once.'

'When?'

'The last time I saw him. Last week. He'd just told me he'd given me an A for the course because of a good exam. He was as pleased as I was, so I gave him a big smacker when he wasn't watching.'

'What did he do?'

'He just sat there looking pleased. Now I want to go.'
She stood up. The tears were streaming down her face.

'Where can I find you?' Salter asked. 'Just in case.'

'Here.' She gave him a card. 'I started work on Monday
as the assistant to the assistant creative director at an
advertising agency, and I have cards already.' She belted
up her raincoat. 'I hope you find this character,
Inspector. What's your real name?'

'Salter,' he said startled. 'Charlie Salter is my real
name.'

'Well, lotsa luck, Charlie.'

They left the tavern and Salter watched her walk away.
Her stride was long and she walked slightly hunched up as
if a gale was blowing. At the corner she turned and saw
him still there, and waved. Salter waved back and
pretended to be looking for his car keys. He would have to
see her again, he decided.

That night, after supper, Annie said, 'I've invited your
father to eat on Sunday.'

Seth groaned theatrically. 'I'll miss Walt Disney. He
doesn't like the TV on.'

Angus said, 'I have to do my essay in the main library
on Sunday. I'll just have a hamburger at Mac's.'

There was a silence while they waited for Salter to start
shouting.

Annie said quickly, 'You can watch Walt Disney
upstairs. And you can come home by six, Angus. Your
grandfather only comes once a month.'

Angus said, 'But this essay is important, Mum. Besides,
I don't like lamb.'

'Nor do I,' Seth said. 'I hate lamb and stuff.'

Annie said, 'It doesn't have to be lamb.'

Salter said, holding on to his temper, 'You can have a
choice, lamb or beef.'

Angus said, 'Couldn't we have poached salmon with that terrific white stuff on it?'

'You know bloody well your grandfather doesn't eat salmon.'

'Lasagna, then.'

'Or any Italian food. Or French, or Greek, or Chinese food. Now knock it off you two. We'll have roast beef, and you'll like it, and you can watch the upstairs TV turned down low. After you've said hullo to him.'

'Walt Disney's no good in black and white.'

'Fine. Don't watch him, then. Now shut up, the pair of you.'

This was the true clash of cultures in the Salter home. Unlike the thoughtful, ever-accommodating relatives of his wife, his own father was a narrow-spirited misanthrope who was getting steadily worse in his old age. He watched television, calling most of it 'bloody American twaddle', and visited the tavern at the end of his street to moan with one or two cronies. He was a former maintenance man with the Toronto Transit Commission who had retired to a tiny flat in the East End of the city near the street-car barn. They saw very little of him, because he was an ordeal. Salter telephoned him once a week, and visited him whenever he was in the area. Annie, however, insisted on their duty to him and he ate his Sunday dinner with them once a month. She had tried him with every delicacy in her repertoire, and he ate them all with the same comment, 'Very nice, I suppose, but I like a proper dinner on Sundays. So did Charlie, once.' A proper dinner was one with gravy and custard. In spite of all attempts by Annie to make him smile, his visits were joyless. The real difficulty lay in coping lightly with his prejudices in front of the children. He was anti-semitic from his youth, and he had since developed a prejudice against every class and race but his own, the poor Anglo-Saxons. No visit was complete without some reference on

his part to 'them Jews', the 'Eyeties', or the 'Nig-nogs' who
were responsible for his depressed social and financial
condition. He watched Annie for any sign that she was
patronizing him, and criticized the behaviour of the boys
continually until he provoked a flare-up of reaction in
Annie or Salter. After a small row, he shut up, satisfied,
with a remark like, 'Sorry I-spoke. I was just trying to be
helpful.' Once he caught Angus in a kilt (another family
tradition that Annie had brought to Toronto); this
offended the old man in several ways at once, including
his anti-Scottish prejudice, and he wondered loudly to
Salter, if the boy wasn't turning into 'a bit of a pansy.'

Now Salter cut the conversation off and brought out his
notebook. 'I've got some phone calls to make,' he said.
'Stay off the phone for half an hour, will you.'

The boys disappeared, still grumbling, and Salter sat
down by the phone. He looked first at a list of numbers
that he had transcribed from the scrap of paper in
Summers's wallet. 'Do these numbers mean anything to
you?' he asked his wife. 'A couple look like phone
numbers, but the others don't.' He handed her the list.

She studied it for a while. 'Hold on,' she said. I thought
so. This one is his Eaton's Account; this one is the number
he used to get money from one of those banking
machines. Those two are phone numbers. That one I
don't know. It looks like the combination for a lock.'

'Well done. Now all I have to do is phone these two and
I'll know all about his private life.'

'Any ideas yet?'

'The same one I started with. It looks like he was done
in by accident, by a prostitute or her pimp. In the
meantime, I've got interested in the guy, and I'm trying
to find out what kind of person he was, just in case we
have one of those clever murders, complete with motive
and everything. So far, I've found out he wasn't a bad
teacher, and some people liked him and some didn't. He

had one real enemy and two good friends in the department.'

'Both men?'

'A man and a woman. And there is a student who liked him. And a woman he used to have a drink with, once a year, out of town. That's it.'

'Did the woman in the department like him a lot?'

Salter gritted his teeth. Annie's remark grew from the problem that always lay between them. She was everything a man could want in a wife except for a continual low-burning jealousy, which had grown partly out of the swinging times they lived in. As she understood the scene, no one was faithful these days, and she was constantly alert to the possibility that her husband, whom she saw as an ideal prize, would be picked off by some other woman. As Salter put it once to a woman whose friendship he had retained in the teeth of Annie's hostility, 'Her friends tell her how lucky she is that I don't screw everyone in sight, and she takes that to mean that they are all ready to lie down whenever I say the word. They are all divorced and it makes her nervous.' In fact, Salter had been unfaithful (with the same woman friend) only once, and he was such a poor liar that Annie had suspected immediately. After that he found fidelity the comfortable way to live. He loved his wife, and wished she would relax. When he tried to tell her this, she said only, 'If I relax, you might,' And that, as his woman friend pointed out, was probably true.

Now Annie asked, 'They weren't lovers, then?'

'She says not,' Salter replied.

'You asked her?'

'I'm a copper,' he shouted. 'I'm trying to find out who killed someone. You start by trying to find out who might have wanted to.'

'Is she attractive?'

Oh, fuck it. 'The interesting thing,' he said, 'Is that I

like everyone who liked him, man, woman and child. But I didn't much take to the ones who didn't. That doesn't mean that this woman gave me a hard-on, or that Summers was banging her after hours in the library. It just means that I might have liked Summers, too.'

'All right, Charlie, make your phone calls.'

The first phone call was embarrassing. The number turned out to be that of Summers's squash-playing friend, Bailey, whom Salter had seen at the funeral. 'Sorry, Mr Bailey. I just wanted to check our appointment. Four o'clock tomorrow, at the club? Thanks. See you then.' There was no reply to the second number. Salter consulted his notebook and dialled again. 'Miss Homer? Miss Jane Homer? Inspector Salter here. Metro Police. I'd like to talk to you about Professor Summers. I believe you were in contact with him in Montreal.'

The voice was thick and strained. 'Yes. I never saw him, though. What do you want?'

'To talk to you, please. Mainly about Summers's background. May I come to your office in the morning?'

'All right. I get there about ten o'clock. I am the Dean of Women at Wollstonecraft Hall. On Harbord Street.'

'I'll find it. At ten o'clock, then. Fine.'

Salter consulted another piece of paper, Summers's hotel bill with the record of two calls Summers had made on Friday afternoon. Again, there was no reply to the first. The second one produced a recorded message to the effect that the offices were now closed and he should call again tomorrow. That was that, then. Salter put his notebook away, and went upstairs to his wife's sewing-room, where she kept all her old college books. He found what he was looking for, Volume II of *Representative Poetry*, and thumbed through it looking for Wordsworth and Keats. The first Wordsworth poem he found was about fifty pages long, and he kept looking until he found one that had fewer than a hundred words. Slowly, stumblingly, he learned the first two lines, a total of fourteen words. When he was sure of them, he turned to Keats. Again he had trouble finding one to his purpose, so he chose, arbitrarily, the last poem and picked out two lines in the final verse that sounded 'poetic'. Once more he set himself to learn them. More difficult, these, because he was not sure what the lines meant. He sat there, mumbling, as his wife appeared. 'What's going on, Charlie?' she asked, staring at the book.

'It's Summers,' he said in some confusion. 'He specialized in Romantic poetry. I was just trying to see what that was all about. Not very lively, is it?' He smiled falsely.

'Who have you been talking to today?'

'Oh, for Christ's sake,' he shouted. 'I'm just getting into the man's mind. That's all.'

She looked surprised at his reaction, but did not press him further, merely picked up a piece of material she had come for and went back downstairs.

Salter waited until she was well out of hearing and went back to his homework. He had Wordsworth cold, but had to mumble away at the Keats for another five minutes before he felt sure of it.

CHAPTER 4

At the office the next morning, Gatenby greeted him with a message from the Superintendent. 'He wants to hear from you about how this Montreal case is going,' he said.

'I've got an appointment at ten. Is he free now?'

'He said he would be in all morning. He was very keen to hear from you.'

'All right. I'll do it now. I'm going to be out the rest of the day.'

'Quick cup of coffee first? Won't take a minute.'

'All right.'

'Little bit of sugar, just to take the edge off?'

Salter had recently been making a stab at dieting. Gatenby showed his interest by tempting him continually, like an old granny with a pocketful of sweets that the children are forbidden to eat.

'No, Frank,' Salter said, hardly irritated at all. 'Annie said I mustn't.'

Superintendent Orliff was not a friend of Salter's, but neither was he an enemy. The Superintendent had no enemies, a state he had achieved by keeping his distance from anyone who made a lot of waves. He was a small, neat man whose desk was stacked with a dozen tidy piles of paper, each one representing some aspect of his work. He kept records of everything, including all verbal transactions, and the piles grew until the particular project was, or seemed to be (for Orliff was a careful man), finished, when it was put with other piles on the shelves lining his office. Eventually the piles were put into cabinets, but not until they had been dead for a long time. Orliff saw himself as a civil servant surrounded by politicians, and while his opinion was regularly sought, he rarely gave it, offering instead only information. He did not bury himself in his work (one of the piles on his desk contained material about his retirement plans; another charted the progress of a cottage he was building), but he recorded it thoroughly. While the various factions in the organization grouped and regrouped themselves, he sat back, available and promotable. His superiors could trust him to be loyal: his subordinates knew he had no favourites. When the former Superintendent had been promoted, he had taken over the job without opposition. He sat in his office now, waiting for Salter to deliver his report.

Salter said, 'As of now it looks like a mugging. I still have a couple of people to question, but those I've seen so far don't look very likely.'

Orliff put his finger on the transcript from Montreal. 'No robbery,' he said.

'No robbery,' Salter agreed. 'But they probably panicked. Hookers who try this trick are not killers. Maybe she had a new boy-friend who was showing off.'

'They agree in Montreal?'

'I speak to Sergeant O'Brien every day. He'd rather have me find a killer with a nice motive here, but, yes, he's looking for a likely pair.'

'So. A middle-aged English Professor goes to a convention, has a little fling and he's unlucky.'

'Yes, sir. That's funny, because he told everyone that it was his lucky day.'

'What did he mean?'

'I haven't found out yet.'

'Uh. So someone sees a party of profs, a bit pissed, our man throwing his money about, at a tit-show, you say?' Orliff smiled companionably at Salter. 'As one middle-aged man to another, being middle-aged, the young girls get him going, so he dumps his friends and finds himself a hooker. Not so hard because she has already got him picked out and is waiting for the nod, maybe already arranged while his friends weren't looking. Back at the hotel he gets undressed, they have a drink, the boy-friend arrives. Our man objects—maybe threatens to call the police—you never know—and all hands panic. Boy-friend clobbers him, then the real panic. That it?'

'I expect so, sir. Something like that.'

'What's the problem with it?' There was no aggression in the Superintendent's voice. If there was a problem he didn't want Salter to make a fool of himself.

'I'm not happy with it yet. There's something screwy. He'd drunk too much. As one middle-aged man to another, sir, he wanted his bed.'

'He was a professor. Maybe they can keep going longer.' Orliff smiled to show he was joking.

'Nobody at the hotel saw a whore, sir.'

'Like I say, he was a professor. Cunning. He would have slipped her past them, all right.'

'Even drunk?'

'Sure.'

'It's possible, sir, but it's got no life in it. It lacks verisimilitude.'

'Say that again.'

'Verisimilitude, sir. It means believability.'

'Does it, by Christ. You mean it may be true, but it won't play?'

'Well, yes, but in this case I think that means it may not be true.'

'It sounds likely to me,' Orliff said agreeably.

'It's probably true, but . . .'

'Now what?'

'I'm just trying to put myself in this man's shoes. Here I am in Montreal, feeling good because I've just had a stroke of luck—any kind, but it probably involves money because I'm taking the boys out for dinner, a hundred and thirty dollars' worth. (My guess is that professors are a tight lot.) So, I've drunk a fair amount and I feel good, all the time I'm thinking about my luck, whatever it is. Would I feel like a whore? Right then and there? I don't think so. I think Summers just went home in a cab.'

'I see—psychology. After a big win at the track you feel like celebrating, not screwing.'

'More or less, sir, yes.'

'I don't know, Salter. I've never won a lot of money. Tit-shows make *me* horny, don't they you? They are supposed to.'

'Well, yes, sir, and I expect they made the others feel that way, which is why they are all suggesting that

Summers must have picked up a whore. But . . .'

'All right, all right. So what's your theory?'

'If there was a whore, sir, I think it would happen later, after he'd climbed down a bit from his high. He would have had to use the bell-boy—he wouldn't know any call-girls in Montreal, or anywhere else. And O'Brien says the hotel staff swear they saw and heard nothing like that.'

'The bell-boy is lying,' Orliff offered.

Salter felt all the weight of a weary and unintelligible world fall on him. He gave in.

'All right, sir. I'll pack it in. I'll phone O'Brien and tell him that's it.'

'No, no. I'm just doing my job. Giving you a hard time. What's the rest of your alternative theory?'

'There's a piece missing somewhere, probably connected with his lucky day. Whoever killed him did it for more money than was in his wallet, or for envy or revenge. He could have told someone what his lucky day was all about.'

'This guy Dunkley. We've got him on file, you say?'

'He was arrested once for disturbing the peace outside the American Embassy. He's in most of the protests.'

'One of them, is he?' Orliff was mildly interested. It was his strength that he did not feel any enmity towards the citizens who tried to make life difficult for him, the robbers, the rapists, and the civil disobedience crowd. 'Without them,' he would say, 'we wouldn't have a job, some of us.' He fingered the report for a few moments. 'You want to stay on this?' he asked. 'We aren't too busy at the moment.'

And you can always spare me, anyway, thought Salter. 'Yes,' he said. 'Until I find out more about Summers and his luck.'

'Many more possibilities?'

'I haven't talked to the wife yet. Then there's this Jane Homer woman. And I have to talk to his pals at the

squash club. At least I want a better idea of the man who
got killed, and the kind of man who might have killed
him.'

'All right. Don't spring any surprises on me, though.
Keep me in touch.' Salter got to the door before Orliff
spoke again. 'By the way, this isn't the dregs. I talked to
the Deputy in Montreal. He said O'Brien speaks highly of
you. I told our Deputy. He was pleased because we owe
Montreal a favour. It wouldn't do you any harm if this
squared the books.'

Salter understood. Just possibly, if he got lucky, he
might find himself moving across the desert again, on the
way to the fertile land on the other side.

He still had some time before he had to meet Jane Homer,
so he paid a rare visit to the canteen for a cup of coffee.
The only other occupant was an inspector in the homicide
division whom Salter had known slightly in the old days.
They nodded to each other, and Salter sat down at the
same table.

'What are you up to these days, Charlie?' the detective
asked, pleasantly enough. His name was Harry Wycke,
and Salter had no real reason to suppose him hostile.
They had never crossed each other, and by now most of
his old enemies, like his old cronies, rarely bothered him,
but he assumed they were all still relishing his demise.
Annie said he was paranoiac, to which Salter replied that
even the constable in charge of records gave his requests
for information a very low priority when he was busy.

'I'm investigating a murder—in Montreal,' Salter said.

'How does that work, then?'

'A Toronto professor got himself killed in Montreal.
I'm helping out at this end.' Was this a problem? Was he
poaching on homicide's territory?

'Tough shit. What are you doing, exactly?'

'I think I'm supposed to be looking for a motive. Just in

case there's someone here who might have done it.'

'Wife? Lover?'

'Not the wife. And no lover so far. Someone clobbered him in a hotel room.'

'Whore, maybe?'

'Or a pimp. It looks possible, but they left behind a wallet full of money.'

'They got scared. Did he have any enemies?'

'That's what I'm supposed to find out. So far, I haven't found anyone who looks like a killer.'

'What do killers look like, Charlie? The ones I know all look different. Couldn't be a professional, could it?'

'The mob, you mean. Christ, I don't think so. He was a *professor*. Besides, don't they warn you first, like breaking your legs?'

'They've given that up now. Too much publicity. Now they just leave a little bomb. Then it could be anybody, unless you are on the inside and know who sent it.'

'This guy *was* a gambler, Harry. You think that a bookie would do that?'

Wycke laughed. 'No, I was just kidding. Well, I wish you luck, Charlie. Most killers are easy—you find them two blocks away covered in blood. The thoughtful ones can be very, very hard. How come they gave it to you?'

'I think you boys were too busy. And I'm just helping out,' Salter said cheerfully.

'That's right, we are. We probably looked at it and gave it back. Still, if you need any help, let me know.'

'Thanks.' Salter dipped his toe into the waters of fraternal feeling. 'This stuff is pretty new to me. I might be glad to give you a shout if I get in too deep.'

'Any time. You know where my office is.' Wycke finished his coffee and stood up. 'I won't trip you up,' he said.

Salter understood, and felt a twinge of grateful

warmth. He had been lonely for some time. 'Thanks,' he said. 'Thanks.'

Wollstonecraft Hall, a red sandstone building on Harbord Street, was built by a dissenting church to protect young ladies from the city when they were not in class, but in the 'sixties it had been forced to swing with the times and had become a mixed residence. As he walked through the halls, Salter passed young men and women in about equal numbers, chatting in groups and pairs, and, in one case, embracing feverishly as if war had been declared.

The Office of the Dean of Women was open, and Salter pushed the door back and walked in. A secretary looked up from her typewriter, and he introduced himself. She was the drabbest girl he had seen for some time; she looked as though she had been hired for her plainness by the original sex-fearing governors of the residence. Her glasses, steel-rimmed, round and tiny, were balanced on the end of her nose; her thick blonde hair was cut in a straight line, parallel with the bottoms of her ears; she wore a brown smock that looked like a shroud. Salter was appalled and piteous. 'Is Miss Homer in?' he asked. 'She's expecting me.'

The girl stood up, took her glasses off, and smiled, transforming herself like the heroine of a musical comedy. She had beautiful teeth, and the shroud, when she was upright, clothed a perfect figure. It's a style, thought Salter. They do it deliberately.

The girl went into the inner office and reappeared with another wonderful smile. 'Miss Homer says you can go right in,' she said. She put her glasses on and went back to posing as a hag in front of her typewriter.

Miss Homer was another surprise. She was about thirty-five, light gold hair, a buff-coloured denim suit, brown-and-white striped shirt, gold bangles on each wrist, gold rings in her ears, and shoes made of tapestry. At first Salter thought she was sun-tanned, but as he approached to shake hands he realized she was so thickly freckled that the freckles seemed alive and she seemed to be blinking to keep them out of her eyes. Salter, who had been expecting a grey-haired matron in golf shoes, found himself shuffling his feet.

'Would you like some coffee?' she asked.

'Thanks. Yes, please.' He sat down in the armchair she indicated, one of a pair arranged by a low table. To his further surprise, instead of calling her secretary, she went to a table by the wall and poured two cups from a percolator. Ah yes, he thought. Secretaries do not make coffee these days, especially on the frontier of the movement.

The room was a relief after the utilitarianism of Douglas College. On one wall a huge block of photographs of various kinds formed a mural. On another hung a large framed thing made of bits of cloth. The desk was a sheet of heavy glass on two trestles. All this Salter had time to take in before she returned with the coffee.

She hunched over her cup and waited for him to begin.

Salter showed her the note which she barely glanced at.

'Yes, that's my note. I'd forgotten about it. Is that why you are here? I never saw Professor Summers.'

'Were you a good friend of his?'

'Once. Not any more. David was an old colleague. I taught at Douglas while I was doing my thesis.'

'How long ago?'

'Six years. I graduated five years ago, and got this job.'

'Did you often see him in Toronto?'

'No, never. Except by accident, of course.'

'But you arranged to meet him at the conference?'

'At conferences like that you pick up with people you don't otherwise see. I often had a drink with the Douglas College people.'

'Were you and Professor Summers in the same field?' Salter asked out of his new knowledge.

'What? Oh no. My field is women's journals.

'Like *Chatelaine*?' Salter asked, surprised at what English Literature covered.

'No, no. Diaries. I got interested first in Dorothy Wordsworth, and went on from there. As a matter of fact, David was interested in my thesis topic, which concerned journals as literary forms. I think he started one of his own because of me, but I never saw it.'

'Let me see, then. You arrived at the conference and left a note in his box. Wasn't he in his room? What time did you leave the note?'

'About six. No, there was no answer from his room.'

'And that's all the contact you had with him?'

'Yes.' She got up to refill her cup.

'How long did you stay in Montreal?'

'I left on Saturday afternoon, with the people from Douglas. Everyone heard at lunch-time what had happened and I was too upset to stay. Besides, people were talking about it, people who didn't know him, as if it was an exciting thing, like a president being assassinated.' As she replaced her cup on the coffee table it rattled in its saucer.

'I see. That's that, then. You have nothing more to tell me?'

She shook her head and then began to shiver, trembling at first, then violently. When her teeth began to chatter, Salter shouted for the secretary, who ran in and held her until the shivering subsided.

'I'm sorry,' the Dean said, when she had recovered enough. 'I seem to be a bit of a mess.'

'Delayed shock, I should imagine,' Salter said. 'I should go to bed and call your doctor. If I want you again, I'll let your secretary know.'

In the outer office Salter asked the secretary. 'Has that happened before?'

'Yes. A lot. She's hardly stopped since she came back from Montreal. I thought she was all right today, but you set her off again.'

'I didn't realize she was so fragile, miss.'

'She's not. I don't know why this is so hard on her.'

Salter left. Dean of Women overreacts to routine questioning, he thought. I wonder why?

It was a long time since Salter had gone home for lunch. From the early days of their marriage he associated it with 'nooners', making love in the daytime, preferably on the floor. Did the young officers still do that? He and Annie had not done it for years, but now as she stood at the sink he put his arms round her waist and squeezed her in something more than a friendly hug. She twisted in his arms and looked at him, startled and worried, but game. 'If you want,' she said. 'But I'll have to turn the pot down to simmer.'

'Fuck the pot,' Salter whispered, and hugged her close. 'All right,' she said. He let her go. 'We'll save it,' he said.

'Who have you been questioning today?' she asked suspiciously.

'Just an old bag who looks after the morals of young ladies. You are the one who turns me on.'

Over their soup and sandwiches, he talked. He came finally to the Dean of Women..

'She's hysterical, and she's lying, because she's frightened, I think,' he said. 'But I don't know why. I don't think she's a villain.'

'Then why is she so upset?'

'I'll find out. Whatever it is, it is something to do with Summers.'

Before he left, Annie asked him about the holidays. He felt like being gracious. 'Make whatever arrangements you like,' he said. 'The boys will be happy, and I don't have a better proposal.'

'What's got into you lately, Charlie?'

'I'm busy,' he said, and opened the front door. As he stepped out he almost walked into a small dark-haired woman in an apron who began screaming at him.

'You Mr Salter?' she asked. 'Come quick. Lady I work for gonna be killed. Come quick.'

Annie reappeared from the kitchen. 'It's Rosa. Mrs Canning's cleaning lady. Quick, Charlie. Something must be wrong.'

It was one of the penalties of being a policeman.

Salter and Annie followed the cleaning lady at a trot across three front yards to Mrs Canning's house. There in the kitchen they found her, standing terrified in the corner, clutching her two young children. 'He's upstairs,' she said. 'In the front bedroom.'

Salter climbed the stairs cautiously to the second floor and went along the hall to the front bedroom. The door was closed, and Salter shouted through it without getting a response. Then he threw the door open and stood back. Nothing happened. Salter moved to the doorway and looked around the room. All the curtains had been drawn so that there was only a gloomy orange light to see by, but it did not take much light to see that the room had been wrecked. The bedroom was also used as a study, and the floor was two feet deep in books and all the other bric-à-brac—clocks, mirrors, ashtrays, lamps—that had formerly stood on the tables and shelves. In the big double bed, under the covers, was a young giant, his eyes open, watching Salter.

'What the hell do you think you're doing?'

'You are trespassing,' the boy said. 'This is my room.'

Salter left, closing the door behind him, and called down the stairs to Mrs Canning. 'What's going on?' he asked. 'He says that's his room.'

'It's *my* room. Mine and Albert's. This is *my* house. He just appeared half an hour ago asking if I was running a baby farm. He's got bathing trunks on.' Mrs Canning was nearly demented. 'I had to keep talking until Rosa came back. I've never seen him before.'

Annie said from beside her, 'He must be mad, Charlie. Be careful.'

'Phone Frank,' Salter said. 'Tell him what's happening. Tell him we need a car and two big men. I'll stay here.'

While they were waiting for help, Mrs Canning calmed down a bit and suggested where the intruder might have come from.

'We rent the third floor to a girl at the CBC,' she said. 'He must have been up there and come down when she left this morning.'

'Phone her,' Salter said.

In a minute it was confirmed. He had arrived from Europe the day before and had been given a bed for the night on the third floor. He had seemed very tired, but the girl had not noticed anything strange about him.

Very quickly the squad car arrived, bringing not only two constables but Gatenby himself. 'You don't mind, do you, boss?' he asked like a child pleading to be allowed up late. 'I haven't been outside the office for months.'

The assault party formed up in the hallway on the second floor. Salter explained the situation and the two officers pulled out their guns, causing the women on the stairs to make frightened noises, but they only emptied the shells into their pockets and re-holstered the weapons. One of the constables said something to Salter, and he turned to his wife.

'They won't hurt him,' he said. 'But they might have to hold him tight, or even handcuff him so that *they* don't get hurt. You'd better go back into the kitchen.'

They got ready to move down the hall, and Gatenby stopped them. 'Let me have a go, first,' he said. 'I might be able to talk to him.'

The others looked doubtful, but Gatenby pleaded. 'Is there a dressing-gown in the room, lady?' he called down the stairs.

'On the door,' she said.

'Right you are.' Gatenby turned to the others. 'Come and get me if I holler,' he said with a wink, and walked into the bedroom, closing the door behind him.

There was a murmuring of voices from inside the room. One of the constables asked Salter, 'You sure he's all right, sir? He seems a bit old for this kind of thing.'

'I don't know what the hell he's up to,' snapped Salter, 'We'll give him five minutes, then we'll go in.'

But in another minute Gatenby reappeared with the boy, dressed now in a tiny striped robe. Gatenby had his arm around his shoulers and was talking to him soothingly, like an old granny. 'Here we go, then. We'll just go downstairs, won't we, that's it. Out to the car, and we'll take you where we can get you all fixed up.'

Salter led the way and opened the door of the squad car as Gatenby talked the boy into the seat, closing it gently behind him.

'All yours, lads,' he said. 'Take him down to the Comical College. Don't shout at him.'

The policeman looked at each other and at Salter, who shrugged. 'Take him away, lads,' he said.

Salter and Gatenby drove back in silence for a few blocks, then Salter said, 'All right, Frank. What the fuck did you do in there?'

'I used psychology, chief,' Gatenby said, chuckling happily. 'I could see he was just a kid, so I went over to the bed and said straight away, "Do you love your mum?" He said, "Yes." So I said, "Well, if you love your mum, she loves you, so come on up and we'll go and see if we can find her." '

Salter waited. 'And that's it?' he asked, finally.

'That's all. He got up quiet as a lamb and put on that dressing-gown, and that was that.'

'Jesus Christ,' Salter said, after another long pause. 'Jesus H. Christ.'

The interlude over, Salter went back to brooding about Summers. What was his responsibility to O'Brien? To ask questions, watch the whites of their eyes, and see if anyone was lying. So who was? At a guess, he thought, everyone except Usher. But what about? Begin with Carrier. It was possible that Carrier was being his natural gerbil-like self, but he certainly acted like a man with a secret. But a killer? Unlikely. Marika Tils? Even more unlikely, and yet she had seemed to be evading him at the end.

Dunkley was still the obvious choice. Hard to tell if he was lying, because everything he said sounded like rehearsed dogma. He was a man of principle, or a self-righteous prick, depending on how you reacted to him, but did that make him suspicious? Would he lie, much less kill, on principle?

Which left Jane Homer, the Dean of Women. There was also someone with a story she wasn't telling, but what? Did Summers try to rape her, after all these years? Hardly. If she knew anything that would help him she would surely have said so. They were old friends, she and Summers.

What about Summers? He was drunk, he had seen a girlie show, he was in his dressing-gown, there was lipstick on the glass, and he had had a lucky day. Any famous detective would have solved it in five minutes, but all Salter could come up with was the classic 'whore-and-pimp' solution. In the meantime he could think of a number of things he ought to do before he went back to cleaning up Yonge Street. Like having a look at the scene of the crime. And seeing Molly Tripp again.

Back in the office, Gatenby picked up their messages.
'They've all been calling,' he said as if he were reading a
children's story to a four-year-old. 'Chiefie, DeeCee, the
copper from froggieland. There's no mail, though.'

Wonderful. Not a single silly assignment, or request,
for three days. Was it really passing? The Chief was, in
fact, the Superintendent's secretary, asking if a written
copy of the report on the Montreal case would be
forthcoming; the message from the Deputy was to ask if
he needed any help. Deduction. He was on the case the
Deputy was interested in. A pity he was getting nowhere,
even if he was having fun. He phoned O'Brien.

'I have talked to everyone in the area, Charlie. They
remember him in the bars, but that's all. I think I've
talked to every known character who was in Les Jardins
du Paradis when Summers was there, but I can't smell
anything.'

'The hotel staff remember anything?'

'I question them every day, just for practice, and to see
if they start remembering. Nothing. Why don't you come
down and try it yourself?'

'It's your turf, Onree,' Salter said, but thinking, Why
don't I?

'My what?' O'Brien asked.

'Your turf. Your manor,' Salter explained.

'Ah yes. Mon fief.'

'I guess so. Onree, I've had a thought. Maybe I will
come down. Not to help you out, but just to get a feel of
what happened on Friday night. When are you free?'

'Monday would be good.'

'Perfect. I'll come down on the afternoon train.'

'I'll meet you, Charlie. Look for me.'

At 3.30 Salter left for the squash club.

Salter was aware of the new concern for health which had
filled the streets of Toronto with men and women trotting

about in shorts, and had created an industry devoted to selling fitness. One of the products of this concern was the huge growth of racquet sports, especially squash. Annie had suggested to him more than once that it was a sport that might answer his own need for exercise. Salter watched his growing belly, and listened to himself puff up the stairs, and toyed with the idea, but his overwhelming concern not to look, sound, or feel a fool under any circumstances had kept him from enquiring further. Now he had an official reason to look inside one of the new clubs and he was looking forward to satisfying his personal curiosity.

The Simcoe Squash Club is on the edge of Toronto's downtown shopping district, which is also Toronto's business district. The location makes it ideal for the man or woman who wants a game on his way to or from work, and it is at its busiest in the early morning, the late afternoon, and at lunch-time. It is housed in a converted warehouse, and Salter found it easily, at a few minutes before four, by following the trickle of men with athletic bags who were converging on the large brick building.

A girl seated at the desk inside the door was checking off members as they arrived, confirming bookings in a ledger and taking money. Salter did not introduce himself officially, saying merely, 'I'm meeting Mr Bailey here. He's a member.'

She nodded, and picked up the phone at the same time. 'If you follow those guys—Hi, Joe, that was a real wingding last night—down the stairs—Just a minute, "Hello, Simcoe Squash Club"—hang on, Mary Lou, I've gotta talk to you—Gerry! How *are* you?—through into the lounge—hang on a second—no, sir, all booked at four-forty—don't go away, Mary Lou—you could get a cup of coffee and—WAIT, Mary Lou—OK? He'll see you when he comes in. OK?—now listen, Mary Lou, you know what happened last night?—'

Salter picked out the bits of this that were his and
followed the crowd into a large area full of tables and
chairs. The crowd disappeared, one by one, through a
door in the far corner, and Salter found himself a seat
and looked around. Half a dozen pairs of members
dressed in shorts and looking more or less exhausted and
sweaty were drinking beer. Most of them were in their
twenties, but one pair was white-haired and ten years
older than Salter. One wall of the lounge was made of
glass and formed the back wall of a pair of courts. A game
was in progress on one of the courts, and Salter tried to
follow it. The players leapt and ran, hitting the ball
alternately, sometimes seven or eight times, before one of
the players missed. Salter couldn't follow the ball and
instead concentrated on the players, marvelling at the
way they ran round each other, never crashing into each
other, rarely touching. As he watched, one of them dived
to retrieve a ball low against the wall and smashed his
racquet in two. It looked like an expensive game. Would
he be able to play it? Salter had been a mediocre though
enthusiastic athlete in his youth, reduced in the last few
years to golf, and not much of that. He had left behind all
team sports, he hated the idea of jogging, and his
attention span for formal calisthenics was about a
minute. In fact, apart from golf, he hardly exercised at
all, which is to say for about nine months of the year. He
felt the need. This game looked as though it might
provide the answer—half an hour of competitive frenzy
leading to renewed fitness or a heart attack.

'Are you a member, sir?'

The young athlete standing beside him in squash gear
was obviously an official of some sort.

Salter decided on a touch of rudeness. 'No,' he said.
'Are you?'

'I'm the club pro, sir. In the afternoons I'm also the
manager. Can I help you?'

'I'm waiting for Mr Bailey.'

'Oh yes. Old Bill. Mind if I sit down?' The pro pulled out a chair. 'You thinking of joining?'

'I'm not thinking of anything right now, Mister . . . ?'

'Larry.'

'Right now, Larry, I'm watching these two, and waiting for Old Bill.'

'Do you play yourself, Mr . . . ?'

'Salter, Charlie Salter.'

'Do you play, Charlie?'

Salter continued to be offended by this boy with dark ringlets cascading down his back, now putting himself on first name terms without permission, but the pro's easy manner, like that of a new wave priest, disconcerted him.

'No. I've never even seen the game until today.'

'Like me to explain it?'

No. Why? 'Yes,' he said.

Larry outlined the objectives of the game, the elementary strategies employed, and then supplied a brief commentary on the game in progress. Salter was intrigued. The pro said, 'Like to have a go?'

'Now?'

'Why not?'

'I'm not dressed for it.'

'I can fix that. We have cupboards full of stuff that's been left behind in the washing machines. All clean. Shoes, too. I'll find you a racquet.'

'No. Some other time maybe.'

'Tomorrow? Come down in the afternoon. I'll give you a lesson. Show you around.'

'Why?'

'If you like it you might become a member. I get a commission on everyone I sign up.'

'No secrets with you, are there, Larry? What does it cost?'

'I won't charge you anything for tomorrow.'

'I know that. I mean this place, a year.'

'Three hundred the first year. Two hundred after that.'

'And the cost of each game?'

'The courts are free except between eleven-thirty and one-thirty, and after four. If you played during the day it wouldn't cost you anything.'

'Who would I play?'

'No problem. Lots of people looking for a game.'

'My age?' Salter asked shyly.

'Our oldest member is seventy-two. We have lots of members in their fifties and sixties.'

'I'm forty-six.'

'No problem. I'll see you tomorrow, then, about three.'

'What? I don't know. Yes. Maybe. All right. I'll let you know if I can't come. By the way—' Salter looked at the clock; he still had five minutes—'did you know Mr Summers well?'

Larry looked pious. 'Yes. He was a good friend of Bill's, of course, that's how you would know him. Terrible thing to happen.'

Salter let this pass. 'Did he play much?' he asked.

'Every day. He and Bill used to get into a battle royal every day. Bill is going to be lost without him.'

'A battle royal?'

'They played hard. Not terrifically good, but they went at it like a couple of one-armed rug-beaters. The loser paid.'

'Paid what?'

'They always played for beer. The loser paid for the beer. Hey, Susie,' he called to a waitress. 'This is Mr Salter, a friend of Dave Summers. I was just telling him about the great games he used to have with Bill Bailey.'

The waitress struck a sad attitude. 'Oh, those guys used to really beat up a storm, you know? And you always knew who was going to pay, like. Real kids they were. I mean, you know, for men, like, mature men, it was funny to see how bad it was for the one who lost. Especially Mr Bailey.' She raised her eyebrows, shook her head, pursed her lips, looked around stagily to see if she were being overheard, all to indicate that Bailey was a poor loser. 'They were at it every night,' she concluded.

'Did they play last week.'

'Oh, sure. They played Thursday night before Mr Summers went to Montreal.'

'Who won?' Salter fixed an expression of warm, sad, piety on his face. He calculated that he had about two more questions before the waitress or the pro asked him why he was asking.

'Oh, gee, I don't know. Wait a minute. Yes, I do. Mr Summers must have won, because he was teasing Mr Bailey, you know, pretending to explain the game to him. Wait a minute, though, he couldn't have won because he paid for the drinks. I think. No. Oh, gee, I don't know. I guess Mr Bailey must have paid, because he was the loser all right.' All this was delivered in the form of a passionate argument with herself.

'I see you're ahead of me, Inspector.' Bailey stood by the table. As the meaning of his words got through to the others, the waitress scuttled, terrified, back to the bar, where she locked herself in conversation with the barman. The pro, however, looked quizically at him. 'Toronto's finest, eh? Here on official business? I guess you don't want a lesson after all. You might have let me know, Inspector.'

'I'd still like a lesson. Do you let coppers join?'

'This is a club for the downtown professional man. That would include you.'

'Then I'll be here tomorrow, at three.'

The pro ducked his curls in a graceful bow, and left, looking like a Restoration beau about to sneak the immortal 'Anyone-for-tennis?' line into the wrong century.

Bailey sat down. 'Thinking of joining the club, Inspector?' he said, too cheerily.

No one is comfortable with the police, Salter thought. 'I don't know. He asked me to give it a try. I might.'

Bailey affected a hearty look. 'If you want some practice, I'll give you a game.'

'I guess you need a new partner. You used to play Summers all the time, you say.'

'We played a lot. We joined together a couple of years ago and we've been kind of seesawing back and forth. Did, I mean. It's hard to start thinking in the past.'

'Did you play him last week?'

'Oh, sure. Every day until he left.'

'Who won on Thursday? The waitress said you had quite a game.'

Bailey thought for a moment. Then, 'He did, I think. Yes, he did. Why?'

'No real reason, Mr Bailey. But it might be useful. For instance, all day Friday, Summers talked about having had a lucky day, and he paid a big dinner bill on Friday night. Now if his wife tells me he was feeling very happy on Thursday night, I'll know it was just squash, nothing to do with whatever was making him so happy on Friday. See.'

Salter felt proud of this pile of rubbish, invented on the spur of the moment to divert Bailey. The reason was that the more he knew about Summers's relationships, the more he would know about Summers, and that included knowing whether he was a good loser or a bad one, and what kind of winner he was, too.

Another man appeared at their table, about fifty, bald as a melon except for a fringe, with the calm, kindly face of a contented accountant. He was clean-shaven, and the fringe of hair had been cut to give him an ecclesiastical air. He looked out of place among all the young stockbrokers and lawyers, but seemed completely at home.

'We were talking about David, Percy,' Bailey said. 'This is Inspector Salter, Percy. Percy Cranmer.'

Cranmer had the hand of a farmer, and he gripped Salter's warmly. 'Very sad,' he said. 'What about his home life? Did he leave any little ones? His wife all right?'

'I think so, Mr Cranmer. He only had one daughter. 'She's at college.'

'Is that right? We don't know much about each other here, except for squash. I never met Dave's wife.'

Bailey stood up. 'We have a game, Inspector, if that's 'it.'

'That's it, Mr Bailey. Thanks very much. If I want you I'll know where to find you.'

'Like Percy said, Inspector, we don't know much about each other here. I wouldn't have a lot more to tell you about old Dave.'

'I meant about that practice you mentioned. If I join the club.'

'Oh. Right. Sure, Inspector. Any time. Come on Perce.'

Cranmer said, 'Good luck, Inspector. I hope you catch the fella. Poor old Dave.'

Salter did not leave at once. When the two men had been gone for ten minutes he found the staircase connecting the courts, and climbed. There were three levels of court, arranged in blocks of eight, twenty-four in all. On one of the top levels Salter found a gallery overlooking the courts below and he stopped to watch. Bailey and Cranmer were playing in one of the end courts, and by standing back, Salter could watch them without being seen. He was surprised to see that the burly accountant played a delicate game, all flicks and soft shots, while Bailey bashed the ball whenever he got a clear shot. By the frequency of service changes, Salter judged that the two men were about even. They were also, compared to the players Salter had been watching in the lounge, very bad. Bailey constantly mis-hit the ball, and Cranmer was only effective if he could flick it around the front wall. They bumped into each other all the time, often interfering with each other's shots. Bailey was as unsmiling and fierce as the good players downstairs, while Cranmer retained his fatherly smile throughout. Salter came to the conclusion that he should be able to beat either one of them in a week.

It was five o'clock, just the right time to telephone Molly Tripp, the student at the funeral. He was lucky. She was going to an early movie on Bloor Street, but she agreed to meet Salter for a sandwich first, so they arranged to see each other at a café on Cumberland Street.

He arrived before her and ordered a beer. The café was almost deserted for no reason that Salter could see, because he had passed two similar establishments on the street that were jammed with people meeting after work. While he was wondering, Molly arrived.

'Hi,' she said, standing squarely before him, smiling like a child, sure of her welcome. She wore a pair of old blue jeans and a sweat shirt, and she was carrying a yellow slicker.

He stood up. 'Let me get you a sandwich,' he said. He pointed to the menu on the wall which listed a dozen kinds of sandwiches, all unfamiliar to him. 'I'll have a "Reuben, Reuben",' she said. He ordered it, feeling foolish.

'What's a "Reuben, Reuben",' he asked.

'A double Reuben, like a double corned beef on rye.'

'What's a Reuben?'

'Oh, it's great. Corned beef, cheese, and sauerkraut.'

'Uh. You want something to drink? Beer?'

'No. I'll have a sip of yours, though.' She picked up his

mug and took a mouthful. Salter looked nervously around but no one seemed to be watching them.

'There,' she said. 'Great. I love beer but I want to stay awake for the movie. I'd like a coffee, though.'

He placed the order, and they settled down opposite each other.

'You wanted to ask me more stuff about Professor Summers?' she invited. 'I was upset yesterday, but I'm all right now.'

'Yes.' Salter nodded. Her hair which had seemed messy at the funeral now seemed just right. Was it 'carefully tousled' as they used to say? She had a pleasant face which was made more appealing by a slightly affected use of gesture—her eyes went wide with wonder, the corners of her mouth turned down in despair or disappointment, and joy switched on the sun in her face. And she was wearing no brassiere. Salter smiled at her, 'Yes,' he said. 'As I told you yesterday, I am trying to learn as much about Summers as I can. What kind of man he was. Whatever you can tell me about him.'

'So go ahead. Ask.' She smiled encouragingly.

'Was he a good teacher?' Salter asked, again. Who cared? All he wanted was an excuse to keep this girl with him.

'You asked that. I told you. But I've thought about it since then. I still don't know. On the plus side, he knew his stuff, he liked it, and he got excited about it. On the minus side he didn't lay it out in a way that was easy to take down, if you like a lot of notes. So some of the students, especially the girls, got a bit uptight when the exams came around.'

'They didn't all fall in love with him?' Why was he feeling jealous?

She roared with laughter. 'You're a bit out of date, Charlie. Nobody sits swooning in class these days.'

'What do they do these days? Lie down in the

professor's office between classes?'

She sat back in her chair. 'No. Usually we just grab the ones we like by the balls when we meet them in the hall. What kind of question is that?'

Salter felt as if he had just pinched her, spitefully. 'I'm sorry,' he said. 'I don't know what goes on in colleges these days with your generation.'

'What do you *think* goes on?'

'I don't know.' Salter was miserable. 'You hear about swinging professors, you know.'

'Summers didn't swing. I told you, he taught poetry.' She was still sitting back watching him. 'What was it like in your day? Did you go to university?'

'For a while. Listen: "A slumber did my spirit seal; I had no human fears." '

She sat forward, smiling. 'That's Wordsworth. It was one of Summers's favourites.'

'Was it?' Salter clawed his way back into her favour. 'Here's another bit: "While barred clouds bloom the soft-dying day, And touch the stubble plains with rosy hue." That's Keats,' he said.

' "To Autumn",' she said. 'Right. He liked that one, too. 'Are all you guys romantics?'

'No, just me. That was my favourite course,' he lied. 'I dropped out of university after second year.' They were nearly together again, and slightly excited by the exchange.

The 'Reuben, Reuben' arrived and she began to eat while he sipped another beer. Nothing was said until she had made some progress with the sandwich.

Then, 'Good sandwich?' he asked.

'Here,' she said, offering him a bite. He leaned forward to take the corner of the sandwich between his teeth. If anyone is watching this, he thought, they will think we are doing a Tom Jones.

'Nice,' he said, chewing, and taking a sip of beer. 'So.

I've learned about English professors, and I know a little
bit more about Professor Summers. Tell me some more.'
    She considered. 'He was enthusiastic — have I said that?
Sometimes he went pretty far and got worked up about
what he was saying.'
    'Very emotional?'
    'I thought he kind of looked for highs in class.'
    'How?'
    'He liked the room to turn on to what was happening.
If we just sat there, he wasn't much good. He didn't seem
to have many notes to fall back on. If he didn't get much
response you had the feeling he would just wrap up what
he was saying and go on to something else. On a bad day
he could do *Paradise Lost* in twenty-five minutes.'
    'All twelve books?' Salter asked smugly. In his university
course only the first two books were assigned, but it was
well known that there were ten more.
    'Yes. It didn't always work, though.'
    'What about outside the class?'
    'What do you mean?'
    Salter took a deep breath. Most of all he wanted to
avoid sounding like a dirty old man, but one part of him
continued to conduct a police investigation. 'Students
sometimes know what is going on outside the room,' he
said. 'Was there any gossip about Summers?'
    'Here we go again.'
    But Salter had considered his question. 'All right,' he
said. 'I would like to know if you thought he had any close
friends or enemies in the college.'
    'Or lovers.'
    'Or lovers.'
    'We wondered about one of his colleagues. This isn't
any fun, Charlie.'
    'Nor for me. Which one?'
    'Marika Tils. They kissed each other hello and goodbye
a lot.'

'Everybody does that now. It's called the Elizabethan kiss of greeting,' said Salter, who had read about it in Saturday's paper.

'Yes, well. That's it. She was an Elizabethan friend, then.'

'But no students.'

'I don't think so. He probably had someone like me in every class. But, as I said, it was all poetry.'

'No enemies?'

'Not that I could see.' She finished her sandwich and picked up the check. 'Movie starts in twenty minutes, Charlie. Want to come?'

He took the check from her. 'No, But I'd like to see you again.'

She looked bewildered, and then she laughed. 'Do you think we ought to go on meeting like this?'

Grateful, he said, 'Sometimes new questions crop up and you like to be able to come back.'

'Any time, Charlie,' she said. She looked at the clock. 'My turn?'

'What?'

'My turn. One. Why did you become a policeman?'

Tell her the truth. So he did, just as if he were talking to a stranger in a foreign country, someone he would never see again.

'I was fed up,' he said. 'I'd dropped out of university . . .'

'Why?'

'I found myself counting the number of bricks in the classroom wall while the lecturer was explaining why some poem I hadn't read was so witty. It wasn't his fault. I hadn't tried to read the poem, because it seemed to be in code. To understand the jokes you had to know the Bible. But I was doing the same thing in History, Economics, and Sociology, especially Sociology. I was about to fail the lot, so I quit.'

'Then what?'

'I looked for some action. I tried to get on a ship, but you have to be a member of the Union; if there had been a war on I would have joined the army. I was bored stiff, but everything I thought of trying took five years' training.'

'It sounds a bit adolescent.'

Salter nodded. Strangers were allowed to say things like that. 'Childish,' he agreed. 'I wasn't ready to settle down so I guess I hadn't grown up.'

'So why the police?'

'I met a guy. I played hockey on the weekend pickup team—you know, the only ice time you can get is twelve o'clock on Sunday night—and one of the guys on the team was a detective. I'd just been rejected for a job I didn't want anyway, selling insurance, and he said why didn't I try out for the police? So here I am.'

'Did you like it?'

'I loved it. I was lucky. I did a little bit of everything at first, before I got into administration.'

'That sounds dull.'

'It wasn't. I was full of ideas and I lived and breathed the job. I got sent on study tours to look at other police forces; I got to say what I thought we should change—I had a terrific time. The three stripes came early, and then I got to be an inspector. That was five years ago.'

'Then?'

'Then the man who was looking after me all this time, who I thought would become deputy, didn't, and he retired and I found I had made a lot of enemies, so I was out in the cold.'

'Sounds like General Motors.'

'I guess so. Anyway, I got shifted out of the centre of things and I've been doing errand work ever since.'

'Is it all over?'

'I thought it was. Now, I'm not so sure. I'm enjoying

myself this week.'

'Are you married?'

'Yes, twice.'

'What happened the first time.'

'It lasted a year.'

'Yes, but what happened?'

'We broke up, got divorced.'

'Yes, but why?'

'She became a hippie, one of the first. She didn't like being married to a square, and I wouldn't let her smoke pot. It was a big deal then.'

'But you got lucky the second time.'

'Yes. It's not all hearts and flowers but I'm still married.'

'Is she pretty?'

'Everybody else says so.'

'Do you have a good sex life?'

Salter looked around again. 'I haven't compared lately,' he said. 'But it's a bloody sight better than I was having at your age.'

She laughed. 'Good,' she said. 'Now I have to go.' She put out her hand in a weirdly formal gesture. 'Once more, Charlie, I hope you catch him.'

He still had some beer to finish so he stayed in the café and watched her cross the parking lot and walk between the two buildings on her way to Bloor Street.

After dinner, overwhelmed by a desire to be agreeable, he helped his wife with the dishes, taking the opportunity to kiss her on the neck, an area he was fond of.

'Go away, goat,' she said. 'Or I'll cover you in suds.'

He dropped the dishtowel on her head to blindfold her, undid the button on her slacks and nearly got the zipper down, preparatory to raping her, dramatically, up against the 'fridge. ' "Strange fits of passion I have known," ' he said.

'Not so strange,' she said dodging. 'But you'll have to wait. Dorothy is coming in from next door to show me how to make a new kind of patchwork square.'

Half an hour later she came upstairs to look for the sewing-basket and found him posing in front of the mirror wearing a jockstrap.

He failed to look embarrassed, so she tried a joke. 'If you want to try my underwear on, don't tear it,' she said.

'Me Thor,' he said, in reference to an old love-making joke. 'For your information, madam, I am going to play squash tomorrow.'

'In that?'

'And my old tennis stuff. Do you know where it all is?'

'What's this all about?'

'I'm going to play squash. Get fit again, like you suggested.'

'Why now? What's going on?'

'Oh, for Christ's sake, nothing's going on. I just decided to take up squash, is all.' He told her the story of Bailey and the club, and his curiosity about Summers's passion for the game.

'Well, enjoy yourself. But take it easy.' She looked at the slight belly. 'I don't want to be widowed by a heart attack.'

'You think I'm too old?' he asked.

'Of course not, dear.' She tried to make up by tweaking his jockstrap, letting it snap back against him. 'Have a good game,' she said: 'But leave something for me.'

'Ha, ha, ha. Randy bitch.' Salter turned happily back to the mirror. He felt as if he were on holiday.

CHAPTER 5

He woke smiling from his first good dream in a year. He
sat up and grabbed at the memory before it faded. He
was in charge of a World Centre. People came to him
with their problems. He was the World Centre for All
Problems. Telephones rang. 'World Centre here,' he
would say. 'Can I help you?' He solved them all. Salter
shook Annie awake, 'I'm the World Centre,' he said. 'Can
I help you?'

'Orange juice,' she said, pulling her nightdress tight
around her knees and turning away.

'Right,' he said, and jumped out of bed to fetch it.

He was not looking forward to interviewing Summers's
wife, and he had put if off as long as possible. Now she
was the last one, and he had an appointment with her for
ten o'clock that morning. Her house was on Stouffville
Avenue, in an area known as Deer Park, no more than a
mile from his own house, and he decided it would be
pointless to travel down to the office first. He considered
hanging about the house for another hour, but since this
would certainly involve him in tying up newspapers for
the weekly pickup, or washing out the garbage cans with
disinfectant, or any of the other husbandly duties he did
not usually mind, but did not want to be asked to do this
morning, he said nothing, and left the house at his usual
time, pointed virtuously towards the subway station.

He could go two ways. One way led him through
upper-middle-class residential streets, across the park,
and past his son's school—a pleasant, leafy stroll on a fine
spring morning. But Salter was a townie; he liked shops
and people and a bit of life, so he headed for the local

portion of Yonge Street (the longest street in the Commonwealth), and began his stroll by walking beside the morning rush-hour traffic. He bought a paper and a cup of coffee; and sat in the mall at the entrance to the subway, enjoying the sense of playing hookey as the morning crowds poured down the stairs. When he had had his fill, he threw the paper into a bin and crossed Eglinton Avenue to walk south. He particularly liked this bit of the street, with its Chinese greengrocers, delicatessen shops, and the hardware store run by six cheerful Australians (or were they New Zealanders?) He paused at each of the three sporting-goods stores and looked at the windows, pricing the squash racquets, and he wondered again how the seven unisex hairdressers made a living. One more gas station had disappeared to make way for a fast food outlet — that made the third in the last few years. Three more restaurants had opened since he last counted, along with a shop that sold only coffee, another that sold sexy underwear, and two travel agents. Hard times? thought Salter. This town stinks of money.

At Davisville subway he turned along Chaplin Crescent into Oriole Park. Here nothing had changed in ten years. The same young mothers were watching the same babies crawl about the sandpit; the same old people were sitting on the benches; the same air-hostesses and night-workers were lying about the grass, trying to get a start on their summer tans. It was all as it was when Salter used to bring Angus and Seth here to play when Annie managed to nail him for baby-sitting on his day off. And here were the same bloody dog-owners. Salter decided to do his duty. 'You,' he called to the swaggering owner of a Doberman pinscher which was bounding about the park, preparatory to savaging one of the children. 'That your dog? Put it on a leash, and don't let it wander here again out of control.' He showed his card. 'What's its licence number?' He made a show of entering the number in his notebook. 'Right,' he said. 'Don't forget.' Across the park he saw another one, a German Shepherd, a breed he disliked and feared almost as much. He walked over to the owner, a middle-aged woman in a headscarf, standing under the trees, smoking. 'Get that dog chained up, madam,' he shouted from far enough away to justify shouting. 'There are children here and it's against the law to let your dog run wild.'

'Go to hell,' she said. 'Who are you?'

'Police Inspector,' Salter said, showing his card. 'We've had complaints. Get it under control.'

'He is under control. He wouldn't hurt a fly, unless I order him.'

The dog leaped up and took a bite at Salter's hand. 'Right,' said Salter. 'Your name, please, madam, and the dog's licence number. I'll send a man round with the charge.'

'Goddam nosey-parker,' she said. 'Why don't you clean up Yonge Street instead of bothering decent people?'

'I'm not arguing, madam. Chain it up and keep it chained up.'

'Interfering bastards,' she said. 'Here, Luba.' She got the dog on a chain and allowed herself to be hauled away, cursing through the smoke. Salter looked around, but the word had spread. All the dogs were now on leads. He went on his way satisfied, telling himself, as always, that he didn't mind the dogs, it was the owners he didn't like.

He felt much more ready to meet Mrs Summers.

Stouffville Avenue is several blocks south of the park, and Salter still had some time in hand when he arrived at Summers's house, so he strolled by it at first on the other side of the street. It seemed to him a genuine old house that had been tarted up, like so many in a district which was festooned with the signs of building renovators and architects. It was a small white house, and from the front it looked like an old cottage with a single bedroom under the roof. From the side, Salter could see that there was a new bit stuck on behind, adding at least two more rooms, one on top of the other. The front yard had been dug out and bricked in to make room for a car, even though a driveway led past the house to the back. Salter recognized the marks of a white-painter, someone who saw a perfectly good house as an opportunity to take it apart and make it into something else. He had suffered from this himself as Annie had called for more (or less) light, another bathroom, a new kitchen, and much else. Salter refused to lift a finger to help on the grounds that he was a policeman, not a carpenter, and he objected to the cost, but Annie had found the money anyway, and no longer asked him to lend a hand. The results were always pleasant, but he still fought each new suggestion bitterly.

He wondered how much Summers had done of all this, and how much he had had to put up with. Salter crossed the street and walked down the drive to the white picket fence enclosing the back yard. A woman was kneeling with her back to him, fiddling with a plant. The yard would have met with Annie's approval. Around a central grass plot were a lot of different coloured flowers, several of which looked familiar from his own back yard, a surprising number of them in bloom considering that frost was still hanging about the suburbs. The grass was littered with gardening tools. A lot of work here, thought Salter. Against the house a small patch was sown with vegetables—tomatoes and lettuce—which would ripen at the same time that they could be bought in the markets for next to nothing, the reason Salter always gave for not planting any himself.

He coughed and the woman looked up. She was thin, in early middle-age, with pretty silver hair.

'Inspector Salter,' he said.

'Yes, I know. Come in,' she said, pointing to the gate.

She threw her trowel on the grass with the rest of the tools, tossed her gloves after it, and let him in through the back door, into a kind of sunroom furnished with white wicker.

'In here,' she said. 'Do you want coffee or anything?' It was not an offer, but a request to know if it was now his coffee-hour, and was it her duty to make some.

'No, thanks,' Salter said. He waited for her to sit down before sitting opposite her.

'Would you mind if I asked you some questions about your husband?' he began.

'Ask the questions, and I'll tell you. I don't know who killed David, or why, and I don't care. It doesn't matter to me.'

This is not going to be much fun either, thought Salter. He said, 'The Montreal police have asked us to help them, and we have nothing to go on.' Salter paused. Should it be 'nothing to go on *with*? What did 'nothing to go on' mean? Would the fat chairman be interested?

Mrs Summers was waiting. Salter continued, 'He was found in a hotel room with a fractured skull, after, apparently, a good night out with his colleagues.'

'A perfect murder, then. How can I help? I was here in bed.' She was not so much hostile as indifferent, continually looking out at her garden.

'There was one clue, ma'am.'

'The killer dropped his Esso card?'

'Not quite. But there was a glass with lipstick on it in the room.'

She said nothing, as if this was no news to her, and stared at her garden.

Salter decided to give her time to respond, and he looked around, taking in the details of the room. It was agreeable and untidy: a tin of shoe-polish seemed at home on an end-table, the top of the television was a storage space for a pile of magazines, and a tea-towel

hung over the back of an armchair. House and garden
had the air of being left in mid-task, like the *Marie
Celeste.*

Eventually she said, 'So he had a woman in his room.
Who was she, do you know?'

'We don't know, ma'am.'

'Nor do I.'

'It doesn't surprise you, ma'am?'

'He was a big boy. Your age. *You* guess.'

'I'm trying to. Did he have any women friends you
knew about?'

'Marika Tils. He was fond of her, all right.'

'Anyone else.'

'Not that I know of, Inspector. Last week I'd have been
certain, but now I don't know. You people come across all
kinds of secrets, don't you? As far as I know, or knew,
David didn't have a mistress, nor did he hire prostitutes to
do things I wouldn't do for him. That help?'

'That's very helpful.'

'Good. We had a fair sex life, and he had me often
enough to make me pretty sure he had no one else on the
side. But at your age you guys get funny, I hear. So, if you
are searching for a woman, let me see, how can I help,
yes, look for one with teeth marks on her.'

Salter said nothing.

She continued. 'Yes, he liked to bite—ears and neck,
mostly, but he would take a nibble anywhere. Otherwise
it was pretty conventional—missionary position except for
Father's Day, when I got on top. I expect we had a sex life
much like yours, Inspector.'

Salter said patiently, 'Did he have any enemies?'

'Nothing fierce. He sometimes called this or that
colleague an asshole, to me, in private, but I expect you
do that, too, eh, Inspector? He wasn't very tactful to
them, either, so a lot of people were wary of him. How
about you, Inspector? Are you careful of your tongue?'

'His colleagues have mentioned a feud with Professor Dunkley.'

'Oh no.' She broke her pose and sat forward. 'Oh no. Don't go off on that track. He and Dunkley were poles apart, and Dunkley *is* an asshole, but he wouldn't kill anyone. He's nasty enough to, but he couldn't justify it within his moral system or his political ethos, or whatever. Oh no. Dunkley doesn't believe in violence.'

'Then why did they dislike each other?'

She looked round the room. Then she said, 'Maybe I should make some coffee after all. I'd like some. Then I'll tell you David's life story, or the bit that matters, including the "affaire Dunkley". I feel a bit better now. I'm sorry to be rude, but this all seemed such a waste of time. David's dead and I'm trying to tell myself it was like a traffic accident. What do I care who killed him? But I can't stop thinking about him.' She got up and led the way into the kitchen which occupied the old back room of the house. Another renovation, thought Salter, noting the clear pine, the quarry tile, and the butcher's block table—all the staples of the Toronto renovated kitchen. She heated water and poured it through a filter, occupying the time while they waited for it by putting a lot of dishes in the sink and clearing the counter. Salter perched on a stool at the table and waited. She served two cups of coffee and pushed one over to him with a carton of cream and a wet spoon she fished out of the sink. She's a bit of a slob, he thought, delighted. I wonder if Summers minded? They sipped the coffee in silence for a few minutes. Then she began.

'David was nearly fifty and he was just getting used to the idea. For the last few years he had thought of himself as a failure, but he was just about through that.'

'Why a failure? He was a good enough teacher, according to one of his students, anyway.'

'Until lately he thought of himself as more than a

teacher. He was chairman of the department for a while, and after that ended he felt—what do you call it?—unfulfilled. But in the last year he had become more at home with himself. His teaching was better than ever, and he didn't care about it so much. In the past he had cared too much—a bad class could ruin his weekend and a good one would leave him flying, but he'd achieved a bit of detachment lately. He was still obsessional about it, though, preparing stuff he'd been teaching for years.'

'Was he fired as chairman?'

'Oh no. They rotate the job every three or six years. But he'd started to live and breathe it, and it was hard on him when it ended. He expected to be offered a job in the administration, and when that didn't happen he started to feel like a failure.'

'Why? Why did he expect it, and why didn't it happen?'

'His mentor quit. The vice-president David was gung-ho for took a job somewhere else, and the new one didn't like David. Simple as that. David went back to teaching, but he's only lately got used to it again.'

Salter listened, uncomfortably aware of the parallels with his own life. *This*, he thought, is the bloody Conrad story. I must tell that fat chairman one day. Thinking this brought him around to his task.

'Was it while he was chairman that he fell out with Professor Dunkley?'

'I told you, Inspector, don't bother with that one. Dunkley wouldn't hurt a fly, on principle, although he made a principle out of hating. They were opposed, of course. Those were the days of the end of the student revolution. David had a few confrontations, and dug down deep in his heart and discovered he was a wishy-washy liberal who believed the students were entitled to run everything except the classroom. Dunkley was involved in all of the sit-ins and supported the students' right to decide everything—including what they should be taught. There was an incident almost every day and those two were always on opposite sides.' She paused, and looked as though she were gathering energy for the rest of it. 'But that wasn't the whole of it. You see—oh, shit—about that time Dunkley became separated from his wife, and just shortly thereafter David and Dunkley's wife became lovers, and Dunkley found out, and they didn't talk to each other after that, even though, according to Dunkley's principles, his wife was free to do what she liked. OK? Now you know it all.'

'How did you hear of it?'

'David is a poor liar. Sorry, "was", so I would have found out soon enough, but in this case Dunkley's wife told him, to spite him, I think—poor Dunkley, no one likes him—and Dunkley told me.'

And that was the end of that, thought Salter. But it gave Dunkley all the motive in the world. He returned to pick at his own new-found relationship with Summers. The parallel fascinated him.

'Why did he seem better lately?' he asked. 'What made the difference?'

'You probably know the answer, Inspector, or you will. How old are you?'

Startled, Salter told her.

'David was nearly fifty. We have some money now, and we were beginning to get around more. Travel. There was no need for him to spend all his time upstairs at his desk, though he still did, most of the winter. But we went away at Christmas, and for a few weeks during the summer.' She looked at him calmly. 'Our sex life improved, and he started to have some fun. He even began to write poetry—no good, but nice. He took up the bits of adolescence he never had, and finished off growing up.'

Salter got annoyed. 'Why does it have to be adolescent?

Maybe he just enjoyed playing squash.'

'Don't get uptight about it, Inspector. You didn't even know him. I think everyone walks around with every age inside him, especially adolescence, but some people get a chance to let the other ages out—the lucky ones.'

This sounded to Salter like one of those conversations that end up discussing whether we are all faggots, really, if only we would relax, and he cut her off.

'You had no money worries?' he asked.

'Nope.' She pointed to the ceiling. 'The house is paid for. Our daughter is nearly through college, and I'm making money. I work for an agency. We find new jobs for executives who have been fired or want to quit. I'm good at it and I make a lot of money. I wanted to help David—I could have slotted him into a new career without any trouble, but he wouldn't allow me near him on that one.'

Bloody right, thought Salter.

'And David was making money himself, on the side,' she added.

'How?'

'On the futures market. It was another thing Dunkley didn't like about him. He called David a capitalist. Silly prick. David was a *gambler* in a modest sort of way. He was watching TV one day and saw a commodities broker who impressed him as a man who knew where it was at. The next day he phoned the broker and opened an account. It's a kind of betting on the future prices of things. David had tried the stock market, but that's rigged in favour of the brokers and the insiders, he said. He had spent a year playing the stock market and earned ten thousand in commissions for the broker and five hundred for himself. This commodities thing was different. He had a good trader—a woman, by the way—and she made him some money. He took back his original stake in six months—I think he put fifteen thousand in originally—and he's been playing with his winnings ever since. Right now he was in cotton, copper and the Swiss franc.

'But Dunkley didn't understand anything about it. He thought that if you made a bet on the future price of pork bellies you were playing with the food of the poor. Even if you lost your shirt. I warn you, Inspector, if you ever get into the futures market, don't tell anyone. They'll be jealous and righteous if you win, and bloody happy if you lose. Which reminds me. I should find out what is happening to us. It's a joint account and all our accounts were frozen until the will is probated, but the positions can still change. Excuse me.' She went to the phone and dialled a number which she read off a list pasted above the receiver. 'Leslie Stone, please. This is Mrs Summers, David's wife. Thank you. I just wondered how we were doing. Good. Thanks. I'll be in touch as soon as they unfreeze things.' She hung up and came back to the table. 'David trusted her totally,' she said. 'Apparently we are making money today.'

Salter was struck with an idea. 'Would you call her again,' he asked, 'and authorize her to speak to me?'

'Why?'

'I'll tell you if I'm right. I just had an idea.'

'OK. Hang on.' She dialled and spoke once more to the broker, and handed the phone to Salter. The broker's voice was cheery with a touch of metal in it 'Hi there, Inspector,' she said. 'What's up?'

'Probably nothing, ma'am. There are some questions around Mr Summers's death, that's all.'

'I won't be much good. I never even knew what he looked like.'

'You never saw him, *ever*?'

'Nope. I'll miss him, though. He was an easy client.'

'How so?'

'He never cried when he lost. Some of my clients cry the

house down every time they lose a thousand dollars.'

Christ, so would I, lady. 'Can you remember the last time you talked to him?'

'Sure, last Friday when he called from Montreal.'

'Did you do any business then?'

'No. We didn't buy anything or sell anything. I had some good news for him, though. He made two thousand dollars that day.'

'How?'

'On the sovereignty referendum. He bought two Canadian dollars, and when the sovereignty results came in he had made a full cent.'

'Two cents?'

'A thousand dollars a cent. A hundred points.'

'I see. He bought two hundred thousand dollars the day before and now they were worth two hundred and two thousand. Right?'

'That's right, Inspector. More or less.'

'That's a lot of money, isn't it?'

'It's two contracts.'

'He must have had over two hundred thousand dollars on deposit with you?' Salter saw Mrs Summers smiling to herself.

'Inspector, I'm very busy, but I'll give you a short course in commodity trading. To buy a hundred thousand Canadian dollars you only have to put up thirty-five hundred, the amount you might lose in a bad week, say. David used seven thousand, or about half of his equity on those two contracts. He was one of our teeny-weeny accounts. If everything went bad he could lose the lot in three days.'

'Could he, by Christ. But this time he won?'

'That's right. And you know why he was so happy? He did it himself. I advised against it and he always took our advice, but this time he wanted to make a bet on his own. I can't get it up for the Canadian dollar, but he was sure of this one. He was happy as hell when he won. I'll miss him.'

'Thank you very much, Miss Stone.'

'OK, Boss.'

Salter had a thought. 'By the way, if I wanted to get in on this, would you take me on?'

'Sure. We've upped the ante, though. You'd need a bit more cash.'

'How much?'

'Seventy-five thousand would get you started. A hundred would be better.'

'Thanks.' Salter hung up, and returned to his chair. 'That clears up David's lucky day,' he said. David? Since when did the corpse ·have a first name? This was all getting a shade cosy.

Mrs Summers said, 'He's won that much before. I wonder why he made such a big deal of it? Still, that's it, then. End of mystery. Would you like some lunch, Inspector? I could make some scrambled eggs.'

Salter shook himself. 'No, thanks, ma'am. I have work to do. I know now about his lucky day, and I also know about one of the phone calls—it was to her, the broker.' He felt the wallet in his pocket, and handed it to her. 'Your husband's wallet, Mrs Summers. Would you check it, and give me a receipt for it? We've photostated everything in it.'

She took it gingerly, and turned it over. Then she laid out the contents on the table and checked them against the itemized list that formed the receipt. 'Money, credit cards, driver's licence, charge slips, receipts, lottery tickets—I'll have to check those, I suppose—library cards, squash club membership. Here you go, Inspector,' she scribbled her name, and put the wallet in a wicker basket full of bills and unanswered mail. 'I'll look at it all later.' There was a pause. The interview seemed over, but Salter did not feel like going immediately.

She sensed this, and asked, 'More coffee? Might as well finish it.'

Salter put out his cup. 'Was your husband reading a paper in Montreal?' he asked, by way of keeping things going.

'Oh no. He didn't go to Montreal to read papers. I don't think many of them do. David just wanted to see if there was anything left of Baghdad there.'

'Baghdad?'

'A family joke. David coined it with a friend one day when they were talking about travel. His friend said that he had never wasted a dollar he spent on travel, and David felt the same way. But he was always looking for a Baghdad to travel to. Baghdad was the place, the mysterious city—always a city—where things were new and strange, the place where something interesting could happen to you. Paris was Baghdad. David had been several times and it turned him on so much he hardly went to bed. He used to wander round meeting people, finding himself in places, letting things happen to him. New York was Baghdad, so was San Francisco. Some places stopped being Baghdads before you got around to them—Dublin was one of those. He wanted to go to Dublin for years, and then he didn't. Other places were Baghdads once, but not the second or third time. London was one of those. Well, Montreal used to be a Baghdad and he wondered if there was anything left of it.'

Salter asked delicately, 'Did you go with him to these Baghdads?'

'Yes and no. We went to New York together—I have to go sometimes on business, but though we had a great time, it wasn't Baghdad when I was around. I think he got a bit of it in the daytime when I was busy. The only place I know of that was Baghdad when I was with him was Corfu.'

'So part of Baghdad is being alone?'

'Sure. Some part of it was the lovely dark-haired lady who beckoned from the doorway. That's why he liked to take a trip by himself once a year, even to an academic conference. You could always keep your eyes open for Baghdad.'

'Mrs Summers, are you telling me that he might have found a bit of Baghdad in Montreal, and she killed him?'

'No, Inspector. It's possible, but unlikely. I'm just saying that Baghdad was a romantic fantasy, and at the right age it includes sex. But it didn't have to, and for the last twenty years it probably didn't. To come down to earth, David would not have found anything interesting or mysterious about a Montreal whore. Anyway the idea of David in bed with a prostitute anywhere is absurd, unless he had spent the previous six months in the Arctic, and not even then, probably. He would never have been happy in bed except with someone who liked him. It's just — well, there are no whores in Baghdad. Am I making sense?'

Too much, thought Salter.

'Thank you, Mrs Summers,' he said formally. 'You have been very helpful.' He finished his coffee and stood up. 'One last thing. One of his colleagues told me your husband kept a journal, a diary. I didn't find it in the office. Have you come across it? If so, may I look at it? There's always the chance that he may have been involved in something he told no one else about, not even you. But he might have put something in a diary.'

She laughed and got up. 'I read it last night.' She took a thick notebook from the wicker basket where she had put the wallet. It seemed to be her filing system. 'Here. Nothing very scandalous or embarrassing in it. Maybe it will give you some ideas of him. Have a look at it, but bring it back, please.'

He put it in his pocket and moved to shake hands as he left, but suddenly overcome, she shook her head and pushed him through the door without speaking. He left the house and headed for the Kensington Market, where he was meeting Molly for lunch. Baghdad.

She was waiting for him, seated at an outside table of a café specializing in health foods. She had on the same jeans and T-shirt as before.

'Hi, Charlie,' she called when he was fifty yards away, making him slightly self-conscious. He habitually wore a tweed jacket and grey flannel trousers, even in summer—these were the casual clothes of his youth, and he was stuck in them—and on this day he had added an open-necked sports shirt instead of a shirt and tie because he wanted to change easily at the squash club. He had felt very informal talking to Mrs Summers, but in these surroundings he felt like a banker. All round them the counter-culture was on display; most of the people were under thirty, dressed in blankets and sacking. At one table a boy sat with his eyes closed and his hands in the air, making two circles with thumbs and forefingers. Meditating? At another, two young mothers tented in curtains were demonstrating the joys of breast-feeding to the passers-by.

'Have a fellafel burger,' Molly suggested.

Salter looked at the menu but could recognize nothing, and he shrugged and nodded. When it arrived it turned out to be a giant sesame-seed bun filled with weeds and roots. Salter found it tasty.

'I'm having mint tea,' Molly said. 'They do have coffee for addicts,' she said.

'That's me. Coffee with extra caffein, please, and two spoonfuls of white, cancer-inducing sugar.' You've got to stand up for your own, he thought.

After the food she sat looking expectant, like a good student. Salter began, 'I'd like to know about the other teachers at Douglas. How did Summers compare, as a teacher, with the others in the department that you had?'

'I only had two others. Dunkley taught me Canadian Literature, and a man named Philpott, an Englishman, taught American Lit. He's not there now.'

'What happened to him? What are you smiling about?'

'He left in mid-term and Professor Browne, the chairman, finished the course.' She laughed. 'Philpott never turned up much and we complained about him. A lot. We called him the Great Canadian Doctor.'

'Why?'

'It turned out he was a fake, no degree, nothing. By rights, according to the proper rules of fiction, he should have been brilliant, but he was a joke. When he did come to class, about once a week, he used to read book reviews to us that he'd got from the library. Browne hushed it up and everybody passed the course.'

'And Dunkley?'

'He's OK. He is supposed to be very left-wing and he wears all the gear, but he's really an old-fashioned schoolmaster. He made us work. In theory you could choose your own way of passing his course, but by the time you had finished discussing it with him you had already done more work than you would have done in a conventional course. He made you do your own course outline, and to do that properly you had to know all the material before you started.'

Salter had run out of questions.

'Anything else?' she asked brightly.

'I guess not. I don't suppose I'll have to bother you again.'

'Hardly worth meeting for, was it? Or was it just an excuse?'

'It was just an excuse. I wanted to see you,' he said nervously.

'That's nice. Do you want to see me again?'

Salter floundered. She rescued him. 'I'm not

propositioning you, Charlie. But we can get together if you like.'

But, Salter thought, you are twenty years old and I am forty-six and you cannot have any idea of how foolish I feel. Summers may have liked your essays as well, but he must have enjoyed you as much as I do.

'I may need your help later on,' he said, dodging.

'You don't have to need my help. Just call me. Or I'll call you—for a beer.'

'No, don't do that.'

'I see. Your wife would mind?'

That didn't take much thought. 'Yes.'

'Don't worry. I won't let you do anything silly.'

The middle-aged police inspector who had seen everything smiled shyly. 'All right,' he said. 'It's nice to see how the rest of the world lives.'

'Isn't it? Now I have to go. Are you buying my lunch? You won't feel compromised?'

'No. I'll put it on expenses, then I'll know it was business. I'm still conducting an investigation.'

'Good.' She touched his hand. 'Finish your coffee.' She walked away, threading between the tables, waving at him as she reached the kerb. Salter hunched happily over the dregs of his coffee.

Salter changed into his old tennis clothes, and wondered what to do with his valuables. The attendant showed him a row of little wooden cubby-holes with locks, and Salter chose one and deposited his wallet and watch, putting the elastic wristlet with the key in his pocket in preference to wearing it. The pro was waiting for him on the court.

'Like this,' the pro said. He dropped the ball on to his racquet and hit it against the front wall of the court. Salter swung at it and missed. 'And again,' the pro said. Swing and hit, with the handle. 'And again.' Swing and hit, straight up to the ceiling. 'That's it,' the pro said. 'I can see you've played a lot of tennis.' Salter smirked. They kept at it for ten minutes, sometimes keeping the ball in play for as much as four successive hits. Then the pro suggested a rally. 'Just keep the ball in play,' he said. Ten minutes later Salter thought it was all up with him. His lungs were heaving, his heart pounded in his ears, and he could barely see for the sweat. 'How's your condition?' the pro asked. He had gooseflesh from the chilly court.

Salter took a deep breath. 'And again,' he sobbed, and hit the ball hard, and properly.

'Terrific,' said the pro, and returned it from behind his back without looking.

At the end Salter said, 'I want another lesson tomorrow.' They left the court and Salter walked down the corridor to the changing-room which was now crowded. He took his clothes off, feeling ill at ease among a lot of nude lawyers, self-conscious about his varicose veins and his old gall-bladder scar. But under the shower, and then, in the whirlpool, he forgot himself in the pleasure of having stretched his body.

He dressed and waited in the lounge, and soon Bailey appeared for his game with Cranmer, the accountant. He dropped his eyes when he noticed Salter, then looked up very quickly and greeted the inspector with a lot of noise. 'How's it going, chief?' was one of the things he said.

'I've just had my first lesson,' Salter said. 'I think I'll join.'

'Really? Maybe we'll have a game, sometime.'

'When I've had a couple more lessons.'

They sat quiet then, waiting for each other to speak. Bailey broke first. 'Any news on Old Dave?' he asked.

'None. I'll tell you, Mr Bailey, we are baffled. It looks as though it must have been a casual set-up.'

'He got rolled, you think?'

'Something like that.'

'Poor old Dave, eh? Well, I'd better change. Percy is always on time.' He bustled about with his racquet and bag.

'One thing, Mr Bailey. I was just checking on a few odds and ends. Summers made a couple of calls from Montreal on Friday afternoon . . .'

'That's right, Inspector, I forgot to tell you. One of them was to me, to tell me he couldn't play squash the next Monday. He'd forgotten to tell me when I saw him on Thursday that he was going to Montreal for this conference.'

'I see. That was all, was it? Did he sound very excited?'

Bailey considered this. 'Excited? No, I wouldn't say he sounded any different from his usual self. No.'

'Why would he phone to cancel a game if you hadn't arranged it?'

'Oh, it was a standard arrangement we had. We only got in touch when we couldn't make it. Otherwise my secretary booked the courts for us every day.'

'I see. It must have been an exciting game on that Thursday to make him forget.'

'Yeah. We always went at it pretty hard. That it, then? Here's Percy now.'

Bailey and Cranmer went off to the changing-rooms and Salter went in search of the manager to make preliminary enquiries about joining the club. Once he had started the process, he decided to go ahead and become a member there and then.

CHAPTER 6

The next morning Salter woke with the thought that one of his many enemies had finally caught up with him in an alley. As well as having two broken legs, he had obviously been worked over from the neck down. So this is what it feels like, he thought. Then he remembered the cause and began to enjoy his pain, the product of his first serious exercise in ten years. He had slept like an athlete, too, and he lay there, thinking of the day before, and watching the stirrings of his wife who slept high on her pillow, her waist almost level with his face. It was seven o'clock and Salter watched her dig deeper into the pillow for a few extra minutes. He waited until she was still again, then he peeled the duvet back, lifted up her nightdress, and bit her gently on the bottom.

She didn't move. 'What's this?' she asked.

'Bum-biting,' he said. 'A traditional arousal technique. I thought I'd try it.'

'Like it?'

'Not much.'

'Good.'

'Want me to try something else?'

She turned and lay on her back. 'I'm not terrifically in the mood,' she said. 'But you are. So how about a Victorian quickie.' She pulled her nightdress up around her waist.

'Right,' he said and rolled towards her. 'Aaaargh, Holy Christ. I can't move. Aaaargh. I played squash yesterday. I can't move.'

'What a vicious circle,' she said. 'You play squash to get fit to improve your sex life, and now you can't move. OK. When you are convalescent, let me know.' She stepped out of bed and into the bathroom.

He lay back among his aches. 'You'll pay for this,' he shouted. 'I'll walk again, you'll see.' After a while he clambered slowly out of bed and edged into his dressing-gown. Downstairs, some minutes later, he met the wondering stare of his two sons, who had heard him shouting and now watched him limping about the kitchen.

The hell with them, he thought. Let them wonder.

He forgot his pain the instant the pro hit the ball to start his second lesson later that morning. This time he hit the ball nearly every time, even essaying some rudimentary placing and shot-making. 'Wow!' the pro said, between looking at his watch. This time the lesson cost him ten dollars for half an hour.

'Found a motive, yet, Charlie?' Harry Wycke stood in the door of Salter's office as he got ready to leave for Montreal.

'You want to hear about it, Harry? I've got a few minutes before I leave.'

'Sure.' Wycke sat down on the hard little visitor's chair and looked around the office. 'Not exactly top-of-line here, is it?' he said.

'It's what they had left over.' Was Wycke about to patronize him?

But the detective just shrugged, and waited for him to speak.

Salter summarized the story so far, and Wycke listened carefully.

'What next?' he asked, when Salter had finished.

'I'm going down to Montreal this afternoon to have a look round. You have any advice?'

Wycke shook his head. 'I wouldn't look for anything complicated. Sex. Money. Both.' He stood up. 'Want me to check out the bookies here? See if he was known to be over his head?'

'Yes, thanks, Harry. But I can't see it.'

'Nor can I. But it's an obvious one, so we'll cover your ass on it.' He winked and left.

The afternoon train from Toronto to Montreal takes a little less than five hours. Salter carried along Summers's journal to pass the time, hoping, in spite of Mrs Summers, to find it interesting as well as useful. He treated himself to the first-class section so that he could drink beer and read in comfort, and was assigned a seat by the window; ideal, because, although there is nothing worth looking at on the Montreal-Toronto journey, staring out the window, or appearing to, was the easiest way of avoiding conversation with the other passengers.

The first few pages of the journal depressed him. It was declared immediately that this was Summers's first exercise in journal-keeping, and the early pages consisted of a long, rambling, 'literary' account of the author's condition—mental, physical, psychological, sexual (too coy to be interesting), social, paternal, marital, fraternal, spiritual ('I know, finally, that I must die;' for Christ's sake, thought Salter), and professional. Salter thumbed through the first hundred pages. About thirty pages in, Summers had written: 'Joyce feeling larky today, and we had a nice time before we got up this morning.' This was more like it. Salter ordered a beer and settled back with page one.

Gradually as he read on, Summers's life emerged from his literary concern with the writing of the journal. The entries grew shorter—soon a page was a long entry—and the journal came alive as it became a record of what was happening to Summers rather than a collection of *pensées*. It began with an enquiry into the writer's depressed state. He was sleeping badly, waking up anxious, and savouring little, it seemed. Salter recognized the condition as his own and reflected that it was probably widespread, normal, and boring. What was more interesting was the upward movement of the journal, marked by the disappearance of introspection, and Salter read more closely to see how Summers had come out of it. The appearance of his new hobby, squash, was the first sign that Summers had gone beyond his fascination with his own melancholy to doing something about it. After about two months, Summers began to mention his games regularly, especially those with Cranmer and Bailey. Soon Cranmer faded, but the games with Bailey were regularly recorded, together with comments. Once Summers wrote: 'Exhausted. Played Bailey today—beat him—he wanted to play again—beat him again. Almost felt sorry for him, and offered to buy the beer. He got very snotty about it. Said I would be buying the beer soon enough. Ho. Ho. I look forward to it all day. We are dead even, but I am feeling up this week. Sometimes I feel a bit embarrassed about this new obsession, but there's a distinguished professor over at the U. of T. who doesn't give a shit for anything except his horse.' A later entry read: 'Lost to Bailey today. My eye still black from last week. I think he's been taking lessons, too.' During a squash tournament, apparently among the 'D' players at the club, the journal stopped for ten days, and Salter reflected that this kind of journal was probably only kept up when the writer felt sad.

Sometimes Summers reprimanded himself for not keeping it conscientiously. The first entry of this kind occurred about a third of the way through, and was the result of Summers himself having read the first six months of his journal and having found it fascinating. Food appeared occasionally as Summers described the meals he had eaten in restaurants, along with the prices. Here, too, he was beginning to see the interest such information might have for him in the future. Sometimes he recorded the movies and plays he had seen and included a considered, literary reaction. More to Salter's taste was: 'Saw a lot of frauds farting around the stage of the St Lawrence Centre last night', and 'Fell asleep during concert yesterday. Drooled a bit, but no one noticed.'

Douglas College was a major theme. All the 'great' classes as well as the total failures were recorded—there seemed to be about one of each a week. Then, among the more detailed comments on the classes, Salter began to detect the figure of Molly Tripp. She was called by name, in the last fifty pages, but Salter recognized her very early as 'a nice girl in the second row with curly hair and blue jeans.' She appeared several times as someone who 'saved' a class on Wordsworth or someone, just as it was collapsing. Then she turned up at the office to talk about an essay. Soon she was identified as Molly Tripp, and Summers started having coffee with her. He wondered (but not to her) if she always wore blue jeans. Then he wondered it again. In the second term, about half way through the journal, she turned into plain Molly, and Summers indulged in a mild, erotic fantasy. 'Just once,' he wrote 'I'd like to see her without her jeans on. (Maybe, though, she has wizened or hairy legs, like Geraldine.)' Salter wondered who the hell the unfortunate Geraldine was—one of Summers's relatives? Significantly enough, Molly turned into 'M'. Summers never took the final step into real intimacy in the journal, seeming always to be wary of an eye over his shoulder, but the adoption of the initial was surely a sign of his heightened, illicit interest in the girl. ' "M" came,' he wrote, 'and I managed to keep her for an hour. Next week she is going to have a beer with me.' Then came the lie. 'Without a few students like her, this job would be impossible,' clearly to assure an outsider (reassure his wife?) of his proper interest in Molly.

The beer did not take place, and Summers's other interest in the girl never was spoken between them. She appeared twice before the exams to chat, and Summers wondered if she saw more in him than a teacher. She came after the exam to say she had enjoyed the course, and Summers wrote: 'So I told her about her "A". She was as pleased as I was. Hung around a long time, but I couldn't make anything out of it. Does she know what's going on?'

That was the last of Molly. By watching her progress and guessing at the degree of emotion involved, Salter was able to make sense of some of the relationships of the other characters to the journalist. Joyce Summers occurred regularly, usually in reference to some outing they had enjoyed. There appeared to be no serious fighting, but often a day or two of squabbling, usually resolved by, in Summers's phrase, 'a nice lay'. Summers was mostly pleased with his wife. Marika Tils was his confidant. She interpreted his dreams, cheered him up after bad classes, and gossiped with him about their colleagues. She never came to the house, apparently, but Slater decided that the fact that she was fully identified meant that they had no sexual interest in each other. Two other initials cropped up from time to time. A woman identified as 'S' was the subject of romantic fantasies; the two had lunch sometimes, but there was nothing urgent about their affair, if such it was. Apparently Summers fancied himself in love with her and enjoyed the idea without any impulse to lose the world for her. In the references to 'S', Summers's literary spark glowed again, but without much heat.

In the last third of the journal Summers began to record his new interest in the commodities market. He was fascinated by the possibility of making his fortune, and every weekend he calculated the week's profit or loss. As Mrs Summers had said, he did surprisingly well. The last entry concerned the Montreal conference. 'Looking forward to Thursday. Have not been to Montreal for ten years. J. coming. Our fifth anniversary.'

Salter put the journal back in his bag and ordered a third and last beer. The train was passing through Cornwall. Who was J? Who else but the Dean of Women? The journal held no other surprises, in form or content, but there was one omission that puzzled Salter. The entries about his colleagues were rare enough; mainly they concerned Marika Tils, although the others were mentioned here and there, usually in connection with departmental politics, all except Dunkley who was not mentioned once. Salter wondered: If 'D' is more significant than Dunkley, as indicating a higher degree of emotional involvement, was the omission of D even more significant? They must have hated each other.

O'Brien was waiting at the terminus to take him in hand. He was dressed in a sports shirt with an insect embroidered on the pocket, and a pair of white trousers. Salter couldn't resist it. 'You look like an RCMP narcotics agent,' he said.

O'Brien made a face. 'We are going out on the town, Charlie. I am trying to look like a Toronto professor in search of a piece of French tail.'

'That, too,' Salter said comfortingly. O'Brien's Volkswagen was illegally parked in the taxi-rank outside the terminus, and they drove off after he had thrown away the ticket he had acquired.

'How are the plans for St Jean Baptiste day coming? Need any help?' Salter asked as they drove along.

'You know about our cultural festivities, eh?'

'I know somebody threw a Coke bottle at Trudeau one year. Are you expecting any excitement this time?'

'Fireworks. Real ones. We could use a couple of hundred mounted police. You have influence?'

'There's just me and Frank. He's got piles and I can't ride.'

'You should learn how. Then when Québec separates you could join the cavalry and lead the charge down Highway 401.'

'No good. Your road is so bad we would never get across the border.'

'Ha, ha, ha. Are you finished with the jokes, Charlie? Can I talk about the case? Something has cropped up.'

'OK. Go ahead.'

'Summers used two keys to his room. You remember we found two keys.'

'Right. He took one when he checked in, left it in his room by mistake, and needed another one to get in when he came home that night.'

'No one remembers him asking for the second key. This is not a busy hotel, Charlie. They would have noticed.'

'But they didn't.'

'He didn't ask for a second key. I've been talking to the clerks again. The one who checked Summers in remembers somebody asking for a second key that afternoon.'

'So he forgot it right away. What is this, Onree? Why are you picking at this?'

'Those two keys bothered me. Now, listen.'

Salter sighed. He enjoyed O'Brien, but if he was one of those people who say 'listen', their friendship would wither quickly. 'Yes,' he said. 'I'm listening.'

'OK. Now. This same desk clerk remembers someone—it could have been Summers—giving him an envelope to put in another mailbox. The envelope had something in it which could have been a hotel key.'

'Was it a key or not, Onree?'

'Of course it was. This clerk doesn't want us to know that he goes through the mail and shakes all the envelopes. You know. A pointed-nose one.'

'So Summers left his key in someone's mailbox. Case complete. Whose?'

'Jane Homer's. The clerk knew because she wrote a note for Summers.'

'The one we got.'

'Yes. It must be.'

'He didn't read the note?'

'No. He says not.'

'Look, Onree, why don't you pour a litre of olive oil down his throat to start with, then staple his ears to his head, then put his testicles in a garlic press, one by one. Maybe he will remember what was in the note and who sent it to who.'

'We can't do that here, Charlie.'

'We do it all the time, only we use nut-crackers because there's no garlic in Ontario.'

'This is very droll, Inspector, but I thought it was important.'

Salter took warning. 'Sorry, Onree. I woke up feeling good, but it's wearing off. All right, so he left a key for Jane Homer to let herself in. I'll talk to her again. She's no killer, though.'

'Did she admit she was in his room?'

'She said she never saw him.'

'When will you talk to her?'

'As soon as I get back. If I learn anything interesting I'll call you.'

By now they had crossed the centre of Montreal.

'I've booked you in Summers's hotel,' O'Brien said. 'We will retrace his footsteps.' He had driven them neatly through the rush-hour traffic to the Hotel Plaza del Oro, and parked in the hotel lot. As they went through the front doors, O'Brien said, 'This is the main entrance, but as you see, the killer did not have to come through here.' The front desk was directly in line with the door, but on either side of the lobby there were smaller doors exiting on to the street. 'You see, he could have walked through that door and stepped straight into the elevator. No one would stop him. I have already registered you so we can go right up to your room.'

The room was standard North American middle class. Two large beds, a television set, two chairs, five coffee tables, and a closet big enough to take twenty suits of clothes. Also a bathroom with an extra coloured lamp in the ceiling which soaked you in ultra-violet light while you were sitting on the toilet.

Salter was wearing his sports jacket, and in deference to his colleague, he took off his tie and put his pen in his inside pocket. 'The best I can do,' he said.

'You look like a Toronto professor who has forgotten to put his tie on,' O'Brien said.

'I could comb my hair forward.'

'Don't worry. Together, we are hard to read, I'm sure. Now. This is it. Every room is identical. Summers had one on the next floor up.'

'Show me how it looked.'

O'Brien arranged the chairs. 'Like this. Two chairs opposite each other. Summers on the floor. Blood everywhere. The whisky bottle here. One glass here. Over here, his suitcase, open but unpacked. Here, by the bed, his clothes, in a heap. The bed was not touched. He had took off his clothes and sat drinking in the chair, I think. The newspaper was here.'

That's the first English mistake he's made, thought Salter.

'It looks as though he was expecting someone, and that's all we know,' O'Brien concluded.

'We know he was expecting Jane Homer. But who else?'

The men stared around the room for a few minutes, then O'Brien said, 'Let's go to the college.'

They left the hotel and walked for two blocks until they came to the building where the Learned Societies meeting was still going on. The French teachers were currently in session—the whole conference took several weeks to run through all the disciplines—and Salter and O'Brien were able to look over the scene of the conference very much as it had been when Summers was killed.

O'Brien said, 'Summers arrived, spent some time in his hotel room, then probably walked to the conference in time to go to the bar after the last session of the day, at four-thirty.'

They passed through the main doors into a crowd of delegates with name tags, standing about in groups. O'Brien led them along a corridor to a bar, a converted classroom, just opening for business.

'This is where he first appeared, Onree?'

'Yes. The others met him here, and they had a drink and went off to dinner.'

The two men looked around. They were learning nothing.

'I didn't put out a request for information,' O'Brien said. 'There were thousands who might have seen him, but if anyone had anything to tell us they would have come forward. That is what the Chairman of the Association thinks, and I agree.'

They walked outside and turned back towards the hotel, along the Rue St Denis, and Salter thought: How bloody easily they do it here. The sidewalk cafés were designed for sitting outside in the summer, and both sides of the street were lined with tables, filled mostly with students drinking beer. Compared to this, Salter thought, in Toronto, for a price, you could sit on two feet of pavement stolen from the sidewalk. Why? Why did they build the sidewalks like this in Montreal and like that in Toronto? The climate was the same. Was it part of the difference between England and France, between London and Paris?

'Let's have a beer,' he said. 'Here. We've got some time to spare.'

They sat down and Salter took in the scene. Baghdad?

The Maison Victor Hugo was two blocks away, a converted house with a small painted sign over the door to indicate its present business. Inside, a table was waiting for them by the small window, and O'Brien placed his colleague so that he could see the street.

'They had that table,' O'Brien said, pointing to one in the centre of the room. 'The waiter remembers them because they were having such a good time.'

'*Bonjour, Monsieur Sergeant.*' The manager was standing by his table. He spoke some more in French.

In English, O'Brien replied. 'I'm off duty tonight. My friend from Toronto is in town and I have brought him here to preserve the reputation of the city. Monsieur Salter,' he added as an introduction.

The manager bowed, shook hands, and spoke again in French. He bowed again and left.

'What was that?' Salter asked.

'He said, "Have a good time and enjoy your meal." If you come here on your own you should buy a phrase-book, Charlie.'

'I know. Especially if you separate.'

'Oh, if we separate it won't matter. We can speak our language and you can speak yours. It is having to speak yours that pisses us off.'

'O'Brien isn't French, Onree. Why do you say "we"?'

' "We" means "Québécois". My name is Irish from my great-grandfther who was a labourer on the railroad. He met my great-grandmother when he was working on a repair gang near Saint Agathe. He settled down, went native, became a Québécois. He was Catholic already, so it was easy. What about you? "Thank God I'm English," and all that?'

'My father's family were, yes. My mother didn't know what she was. She came over as a domestic servant, sent by an English orphanage. I grew up in Cabbagetown, like your St Henri, then—but we moved out of it after the war because it got too slummy, even for us. Now it's very trendy.'

'How do you know about St Henri?'

'*The Tin Flute.* We did it in college.'

The waiter appeared, flourishing a pen. Salter let his host do the ordering, and they ate some carrot soup, a veal stew that tasted agreeably of liquorice, and a big piece of soft, white cheese with some strawberries. They ate a lot of bread with it and drank a big bottle of wine. Salter was not a connoisseur, but he had eaten enough bad food to know the good when he tasted it, even if the upper levels of discrimination were beyond him. This all tasted all right.

'How much, Onree?' he asked at the end.

'My check . . .'

'All right, but how much? Summers spent a hundred and thirty dollars here on five dinners.'

O'Brien picked up the check. 'Thirty-eight dollars. They must have drunk a lot of wine. OK, Charlie, let's see what's next on the agenda.' O'Brien paid the bill, leaving what seemed to Salter a huge tip. Salter used the washroom before they left, and was pleased with himself for being able to translate the slogan above the urinal—'*A bas les anglais.*' He wondered if he could still pee that high, and the thought was father to the deed. Just a short burst, but enough to satisfy.

They began with a cognac at the outdoor café next door. Now the street was full of strollers, cyclists, and people drinking. Students sat in windows on the second stories, calling to their friends on the street as the curtain rose on a perfect evening in early summer in the quarter.

'And now to the first bar,' O'Brien said. They walked south, to a sign which announced simply, '*Danseuses*'. Inside, an ordinary bar counter ran from the door along one wall. The rest of the long room was filled with tables and chairs. The two men sat at a table near the bar and ordered beer.

'They came here first and had one drink. Summers was still paying,' O'Brien said.

Behind the bar a middle-aged couple filled the orders,

and chatted between drinks with a similar middle-aged couple seated at the bar. The scene was domestic and suburban, except for the bare breasts of the waitresses. Then, at the far end of the room, a spotlight lit up one of the tables, and a waitress climbed on the table and took off her skirt. Underneath she was naked. It was still early in the evening, and there were only about a dozen people in the room. The patrons all got up from their tables and moved closer to the girl who was wiggling in time to the juke-box. She jigged for about three minutes while the drinkers watched, then she jumped down, put her skirt on and began taking orders for drinks. Her place was taken by the other waitress who put herself in a back arch on all fours and walked around on the table in this position, like a giant crab.

O'Brien and Salter stayed where they were by the bar in spite of polite urgings by the bar-tender to move closer.

O'Brien saw Salter taking in the whole room, and said, 'They are not here, are they?'

'Who?'

'The whores. The muggers. The hoods.'

Salter confessed that he had been looking for them, and that the room was utterly without any sign of the lower depths. Except for the nudity, it might have been Monday night at the Canadian Legion.

'*Allons,*' O'Brien said. 'The next one is more lively.'

They crossed the street and walked south for a block until they came to a store-front whose windows were covered with posters advertising '*nus*'.

'Les Jardins du Paradis,' O'Brien said.

They pushed a cloth curtain aside and were met by a youth sitting at a card-table. 'Two dollars, messieurs,' he said. 'And two dollars for me if you want a good seat.'

'*Bonjour, Paul,*' O'Brien said. The youth looked up. '*Ah. Monsieur le detective. Encore.* For you a good table is free but it is still two dollars to get in.' He stood up and guided them through a second curtain into the main body of the old store. Once more the scene was simple. A small stage of planks about ten feet square was set up against one wall. Around it and filling up the room were plastic tables, each with four chairs, which were mostly occupied. The boy led them to a table right by the stage, one which the waitresses used to rest their trays between orders. He set a couple of drinks at it, and the two men sat down.

The crowd was young, young enough to make Salter feel self-conscious. Although there were more men than women, there were plenty of couples in the room. Salter ordered beer from a waitress and was amazed to find it cost no more than it should. The music began and the routine at the first bar was repeated. Their waitress was first, and she performed a brisk striptease for about ten minutes. During the first song, she took off her skirt and pants; during the second she unhooked her brassiere; finally her underpants came off and she shook herself vigorously for two or three minutes with an absent-minded air, like someone doing her morning exercises while thinking of the day ahead. The effect was to make Salter feel he had nothing to fear by way of embarrassment from these girls.

The next dancer ended that. Some quieter music began, and a girl ran up on stage in jeans and a T-shirt, a girl with curly hair and a striking facial resemblance to Molly Tripp. Salter wondered for a second if some trick was being played on him. It was an absurd idea; nevertheless, he had the feeling that he was about to watch Molly undress herself and shimmy, naked, and the thought filled him with tension.

She started to dance, and almost immediately peeled off her T-shirt. Fascinated, Salter nodded. That is how she would look under her shirt. The music started again, and the girl took off her jeans; she had thin, brown legs, neither hairy nor deformed. Soon she kicked off her underwear and jigged happily around the little stage. As she came near them, Salter was sorry they had such a good table, because the following spotlight lit up O'Brien and him. He heard the music end with relief, but almost immediately it started again and the girl began a series of acrobatics designed to reveal her delicate and tender parts from all angles. Salter tried to look indifferent, but this made the girl mischievous, and she came to the edge of the stage and wiggled at him, her crotch only a yard from his face. He was appalled and he picked up his beer in defence, and the girl pouted at him, turned, and bent down to thrust herself in his face. Then she poked her hand through her thighs and stole his beer. The crowd cheered her wit, and after a bit of applause the spotlight finally went out.

The house lights went up to show O'Brien grinning at him. Salter looked around the club, and everyone else seemed to be grinning at him, too.

'You think you will recognize her again, Charlie?' O'Brien asked.

Salter realized, then, what was going on. 'You set that up, you bastard,' he said.

'It's a regular part of her act. You can order it for a friend, so tonight I asked them to honour you. Nice?'

Salter decided to tell his colleague of the extra dimension. 'If that happened to Summers, I can understand why he went home. That girl looked exactly like a student he thought he was in love with.'

O'Brien stopped grinning. 'It must have upset him. It looked as though it upset you.'

'Yes, and I hardly know the girl.'

After this the men walked back to Salter's hotel where they had a last quiet drink and reviewed their case.

'You don't think this Dunkley is likely?' O'Brien asked.

'On paper, yes. But not when you meet the man. He is

a good hater—almost enough motive in itself—and he must have got pretty jealous of Summers's lucky day. And he was already jealous of what he thought was going on between Marika Tils and Summers.'

'And you call this "on paper"? It would look pretty bad for Dunkley to someone who didn't have your feeling about him.'

'I know, and you'll probably have to prove he didn't do it, just to avoid arresting him for it. He's got a good alibi, though, along with Carrier. The one who knew Summers who doesn't have an alibi is Marika Tils, and I can't find anything phoney about her feeling for Summers.'

'So what do you think happened?'

'Either Summers was killed by an unknown stranger, or by an unknown (unknown to us, that is) friend.'

'Summers let them into his room, or they had another key. You don't think this Homer woman did it? *Her* story would look bad to a jury, too.'

'I know. No, I'm stuck with the whore theory, Onree. This must be your problem.'

'My instinct about the whores in this district is like yours for Summers's friends. I don't believe it, but I'll go through the motions. What we need to prove us both right, Charlie, is an unknown friend of Summers with all of Dunkley's motives and a taste for murder.'

'Right. Let's keep our eyes open.'

O'Brien offered to take the next day off and show Salter something of Montreal, but Salter declined, having a number of matters that required his attention in Toronto, including a squash lesson and a drink with Molly Tripp.

CHAPTER 7

In the years since Salter had courted Annie there, the
Roof Bar had changed, but it was still the best bar in
Toronto. The waiters still knew him, and watched now as
Molly climbed on to the table. She took off her T-shirt
and started to dance; then, as the waiters rushed to stop
her she jumped up on to the stone balustrade that ran
round the edge of the roof, and stepped out of her jeans,
to pose for a second, naked. Salter jumped up after her,
and she took his hand and stepped with him off the
balustrade into space.

Salter awoke with a bump, sweating. Probably he had
been shouting, too, but in a hotel bedroom in Montreal a
little shouting is allowed. He showered and dressed
quickly and took a cab to the station to eat his breakfast
there while he waited for the train. He wanted badly to
read a Toronto paper with his morning coffee to get back
to normal.

In Toronto he phoned his wife and Sergeant Gatenby,
and then, without calling ahead, took a cab to Jane
Homer's office in Wollstonecraft Hall. The secretary tried
to intercept him, but as she was announcing him he
walked past her into the Dean's office. Jane Homer was
calmer now. She still looked unhappy at seeing him but
she no longer shook with misery, or fear. Salter came to
the point quickly.

'When did you visit Professor Summers's room, Miss
Homer?'

She protested, so he retreated a step and gave her the
background of his question. 'We know that he put a key
for you in your mailbox,' he said. 'At around two o'clock.
We know that you got the key and wrote him a note — we

have that note. We found the key in his room, and the desk-clerk remembers the rest. Now, when did you go to his room?'

'I went up there during the evening—about nine o'clock,' she said finally.

Salter waited.

'I know it sounds odd. But David left me his key so that I could let myself in and pour myself a drink while I waited, which I did. But he didn't come home early enough, so I went back to my room and to bed.'

'And that's that?'

'Yes.'

What a poor liar, Salter thought. What would this woman's motive for lying turn out to be? A good deal less than murder, he was certain.

'You have nothing else to tell me?'

She opened a desk drawer and took out a scrap of paper. 'This note was in the envelope with the key,' she said.

Salter read, 'If I'm not here when you get back, try later. I've had the most fantastic piece of luck.'

'Why didn't you show me this the other day?'

'Because I wanted to stay out of it. Because I was not involved in David's death and it would not help anything to know we were going to have a drink.'

'Did you? Have a drink? Just so that I know what else you don't think would help.'

'Yes. I poured myself one while I waited for him.'

'How long did you wait?'

'About half an hour.'

'What time, then, do you think you left the room?'

'About nine-thirty.'

'Anything else?'

'What do you mean?'

'I mean anything else, Miss Homer. *Anything else?*

'No. I went to David's room to have a drink. He did

turn up. That's all.'

'Did you often drink with Summers in hotel rooms?'

'That's enough, Inspector. I am just unlucky to be caught up in this. You know that.'

'I don't know anything, Miss Homer, except what I read in the papers and what people tell me. That's it, then?'

'There is nothing else. Now I have an appointment, please.'

Salter considered. He decided to keep what he had read to himself for the moment. 'All right, Miss Homer. Please don't go away, though, will you? I think we'll be in touch, shortly.'

She said nothing as he got up and left.

He walked back along College Street to his office where he was greeted by Gatenby with the news that the Superintendent wanted a report on the progress of the case by Monday. 'What case?' Salter grunted. 'What progress?'

He sat behind his desk and considered the note that Jane Homer had given him. It was bothering him, and he wanted to ask someone why. Then he isolated the phrase which troubled him, and phoned Mrs Summers.

'Inspector Salter here, Mrs Summers.'

'Hello. I wanted to thank you for coming by. I felt better after talking to you. Not terrific, but better. What can I do for you?'

'One of your husband's colleagues has remembered another phrase that he used on Friday when he was talking about his lucky day. He said your husband said he had had a "fantastic piece of luck". My question is simply: Would he have described the two thousand dollars he made in trading the Canadian dollar in those terms?'

'Your instincts are sound, Inspector. No, he wouldn't.

He didn't tell anyone much about his dealings, but, like I said, he made two or three thousand in a day several times. Lost it, too.'

'That's what I thought. Then what would he have called fantastic?'

'In money? A lot. Fifty thousand or more.'

'Could it be anything else?'

'Search me, Inspector. It sounds like money.'

'Have you had a chance to check his wallet? Maybe there is something there that we didn't notice?'

'I'll look for secret compartments, shall I? See, I'm joking already. No, I'll look, but I don't know what I'm looking for.'

'Nor do I. But the clue to your husband's behaviour that night was this stroke of luck, and if I can find out what it was we might be able to guess who he told, or who told him.'

'I'll look at it this afternoon.'

'Thank you, Mrs Summers.' Salter hung up the phone and stared at the note until it was time for his lesson.

They played for fifteen minutes without pause. Salter was splashing sweat on to the floor, but he was thrilled to note that his heart and lungs, while bursting, seemed to be getting used to the condition.

'Now,' said the pro. 'Let's have a little game. Best of five.'

They played a little game, the best of five points. 'Nice going,' called the pro, as Salter lumbered and dived after the ball. 'Terrific.' The pro won 3-2 and patted Salter with his racquet, one jock to another. 'Great stuff, chief,' he said. 'Tomorrow, same time?'

'Yes,' Salter wheezed. 'How do you think I'm doing? Could I play anyone around here, do you think?'

'Sure, Charlie. You could give Bill or Percy a game.'

Salter sat afterwards in the lounge, open-pored and

aching, watching the door. Bailey came through, on time, and Salter waved him over. He came to the table, somewhat reluctantly, Salter thought, and sat down:

'How about a game?' Salter asked.

Cranmer appeared, smiling like a shepherd. 'You could play on Monday, Bill;' he said. 'I have to cancel our game.'

Bailey looked irritated. 'Sure,' he said. 'Inspector . . .'

'Charlie,' corrected Salter.

'OK, Charlie, tomorrow, then. Four o'clock on the court?'

'Thanks, Bill.'

On Friday, after two days of doing nothing, except playing squash and waiting for O'Brien to call and say he'd found the killer, he met Molly, not on the Roof, but in a bar converted from a defunct gas station on Church Street where, thought Salter, instant food had replaced instant gas. He thought of an obvious joke but let it go as too obvious. 'Listen,' Molly said. He listened. Banjos and guitars and wailing voices. Country music. 'Ah!' he said. Salter did not have much music in his soul but this made his feet tap. 'What is it?' he asked.

' "The Lady's Choice Blue Grass Band!" Terrific, isn't it?'

'Nice,' he said cautiously. His night out in Montreal, followed by the nervous dream, had left him feeling disqualified from flirting with her, and he resolved that this would be the last time he would see her. He had thought about her, on and off, all day, and been unable to decide whether the dream represented desire, or fear, or what. Did he want to take her clothes off and grapple with her? What was he to her—Dad? He looked in the mirror behind the bar. One middle-aged policeman and one pretty (young) girl. When she looked in the mirror, what did she see?

It was time to go. She said, 'Let's go round the corner
to Sam's. I want to buy a record.'

They finished their beer and walked through to Sam
the Record Man on Yonge Street. 'Here,' she said,
thumbing quickly through one of the country music
racks. 'Here it is.' She pulled out a record of 'The Lady's
Choice Blue Grass Band'. Salter reached for his wallet,
but she pulled the record away from him and put a finger
to her lips to indicate a secret. When she had paid and
they were out on the street she turned to him and put the
record in his hand. 'Happy Birthday,' she said.

'Christ, I forgot,' he said. It was one of the first things
she had asked him.

She leaned up to him and kissed him beneath the ear
and ran across Yonge Street, leaving him looking after
her on the sidewalk.

At home there was a cake, a round of 'Happy Birthday to
you', a new fountain-pen from his wife, and a set of jump
cables from his sons. After dinner, Salter produced the
record. 'Look,' he said, 'I heard this record today while I
was having a cup of coffee, so I went and bought one. It
was on a juke-box.'

Annie took the record and read the cover. The boys
looked over her shoulder and broke into hysterics. Salter
was mystified until Annie led him into the room
containing the stereo where she pulled a record from a
pile and showed him the cover. It was the same record.

'It's a Halifax group,' she said. 'My brother sent it to
Angus for his birthday in March.'

'Have I ever heard it?'

'It's the one you are always yelling at Angus to turn
down.'

'Is it?' Salter could think of nothing to say.

Annie said, 'Come upstairs.'

In the bedroom she asked, 'Who bought it for you? The

woman you were with this afternoon? The one you are
having the affair with?'

'Yes,' he said. 'Yes, she did. But I am not having an
affair.' And he told her the truth, or as much as he
understood himself about Molly Tripp.

'Your father called,' Annie said on Sunday morning.
They lay in bed after the most astonishing weekend in
their marriage. The inevitable discussion of Molly Tripp
had led to a much closer discussion of their own
relationship which, though full of goodwill, had not been
sharpened on the whetstone of a good talk for a long
time. The result had been a miniature courtship,
climaxing in a small honeymoon, so that they had spent
most of the weekend making love with more enthusiasm
than they had shown each other for years. The effect on
Salter was a mild case of priapism. Even now, spent, and
talking about his father, he lay rigid beside her.

'Not coming?' Salter asked, hopefully.

'Yes. He wants to bring a friend.'

'What!'

'A lady.'

'A girl-friend?'

'I imagine so. Maybe he's going to get married again.'

'For Christ's sake.' Salter withdrew into the bathroom.
There he stood under a cold shower for several minutes
before turning on the hot water to scrub himself. He felt
purged, battered and clean. Annie came into the
bathroom, and he put his arm up defensively.

'You playing squash this morning?' she asked.

'If I can,' he joked.

Annie ignored the facetiousness. 'Bring home some
Brussels sprouts from one of the Chinese stores on Yonge
Street. Your father is always asking for them.'

The pro played with his left hand, supplying the lesson

with a much-needed element of surprise. He still won
easily enough, but Salter got several points intentionally.
The weekend had made him feel lighter on his feet, and
he looked forward to meeting Bailey on the court.

His father arrived at six o'clock, accompanied by a stout
lady in her fifties dressed in a mushroom-coloured outfit
and wearing a hat like the Queen Mother's.

'This is May,' his father said, pointing at her as he did
so. He acted throughout the evening like May's owner,
drawing attention to her finer points when she was under
discussion, ignoring her when the conversation was
general. May said nothing whatever during dinner,
placidly eating Annie's roast beef, Brussels sprouts and
Lunenburg Pie like a large, well-trained child.

After dinner the boys disappeared, and Annie took
May for a walk so that the two men could chat in private.

His father said, 'I've been walking out with her for two
months now. She's Fred's widow. I expect you are
surprised.' He sat like a man in sudden possession of a
fortune, puffed-up and happy.

'I'm pleased, Dad. Annie is, too.'

'What about?'

'Well, that you've found a friend.'

'She's more than that.'

Salter blushed. As a child, he did not remember the
smallest reference to sex ever occurring in his parents'
house, and his father and he had kept up that
relationship. His father's remark sounded shockingly
bawdy.

'That's your privilege,' he said. Jesus Christ.

'We aren't going to get married,' his father said. Now
he was leering. 'We are going to live together.' He stared,
belligerent and proud, at his son, to see if he understood.

'Ah. Yes. Well, then. You won't be alone, will you?'

'It's not just for the company. I'm only sixty-seven. We

are having an affair.'

'Oh, well. That's all right then, isn't it?' Would the old
(new) goat never shut up?

'It's more than all right. It's what my old man used to
call "a bit of all right".' He leant forward and touched
Salter's knee, and leered again. 'You know what I mean?'

Salter treated the question as rhetorical. 'Good for you,
Dad,' he said loudly. 'Enjoy yourself while you can, eh?'
Would you like some dirty magazines from the exhibits
down at the station?

His father came to the second point. 'I've left
everything to you, of course. Don't worry about that.
We've both got good pensions.'

Salter was embarrassed. 'Spend it on yourself, Dad,
and on May. Have a good time. We're all right.'

'I know that. I know *she's* got plenty.' His father always
referred to Annie as 'she'. 'But I thought you might be
expecting a bit from me.'

'Spend it, Dad. Spend it.' How much was involved? A
thousand? Five?

'Right.' His father stood up and stroked his chest. 'We
won't be having any çelebration. She's no blushing bride,
after all, though she's made *me* blush a couple of times.
The boys out, are they? Never do say cheerio properly, do
they? Still. Here. Give them this.' He held out two ten-
dollar bills.

'Nobody gives kids money when they visit any more,
Dad.'

'I do. Here.'

Salter took the bills to avoid an argument and put them
on the sideboard. Just then his wife returned with May,
who was still silent but beaming and pink. His wife took
charge, chattering appropriately. She kissed his father,
who took her head in his hands and kissed her hard in
return. Annie said, 'Isn't it great, Charlie? We're giving a
party for them on July 5th.'

Salter wondered what had happened to the idea of no celebration, and he wondered, also, if his wife remembered that they were going to the Island on July 3rd. Before he could point out either of these objections, Annie said, 'I suggested it. So all you have to do is turn up.' This last remark was addressed to the happy couple.

In bed that night, Salter started to express his surprise, but she cut him off. 'Look at it selfishly,' she suggested. 'With luck, you have at least twenty years of it left.'

Salter stroked her back. 'Not at this rate,' he said, and curled, unmolested, around her.

Before he fell asleep, he asked, 'Is everybody doing it?'

'What?' she asked.

'I'll tell you tomorrow.'

Looking for Baghdad, he thought.

CHAPTER 8

On Monday morning Salter wrote up his report to date. Most policemen detest this aspect of their work, and Salter was like most policemen. An incompetent bank-robber may be caught in ten minutes, but it takes the rest of the day to write up a report on the incident suitable for Deputy Chiefs, Crown Attorneys, and the Supreme Court. In this case, however, he did not mind so much because he had nothing else to do that he could think of, and the sheer act of writing the report would enable him, force him, to review it systematically. He had been writing for two hours when he got a phone call from Mrs Summers. She had checked the wallet, and none of the lottery tickets were winners, although one would not be drawn until the following week. There was nothing else.

Except, 'There is one ticket missing, though,' she said.

'Missing? How do you know? Which one?'

'The local one. The weekly one. I was with him when he bought it the day before, so I know he had it. He must have checked it and thrown it away.'

'When was it drawn?'

'Thursday. The results are in the paper on Friday.'

'You are absolutely certain? And the ticket is not around the house?'

'Yes and no. I was with him, I told you. And he put the ticket in his wallet, like he always does.'

Now what? Salter felt as if he had won a lottery himself, but was too frightened to check the ticket carefully in case he was wrong. He tried to give himself breathing space by returning to the report, but he was unable to write a sentence. After a few minutes of indecision he phoned O'Brien in Montreal and told him of his conversation with Mrs Summers. Then he asked, 'Is there any way that the ticket could have been overlooked when the room was searched, Onree? The waste-basket, anything like that?' Salter's voice was plaintive.

'Wait, Charlie. Here is the man who looked after the scene. Speak to him.'

A detective with an accent much thicker than O'Brien's came on the line and Salter repeated his question.

'There was no ticket in the room, Inspector. You know those 'otel rooms. It was not an 'ard search. There was his clothes, the Scotch whisky, his suitcase, and the news-paper. And that's all. I checked the waste-basket myself. Not even a chewing-gum wrapper. Sorry, Inspector.'

'That's fine, Officer. Just fine. Thank you. Let me speak to Onree again. Thank you. Onree? Listen. I think I've got something. I think I've figured out what his lucky day was. I think he won a big lottery prize, and that he was killed for it, the ticket I mean. It's the only thing that was so big that he didn't want to tell anyone but couldn't keep it to himself, if you know what I mean. What do you think of that, Onree? Pure urcewl pworro.'

'Pure what, Charlie?'

'Pure urcewl pworro. You know. The guy in the stories.'

He heard O'Brien repeating the words to himself several times, then a shout of triumph, followed by some rapid French as O'Brien relayed something to his colleagues. Then, 'There are some flaws, Charlie.'

'I know that. It may all be bullshit, and it's certainly pure conjecture, but what do you think?'

'I think it's nice, Charlie. Let me think some more and we'll try to figure out how to prove it. I'll call you back this afternoon.'

Now. Salter found the number of the lottery organization and held his breath while he asked his first question. The answer was that no one had yet claimed the previous week's grand prize. The answer to the second was that the ticket had been bought in Mississauga. As far as he knew, there was no connection whatever between Summers and Mississauga. Shit.

Salter went to lunch.

Sergeant Gatenby poked his head round the door and addressed Salter who sat brooding after lunch. 'Visitors,' he announced in a stage whisper, gleefully.

Salter looked at him without interest. 'I'm busy,' he said. 'On a case.

'Oh, these *are* the case,' Gatenby said, rolling his eyes. 'A lady and a man. Miss Jane Homer and Professor Pollock.'

Now what could this mean? 'Show them in, Frank.'

Miss Homer entered first, pale and frightened. Behind her came Pollock, pipe in hand and boots ajar.

'Sit down,' Salter said, and waited.

Pollock began. 'I have been talking to Miss Homer, Inspector. I think she's been unwise and I've advised her to come and see you. She asked me to come with her.'

'Fine. Wait outside, please.'

'Miss Homer would prefer me to stay, I think.'

'Mr Pollock, I am conducting an inquiry into a brutal murder, not a student appeal. If Miss Homer wants to make a statement, I'll have it witnessed by my sergeant. If she wants a lawyer, I will phone for one. Are you a lawyer? No. Right. Wait outside.'

Pollock looked at the woman. 'I thought it might be like this,' he said. 'I'll wait outside. If you need your lawyer, I'll make sure he gets the message.'

Jane Homer said nothing, and Pollock left.

'Now, Miss Homer. You are going to tell me what fifth anniversary you were celebrating with Professor Summers, are you? I'll get Sergeant Gatenby.' Salter watched her start to shiver again and he went to the door to send the sergeant for a cup of tea. When Gatenby returned, he brought his notebook and a pencil.

Salter began. 'Miss Homer wants to make a statement. After she has finished, type it immediately and she will sign it. Go ahead, miss.'

She began in a tight, mechanical voice. 'When I arrived at the hotel in Montreal, there was a key waiting for me and a note from Professor Summers telling me to wait for him in his room.'

'We'll put the full note in the script, Miss Homer. I'll give it to the sergeant.'

She resumed. 'I went up to his room about nine, but there was no one there. So I left after half an hour.'

'Did you do anything while you were there?'

'I had a drink, and watched the television.'

'I see. And when did you come back?'

'At eleven-thirty.'

'To spend the night.'

'Yes.'

'To have intercourse with Professor Summers?'

'Yes.'

'He was expecting this?'

'Yes, we met every year.'

'At the conferences?'

'Yes.'

'You slept with Professor Summers once a year at the conferences?'

'Yes.'

'You never met him in Toronto?'

'No.'

A phrase occurred to Salter about the groves of academe.

'I see. Go on.'

'When I came back at eleven-thirty, I found David.'

'Dead?'

'Yes.'

'Would you describe the position of the body, and the state of the room, please?'

She did so, accurately.

'So. Why didn't you raise the alarm?'

'I am the Dean of Women at . . .'

'I know. You are the Dean of Women at Diddle-the-Girls Hall. So to avoid having your annual adultery exposed, you kept quiet about a murder.'

'Yes.'

'And then?'

'I left the next afternoon.'

'And that's that?'

'Yes. And now, I suppose, everyone will be involved.'

'Not necessarily. If what you say is true, it has nothing to do with my case and I won't involve you unnecessarily. It is possible you will be needed to substantiate the time of the death, which might be important, but I can't do anything about that. First, though, I have to decide whether I have the whole story from you.'

'You think I'm lying.'

'I don't think anything. I've had three separate stories

from you so far, and I now don't believe or disbelieve any of them.'

'You think I killed David?'

'No, I don't, Miss Homer, but what I think is irrelevant. It's my job to be suspicious, especially where I have cause.'

'Are you going to arrest me?'

'Not unless this story turns out to be phoney, too. Will it?'

'Of course not.'

'Then, no. But, once more, Miss Homer: Do you have anything more to tell me?'

'No. I have nothing to do with any of this. I think like everyone else that poor David was probably killed by a prostitute or her associate.'

'If he was waiting for you, that's hardly likely, is it?' Salter asked, though he wondered himself. Who could say what the effect of seeing Molly dancing naked on the table was on the slightly infatuated professor of romantic poetry?

'May I go now?'

'Would you wait in this office, please, while the statement is being typed.' Salter led her into a little side office, like a cupboard. Gatenby looked up from his notebook when the door had closed. 'These academic conferences,' he said. 'Just a sea of heaving arses, you might say, eh, Inspector?'

Salter grunted at him. 'Type the report, Frank, and tell Pollock to come in here.'

Pollock came in and sat down. 'May I smoke, Inspector?' he asked, indicating the pipe and his tobacco pouch.

'No. You know what Miss Homer told me?'

'Yes. I told her to come and make a clean breast of it. The smell bother you, does it?'

'Should I believe her?'

'Oh yes.' Pollock still had not put his smoking materials away.

'Oh yes? Why?'

'Because I know who killed David,' Pollock said, and now with the air of a man who had earned the right, he began to fill his pipe.

Salter watched him for a few seconds, a long time, feeling all the professional frustrations and the private emotional turbulence of the last few days pile up, and he went mad.

'Professor,' he shouted, making the title sound like a term of abuse, 'if you know anything about Summers's death you have an obligation to the law to reveal it. If you've just been doing a little theorizing in your office, then forget it. What I do need, if you have any, is information. Now. You've got something to say? *And don't light that bloody pipe!*'

Pollock weathered this fairly well. 'No,' he said. 'I haven't. But Professor Carriér has. He should be here now. May I see?' Without waiting for a response he opened the door to the outside office. 'There we are. Come on in, Paul.'

Carrier came in, looking distraught. He allowed Pollock to lead him to the chair and sat down. Pollock placed his boots at right-angles and stood at his shoulder, sucking his unlit pipe.

'Go ahead, Paul,' Pollock said.

Carrier looked up at Pollock, who nodded and pointed with his pipe at the inspector. Carrier began, 'Dunkley wasn't in my room on Thursday night when David was killed. He must have done it.'

'Hold on, please. I gather you are now changing your story, Professor. Let's have it again. When wasn't Dunkley in your room?'

'Between ten o'clock and twelve o'clock.'

'Why did you tell me he was?'

'He asked me to. He swore he had nothing to do with David's death, but he was honour bound not to tell me where he was.'

'Oh, great. And you swore, on your professor's honour, not to let him down, did you? But now you think he might have killed your friend. Before, you didn't think so. Now you do. I see. This is wonderful. What made you change your mind?'

Pollock said, 'I did, Inspector. He confided in me and I told him to come and see you.'

'You did, did you, Professor? When?'

'He told me about it right away, last weekend. But I only advised him to see you today.'

'I see. Just before I charge both of you with making false statements and withholding evidence, do you mind telling me why?'

'Jane Homer confided in me yesterday. She said you had interviewed her twice. I thought you might suspect her, so I thought it was time you got the whole of Paul's story.'

'Now let me see. You didn't think Dunkley could have done it until you thought I was accusing Miss Homer. Then you thought he might have. What a detached witness you make. That the academic mind at work, Professor? The literary mind?'

'I was about to tell you, anyway, Inspector, or advise Paul to. I changed my mind because Dunkley is obviously cracking up!'

'Is he? Why is that? You know why, of course?'

'What else could it be?'

'Perhaps he's terminally ill. Perhaps his cat has died. I could give you a thousand reasons. All right, Mr Pollock. Let me tell you what you are going to do. I haven't made up my mind how much to charge you with yet, but in the meantime you are going to go back to your study and stay there, keeping your mind open and your mouth shut.

162

Don't speculate about this case with anyone, unless the
killer asks your advice in which case discuss it with me.
Now get out, please. As for you, Mr Carrier, I'll get a
statement from you and ask you to wait, too, while it is
being typed. I may hold you for further questioning. You
realize, of course, that if Dunkley has no alibi, then
neither have you.'

Pollock said, 'Oh, that's ridiculous, Inspector.'

'Shut your goddamn face, you. Get out,' Salter
screamed. 'Go on. Out!'

Pollock, shaken finally, moved to the door. 'I think you
are making an error, Inspector,' he offered.

'Frank,' bawled Salter. The sergeant put his head
round the door. 'Frank, I want Professor Pollock charged
with withholding evidence. He can have bail. Back here
at ten in the morning.' Salter dismissed Pollock and
turned to Carrier. 'Now. Your statement, please,
Professor.'

Pollock was led out looking dazed, still sucking his
pipe.

While he was waiting for Carrier's statement to be
typed, Salter phoned Montreal. He was connected with
O'Brien immediately.

'Onree,' he said, 'a few developments. First, it looks as
if you can forget about the whore theory. I found out
whose lipstick that was on the glass.'

'Jane Homer's?'

'Right, but I believe she had nothing to do with this.'

'She was in the room, Charlie.'

'They were lovers, but she never saw him that night
until he was dead. She let herself in at eleven-thirty and
found him dead.'

'You believe this, Charlie?'

'Yes, I do. They used to meet once a year. I read about
it in his diary. This was their fifth anniversary. Somebody
wrote a play about this kind of thing. It happens all the

time, apparently. It's a cliché.'

'Romantic. Anything else?'

'Yes,' Salter said reluctantly. 'Two of the people he had dinner with have no alibis for the time Summers was killed. One of them was his worst enemy.'

'Ah?'

'Ah nothing, Onree. Tell you the truth, I think this is what these people would call a sub-plot, but Christ knows how it will tie in.'

'But you will question this . . . ?'

'Dunkley. Oh, sure. It's all a bit phoney, though. He hated Summers and Summers disliked him.'

'So therefore he didn't kill him? This is Anglo police thinking?'

'No, no, don't start calling me a Wasp, Onree. But everyone, including people who don't like Dunkley, has said he couldn't possibly have killed Summers. His wife, even. And Jane Homer.'

'But you *will* pick him up?'

Salter sighed. 'Yes, tomorrow. I'll call you.' He hung up, and dialled the number of the chairman of the English Department.

'Professor Browne? Salter here. No, we don't have a 'Yard' in Toronto, Professor. I want you to do me a favour. First, do you know where Mr Dunkley is?'

'Yes, he's right here in the office.'

'Oh shit.'

'No, no, Inspector. *Nil desperandum.* I meant only "at work" rather than "at home". He's in his own office. He can't hear us.'

'Good. Would you make an appointment with him to see you at ten in the morning? I want to make sure that he stays in town, but I am afraid that if he knows that I want to see him he may disappear.'

'Really, Inspector? Blood on his hands?'

'Don't be silly. I think he might just not want to talk to

me. And, Professor. Please. Not a word to anyone.'

'Mum's the word. I'll think of some excuse.'

Salter hung up and called out to his sergeant, 'I'm going downtown, Frank, on some errands. I'll see you in the morning.'

But Gatenby had seen Salter's appointment book. 'Have a good game, boss,' he called back cheekily.

Salter was going to lose, there was no doubt about that. Bailey was not very good, but the policeman had not been playing long enough to get to his level. Nevertheless, he was giving him a game. The first one he lost 9-0, the second, 9-3, and the third, 9-1. End of set. Now Salter was serving to open the second set. He served, and Bailey smashed the ball into the corner, too low. Salter served again, and the ball dropped dead in the back corner, giving Bailey no chance. 2-0 to Salter. He served again and Bailey made a good return, curling the ball along the left side wall for a certain winner. Salter dug at the ball, two-handed, like an idiot playing golf, and managed to scrape it back along the wall, catching Bailey off-balance. Bailey stared at the ball for a moment, then said, 'Shovelling is illegal.'

Salter said, 'Your point, then?'

'No, no. Just mentioning it, see. In a needle match you wouldn't be able to do that.'

'Let's play it like that, then.'

'No. no. That's fine. Go ahead. I was just pointing it out.'

Salter prepared to serve. He had no sense of having 'shovelled' the ball. There had been a hitting sound when he connected, soft but clear. He served again. Bailey returned the ball carefully, and Salter rushed at it. He connected with the handle of his racquet and the ball dropped soggily off the front wall. Bailey threw himself at it and got it on the second bounce. Salter let the shot go past him, and bent to pick the ball up. Bailey put out his hand for it.

Salter said, 'I thought it bounced twice.'

'No, no,' Bailey said. 'I got it.' He took the ball and got ready to serve.

Now Salter knew what he was up against. During the first set Bailey had roared around the set like a man chasing chickens. He slowed down when he was well ahead in the second set, offering Salter a few tips until Salter won two points in a row, then he started roaring and smashing again. In the third set Salter had tried only to defend himself as Bailey raged about him. The level of body contact increased, and twice Bailey hit him with the ball, as it seemed to Salter, intentionally. This was the first time he had actually cheated, though. Salter decided to have a go.

Bailey served, Salter returned it and Bailey banged it back. Salter tipped it gently against the front wall as he had seen Cranmer do, and crouched out of the way. Bailey hit him in the ankle with his racquet, and shouted, 'Let.'

'What?'

'You were in the way of my shot,' Bailey said. 'We play the point again.' He served again. This time Salter tipped it immediately against the front wall and jumped clear of any possible 'let'. Bailey dived for the ball and crunched himself against the wall. He got up and shook himself. 'I can't stand that soft shit,' he said. 'Summers used to do it. It fucks up the game.'

It's legal, though, thought Salter, and served. Bailey smashed it, below the line. 4-0 to Salter. Salter served again, and this time Bailey tried a soft shot against the front wall, and missed. 5-0. Salter had not enjoyed himself so much for years. He served again, but Bailey now hit a perfect return which Salter missed. Bailey served, very aggressively, and ran to the centre of the court ahead of Salter's return. The ball hit him in the back. 'Jesus Christ you've got the whole fucking court,' he shouted.·'But you were standing where I wanted to hit it,' Salter said mildly. He served again and Bailey smashed it home for a winner. Now Bailey served carefully, and by playing warily won the next five points without any difficulty. 5-5. The lights went out at that point and the two men walked off the court, dripping.

Over the beer, which Salter insisted on signing for, Bailey recovered himself as Salter asked him to explain what was legal, what was 'fair', and what was unsporting. Bailey explained, rising to the bait of Salter's mock humility. 'That soft stuff is "legal",' he said, 'but it ruins the game. In my opinion, anyway. Old Dave used to do it a lot. You noticed when we started playing properly how the game got better.'

'Is that how he won the last game you played?'

Bailey looked confused. 'Well, yes,' he said, after a few seconds. 'He couldn't beat me in the open court. But he could work that soft shit real well.'

They were interrupted by the waitress with the charge for Salter to sign.

'Want another, Inspector?' Bailey asked.

'Sure. Tomorrow?'

'I meant a beer. But OK. Same time, then.'

Cranmer appeared at their table. 'Beating Metro's finest, Bill?' he asked, nodding at the slip the waitress was returning to Salter. And then, 'Any news, Inspector?'

Salter shook his head. 'Lots of suspects, but no clues, Percy. We are continuing our inquiries.'

No one wanted to pursue the subject, and the two players rose to go to the showers. 'After you, Charlie,' Bailey said, with a flourish of courtesy.

The next morning Salter waited in the chairman's office. It was five to ten and they were expecting Dunkley. 'You want me to become invisible when he arrives?' Browne asked.

'If I could use your office, it would probably be best.'

'I shall be in the library if you want me. Ah! Come in, Stewart, come in. I'm afraid I've deceived you. It is the Inspector who wants to talk to you.' Browne smiled falsely, and slid his bulk through the door, closing it scrupulously after him.

Salter pointed to a chair, but Dunkley remained standing. 'I presume this is still in regard to Summers's death?' he asked.

'Unless you've anything else on your conscience, Professor?'

Dunkley folded his arms and said nothing.

'Sit down,' Salter said sharply.

Dunkley sat down then, and refolded his arms.

'Now. I'd like to know where you were between ten o'clock and twelve o'clock on the night Summers was killed.'

'I see I have been betrayed. I have nothing to say.'

'In that case you can get your hat and say nothing down at the station.'

'I'm ready to go now.'

Salter stood up. 'Let's go, then.'

Dunkley preceded him, still with his arms folded, out to the corridor where they found Marika Tils and Paul Carrier in close and agitated conversation. Shit, thought, Salter, I forgot to remind that fat chairman to keep his mouth shut. Carrier looked white, and Marika Tils clutched at Dunkley as he went by, but Dunkley shook her off and marched down the hall to the elevator. The two men left the building and drove to the station.

'Now,' Salter said, when they were in his office. 'You are entitled to have a lawyer present, and to stay silent if you want, because you are under suspicion, but I'm not charging you with anything yet. I simply want the true story.'

Dunkley looked out of the window and crossed his legs, locking himself up tight.

'For Christ's sake,'. said Salter, 'You are a well-known enemy of Summers, you were in Montreal, and you refuse to say where you were when he was killed. What do you expect me to do?'

Dunkley stared out of the window.

Salter tried again. 'If you won't speak, I shall have to send a squad to your residence to look for evidence—blood, whatever—and if it's there, they'll find it.'

Dunkley spoke now. 'You won't find anything,' he said. 'I didn't kill Summers.'

'Then would you mind telling me *why* you won't say where you were?'

'I was not alone. That's all. It's a matter of loyalty. I told Carrier that, and he gave me his word.'

'Oh, fuck this,' Salter said exasperated. 'Sergeant! I want the boys to go to this man's house and look for the usual. Hold him here for obstructing the police.'

Dunkley broke his pose. 'I'm under arrest?'

'Of course you are under arrest. What do you think? Frankly, Professor Dunkley, I'm just covering my ass. I may be wrong, but I don't think you've the guts to kill a mouse. I think you are on some kind of trip, right now, and I'm too busy to find out what it is. When I have a moment, I'll question you further, just because I'm curious about what you are up to.'

'In the back room? Where no one can see, or hear?'

'No. I think you might enjoy that. No, right here. I may invite a few friends, though. Now sit there and don't resist arrest. My sergeant is liable to give you a nasty pinch if you try to run away.'

For something had been bothering Salter all night. He

borrowed an empty office and sat down with a pad of paper to go through the exercise of writing the report once more. After half an hour of laborious detail, he stopped and went back to the first page. He read the list of items that had been found in the room, again and again. Then, he read the account of the discovery of the body and got his first solid confirmation that he wasn't going off half-cocked. He phoned O'Brien, who was out, but then he was put through to the detective who first went into Summers's room.

'There was a *Globe and Mail* in the room,' he said. 'What state was it in?'

'There was some blood on it.'

'No, Officer. I mean, had it been read?'

'It was open, yes.'

'What section? The *Globe* is in three or four sections.'

'The front section. The first page inside.'

'And the other sections—Business, Sports?'

'You can see in the picture. They 'adn't been touched.'

'Thank you, Officer. Tell Sergeant O'Brien I called, will you? And tell him I still think I'm right.'

In a fever he dialled Mrs Summers's number. When she replied, he asked, 'You say you drove your husband to the station on Friday morning. Was he very late?'

'He had to run like hell, Inspector. I was surprised that he made it.'

'He didn't stop to buy a paper?'

'No, I told you. He was *late*.'

'Sorry, Mrs Summers. Now did he get a chance to read the paper at home?'

'We don't get it delivered. I stopped it when he got interested in commodities, because he spent the first hour of the day adding up his winnings, or his losses. It drove me mad.'

'Thank you, Mrs Summers.'

One more check, the broker. 'Leslie Stone? Inspector

Salter here. I want to ask you a question you've already answered, but I want to be sure of it. When you told Professor Summers about his profit on the Canadian dollar, was that news to him?'

'Absolutely, sherriff. He cheered and said something about the gods were smiling on him, this really *was* his lucky day.'

'What do you think he meant?'

'It sounded to me like he'd heard all kinds of good news that day.'

'That's what I think too, Miss Stone. Thanks.'

'You're welcome.'

Now. Which one of them had Summers told about his ticket? The fact that the ticket had been bought in Mississauga, a fact which might make nonsense of his hunch, would clear itself up, he felt certain. Mississauga lay just outside Toronto along the Lakeshore, towards Oakville. Lots of people lived there and worked in Toronto, and the other way round.

He sat there wondering what to do next. He was utterly certain now of why Summers had been murdered; he was also certain he knew who had done it if only his brain would disgorge the information. He phoned O'Brien again in Montreal and found him in. After some pleasantries, Salter said, 'I'm sure of it, Onree. Summers bought a lottery ticket, he was checking the results on page two of the *Globe* on Friday afternoon in his hotel room; he told everybody after that that that was his lucky day. Whoever killed Summers has the lottery ticket. There's only one flaw: the winning ticket was bought in Mississauga, and there's no way Summers could have bought it. Even if he did, the one he bought, that his wife saw him buy, is missing.'

There was a long silence. Then O'Brien said, 'Charlie, you must be right, but there's something missing. You will have to wait to see who cashes the big winning ticket.'

His voice was comforting.

'Yeah, right. And if it is a little old lady in Mississauga, I'll clap her in jail on a charge of having been in Montreal that night, having heard about Summers's win, having beaten him over the head, and having snuck back to Mississauga without anyone noticing.'

'Do you have any other suspects, Charlie?'

'I'm holding Dunkley, and there is one other left, a quiet little guy, colleague of Summers, who looks harmless, but I'm learning a lot about absent-minded professors who aren't what they seem.'

'My advice is to give it a rest for a while, Hercules. Let your grey cells go to work on it.'

'How do I arrange that, Onree?'

'Go to the races.'

Salter hung up and sat with his cobweb theory dissolving in his hands but unable to get clear of it. He could see nothing to do. He sat at his desk, doing nothing, until it was time for his game with Bailey which, he reflected, as he stood up to go to the squash club, might qualify for O'Brien's approval as a sufficiently absorbing activity to release his mind to get on with its work unconsciously, without interference from its owner.

Bailey won again, but this time Salter nearly won a set. Bailey said, 'You're getting pretty good, Charlie. I can't let down at all.'

Next time, buddy, Salter thought.

'Beer?' he asked.

'Sure. It's costing you a few beers, learning this game.' Bailey was trying to be a good winner, but it was hard.

The two men drank their beer, while Salter listened to some helpful tips from his opponent and master. What was even worse was when Bailey, in a burst of expansiveness, and contrary to all the agreed etiquette, tried to pay for the beer. Salter grabbed the charge slip from the girl's hand and said, 'Loser pays.'

'OK, OK,' Bailey said. 'But it could be expensive.'

Salter drank his beer quickly, trying to look agreeable. Christ, he thought, it's just a game. I'm getting as bad as Summers. He left the club and walked over to the subway station, thinking of Summers, and Dunkley, and lottery tickets, and Mississauga, and getting nowhere. He seriously thought of phoning Molly Tripp, but he rejected it, because he could not think of an excuse, and because he did not want to show himself to her in a sour mood. Besides, Annie would probably guess.

He went home, ate his dinner, still brooding, snarled at the kids for watching television day in, day out, turned his back on the tentative advances of Annie in bed, and woke up depressed, just like the old days.

CHAPTER 9

At the office he phoned O'Brien, his only friend, for a chat, but the Frenchman was out, of course. The Oldest Sergeant in the Force brought him some coffee and reminded him that Dunkley was still in the cells.

Salter said, 'He didn't do it, Frank. I'm right back where I started. Whoever killed Summers did it for a bloody winning lottery ticket, or something like that'—his confidence in his theory was ebbing—'and someone knew what Summers's lucky day was.'

'Why don't you try that end?' Gatenby said. 'Ask them again, straight out, if they have any idea of what Summers's lucky day was.'

What an asshole, thought Salter, automatically. Still, it was something to do. He started by phoning Usher. He worked out a twist on the question.

'Mr Usher,' he asked, 'do you remember if anyone was

alone at any time on the Friday night, and was anyone, apart from Summers, acting strangely? I mean, at any time were all of you in the washroom except Summers and one person? Anything like that?'

But Usher was unable to remember anything. Nor could Marika Tils or Carrier.

Salter gave up. 'Frank,' he called. 'Bring Dunkley in here.'

When the professor was led in, slightly unkempt after his night in the cells, Salter tried to be brisk and cunning.

'Mr Dunkley. Before I proceed with the rest of the charges I'd like to clear up one or two details. We know now that you had the motive and the opportunity to kill Summers. What was the straw that broke the camel's back? Was it Summers's piece of luck you couldn't stand the idea of? When did he confide in you, by the way? In the bar?'

Dunkley looked at him in contempt. 'What a pathetic flounderer you are, Inspector. Is this typical?'

Salter looked back at Dunkley, wondering whether to bother charging him with anything, for he was as certain as ever that he was the wrong man. They were interrupted by a commotion in the outer office. A constable put his head round the door to say that a Professor Pollock was causing a disturbance.

'Bring him in here,' Salter said.

When Pollock was led in he immediately ran at Dunkley, knocking him out of his chair. They rolled together on the floor as Pollock tried to punch his colleague.

'You dirty, rotten bastard,' screamed Pollock. 'You slimy, filthy, rotten pig.' And much more besides.

Salter picked the two men apart and held Pollock, spitting and cursing, while Dunkley stood back against the wall, straightening his clothes. When Pollock stopped shouting, Salter relaxed his hold, and the professor launched himself across the room and tried to hit Dunkley again, who crouched without making any effort to defend himself. Salter hauled Pollock away again and dragged him out of the office, handing him over to a constable to 'lock up until he cools off'.

When he returned to his own office, Dunkley was seated again. 'What was that all about?' Salter asked.

'I have no idea,' Dunkley replied, trying to recover his former pose.

'Oh, for Christ's sake! Frank!' The sergeant poked his head round the door, grinning in glee. 'Take this idiot back to the cells, will you? I'll tell you when to do anything about him.'

Gatenby said, 'There's a lady to see you, Chief.' He rolled his eyes to indicate that Dunkley should not know who it was.

'All right. Take his learned gentleman away and bring her in.'

Marika Tils entered, looking frightened.

'Churchey la fucking femme,' Salter said.

'What?'

'It's French. It means I should have known it would be you.'

'You were right, then. Has Professor Pollock been to see you?'

'Yes. Professors Dunkley and Pollock met in my office and tried to have a fight. Or rather, Pollock did. The trouble was that he has forgotten how, if he ever knew, so he didn't hurt Dunkley much. Hitting people is harder than it looks on TV.'

'They were fighting over me.'

'Fighting over your favours, were they?'

'Yes.'

'I was joking. They really were?'

'Yes. Toby had found out that Dunkley had made love to me.'

'In Montreal, of course, on Friday night. Who is Toby?'

'Toby Pollock. Yes, in Montreal.'

'My sergeant was right. These conferences of yours sound like giant games of musical beds.'

'I didn't want to sleep with Dunkley.'

'Tell me the whole story. Who did what, where, why, and most of all, when.' Salter was sick of this gang. His head was buzzing with an idea that had nothing to do with this nonsense, but he had to complete this part of the investigation in case his latest idea was insane.

She began. 'Dunkley has always been jealous of David and me.'

'Not Pollock, your lover, but Summers?'

'Yes. I told you, he knows nothing of Toby and me.'

'He does now. Go on.'

'I told you, David Summers and I were friends, not lovers. But Dunkley thought we were. Lovers, I mean. He saw us always together, and he assumed. He was jealous because he wanted me, but I didn't like him. Several times when there had been drinking, at a party or something, he got me in a corner and asked me to go to bed with him. But I told him and I told him, and I thought finally he had given in because he—what, lay off?'

'Laid off.'

'Yes. It doesn't feel right, grammatically. Anyway, he laid off me. Until Montreal. Then someone told him a bit of gossip about David's annual rendezvous with a lady at the conference.'

'You knew about that?'

'We all did. David confided in everybody about it. But he never said who it was. When David bought us all dinner, and told us about his lucky day, and went home early after *I* went home early, Dunkley put it all together and decided I was David's annual event, his lucky day, so to speak. When he and the others came back to the hotel, he waited for a little while and phoned David's room. There was no answer, because, I suppose, David was already dead. But he decided David was in my room. So he came to my room and banged on the door. I didn't answer at first, but he kept on banging so I told him to go away through the door. But he was shouting that he knew I had David in there and he wouldn't go away, so I opened the door to show him. Then he was sorry and told me how much he loved me and asked me to let him stay with me. This went on and on and on. In the end I thought maybe he would go away if he got what he wanted so I asked him and he said he would, so that's what I did.'

'You let him make love to you, to get rid of him?'

'I was exhausted, Inspector. Besides, it's no big deal.'

'It was for Dunkley.'

'Oh yes. Afterwards he thanked me. I got rid of him then and that was the end of it, I thought, until today, when I realized I was his only alibi and he would never use me because he is a man of honour.' She spoke without passion; she was evidently worn out.

'So you decided to come and see me.'

'No, I was idiotic. I told Toby. He went crazy.' She slumped in her chair. 'What a lot of fuss over a little fuck.'

'I'll sort these two out, Miss Tils. Go home and take the phone off the hook. One last question. Are you sure of the time when Dunkley was in your room?'

'Certain. At eleven he was banging on my door. At ten past eleven he was in my room. At twelve he was in my bed. I had the TV on. The news, the weather, and "O Canada".'

In spite of his irritation, Salter laughed. 'You should have told me all this days ago, Miss Tils. As you say, we have all been put to a great deal of trouble over one little fuck.'

She made a face and stood up. 'You know what pisses me off, Inspector? The three of us won't be able to live in the department after this, so one of us will have to go. Dunkley should go; if not him, then Toby. But I will go. They have tenure, and I'm just a woman they are fighting over. And my appointment is for one year only.' She shouldered her bag, and left.

Salter called in the sergeant. 'Frank,' he said, 'I want you to hold those guys for the rest of the day. Let them go, one at a time, at the end of the day shift, and warn them that if either one speaks to Marika Tils or tries to speak to the other one before I give my permission, it will be a criminal offence.'

'It won't, will it, chief?' Gatenby said, in the voice of a doubting yokel.

'Of course not, you silly sod. But it might keep them apart for a few hours if they think so. Let Dunkley go first; tell the patrol to drive him to his house and sit outside for half an hour. Then come back and take Pollock home; same routine. Then have them park outside Marika Tils's place until I give the word.'

'Right, chief. I'll give her full power when we go over the reef,' said Gatenby, leaving Salter to wonder if he was being made fun of.

When Gatenby returned, Salter was still staring out of the window.

'No good, chief?'

'No good, Frank. Dunkley didn't know. No one knew.'

'Someone must have,' Gatenby said.

In a minute, thought Salter, he's going to ask me if I've looked in all my pockets, just like my mother did when I'd lost something.

Gatenby said, 'Perhaps he told someone else?'

Very rarely, his mother would keep on until she suggested a place he had not thought of, the right place. 'Did you leave it in your raincoat?' she would say. 'You went to school with it on, but you didn't bring it home.'

Salter stared at Gatenby for a very long time. Then, 'Frank,' he said, 'you are a fucking genius.'

'I was only trying to help,' Gatenby said. 'There is no need to be sarcastic.'

'I wasn't being sarcastic, Frank. You are a fucking genius. Now leave me alone.'

He went over the details for an hour. It had to be right even if there was still a piece missing. Eventually he made two phone calls, one to O'Brien and one to the squash club.

O'Brien said, 'You'll have to be careful, Charlie. If he knows what you are up to, you won't find a thing. You may not find anything anyway, if he's destroyed it.'

'I'll find *something*, Onree. He can't cover up a trip like that.'

'If he did it.'

'I *know* he did it.'

'Jump him, Charlie. Frighten him.'

'OK. Onree, I'll call you.'

'Good luck.'

Salter had the afternoon to wait until he could go down to the squash club. He went for a walk along College Street to Parliament Street, then for a long ramble through Cabbagetown, in the area where he had grown up when they still grew cabbages in the front yard. When he had used up enough time he headed for the squash club to intercept Bailey. First he phoned Gatenby.

'Frank,' he said, as soon as the sergent answered, 'send a car to this address.' He gave the location of Bailey's apartment. 'I want the place turned over. I'll get a warrant tomorrow.' He told the sergeant what he was looking for.

'Right you are, boss,' Gatenby said. 'Just like the old days, isn't it? For you, I mean. I was always on traffic duty, myself.'

'Move, for Christ's sake, Frank. I should have done this an hour ago.'

He went back and stationed himself in the lounge by the door. At a few minutes to four, Bailey came in, and Salter hailed him.

'Could I have a word, Bill? Won't take a minute.'

Bailey sat down. 'I have a game with Percy at four,' he said.

Maybe, thought Salter, and took a deep breath. 'Bill,' he said, 'if Summers won his last game with you, why did he pay for the beer?'

Bailey went grey, and Salter should have stopped there, but he was unable to. He continued: 'And when he phoned you from Montreal, did he tell you how much he'd won on the lottery?'

It was a hit all right, but Bailey had now had the few seconds necessary to start him talking. 'He didn't win any lottery,' he said. 'Not that I know of.'

Salter tried a lie. 'He told his broker he'd won a fortune on a lottery. He phoned you right after. Didn't he say anything about it?'

Cranmer arrived, and Bailey stood up. 'No. Not a word. Jesus, poor guy. That it, then?'

'That's it, Bill,' Salter said, and the two players disappeared into the changing-room.

Have I fucked it up, thought Salter, as he waited for the call from Bailey's apartment? Am I wrong?

After five minutes, Cranmer emerged from the changing-room in squash costume. 'Seen Bill anywhere?' he asked Salter. 'He's disappeared and we start at four-ten.'

Salter made a dive for the phone. 'The man is on his way,' he said when he got through. 'Hold him at the apartment. Any excuse. I'll be there in five minutes. He ran down the back stairs of the club, and within a few seconds was able to commandeer a passing cruiser. On the way to Bailey's apartment, he raised Gatenby on the radio.

'News?' the sergeant said. 'I'll say. Your man saw our car outside his apartment and took off. Luther is following him in the squad car. They are travelling along the Lakeshore. Luther wants to know how hard to go for him if there is a real chase.'

'Tell Luther he's wanted for murder. Don't lose him.' The light gleamed within the cave; with a quarter of a mile to go, Salter's horse emerged smoothly from the pack, bearing down on the finish line.

'What's the word from the search?' he asked.

'Nothing yet.'

'Tell him to stay there. I'm on my way over.'

It took another ten minutes to get to Bailey's apartment; they travelled with all the noise and lights the car could supply. Inside the apartment, a detective was sitting down, smoking. He said, 'Phase one is over, boss. No obvious places left. The next stage takes a long time. You want it done?'

'Not yet. Maybe. We might not need it.' Salter looked around. 'He's running, and that's just as good.' He walked around the apartment, glancing at all the drawers the searchers had left open, and picked up a small iron key attached to an elastic wrist-band, which was lying on the kitchen counter.

'Where did you find this?'

'In his laundry basket. We figured it had dropped out of his tennis shorts.'

'Squash,' Salter said absently.

'Is it important?'

'It might be.'

The driver of the commandeered squad car appeared at the door. 'Message for you, sir. The guy they were chasing ran off the road trying to make the turn on to the 417. They are waiting for the ambulance.'

'Take me back to the squash club,' Salter said. He turned to the detective. 'Tidy up here, and wait for me. Don't look for anything else yet.'

In the car, he said, 'You can switch the noise gear off.' Nevertheless, when they got to the club he ran up the steps to the changing-room where the row of little wooden lockers was situated. The key opened No. 23, and Salter peered, frightened, into the cave. Inside were two lottery tickets.

'What put you on to it?' the Superintendent asked.

'The charge slip for the beer at the squash club,' Salter said. 'Right from the beginning I knew that Summers had won the Wednesday night game, but he paid for the beer. Why? Either he was being generous, which would have pissed Bailey off mightily, or the bet was something else. When I got on to the missing lottery ticket, I realized what had happened. They bet their lottery tickets—no big deal at a dollar each—but Bailey's won, and Summers couldn't resist phoning him from Montreal and crowing. Bailey went crazy—not about the money so much as the way he had lost it, and to Summers. So he flew down to Montreal and waited for Summers to come back from his night out.'

'Then he just beat his head in to get the ticket?'

'Not quite. He says he just wanted to get half the winnings, or get the ticket from Summers and throw it away so that neither of them could have it. But Summers wasn't as drunk as he seemed, and he caught Bailey going through his wallet after Bailey thought that Summers had passed out. Bailey knew he was finished then, so, in a panic, he killed Summers, and ran. Afterwards, when he realized he might get away with it—Summers had told him he was waiting for someone else—he kept the ticket, thinking to 'find' it in his wallet in a month's time. After

all, no one else knew about it, and who would connect it
with Summers?'

'This is very cute figuring, Salter. Put it all in your
report. Tell me, why didn't you follow up this charge slip
when you first saw it?'

'I didn't realize the significance of it, sir.'

'Don't put that in the report, then. Put, "When I
rechecked the contents of the wallet, I saw that one of the
charge slips was for a bill that the accused should have
paid." '

'Right, sir.'

'Now. When you found out that the winning ticket was
bought in Mississauga, why didn't you check the addresses
of all suspects? Then you would have found out that
Bailey's company has a factory there.'

'I thought my theory was wrong, sir. I didn't realize
that someone was trying to get his own ticket back.'

'Don't put that. Put, "I decided, then, to check on the
Mississauga connections of all suspects." Then what did
you do?'

'I went to the squash club to talk to Bailey. But before I
could question him properly he left.'

'Jesus Christ. You asked him if he did it? Right there in
the squash club?'

'More or less, yes, sir.'

'For Christ's sake. Put, "I began by checking up on
Bailey, who was then at the squash club. However,
something in my manner must have put him on his
guard, for he left the club quickly. I called for help to
search his apartment and arrest him if necessary." A lot
of this is still guesswork, Salter. Can you prove enough of
it?'

'The guesswork is concerned with his motive, sir. We've
found traces of blood on a shoe, and a charge slip for his
air fare to Montreal that day. We can prove he killed
Summers.'

'You know what, Salter,' Orliff said after a few minutes. 'I wouldn't put in all this bullshit about squash and all. I'd put, "From the beginning I had considered the possibility that the motive was robbery, and when I came to the missing lottery ticket I surmised from the phone calls that Bailey might have known about the ticket." Never mind the rest. Keep it simple.'

'Yes, sir.'

'This is very nice, Salter, very nice. What about all the professors you locked up? One of them is suing us for unlawful arrest. Any problem?'

'I don't think so. That's a whole mess which got in the way, although without them I wouldn't have got on to Summers's big win. These people were all diddling each other while Summers was being killed, but it didn't have anything to do with Bailey. I'll tell Dunkley that the charge of obstructing police is still outstanding, or rather, I'll tell his lawyer. He'll understand.'

'Right. I'll tell *you*, Salter, the Old Man is happy. Your pal in Montreal has written us a letter saying how great you are—brilliant, co-operative—all that kind of stuff. The Old Man is so happy he's wondering if we can find a better spot for you, better than you've had for a year.'

In the distance shimmered the oasis, no longer a mirage, but the real thing, with water, dates, and maybe his own camel. Salter said nothing.

'He doesn't hold grudges,' the Superintendent said, 'Longer than necessary, that is. Nor do I. All right, then.' He nodded to dismiss the inspector.

They were parked near the boardwalk down by the Lakeshore. He had phoned her and picked her up after work to say goodbye. They bought some fish and chips at Nova's and sat eating in the car.

'You know,' he said, 'I read Professor Summers's journal. You cropped up a lot. I think he was more interested in you than you realized.'

'You think? But he didn't want to do anything about it. We were just having a little romance without tears. He might have been a bit soft on me, but it was mainly my beautiful mind he liked.'

Probably. He said, 'He wrote once that he would like to have seen you without your pants on.'

'He wrote that, did he?' she laughed.

'Yes. I know what he meant.'

'Well, hello, Charlie!'

'No, no. I think he just meant that he had always seen you in jeans.' Salter thought of the girl on the table in Montreal. 'I've seen you when you weren't wearing them, once.'

'When?'

'At the funeral, remember?'

There was a knock on the car window. A uniformed policeman wanted to talk to him. Salter rolled the window down and showed the officer his identification.

'Sorry, sir.' The policeman saluted. 'We've had a lot of complaints about couples parked here.' He looked pointedly at Molly.

'This is my daughter, Officer. We are just eating some fish and chips.'

'Right, sir. Right.' The man moved off.

'And now,' he said, to the giggling girl, 'I'll take you home.'

Later that night he lay in bed talking to his wife.

She said, 'It isn't the way you think of professors, is it?'

'How do you mean?'

'The way you tell it, he got killed because he won a squash game. Is that normal?'

'No, but I understand how it can happen.'

'And this annual event at the conference? A bit stagey, isn't it?'

'You mean literary.'

'Do I? And these young female students. I think the wives of middle-aged professors must put up with a lot.'

Salter reached over and put his hand on her belly. 'Shut up, now,' he said. She put her hand on his, and after a few moments they rolled together, and made love in friendly, missionary fashion, as he kept his weight on his elbows like a gentleman. He concentrated on her pleasure and joined her when she was ready. Afterwards, as she curled herself around him, she muttered something into his back. 'What?' he asked over his shoulder. She leaned over and kissed him. 'I said that was nice. By the way, someone called Harry Wycke phoned. He wanted us to go for a drink at his house on Saturday night. I told him I thought you were busy. That right? Who is he?'

'He's in Homicide. I think we might go.'

'But, Charlie, we never socialize with the people you know at work.'

'We never used to. Maybe we should give it a try. Wycke seems OK. Now shut up and go to sleep.'

Wisely, she pretended to.

SMOKE DETECTOR

For Tory and Jessica

Chapter One

September is Toronto's best month. The summer can be hot and sticky, and winter goes on too long, but for a few weeks between the two seasons the city is blessed with warm, dry, sunny days and nights cool enough to sleep.

Salter opened his eyes and looked at the bit of sky framed by the small third-floor window: white branches of a silver birch dressed in yellow leaves, all set against a clear blue sky. He rummaged under the duvet in search of his wife and squeezed her awake. 'Look,' he said. 'Look outside.'

He slid out of bed and crossed to the window, naked and bent-kneed, keeping his bottom half out of sight of all the neighbours who might be watching through binoculars. 'Bloody marvellous,' he said. Then, slightly chilled, he crawled back into bed and reached for Annie, but she had disappeared while he was drinking in the morning. He heard her turn on the shower one floor below and he lay still for five minutes until the noise of running water stopped. Then he ran down the stairs and pounded on the bathroom door. Annie let him in and locked the door behind him, and Salter sat on the edge of the tub and watched her dry herself. It was his favourite way of starting the day.

She was forty, and as far as he could tell she had not changed a wrinkle in the eighteen years since he had first seen her naked. She often pointed out marks of decrepitude on her aging, sagging epidermis; but all the flaws she showed him looked no more than the tucks and rumples that were unavoidable when a human skin was stretched over such a complicated frame. Salter felt a grumbling in his loins as she shrouded herself in a bathtowel. He sighed and turned on the shower.

At breakfast, which they ate while their two sons were getting ready for school, Annie said, 'By the way, there are some things I have to tell you, but finish eating first.'

Salter's euphoria ebbed away. 'By the way' delivered on a descending scale, with a heavy pause after 'way', was bad news, always. He ate two pieces of toast and looked at the paper. Something fairly substantial was coming, he guessed, or Annie would have delivered herself of it immediately. The boys left separately, eleven-year-old Seth first, with a kiss, then his fourteen-year-old brother, Angus, without even a goodbye. Odd, that. Angus had stopped kissing people some months before, but he usually said something by way of an exit.

'Is it Angus?' Salter asked, when they were alone.

'I might as well start with him,' she said.

Christ! There was a *list*.

Annie disappeared upstairs and returned with two magazines which she put beside his plate. He picked up the first one gingerly and opened it at random. A photograph ran across two pages, a picture of a naked girl with enormous breasts kneeling over a recumbent male. Salter picked up the other one. It was devoted to group activities.

'Where did you find these?' he asked.

'In Angus's cupboard.'

'Put them back.'

'Put them back?'

'Right. Where you found them.'

'What are you going to do?'

'Me? I don't know. But if you put them back I'll have time to think.'

'I've already told him I found them.'

'Shit. All right. So. One: Angus has been reading skin magazines. What else?'

'The nurse phoned yesterday. I forgot to tell you. They want you to take some more tests.'

Salter had recently undergone his annual medical and been pronounced fit. 'Why? What for?' he asked.

'It's something to do with your urine.'

Salter's voice became noisy from fear. 'What? What is? What did she say? I've got diabetes?'

Annie shook her head. 'She said there was blood in it.'

'Blood? What does that mean? How long have I got?'

'She said it is probably nothing. But she's fixed an appointment for you to see a specialist today.'

'What's the rush? I thought it took six months to get an appointment with a specialist.'

'You got lucky. This one has a cancellation.'

'What kind of specialist?' Salter's mind raced over all the fatal diseases that strike middle-aged policemen.

'I think she said urologist.'

'A piss-artist?' He laughed in spite of the scenes that were rushing through his head. Had he made a will? 'That's it then? Angus is feeling his oats and I'm dying. Anything else?'

'I will be working late for a few days. Maybe a couple of weeks.'

'Doing what?'

'We're very busy, Charlie, and you just don't turn down new accounts these days.' Annie was a 'gofer' in an advertising agency; she arranged the locations, the sets and the props for filming commercials.

'Okay,' he said. 'Angus is a sex maniac. I'm dying. You're leaving home. Anything else?'

'You are such a help, Charlie. I'm sorry you're worried about the doctor, but I'm sure you're all right. Don't take it out on me.'

'Anything *else?*'

'Yes. The screen door has jumped off its track on the third floor. One of the wheels seems to be broken.'

'I'll look at it tonight.'

In many ways it was the worst news of all, because it was probably the beginning of a month-long saga in which he spent every Saturday morning and some part of the week trying to understand the trouble, locating a hardware store which still sold the replacement part (the door was ten years old), and finally, learning from scratch, by trial and error, how to replace the wheel without any of the tools that the job required. Salter fixed what he could about the house, but he had no mechanical ability, and confronted with a new problem for which there was no standard repairman, he anticipated the ultimate failure of his efforts from the beginning and tackled the job in a temper. He had also lost interest in the house, having reached the age when he preferred to spend his time in the present rather than repairing for the future. The years were passing quickly, and Salter had lost any desire to putter. He got up to go.

'Think about Angus, won't you, Charlie?' Annie asked again.

Salter put on his jacket. 'I'll think about him, and me, and the third-floor screen,' he said. 'How late will you be?'

'If I'm going to be after seven, I'll call you.' Annie got up and opened the refrigerator door. 'There's bacon and eggs, cold roast beef, half an apple pie, cheese, and a cupboard full of canned soup. You can manage.' She put her arms around him in a gesture that was meant to be friendly, comforting and sexy, designed to take care of all his worries.

But as he walked to the subway, the perfect morning weather now seemed an ironic backdrop to his own threatened cosmos.

At the office, Sergeant Gatenby greeted him like an old nanny who knows of a treat in store for her favourite child. Gatenby was not much older than Salter, but he was known as The Oldest Sergeant in the Force because of his white hair and avuncular manner, both of which he had acquired in his thirties. In those days he was known as The Oldest Constable in the Force, and most of his career had been spent performing all those duties which called for a kindly old copper to represent the Force to the public, especially to children.

'Chiefie wants to see you,' he said now. 'I think he's got a job for us.' 'Chiefie' was Staff Superintendent Orliff. As the result of emerging on the losing side of a recent political struggle within the Force, Salter had been an outsider for a year. Then, through a piece of luck, one of the odd jobs he was given provided a chance to solve a homicide case in Montreal, earning him the gratitude of the Montreal police, and thus of his own bosses. He had been let know then that his period of exile could be coming to an end, and also that he had been exaggerating the depth of the hostility to him. 'No one,' Orliff, his new superintendent, had said, 'holds grudges for ever.'

Salter went now to Orliff's office where the Superintendent was waiting.

'Arson and homicide,' Orliff said, tapping the corners of the pile of paper in front of him to make the edges square. His desk was immaculately tidy, and along its outer edge was a row of neat stacks of paper like the one under his hand.

'I'm on the Arson Squad?' Salter asked.

'You're helping out. The squad has its hands full – these things come in bunches and there isn't anyone to spare. That Jamaican case is keeping everyone busy,' Orliff said, referring to a manhunt currently on for the killer of a young black girl who had been raped and murdered on her way home from babysitting. The black community was demanding action.

'What's the story?'

'An antique dealer on Bloor West. Store caught fire last night. The fire department saved the building, but they found the owner dead. Smoke inhalation, probably, but the autopsy will show. The fire started in the basement and the Fire Marshal thinks someone put a torch to the place. The owner has an apartment above the store, although he didn't live there. He had a home on – ' Orliff checked his notes – ' Albany Avenue, in the neighbourhood. I guess he used the apartment sometimes, because he had a bed up there, and some clothes. That's it. You'd better talk to the Marshal's office first, and then go and see what you think.'

'Has the Fire Marshal finished? I thought those boys did their own investigations.'

'Only the arson side. As I said, this is homicide. The coroner has it now and he's told us to get going. The fire was no accident, so the death is homicide by person or persons unknown, as they say.'

'What am I doing? Just filling in until Homicide can spare someone?'

'That's right, Charlie. They'll take over when they can, but you might have it cleaned up by then.' Orliff smiled. 'I told them you were busy on a couple of other assignments but that if they were desperate you would have a look at it. They said they'd like you to do that.' Orliff watched Salter, and waited. He was making two points: first, he, Orliff, was looking after Salter to the extent of making him seem busy, and, second, that Homicide still wanted Salter to help out after they had heard who he was. Together they added up to a significant small improvement in Salter's status. If he turned the assignment down, which he probably could, he might wait a long time for another one.

'Who is over there now?' he asked.

'Constable Katesmark is guarding it. Here's the report from the officer who got to the fire first. And here's the name of the investigator from the Fire Marshal's office. Lotsa luck, Charlie.'

Salter took the sheet of paper which Orliff had prepared and watched the Superintendent make a note to himself that the case was assigned to Salter, with a date and a time. The Superintendent had risen steadily through the ranks chiefly by being careful, and one of his habits was to make a record of everything. Thus by the time a case was in its second day, Orliff had a pile of reports, memos, and notes to himself, recording, literally, everything that had been said and done. These cases he laid in a row around the edge of his desk. On the shelves behind him there were another thirty or more that were not quite dead; in the filing cabinets were dozens more that were finished, but Orliff was not yet ready to put into deep storage. Among the neat stacks were several personal projects: one of them was the Superintendent's continuing investigation into various annuity schemes; another contained the plans for the cottage he was building in the Kawartha hills. The object of working, for Orliff, was to provide for the good life, and he kept his work and its object in front of him all the time.

Salter went back to his office and told Gatenby what was up. 'First murder, now arson – they'll be giving us espionage stuff soon,' Gatenby said, chuckling. 'Charlie Salter, Special Agent. Ha, ha, ha. Anything for me to do yet?'

'Not yet, Frank. Just tell anyone who needs me that I'm busy, on a case.' Salter permitted himself a small smile. The day was improving slightly.

'Oh, I'll tell them.' Gatenby picked up Salter's IN tray. 'I'll tell them. I'll get rid of this first.' He sat down and began referring the assignments one by one back to the sender.

Salter started by reading the police report. The alarm had been phoned in at 1.53 a.m. The police and the fire trucks had arrived together, the report said. The fire was confined to the basement and very quickly extinguished. The owner, who was found at the foot of the stairs leading up to the second floor, was pronounced dead on arrival at the hospital.

Salter phoned the Fire Marshal's office and spoke to the investigator, asking the obvious question first. Could it have been an accident?

'We don't think so. The agent used was gasoline, or something equally volatile – the guys on the truck said they could smell it when they arrived. And there was no container around, which means that someone poured gasoline on the basement floor, lit it and got out right away.'

'Spontaneous combustion?' Salter asked. The question was probably foolish, but he knew Orliff would ask *him*.

'That's something else. Usually it involves something like linseed oil. Look, Inspector, I'm just going to bed. I pass the fire on my way home, or I can do. Why don't you meet me there and I'll take you over it? You're new to this, aren't you? Usually it's Munnings or Hutter on these jobs.' The investigator's voice was friendly, but weary.

'That's right, I am. I'd be glad of any help.'

'Half an hour then. See you there.'

Salter hung up and shoved the report in his pocket.

'I've gone to the fire, Frank,' he said, standing up.
'I'll be back at noon.'

Bloor Street, which once marked the northern bound-
ary of the city, is now a continuous shopping district
running through the heart of Toronto. In the centre,
where it intersects with Yonge Street, the stores are
fashionable and expensive, but within a few blocks in
either direction the character changes as the street
becomes the 'Main Street' of the local district, changing continuously with the economic and racial character of the area.

The building that Salter was looking for was several
blocks west of Bathurst Street, on the far side of a
district dominated by Honest Ed's, a giant bargain
mart decorated like a cross between a circus and an
amusement arcade, covered in coloured lights and
hung with revolving balls, a discount store that
attracts huge crowds with daily specials like chickens
at one cent each (limit one per customer). Partly
through the benevolent whim of the proprietor of this
establishment, Markham Street, which crosses Bloor
just west of Honest Ed's, has developed into a little
colony of artist's studios, restaurants, and second-
hand dealers, which the chief landlord calls 'Mirvish
Village'.

At this point, Bloor Street is a pleasant muddle of
small stores and restaurants, housed in the same two-
and three-storey buildings that were erected in the
early years of the century when the district was
largely Anglo-Saxon. The mix of races has changed,
but the street still looks, as Salter's mother had once
said out of her girlhood memories of South London,

like Toronto's Tooting Broadway, crowded with small clothing stores and greengrocers. Now the travel agents have signs in Greek and Portuguese, and mangoes and red bananas sell as briskly as carrots and Brussels sprouts. Pasta is on sale everywhere, a staple not only of the Italians, but also of the large population of students who live nearby, within walking distance of the University of Toronto, which sprawls hugely across the city to the south-east.

Salter found a parking space a block away from the fire and walked back to the store. The name was still discernible: 'THE BOTTOM DRAWER – ANTIQUES AND COLLECTIBLES (C. Drecker).' The front of the store was boarded with plywood, but the door was open and a policeman stood on guard talking to a grey-haired man about Salter's age. Salter produced his identification, and the other man put out his hand. 'I'm the guy you were talking to,' he said. 'Hayes, Fire Marshal's office.'

He was heavily built without fat, not dramatically dirty, but as Salter got close he could see the line of ash around his boots and the soot in the creases of the man's face that told of a long night's work. His exhaustion was evident in the slump of his body. 'We'd better go inside,' he said, in a voice that also said to Salter that it was long after closing time but he would do what was necessary to fill the policeman in.

'Started in the basement,' Hayes said. 'Want to go down?'

Salter nodded and Hayes switched on the electric lantern he was carrying. 'There's no power, of course', he said. He led the way through to the back of the store, down a flight of steps to the dark hole below,

and shone his lantern around. The room was charred
and blackened and still dripping with the water that
had been poured into it. Surprisingly, the fire seemed
to have burnt only a small part of the ceiling, making
a hole about six feet across at the back of the basement
opposite the stairs.

'They got here in time to save it,' the investigator
said. 'It didn't take much to put it out. The damage is
mostly smoke.'

And water, thought Slater, looking at the sodden
mess. 'What makes you think it was arson?' he asked.

'Okay,' Hayes said, and cleared his throat. When
he spoke again he assumed a formal, pedagogical
tone. 'The firemen smelled gasoline, or something
like it. The fire started on the floor. Look. See this
patch?' He pointed to a bare patch on the concrete
floor. 'Nothing to burn there, but something burnt *on*
it if you get me. Now. The fire took off over here.' He
pointed to a charred mess underneath the burnt part
of the ceiling. 'My guess is that that was a pile of rags,
probably soaked in oil. There's not much else to burn
down here. He didn't use it for storage. So you've got
a gasoline fire which turned into an oil fire. That's
why there was so much smoke.'

'But it couldn't have been spontaneous?'

'You don't mean spontaneous,' Hayes said. 'You
mean could it have been sparked by something
accidentally, right?'

Salter nodded.

'First', Hayes continued, 'there's no furnace. The
whole place is electric – lighting, heating, hot water
– the lot. The wiring runs round the ceiling, see.
Now you do get a gasoline fire set off by an electric

spark – any kind of spark will do – but you've got to
have the right mixture of gas and air up at the ceiling
level, you follow me? Okay. Now, if you get that
mixture you also get one hell of an explosion – it
would take the roof off. But there was no explosion. I
talked to some of the locals who were gawking and no
one even heard a woomp. So the gas ignited almost
as soon as it was poured. That is, somebody poured
gas around, lit it right away, and got the hell out.
Even a couple of minutes would have been dangerous. Another thing, there was no container. We didn't
find a can or anything else in the basement that could
have held the gas. Whoever poured it took the can
with him.'

Salter looked around the basement, following the
investigator's argument. The floor had obviously not
been swept for years. There were several iron coat
hangers, dozens of nails, pieces of wire, hooks and
broken hinges forming a kind of metal rubble all over
the floor, but nothing that could have contained
gasoline. He pointed to a light-bulb. 'What happened
to that?' he asked. 'I thought those things would just
explode.' The bulb bulged distortedly on one side.

Hayes smiled. 'It's one of the ways you can tell the
point of origin,' he said. 'This one is obvious, but if it
wasn't, the light-bulbs would tell you because they
expand in the direction of the heat.'

'What about the windows?' Salter asked. There
were two small windows at ground level, hinged on
the top of the frame and opening upwards and
inwards. The one farthest from the fire was still intact,
the bolts rusted into place. The other window was
close enough to the pile of rags to bave been

scorched. Hayes waited for his pupil to examine it for himself. At some time the glass had been broken and replaced with a cheap plastic storm window. The charred cardboard edging was still in place, but the plastic pane had melted and shrivelled away, and a fresh draught blew in through the gap. The frame, like its companion, was still bolted and rusted shut, and the cross-struts were still intact.

'No one came in there,' Salter conceded. 'What now?'

'Upstairs,' Hayes said, leading the way. 'What's your regular assignment?' he asked conversationally.

Who knows? thought Slater. He remembered Gatenby's joke. 'I'm on the Intelligence detail,' he said. 'Counter-espionage mostly. Other stuff, too, though.' He smiled to show he was joking, but the investigator had his back to him and just nodded to show he had heard.

No more jokes, Salter told himself.

Hayes stopped at the foot of the stairs leading to the second floor. 'This is where we found him,' he said. 'He was in his shorts. There were no marks that I could see, but the pathologist will tell you about that. Smoke inhalation, pretty certainly.'

'Could he have set it himself?' Salter asked, and regretted it immediately.

'You think he might have set fire to the basement and gone upstairs to have a lie-down?' Hayes's voice was tinged with wonder. Then his weariness took over as he explained to this incompetent they had sent (instead of Munnings or Hutter) the stupidity of his question.

Salter cut in. 'Look, I'm sorry. I'm not on the

regular arson detail. I need a refresher course, so I would be grateful for a step-by-step account of how you came to your conclusions. Okay? You're the expert, so tell me.'

Thus appealed to, the investigator softened slightly. 'It's been a hairy three days.' he said. 'Last weekend there were fifty-eight fires in Metro. The average for a weekend is about thirty.'

'No wonder you're tired', Salter said. 'So,' he continued, 'you found the owner here, in his underwear. If, by some kind of magic, he *had* set the fire, there would be a can around. Then I would also have to figure out why he got undressed to set fire to his own store. Right? But the obvious thing is that he was overcome by smoke. Right?'

Hayes nodded. 'That's about it,' he said. 'Let's look at the rest of it, upstairs.' He turned to lead the way.

At the top of the stairs to the second floor a small landing gave access to a tiny apartment. At the back a newly renovated bathroom looked over the yard, which was no more than a parking space for a blue Volkswagen truck. Next to the bathroom, a small bedroom had been used for a workroom, and contained the dismantled pieces of a table and a rocking-chair. There was a kitchen next to the bedroom, and then a living-room which took up the front of the apartment and looked over the street. This room was furnished with a mixture of odds and ends from Drecker's stock: a double bed that opened out from a settee, two odd armchairs, and an old coffee table. The floor was covered with an oriental-looking rug, and a cocktail cabinet in blonde wood stood in the corner next to a television set that was angled so that it could be watched from the bed. There were no pictures on the walls, and the total effect was of a camp rather than of a room used for living. The damage here was negligible, although the room, like the whole house, stank of wet smoke.

'Funny way to live, isn't it?' Hayes said. 'No pictures or anything.'

'I don't think he lived here,' Salter said. He looked around the room. Beside the bed was a bottle of rum, about a quarter full, and a huge empty cola bottle.

'The pathologist will tell us,' Hayes said, 'but my guess is he was too drunk to help himself.'

Salter nodded. 'It makes sense, doesn't it? Let's go downstairs.'

The assortment of soaked and blackened furniture that had made up the stock was still arranged for sale in the store, although some of the shelves were empty.

'The insurance people took a look already,' the constable on guard said. 'Drecker's assistant went off with them. He said he'd be back as soon as he'd finished with the adjuster.'

I wonder what he had that was worth a buck, Salter thought, looking around. Even under the smoke it was easy to guess that Drecker did not aim very high. There was a cheap metal desk, a huge old typewriter, and a filing cabinet that looked as though someone had tried to kick the side in. The floor was bare, and the shelving had been assembled from a lot of old bookcases of different sizes.

'If that's it, I'm going home to bed,' Hayes said, breaking into Salter's thoughts.

'Yes, thanks. Thanks a lot.' Salter shook hands with

the investigator. 'Can I call you if I need more help?'
It was as much an apology for any irritation he had
caused as a request for help.

'Sure,' Hayes said. 'But I guess Munnings or
Hutter will be taking over soon, won't they? You can
go back to catching spies.' He nodded and left.

No more jokes, Salter promised himself.

'He's got us mixed up with the mounties, I reckon,
sir,' the constable said, grinning.

Salter looked at him, searching for the remark that
would relieve his own feelings. In the end he said
nothing, but the constable read his face accurately
and turned away. Salter looked at the man's back.
Another enemy, he thought.

He bent down to look at the front door which the
firemen had smashed off its hinges. There were two
locks, but only one of them was secured. On the back
door, which opened on to Drecker's parking space,
both locks were in place. Did that mean anything?
Salter came to two opposite and equally convincing
conclusions, and set the problem aside. He walked
out on to the street to scout for neighbours who might
have seen something. The buildings on both sides of
the street were all two-storey affairs. All of them had
stores on the ground floor, while most of the second
floors were occupied by insurance and travel agents.
At the end of the block an old three-storey apartment
building offered possibilities, but most of the tenants
would be at work now. Checking the building was a
job for others.

Salter returned to the store and nearly collided in
the doorway with a young man who was also on his
way in.

'Who are you?' Salter asked without preamble.

From inside, the constable answered. 'This is Dennis Nelson, the assistant.' He left Salter to introduce himself.

'Inspector Salter,' the policeman said. 'I would like some questions answered.'

'About me?' Nelson asked. He had bright ginger hair cut in an English style with a drooping lock over his forehead, and a thick fair moustache which hung in points around his mouth. His face was smooth and round like that of a grown-up cherub, with an expression of eagerness approaching glee, giving him the air of a schoolboy on a picnic. He was casually but carefully dressed in chino pants and a thick dark blue sweater. Salter judged his age at about twenty-two or -three.

'About everything here,' Salter said. 'You. Your boss. The regular customers – whatever you can tell me.'

Nelson looked around the blackened store. 'Could we go somewhere else?' he asked. 'I was just going to take the records home for safe-keeping until someone tells me what happens next. Why don't we talk in my apartment? It's not far from here.' He stood with his feet together and one arm pointed at right-angles in the direction of his apartment, somewhere down Bloor Street, giving the impression that at a nod from Salter he would give a little kick and launch himself horizontally sideways, to arrive in a trice at the apartment.

Salter shrugged and nodded. A pixie was a nice change from an exhausted fire marshal and a wounded constable.

Nelson sprang across the room to a single-drawer filing cabinet that stood next to the cash register. 'Everything is in here,' he said. 'If you have a car we could load it in and drive over. I live on Washington Avenue.'

'What's in the cash register?'

'Nothing. There should be a float of twenty-five dollars here.' He dived under the counter and came up with a dirty envelope full of change and small bills, and held it high in the air, inquiringly. 'Everthing else went into the night deposit box,' he said.

'Put the money in the filing cabinet,' Salter said. 'We'll take it with us. I'll get the car.'

When he returned, he double-parked with his engine running, and the two men loaded the filing cabinet into the back seat. The constable looked after the car doors and saluted carefully as they drove off.

'You'd better do a U-turn,' Nelson said. 'You can't go around the block because of the one-way street system.'

They turned east along Bloor, past Honest Ed's, to Spadina Avenue, and then south to Washington, the first street. Nelson lived in a house near the Spadina end of the street, and Salter drove the car up on to the sidewalk outside the house. They carried the filing cabinet into the kitchen and put it on one end of a long counter. Nelson twirled about with paper towels, cleaning the soot off the cabinet while Salter looked around the apartment. It was decorated in a style he faintly recognized, and Annie would identify when he got home: most of the colours were black and white, making the apartment look like the set of an old movie; the rug was white, the small piano was white, as well as the curtains, most of the wall-space and woodwork, and some of the furniture. In the centre of the room was a huge black glass coffee table, and one of the armchairs and a footstool were also black. The ornaments above the fireplace were made of frosted glass, except for a clock which advertised Sweet Caporal cigarettes and belonged in a bus station on the prairies, and another clock of white plastic with a tiny black Harold Lloyd dangling from the minute hand. On the walls were several drawings in black ink of people writhing, clipped between sheets of glass without frames; two whole walls were filled with bookshelves, crammed with books and magazines about art

Nelson stood poised in the doorway of the kitchen. 'Coffee, Inspector?'

'All right.' Salter sat down, choosing the black armchair in case he had any soot on him. In a few minutes, Nelson reappeared, moving as if on roller-skates, bearing a Coca-Cola tray on which he carried two white mugs, a jug of cream, and a bowl of sugar. Salter sipped and found the coffee delicious.

'If you want to smoke, I have an ashtray some-where,' Nelson said.

'No, thanks. Now, Mr Nelson, tell me first about your boss, C. Drecker. What does the "C" stand for?'

'Cyril. What do you want to know? I didn't like him,' Nelson said with a flourish of his cup, looking brightly at Salter to see if he had shocked him.

'I see. This is going to be easy, then. You went out last night and set fire to the store and killed him?'

'O no. I'm sorry he's dead – ' here Nelson struck a

pose personifying Sorrow – 'but only in a general
way.' The smile returned.

'Why didn't you like him?'

'Because I saw him swindling people, and because
he was abusive and flatulent.' Nelson was solemn
now. His brightness was undiminished and he spoke
without rancour, but in a determined clear voice.
'Never speak evil of the dead, and all that, but if the
police followed *that* rule you wouldn't get anywhere,
would you?'

Salter took out his notebook. Nelson obviously felt
free to express his dislike of Drecker without arousing
Salter's curiosity, although he might have decided
that the police were bound to find out about it,
anyway.

'How was he abusive?' Salter asked.

'He made fun of me, or tried to. He was snide.'

'How?'

'He made fun of my lifestyle.'

Salter waved a hand around the room. 'All this?' he
asked. 'Looks nice to me.' What was it? Apart from
the Sweet Caporal clock and the Coca-Cola tray,
everything in the room was black or white.

Nelson looked at Salter speculatively for a few
moments. Then: 'Not my taste, Inspector,' he said.
'My sexual orientation.'

For a few seconds Salter was genuinely puzzled.
Then he realized what he was being told. Feeling like
a yokel, he decided to act like one, but a yokel
without prejudices. 'You're queer, are you, Mr
Nelson?' he asked, like someone enquiring, 'You're
Hindu, or vegetarian, or new to the district?'

'I'm bisexual, Inspector,' Nelson said, like a boy who could not tell a lie.

'Fine, fine. And Drecker made fun of this, did he? How?' Might as well beat the subject to death.

'He used to ask me if I fancied this or that male. And he would fantasize about what he would like to do to the women customers, aloud.'

'And what did you do?'

'When he went too far, I told him to stop. Mostly I ignored him. Once I asked him why he was so interested in the gay scene. That shut him up for a long time.'

'He doesn't sound very attractive, Mr Nelson. Dirty talker, dirty habits.' Salter pretended a bit more sympathy than he felt. Drecker sounded to him no worse than most of the men he knew, even if he had kept the locker-room talk going later in life than usual.

'Only around me, Inspector. Other people thought he was a fine fellow. Especially his girlfriends. They found him attractive, all right.'

'Girlfriends?'

'He always had one, sometimes two at the same time.'

'Was that what the upstairs apartment was all about?'

'Mostly,' Nelson nodded.

'So, he was a pig as far as you were concerned.' Salter said, again discounting something for Nelson's fastidiousness. 'Why did you work for him?'

'I wanted to learn about the Toronto dealer scene. I know something about antiques, and the The Bottom Drawer was a place to pick up the economics

of the trade. The worm's eye view of it, anyway. I
hope to get my own shop eventually.'

'He was also a crook, you say. Enough of one to
have enemies who would want to kill him?'

Nelson shook his head. 'I wouldn't have thought
so. He wasn't that big – more of a chiseller, really.
Drecker was always looking to buy for a dollar and
sell for a hundred, always trying to get something for
nothing.' Gradually, as Salter responded seriously to
his words, Nelson was becoming less galvanic.

'Was he known for it?'

'In the trade, yes. The bigger dealers, the ones
Drecker sometimes sold to, didn't trust him. They
always demanded full provenance of everything he
sold them.'

'They thought he might be a fence?'

'They knew he would be if there wasn't much risk.'

'Who are these dealers? Who did he do business
with, say, in the last six months?'

Nelson pointed to the file cabinet. 'It's all in there,'
he said. 'I could make up a list for you, but it would
take a bit of time.'

'Tomorrow?'

'Sure.'

'Good. Next. Are you aware of anyone else who
had a grudge against him? Any big arguments, that
kind of thing?'

'There have been a couple of shouting matches,
lately. One old lady sold him a harvest table for ten
dollars. He had it cleaned up and put it out for six
hundred.'

'You know her name?'

'No. Drecker dealt in cash when he could. No

receipts for stuff like that. But that was two months ago. Then there was the guy who fixed the bathroom, Raymond Darling. Drecker must have tried to swindle him because he came back last week and they had a shouting match upstairs. He came back twice. I know him – he's a friend of a friend of mine. More coffee?'

Salter pushed his cup forward. 'Write his name down, will you?' he said, pointing to a little block of white notepaper that fitted into a perspex box on the coffee table. 'Along with where I could get hold of him. Now, one more question, Mr Nelson.'

'Where was I last night? Right?'

'Yes. Where were you last night?'

'I was here until one o'clock this morning, and then I left and spent the rest of the night with a friend.'

'A friend?'

'A friend,' confirmed Nelson. 'A *lady*,' he added. His face creased into a 'gotcha' smile.

'Her name?'

'Julia Costa. You want her address, of course.' He wrote it down on the same slip of paper and handed it to Salter.

'And until one o'clock you were here, alone?'

'No.' Nelson said. He was not smiling now. 'Until one o'clock I was here with the person I live with. We were having an argument and I couldn't stand it any longer so I got a cab and went over to Julia's.'

'I see. Your friend could confirm this?'

'Yes. Jake will be back this afternoon. Could I ask you a favour? Would you mind *not* telling Jake where I went when I left him?'

'All right. Why?'

Nelson put his hands in his pockets and pushed himself against the back of the chair. 'He's jealous,' he said. 'It's one of the things we quarrelled about. He wants to know where I am all the time, and I need some kind of private life of my own. I've got to have some air.'

It seemed his proper element.

'I see,' Salter said. 'Jake is your – lover?' He cleared his throat to speak more distinctly next time.

'I thought I had made that clear.' Nelson's eyes widened in mock surprise.

'And he's jealous of this Julia Costa?'

'He's jealous of *everybody*.'

'Possessive, like,' Salter said, feeling every moment more and more comfortable in Nelson's world. Apart from Nelson's taste in partners, it all sounded very familiar. He stood up. 'I'll come by this afternoon and get a confirmation from your room-mate.'

Nelson laughed. 'We have separate rooms,' he said. 'When his mother comes to town we are just regular buddies. Besides, he *snores*.'

Salter smiled. He opened the door, then paused.

'Relatives,' he asked. 'Did Drecker have any?'

'A wife. She's out of town. I phoned her with the news and she's flying in this afternoon. Say, I thought you guys were the ones who were supposed to know all this?' Nelson added in a teasing voice.

'We'd check it all out, Mr Nelson, but it's quicker to ask you. Thanks for the coffee. I'll be back this afternoon.'

He drove back to the station-house and parked his car. It was nearly lunch-time, so he walked over to

his squash club where he had arranged for a game
with one of the other beginners. They lumbered
about the court, oblivious of the world for forty
minutes, and then had a sandwich and a. beer
together. He had been playing squash for five
months, and though he was still no good at all, he
pursued the game with childish pleasure. He and his
partners knew almost nothing about each other (he
told them he worked for the metropolitan government) but the exercise, the anonymity, and most of
all, the pleasure he got from competing again, something he had not had for years, made these games the
high points in his week.

He walked back to his office feeling lighter,
especially in the head, and greeted his sergeant.

'How are you, Frank?' he asked.

'What's that?' Gatenby asked.

'I said, how are you?'

'Nothing wrong with me,' the sergeant said in a
puzzled voice. They had already met once that day,
and Salter was not one of nature's constant greeters.

'I want you to check the neighbours around that
fire, Frank. Find out if anyone saw anything suspicious last night.'

'Right. I'll put the boys on it.'

'Have them check every building that overlooks
the store.'

'All right. Anything else?'

'Not yet. There will be, though. I think this one
will take a lot of checking around.'

'Your wife phoned, to remind you of your doctor's
appointment. Anything the matter, Charlie?'

Salter looked up, startled. Sergeants do not call

inspectors by their first names unless invited, and in taking the privilege on himself, Gatenby was pointing out that the time had come for Salter to acknowledge his sergeant, instead of keeping him at arm's length. Salter felt rebuked and very slightly touched.

'I don't know what's wrong, Frank,' he said. 'Nothing, probably. Some test turned their litmus paper blue. I don't know.'

Gatenby nodded sympathetically, and Salter started to write a report for his superintendent. After half an hour it was time to go back to Washington Avenue and interview Nelson's room-mate. He told Gatenby that if Drecker's widow called, he would see her in the morning, and left.

This time he found Nelson in a very upset state. His friend, Jake Hauser, had come and gone while Salter had been away, but not before their quarrel had been renewed and intensified. Nelson was so agitated he could hardly talk. Another person was with him now, an attractive black-haired woman in her early thirties, dressed in jeans and a T-shirt that left her midriff bare.

'I'm Christine Nader,' she said, after Salter had identified himself. 'I live across the hall. I came over to complain about the noise last night, but poor Dennis was in such a state I stayed around.' She was kneeling beside Nelson's chair, holding his hand, her back half-turned to the policeman.

Nice neighbour. Salter tried to repress the thought that she was wasted on Nelson. It was the kind of thing Drecker probably said. 'You heard the argument last night?'

'Oh yes, indeedy. Loud and clear,' she said over her shoulder.

'Do you want a full account of our quarrel?' Nelson shouted, close to tears.

'No, sir. If this lady can confirm that you were here until one o'clock, that's all I need to know.'

'I can guarantee it, Inspector,' she said.

'Good.' Salter still had not sat down, but he moved across the room to avoid looking directly into the top of her T-shirt. 'And where will I find Mr Hauser?'

'You won't. He's gone for good.' Nelson's voice was defiant.

'Has he? Why?'

'Because I told him to.'

'Nevertheless I'd like to talk to him. Where do you suggest I look?'

'I haven't any idea. His parents live in South Porcupine, but you won't find him there.'

The woman continued to soothe him, patting his hand gently.

'Where does he work?'

'At Queen's Park. He's an accountant for the Ontario Government.' Each statement increased Nelson's distress.

'I'll try there. I'll come back tomorrow and go over that list of dealers.'

Nelson looked away, and the woman grimaced at Salter to go.

From a phone booth on Spadina Avenue he established quickly that Hauser had not been in to work that day and had not called in. No one knew where he was. The first suspect.

* * *

It was nearly three o'clock. He was not due at the hospital until three-thirty, so he filled in the time by attending to an item on Annie's list – the screen door. There was a hardware store on Bloor Street, not far from the burned building, and Salter drove the few blocks to it. He started to explain his errand, but the owner was shaking his head and pursing his lips before he had finished.

'No way,' he said. 'No way. No way. No-o-o way.'

Salter waited for the little performance to finish and the explanation to begin.

'They put those wheels on in the factory,' the man said, shaking his head steadily, so that Salter wanted to lean over and place his hand on the man's scalp to stop him. 'No way you can repair those suckers by yourself.'

'You mean I have to take the door to the factory?' Salter asked.

'That's right,' the man said with the loud, dogmatic confidence of someone who didn't know what he was talking about. 'What make is it?'

'I don't know. Is it on the door?'

'Should be, shouldn't it? What *you* have to do is find out who makes the door and see if they do repairs. Probably means a new door. How old is it?'

'Ten years.'

At this the man closed his eyes, turned sideways to Salter and started shaking his head again. 'They won't be in business now,' he said eventually. 'These factories disappear overnight.'

'In which case, I have to have the whole goddam unit replaced?'

The man shrugged and opened his eyes. 'Looks

like it,' he said. 'Tough tittie. I could be wrong, of course,' he added, leaving the policeman back where he started.

'Thanks,' said Salter, and left the store with the sense that the screen door was going to be a classic.

At the hospital the specialist asked him questions for ten minutes; most of them seemed irrelevant, or suggested diseases that Salter had not even thought of. The doctor seemed indifferent to the answers, even when Salter could not answer at all, as with 'Are you urinating more or less frequently in the past year than usual?'

Salter then undressed and lay down and stared first at the wall, then at the ceiling. The doctor was soon done. 'You can get dressed now,' he said and disappeared. When the policeman was buttoned up he went into the outer office where the nurse was waiting to go home. His next appointment, she said, was on Thursday for the same time, with the X-ray department.

'What for?' Salter asked.

She replied in medical jargon which meant nothing to Salter.

'Did the doctor find anything, did he happen to tell you?' he asked.

'The doctor will send a full report to your family doctor,' the nurse said, adjusting her scarf in a mirror. 'Do we have his name?'

'I don't know. Do you?'

She put down her purse and went to a filing cabinet where she found Salter's file. She looked at the single sheet of paper it contained. 'Dr Blostein?' she asked.

'That's right.'

She switched off the light and eased Salter into the corridor. 'We'll let him know,' she said.

At home Annie was waiting for news and Angus was in his room, waiting. He dealt with Angus first by knocking on his son's door, listening for a reply, and letting himself in when none came.

Angus was sitting in the exact centre of his bed, his knees up to his chin. Salter sat down.

'You got any more skin books in the house?' he asked.

Angus shook his head.

'Good. If you have, get rid of them tonight. They upset your mother. They don't upset me, I've seen them before. You want to talk?'

Angus shook his head again. He met Salter's eyes and looked back down at his feet. By now, Salter thought, he will have checked around at school and found out what usually happened to his pals when they got caught. What did happen? He pondered what his own father would have done in the circumstances, but the question was absurd. In Salter's childhood, pornography consisted of sepia photographs that dated from the Twenties. The women in the pictures looked, to a fourteen-year-old, like aunts, and the men, mustachio'd with gleaming hair parted in the middle, like music-hall performers caught between changes. He had made no connection between the activities of these foreign-looking people and his own desires.

His father had said nothing of any kind on the subject. Talk of sex, like swearing, was forbidden in

the house, and Salter carried into his teens the
impression that his parents had banished that part of
the world from their lives. One day, when Salter was
sixteen, his father suddenly told him a very dirty joke
as they were walking along the street, and Salter
realized that his father was now treating him as a
man, but he was too shocked to reply in kind.

Now he looked at his son and wondered how they
would get through the next five years. Probably it
would not be as long as that. In his own day most
first-year undergraduates were still virgins, but nowadays they were all screwing in grade ten, weren't
they?

Angus continued to observe his bare feet while
Salter tried to find an exit line. There was a small
pustule on the boy's neck, and a hint of hair on his
lip, but underneath there was the innocent ten-year-
old face of yesterday, and underneath *that* was the
little boy he had taken to play in the sandpit in Oriole
Park. Age, Salter thought, was something one's
friends and relatives wore on top of the real person
that you had known all along. The one or two
acquaintances he still knew from his school-days had
not changed in thirty years – they had merely put on
age as they had put on weight, a superficial change
that looked like reality to the outsider, but to someone who had known them all along seemed no more
than a kind of make-up.

He got up from the chair and patted the boy on the
shoulder. 'See you later,' he said. Angus nodded, but
did not look up, and Salter left.

Downstairs Annie was preparing some kind of
curry. He poured himself a bottle of beer and walked

out to the back porch, or 'deck' as it was known in his neighbourhood. Salter had married above himself – his wife came from an Establishment family in Prince Edward Island, and he met her and wooed her while he was recovering from the wreck of his first marriage. His own background was solidly lower-class. His father had been a maintenance man for the local streetcar company; his mother came from England at fourteen, shipped out by an orphanage to work as a domestic servant. Salter was wary of his wife's class, and of his own middle-class status, and he kept his distance from both by calling the garden the 'yard' and by eating his dinner at noon and his supper at night.

'What did you say to Angus?' Annie whispered in his ear.

'I told him to keep the skin books out of the house.'

'Is that all? Aren't you going to talk to him?'

'I don't know,' Salter said, who didn't. 'What about? They get it all in school, don't they?'

'It's not the same. He needs someone to put it all in some kind of context.'

'Shall I tell him how on our first night I put a rose between your legs because I'd read that someone did that in a book to show how beautiful he thought *IT* was? And you woke up in hysterics because you thought the rose was a spider?'

'Charlie, he needs someone to *talk* to him.'

'All right, all right. I'll do something. Leave it alone for now, will you?'

Angus came in the room behind them and sat down at the dining table. Annie called Seth and they began to eat. Annie gave a bright account of her day at work, a day in which she located an old gas station of the Forties, constructed to look like a sugar-candy house in a fairy story – a style widely used once but now nearly all gone. Seth had a story to tell about a temporary master at his school whom he described as a 'real lunch-box.' Angus said nothing and left the table as soon as he had finished.

Annie and Salter took their coffee out on to the back porch where the superb weather was just beginning to turn cool.

'Did you see the specialist?' she asked, when they were alone.

'Yes.'

'What did he say?'

'Nothing. His nurse said I have to go for some X-rays on Thursday.'

'What for?'

'Christ knows. I don't.' Back came the black wave that he had kept at bay for a few hours. He changed the topic. 'I got a new assignment today. Homicide.'

'Are you pleased?'

'It's better than organizing the leave rosters.' Salter waved away a wasp. 'This job of yours going to keep you busy?'

'I think so, for a little while.'

Salter grunted.

He was not yet quite used to a working wife. She had broken him in gently: in June she had announced that she was bored and they had talked about things she could do to get her out of the house; in July she had let him know that courses in French or getting into volunteer work was not what she had in mind. She wanted a job, a real job. She ran the house with

her left hand, the boys were old enough not to set
fire to it, and she needed, she said, a life, maybe even
a career. A sign of the times, but at the bottom of his
mind Salter feared letting her out of purdah in case
she found out what alternatives the world had to offer
to marriage to a police inspector whose career had
come to a halt once and only now was showing signs
of life again.

At first her job had been part-time, between ten
and three, and Salter hardly noticed it and never
inquired. When he thought about it he both believed
and did not believe that she lived in a glamorous
world filled with smooth bastards in Italian clothes.
He had never quite overcome the feeling of enormous
luck at getting Annie in the first place (or rather,
second place, after his brief disastrous marriage to a
flower-child who promptly took up arms against the
Establishment, including Salter, so actively that the
marriage shattered within a year). Salter uas uxorious
without being submissive, and while he had enough
sense not to want to keep Annie in a doll's house, he
feared for his safety whenever she spread her wings.
He could not imagine life without her, but he sometimes thought that he might leave her so that he
would no longer have to worry about her leaving him.

'It's not going to interfere with you. Aren't you glad
for me?' she said.

'Oh, I am,' he lied. He waved another wasp away.
'Goddam wasps.'

'There's a nest. Outside the bathroom window.'

Salter looked up. A small brown globe about the
size of a melon had appeared between the bathroom
window and the screen.

'Knock it down,' he suggested.

'It isn't that easy. You might have to get a head net and some gloves.'

'*I* might leave it. They go to sleep in the winter.'

'Then we'll have to get the screen door fixed. They are coming in the third floor.'

'I found out today that to fix the third floor we might have to take the back wall off the house.'

'Why don't you ask someone about it?'

'Who? What? I've tried,' Salter snapped in frustration. The phrase 'Why don't you . . .' was second only to 'By the way . . .' in making him angry. For all the progress that women had made, Annie, and most women in Salter's experience, responded to a difficult situation with a 'Why don't you'. Usually it involved a tricky or embarrassing situation, such as 'Why don't you ask the captain why the ship has stopped?' The classic 'why-don't-you occurred when they were lost in a car on a trip to New York. Annie said, 'Why don't you ask that policeman if we are in Manhattan yet?' Salter did, and the cop said, 'Well, that's Central Park, bud, and I don't think they moved it lately.' But, as Annie said, she didn't see why women should have to ask all the potentially dumb questions.

'It has to be fixed, Charlie.'

Salter sighed. There was too much going on. 'I know. Right now, though, dear, just at this moment, fuck it, eh?'

He changed the subject. 'What do you know about antique dealers?' he asked. 'A store run by someone called Drecker out past Honest Ed's burned down last night. The owner died in the fire. Ever heard of it? It was called The Bottom Drawer.'

'A *real* antique shop?'

Salter shook his head. 'I doubt if your mother would bother with it,' he said. 'More of a – what-do-call-it – collectibles store. You know, junk. The lower end of the trade anyway. Antique apple-corers, but mostly second-hand stuff.'

'I knew some of the stores on Markham Street. Was it about that level? They are sort of off-Broadway.'

'Not even that, I think. Off-off-Broadway, if anything.'

'No. Never heard of it. But Jenny would know. Why don't you give her a call?'

Salter brightened. 'That's a thought. I'll ask her out to lunch.'

'She'll love that,' Annie said, slightly mocking.

Jenny Schumann was an antique dealer in York-ville, an old friend who had employed Annie occasionally on a part-time basis before she had the children. She had been declaring her interest in Salter, loudly and publicly, ever since she had met him, coupled with the assurance that only her friendship with Annie prohibited her from seducing him. Salter enjoyed the game, Annie was vicariously flattered by it, and Jenny had become the only friend they had in common who kept no secrets from either of them. She assumed that neither Salter nor Annie ever confided in her about the other, and freely passed on to both what the other had said. This ought to have inhibited secrets, but it worked in another way. Once they had come to know her, both Salter and Annie used her as a kind of marriage counsellor, telling her the things – mostly trivial but occasionally something fundamental – that they wanted her to pass on without having the face to do it directly. Annie, for example, once told Jenny that she wished she could have a room of her own, a workroom. This was before she got a job. Jenny immediately told Salter, who then realized that what he had heard for years as a faint and wistful desire was a real need that he should respond to seriously.

'Keep your hands above the table,' Annie said, kissing Salter on the head as she passed into the kitchen.

'Can I take my shoes off?' he called.

'Okay,' Annie shouted from the top of the stairs, 'But not hers, you hear?'

Salter blushed, and laughed.

Chapter Two

Next morning, he began by reading the report of the officers who had checked Drecker's neighbours. Nothing. Nobody had seen or heard anything unusual. The last item on the report dealt with something else. One of the men doing the check had found a gallon can of camp fuel, still half full, among the weeds in the laneway that ran behind the store. Salter reached for the phone, dialled the Fire Marshal's number, and asked for Hayes, the investigator.

'Camp fuel,' Salter said, after identifying himself. 'We've found a can of camp fuel. That would work like gasoline, right?'

'Just as good. It's more volatile than regular leaded gas. It's called naphtha, or white gas.'

'Who would use it, apart from campers?'

'A lot of people. It's a good cleaning agent, so the owner might have had some.'

'So there's no point checking around trying to trace the can and who it was sold to?'

'I wouldn't think so. But that's *your* job, isn't it?'

'Yeah, thanks.' Salter put the phone down. 'Send it off for fingerprints, Frank, and get it analysed,' he said. 'And remind me to put that officer's name in the report.' If you've robbed Peter, he thought, remembering his short-tempered response to the constable guarding the fire, you can pay back Paul.

Gatenby looked up. 'Is it very helpful?'

Salter thought about it. 'It means the fire was probably set by someone who threw the can in the weeds,' he said. 'That's the way it looked, but it's nice to have a piece of solid evidence. If it's covered in fingerprints, it will be even nicer. Anything else?'

'Drecker's widow called. She'll be in all day. I must say she didn't sound too upset.'

'I might as well go over now.' Salter hummed a little and looked at his watch. 'Frank, do you know how I might get a screen door fixed? A sliding one. The wheel has come off.' Salter had no idea why he was asking Gatenby, except that the Sergeant sometimes wore little glasses like Pinocchio's father which gave him the air of a clever old craftsman.

'Who put the door in?'

It was an obvious question. 'Fred Staver. We still have his number. I'll ask him. Thanks. Next question. What would you do if you caught your boy reading skin magazines?'

'I don't have a boy, do I?'

'I know. But what would you do if you *had* one?'

'I know what my old dad did when he caught me.'

'What?' This might be something.

'First of all he took me down to the basement and made me burn the pictures in the furnace. We had a woodburner in those days. Then he explained to me how looking at pictures like that would make my eyes weak and make me old before my time. Then he asked me how I would feel if my mum should see them. Then he told me if ever he caught me with anything like that again he would put me in the Working Boys' Home. He wouldn't have me in the

house, he said. Then he hit me, once on each side of
the head.'

'Did it work?'

'Oh yes. He was a bricklayer. My ears were ringing
for days.'

'Did you hold it against him later?'

'No. It could have been worse. One of my pals got
caught and *his* father set the minister on to him. He
had to go to the minister's house and tell him all he'd
been up to in that way during the week. They used
to get down on their knees together and pray for help
to keep the boy pure. Oh no. My old dad and I had a
good laugh about it later.'

'Did he ever try to teach you anything about sex?'

'When I started out with girls he said to me,
"Remember, son. A standing prick has no conscience." I didn't understand that for years. Then, on
my wedding day, he said, "From now on, whenever
you find yourself laying next to a woman, make sure
she's your wife." He used to talk like that.'

It was news from another age. 'Thanks, Frank. Not
much help now, though.'

'He also used to say, "If you don't know what to do,
don't do anything." I've often found that useful.'

'I wish I could. But Annie's nagging me. She wants
me to talk to him.'

'Take him fishing. You used to like that, and isn't
that what they tell you to do. "Be a pal to your son."'
There was no irony in Gatenby's voice.

Salter looked at him in surprise. 'I think you've got
something,' he said after a few moments. He stood
up and put on his jacket. 'Now I'm off to the bereaved
widow. I'll call in at noon if anyone wants me.'

'If anyone inquires, I'll tell them you're busy. You are, aren't you?'

When Albany Avenue north of Bloor Street was first developed, families were bigger and automobiles fewer, so the houses were built with lots of rooms and jammed close together. Now that many of the houses have been carved into flats, the street is permanently full of cars, and the few narrow driveways all have signs warning against parking in front of them.

Drecker's home turned out to be a duplex badly in need of paint and repairs. The two balconies, one on each storey, looked unsafe, and the steps up to the front porch were starting to rot. Salter pressed the bell and heard someone coming downstairs. A large blonde woman opened the door. Behind her, a tiny hallway led immediately to the stairs to the upper apartment.

'Mrs Drecker?'

'Yes. You the policeman? Come on up.' She had a loud, metallic voice that banged on Salter's eardrums.

He followed her up the stairs, along a bare, uncarpeted passage to a front room overlooking the street. The room was crammed with old furniture, including six ratty armchairs, much of it, Salter guessed, lodged there until it could be sold. A few dusty-looking pictures hung on the walls, and in the centre of the ceiling hung a huge bronze chandelier with a single light-bulb in one of its sockets.

'You want a soft drink? I don't have anything else,' she asked. She was in her mid-forties, dressed in a white linen tunic and sandals. Her yellow hair was braided around her head and her face was bare of make-up. The overall impression was of cleanliness: she looked sauna'd and scrubbed to the bone in contrast to the dilapidated paintwork and wallpaper of her home.

Salter declined the soft drink and produced his notebook. 'Mrs Drecker. You just got back to Toronto yesterday?'

'That's right. I was out west on holiday.'

They sat in facing armchairs. She folded her hands in her lap, looking no more disturbed than if she were responding to a public opinion pollster.

'Where, exactly?'

'Banff. The Solar Inn. It's a health camp. I go there every year.

That accounted for the shining look. 'Mrs Drecker, we have to consider the possibility that your husband's death wasn't an accident. Did he have any serious enemies to your knowledge? Any quarrels, or feuds? Any business deals that might have brought him up against people who would do something like this?'

She brushed the suggestion aside with a gesture. He wasn't a fence, if that's what you mean, though he knew a couple. He didn't mind where the stuff came from (though he liked to *know*), as long as he could make a nice profit. But he didn't deal in the kind of thing that would be worth lifting – jewellery or silver. He stuck to furniture and he stayed inside the law, though he would swindle you if he could.' She spoke of her husband without malice, as an interesting character she had known.

'Had he "swindled" anyone lately that you know

off?' he asked. There seemed no need to beat about the bush.

She shook her head. 'Not in a big way that I know of. When I say "swindled", I mean his idea of a good deal was to buy an old Ontario dresser from a bankrupt farmer for ten dollars and sell it for five hundred.'

And this was everyone's idea of Drecker. 'Doesn't everyone know about the value of stuff like that, nowadays?' he asked.

'You'd be surprised. There's still good pickings around here if you keep your eyes open.'

'And he did?'

'We both did. A lot of stuff these days comes out of garage sales. People moving house. We went round them together – I've got a good eye, myself, and most weekends we picked up a truckload. We usually found three or four things we could put through the shop, and the rest of it we'd get rid of at our own sales.'

'You *held* garage sales?'

'Sure. About once a month.'

'Where?'

'Different places. Lots of garage sales are phoney, didn't you know that? All you need is a place – a vacant lot will do – that you can rent for a few dollars. You can put up a lot of signs, and everyone comes looking for a bargain.'

Bunch of crooks, thought Salter, and made a mental note to tell Annie, who was fond of going round the neighbourhood sales on Saturday mornings. 'I gather you helped your husband run the store?' he asked.

She shook her head. 'We were partners, but I

never went near the store when it was open. I have
my own life.'

'Were you surprised at the news?'

'Sure I was surprised. Cyril was good at looking
after number one. Besides, no one ever threatened
him that I know of. As I said, he wasn't big league.'

Was she stone deaf, he wondered? Her voice
seemed to be coming from an old gramophone,
turned up to full volume. 'Why was he in the store
that night? Did he often stay out all night?'

'I don't know, probably a woman. Look, Inspector,
Cyril and I were partners. We got married ten years
ago, but it didn't take, if you know what I mean. We
didn't live together as man and wife after a few
months. But, as I say, I've got a good eye, and I was
useful to him. Besides, it was my money that set him
up. So we became partners, legally. We still lived
here but we left each other alone. We had separate
rooms, and sometimes I cooked a meal – though I
don't take much to that side of marriage, either – but
mostly we went our separate ways. It worked out well
for me. I play bridge, I practise yoga and go to health
classes, and I have my own friends.'

All with soft, low voices, Salter hoped, unless they
got together in a bomb shelter. 'You say, "some
woman". Did your husband have many woman
friends?' Other people's lives, or 'lifestyles', always
sound weird if you think your own is normal.

'One at a time, usually. He never brought them
here. That was our agreement. Separate lives. He
used the room over the store, but I always knew who
it was.'

'And who was it, lately?'

'Someone who worked in a furniture store at the other end of Bloor Street. Most of his women came through the trade.' Drecker's women might have been a hobby he had, like keeping exotic pets.

'You know her name?'

'It's above the phone in the kitchen. Hold on.' She disappeared into the back of the apartment and reappeared with a slip of paper in her hand. 'Julia Costa,' she said. 'You want her address?'

Salter took it down, checking it against the same address Nelson had given him. A small world. 'Will your husband's death change things very much for you, Mrs Drecker? You don't seem very upset.' What would the signs of grief be in Boadicea?

'Don't I?' She said nothing for a long time. Then: 'I told you, Inspector, Cyril and I were partners. I'm sorry he's dead, but I may be better off because of it. We insured each other and I'll own the business now, so in that way I'll be ahead of the game. On the other hand, it's been convenient for me sometimes as well as for him to be officially married to someone.' She let the remark hang in the air. 'I've been thinking. I'll have to reorganize myself. Yes, I'm sorry Cyril is dead, but I have no deep feelings about it.'

That seemed to be that. 'You'll be staying here for a while?'

'Yes. I own this building now, as well as the shop. I might sell it and move a little closer to my health club. I don't know. I'll be staying here for a few months, anyway.'

Salter stood up and put away his notebook. A thought seemed to strike him. 'What about your husband's assistant? How long has he been working in the store?' He tried to sound casual, ticking off the routine questions.

'Dennis? A year or so. Why?'

'He didn't seem to like your husband.'

'No. He didn't.'

Salter waited for some more.

'You've met him,' Mrs Drecker said. 'He's a pansy. Cy made fun of him, but Dennis wouldn't hurt a fly.'

'What about his friend?'

'What about him?'

'Would he?'

'Because he's gay, you mean?' She was belligerent, challenging.

'For Christ's sake, Salter thought. You started this.

'Whether he's straight, gay, or anything else,' he said.

'I don't know. I've never met him. I doubt it. If Dennis is harmless, his friend is, too, I would think.'

She's probably just defending alternative lifestyles, Salter guessed, having dropped out of the housewife role herself. He nodded to finish the interview, and started down the stairs. It was time for lunch with Jenny.

'Miss Schumann is expecting you. She said she'd be right down,' the assistant said. A nice young girl with a pear-shaped figure and her hair in a bun, an old-fashioned type who reminded Salter of the trainee librarians of his youth. Salter thanked her and walked round the store.

Jenny Schumann specialized in antique silver. Her shop took up the ground floor of a converted house; above it was a shop that sold old maps; the third floor Jenny had converted into an apartment for her own use. She had bought the house for thirty thousand dollars in the Fifties and remodelled it herself. It was now worth three-quarters of a million. Her store was like the chapel of a radical modern religion where the artifacts of an older faith were on display. The rug was rich and dark; the white walls were pierced by several small windows, each of which was lit from within to make a showcase to display a teapot (Georgian, $10,000) or a silver and lead glass desk set (about 1860, English, slight chip, $1,500). On one wall, a row of locked glass cases held a lot of small objects, snuff-boxes and such. The other merchandise was set out on appropriate altars. A coffee service with sharp edges was centred on a long, black, highly-polished table, also for sale. Two objects that were either vases or giants' mead cups were displayed on what looked, to Salter's surprise, like a battered card-table, but turned out to be a 'coaching table' (probably early 19c). In all, about a dozen pieces of expensive furniture displayed a large fortune in silver objects, mostly designed for eating and drinking.

While he waited for Jenny, Salter amused himself by pricing the merchandise, playing the game he usually played in these circumstances, called 'Do I have any taste, of any kind whatsoever?' Because of the one on display in the window, he concentrated on teapots, of which there were three for sale. After looking at all three several times in turn, he had no trouble rejecting a Victorian horror, valuable because of its weight, no doubt, but with none of the quiet classical good lines of the other two, Salter told himself. But he could not decide between these two,

239

one of which was square in design, and the other
bulbous.

'Which one do you like?' asked Jenny, who had
appeared beside him.

Salter decided not to play. 'That one,' he said,
pointing to the Victorian monstrosity, and began
preparing his defence, the view of the common man
who likes a bit of decoration on his teapot.

'You have exquisite taste, Charlie. That's the best
thing in the store.'

You can't win, he thought, but he accepted the
compliment as his by right. He gave her a hug, and
helped her on with her coat. He had booked a table
at the café in Hazelton Lanes, and they arrived early
enough to be given a place in the corner. As usual,
she made it the focus of the restaurant. Pairs of
women had watched them come in and then turned
to each other to wonder what the connection would
be between them. It was not her beauty, although it
was from her that Salter had discovered how attractive a woman of fifty could be. She was carefully made
up (Annie had explained to him once how it was
done), and the effect, as he said to Annie, was like a
softly-lit painting, which made Annie laugh out loud.
Dark hair worn long, with enough grey in it to admit
her age; she was tall and thin, and she liked velvet.
Today the colour was black, with a lot of gold jewellery. Dark grey stockings with, Salter noted, very
pretty black and gold shoes. He had a thing about
shoes.

She was rich, of course, but other people are rich
without having her aura, like, he thought, like – like
– a queen who has been elected. Content with his

simile, and aware of the eyes of the world, he bent over and kissed her. She smoked too much, and her breath smelled faintly of seaweed, but Salter didn't mind that either.

'My knight in shining sackcloth,' she declared in a charred voice that reminded him by contrast of Mrs Drecker.

'What do you mean?' he asked, surprised. He was wearing his normal outfit of grey flannel trousers, dark blue tweed jacket, white shirt and blue tie with red geese. 'Something wrong?' he asked, looking down at himself.

'Wrong? What could be wrong?' she said. 'The same clothes you've had on for fifteen years to my knowledge. How could they be wrong?'

'I bought this coat last year in Eaton's. It was on sale,' Salter protested, and then the penny dropped. 'You've been talking to Annie,' he said. 'Well, these are my plain clothes, see. They are the ones that make me inconspicuous so no one can tell I'm a cop, see.'

She made a charade of nearly falling off her chair laughing. 'Are you kidding? Half the people in this café think you are about to arrest me.'

Salter looked around and a number of heads clicked back into place.

'What do you want me to wear?' he asked. 'A gold windbreaker? Earrings? You want me to get my hair done in ringlets? I'm a square, for God's sake.'

'No, Charlie, no. Just a coat that fits you. And a decent haircut. And even squares don't use the term any more.'

'I just got this haircut. It cost me ten bucks.'

'On sale?' She sat grinning at his wounded pride. 'Tell Annie I tried,' she said. 'Anyway, who cares. If Annie doesn't want you, I'll take you, Eaton's basement wardrobe and all. It's just your body I'm interested in. Superman in his Clark Kent rig, that's you.'

Salter looked smug. The polite greetings had been exchanged; the conversation could now proceed.

'Tell me about antique dealers,' he asked. 'I'm investigating a death by fire of an antique dealer and I'd like to get filled in on how he operated.'

'Cyril Drecker?'

He nodded.

'Not really in my world, although I knew him slightly. He wasn't an antique dealer. He was a second-hand dealer. There's a difference. Let's order first.' There was no Anglo-Saxon business with Jenny of trying to catch the waiter's eye with a genteel wave of the menu. 'Waiter,' she called in a Tallulah Bankhead summons, and he came, smiling, immediately.

She ordered fish and a glass of white wine. Salter ordered a veal and partridge pie, at her insistence, and beer. When the drinks came, he swallowed half his beer at a gulp as she watched admiringly.

'So greedy,' she said, making it sound like a sexual attribute.

He wiped his mouth with the back of his hand so as to be in character, and started again. 'You knew Drecker,' he prompted.

'Very slightly. I bought a Victorian hip-flask from him once. A touch of sleaze about him, I thought. I made sure I got full provenance.'

'Why would he sell it to you?'

'Because it was too good for him to handle. I imagine he did that with a lot of stuff.'

'You mean that he would pick up something dirt cheap, sell it to you for three times what he paid, and you sell it for twice as much again?' he asked, teasing her about the fat profits she made.

She threw the tease back. 'That's right. My father used to say, "You buy something for a dollar, sell it for two and make one per cent profit." He thought people who made twenty per cent profit were greedy.' She made a face at him.

'Did Drecker have a reputation, a bad one, in the trade?'

She shrugged. 'He might have. I don't hear much talk. The dealers I know don't sit around in some antiquaries' handout, swapping thieves' gossip, Charlie. If I have any doubts, I just don't buy. If there are any fences in the trade, I don't know them. Try your pawn squad.'

'What about your own professional association? Would they know?'

'I doubt if he was a member of the Canadian Antique Dealers' Association, Charlie. We're a choosy lot. Besides, I told you, Drecker was a second-hand dealer, not an antique dealer.'

'What's the difference?'

'Antiques are at least a hundred years old – that's the difference. And we don't need a licence to operate.'

'Second-hand dealers do.'

'Sure. And they have to register everything that comes off the street with you, the police, and they can't sell it for fifteen clear days. Ask the pawn squad.'

'I will. I should have already. But what about the guy himself? Did you get any kind of impression? As a' man, I mean.'

'What do you mean?'

'I think he was a bit of a womanizer,' Salter said.

'Was he? I can't help you on that one, either. You know me – I'm only interested in short-haired police-men. Are you looking for a love-triangle?'

Salter shook his head. 'I don't know what I'm looking for.'

The food arrived and Salter got on with his pie while Jenny stabbed at bits of her fish.

'Interrogation over, Charlie? Can you put the lunch on expenses now?' she asked after a few minutes.

'I'll pay for it myself, with cash, so that Annie won't see the charge slip and find out about us.' He leered at her, beginning the game again, and pushed his empty plate to one side. Jenny nodded to the hover-ing waiter, who slid into gear immediately to bring them their coffee.

'Would that we could.' She sighed theatrically. 'Which reminds me about Annie. I saw a Bristol glass decanter to match the two she already has. It's perfect – original stopper and everything. The gold is a bit faded but the label is clear – "Hollands". She has "Brandy" and "Rum", doesn't she?'

'Yes. Where did you see it?'

'I'll give you the address. It's in Hamilton.'

'Hamilton? I thought all the real antique dealers were around *this* area. Hamilton's all steelmills, isn't it?'

'Nice of you to say so, Charlie, but it isn't true. Two of the best dealers in the province are in

Streetsville and St Catherines. The dealer in Hamilton wants three hundred, and he'll keep it until you can get down there.'

'Done.' What a stroke of luck, he thought. Christmas for Salter was infected, poisoned, every year by his inability to find the perfect present for Annie. He had no confidence in his own taste, but he felt a compulsion to surprise her on Christmas morning with exactly the right toy. He had tried spending a lot of money, but that hadn't worked. She took the matched set of cow-hide luggage back to Simpson's and bought a washing machine instead. The clothes he bought didn't fit, and the jewellery was ugly (although he had once bought her a ring she liked, so he bought her a ring every year for the next five years until she asked him to stop).

Solving the problem with a certain winner this early in the year would mean he could look forward to Christmas like everyone else. All he had to do now was find the right book, the ideal record, and a big bottle of bath oil of a kind that she had never used before. A week's work, but a piece of cake now that the chief problem was solved.

'I said "how's everything at home"?' Jenny asked, kicking his ankle. 'Wake up, lover.'

'Sorry. Fine. No. It's not so good.' And he told her about Angus. 'Annie thinks I should talk to him,' he said. 'But I don't know what the hell there is to say. So he's looking at dirty books. So what? It doesn't mean he's a sex maniac.'

'Is that what Annie said?'

'Not exactly.'

'What did she say exactly?'

'She said she wants me to help him put it into a context. That's the word she used.'

'What did you say?'

'I cut her off. I said I'd think about it.'

'Charlie, maybe she doesn't mean it that simplistically. Annie isn't silly. She knows how things have changed.'

'What are you talking about?'

'You're a policeman, Charlie. Gorgeous, but a policeman. Maybe just a little bit conservative. Couldn't Annie be saying the opposite of what you think.'

'I still don't know what you are talking about.'

'Look. If I caught – oh Christ, "caught" – if I found any skin books in one of my kids' cupboards, I'd leave them there. They're his, aren't they? But I would ask him what he got out of them. Then I have a feeling we'd all look at them together, if it didn't bother him.'

'You'd *what?*'

'I'd look at them with him. Then maybe we could get something going about pornography, sex, love – the whole bit.'

'But Angus is fourteen! Anyway, you don't have any kids.'

'If I did, I wouldn't go hairy over a couple of skin magazines.'

'I'm not. Annie is.'

'Oh, for God's sake, don't be so damned dense. Sorry. Look, Charlie, it sounds to me as if Angus is as frightened of you as you were of your father. Frightened to tell you what is happening to him. Your house is full of taboos, and what Annie wants you to do is not intimidate Angus any more. Talk to him. Talk to him like a human being.' Jenny sipped her coffee, slightly agitated.

Salter was very disturbed. Here was all the trendy psycho-jargon that was the staple of the Saturday newspaper columnists, in articles that Salter regularly jeered at, coming to him now from someone real, over the age of twenty-nine. Could it be true?

'You mean Annie and Angus, and maybe even Seth, are waiting for me to relax and talk about sex?'

'It sounds like it to me.'

'Maybe they talk now, behind my back?'

'Maybe.'

'Then why hasn't Annie said anything, done anything?' Salter asked, trying to find an alternative villain.

'She probably has, but you always cut her off. I don't know, I'm not there.'

'You make me feel like a bloody Victorian.'

'I think the boys see the policeman in you more than the father.'

'Thank you, Ann Landers.'

'Look at you now. Let's talk about something else. Who have you arrested lately?'

But Salter was too disturbed to give much attention to any other topic. After a few minutes, Jenny got up to go. She looked around the restaurant, then kissed him on the cheek. 'Whatever else you do, Charlie, tell Angus you love him. If you do, that is. Say "I love you, Angus." See what happens. It's the big thing in pop psychology. That, and touching.'

'I can't do that,' Salter said.

'Why not?'

'I'm a Canadian, he said.

She laughed and patted his cheek.

Salter sat at the table for a few more minutes, feeling too much alone in a changing world. Then he walked through Yorkville to his car and sat in the parking lot for a few minutes. But the mood hadn't passed when he drove off to meet Nelson in his apartment.

'Here you are,' Nelson said. 'Everybody he's dealt with in the last three months. All the ones who demanded receipts, that is.' Nelson had made a neat list. He had calmed down from his distress of the day before, but he looked as if he had not slept.

Salter took the list and glanced at it. 'Any word from your friend?' he asked casually.

'No. Have you?'

'Not yet. He hasn't shown up for work yet. Tell me who these people are. How did Drecker come to deal with them?'

'They are specialty dealers,' Nelson said. 'This one, for instance, is an interior decorator on Davenport Road. He buys any garden ornaments we get.'

'What was this for?' Salter pointed to an item of two thousand dollars sold to a dealer in Yorkville.

'I'm not sure. He's Toronto's biggest dealer in Japanese prints, and I never saw anything around our store he would be interested in. You'll have to ask him yourself. Drecker might have got something from an old Japanese gentleman who's been coming in lately. He bought a wooden box from us three weeks ago, and he's been back twice while I've been in the shop. Drecker used to deal with him upstairs – he always did his important deals up there – and he

never told me anything about him and I never asked.
But after the last time, Drecker told me to say he was
out if the Japanese ever came back. Maybe the guy
wanted his money back, something Drecker never
did.'

'If Drecker were involved in anything crooked,
really crooked, would you know about it?'

'Probably not. He liked me to think he was always
wheeling and dealing, but I think that was mostly BS.
He would never take any risks. He was too wary not
to cover himself six ways at once, even when he was
cheating on his income tax. Still, as I say, if he was on
to anything big he wouldn't brag about it to me. But
I doubt if Drecker was mixed up with the mob.'

'Is the mob into antiques, Mr Nelson?'

'I thought they were into everything.'

'You've been watching too much American television. There's a five-year lag between the US and
Canada, in crime as well as culture. It gives us a
chance to know what to expect. We watch television,
too, to see what ideas our local villains might be
picking up. Do you do any dealing on your own?'
Salter asked suddenly.

'Sometimes. I pick up things at auctions, and
Drecker used to let me sell them through the store,
for a percentage of the profit. Nothing very much,
but I *am* trying to learn the business, and Drecker
didn't pay much. He said I ought to pay *him*, as if I
was indentured or something.' Nelson stared at
Salter, inviting him to share his astonishment.

'Why did you stay there? You didn't like him much,
did you?'

'I loathed him, I told you. But look in the papers.

There aren't many advertisements for "Antique Dealer's Assistant Wanted". I was learning something, and getting to know a few of the other dealers. As soon as anything better cropped up I would have moved. In the meantime I had to eat, and if things got too rough I could always go back to my old trade.'

'Which is?'

'I was a librarian at Douglas College. I left because I couldn't stand the politics.'

'Politics? In a college library?'

'Really. You have no idea.'

'Well, well. Thank God we don't have any of that in the Force.'

Salter put the list back in his pocket. 'I'll have a word with some of these people. Apart from this lot, you know of no other enemies Drecker had? He hadn't gotten into any arguments lately?'

'The man I told you about, the one who remodelled the bathroom.'

'Darling?'

Nelson nodded. 'And me. But you've checked up on me, I suppose.'

'Not yet. Do you ever go camping, Mr Nelson?'

Nelson grinned. 'You mean locally, or the great outdoors?'

'I mean back-packing, Mr Nelson.' It was not a serious inquiry, for Salter found it hard to visualize Nelson waking beside Lake Onatonga, greeting the dawn with a cheer.

'Ah ha!' he said. 'You've found a clue. Someone left a tin of Eddie Bauer's waterproof matches at the scene of the crime.'

'You *do* go camping, then?'

'I did once, Inspector. Once and once only. Jake was keen on canoeing when I met him, and he persuaded me to go on a trip with him this spring into Algonquin Park. What a weekend! To start with, Jake insisted on being very authentic. No artificial firelighters, all dried food – have you ever lived on dried foods for three days? When we came out I had to have four jelly doughnuts immediately. Jake didn't think we should take anything to drink, either – no wine, no gin, nothing. We had a row about that. Can you imagine the voyageurs as teetotallers? I finally insisted on a mickey of scotch for medicinal purposes. I figured one large, very large, drink at night, just for me while Jake drank his bark tea or whatever. Of course, when I opened it the first night he offered to keep me company – without approving of it, mind you – so there wasn't enough to last the trip. The whole expedition was like that. First there were the mosquitoes. At every portage we had to drape ourselves in nets and carry the canoe through thick clouds of them. At night we huddled in this little survival tent, listening to them on the outside, trying to get at us. I was covered in bumps and itching like the owner of a flea circus.' Nelson was getting more and more animated. 'And filthy! My God, does anyone realize how dirty the great outdoors is? What with mosquito repellent, the smoke from the cooking fires, and the grease – everything that isn't dried is fried, Inspector – I've never felt so squalid. And Jake was unbearable. He had bought a lot of equipment – Swiss army knives and gadgets for smoking fish and the like – which he wanted to try out. It nearly finished us, I can tell you. I took a week to get back

to normal and we agreed that he and I would never
share the outdoors again. Yes, I've tried camping.'

And you've told this story a few times at parties.
'And your friend Hauser is an experienced camper
now, I take it?'

'I suppose so.' Nelson quietened down and began
to stammer slightly as he realized the message he had
conveyed to Salter. 'Why? Did you find a clue? Lots
of people go camping, you know.'

'I know. I'm asking them all.' Salter put away his
notebook.

'Have you checked up on my alibi yet?'

'Not yet.' And there isn't much need if you are so
keen on it, Salter thought. Was he trying to change
the subject? 'I still have to see this Julia Costa. I'll do
that this afternoon or tomorrow. Have you spoken to
her yet?'

'Oh, sure. But I really was with her. She was
wonderful.'

That word again. To Salter's generation a 'wonderful person' meant Mahatma Gandhi or Schweitzer in
Africa. You expected to meet maybe two in a lifetime.
Now it just meant 'nice' and he wished teachers in
grade school would warn students against it, as he
had been forbidden to use 'nice' by his seventh-grade
teacher. Salter tried for an unsettling remark.
'Anyway,' he said, smiling, 'as Drecker's girlfriend
she would hardly cover for his killer, would she?'

'You know about that, do you? Well I don't care.
She's a wonderful person.'

'That's nice,' Salter said, and left.

He looked over the list before he drove off. Most
of them could be left to Gatenby, but he decided to

call on the Japanese specialist himself to find out what
was worth two thousand dollars, and that put the
interior decorator on Davenport on his route back to
the office. He drove north on Spadina across Bloor
and became involved in the tangle of one-way streets
that is designed to protect the area from people who
wish to drive through it, streets that change direction
at every intersection, so that navigating them is like
tacking against a high wind. Eventually he fought his
way through to Avenue Road and turned into Cumberland Street, where he made a slightly illegal turn
into the municipal parking lot.

He found MacLeod's gallery tucked away in an
alley. There was none of the hurly-burly of commerce
here. This was a gallery with a dozen oriental-looking
pictures hung on the walls with small price labels
beneath them. Salter spent his usual few minutes
looking at the pictures, trying to see what made the
difference in desirability between those priced at fifty
dollars and one on sale for three thousand. He
decided he liked the three-thousand-dollar picture
best, but only just; say, twenty dollars' worth more.

In the middle of the gallery, behind a desk, a
bushy-haired man was reading invoices. He looked
too young to be the owner of what was obviously a
very successful business (the gallery had half-a-dozen
people in it), but he was sorting paper with authority.

'Mr MacLeod?'

'Inspector?'

'Am I that obvious?'

'I've been expecting you.'

'Have you now,' Salter said, and waited.

'Why don't you sit down?' MacLeod said, gesturing

to a chair beside him. 'We can talk here, if you like. Hajime will look after the customers.' He pointed to a young Japanese who was laying out pictures on a large bench at the back of the gallery.

It was not the place Salter would have chosen, but MacLeod seemed to have a quiet voice, so no one would take any interest in their conversation.

'You know what I've come for?'

'Drecker. I read about it in the paper. I only dealt with him once but it was a big deal for him and I expect you found it in his books. Right?'

Salter nodded.

'He offered me a collection of Japanese prints and I bought some of them. I sold the lot in one go in a way I thought was odd, but now, Inspector, has turned out to be even odder.'

'A good deal for you?'

'I didn't even display them. But the man who bought them has disappeared, hasn't he?'

'You tell me, Mr Macleod.'

'Ah! You don't know about him? Well, I'll tell you. His name is Gene Tanabe – I've sold stuff to him for years, ever since I opened. He's a dealer himself, but one of those who hates selling anything he really likes so he's got a pretty good private collection. I called him when this lot came in from Drecker and he flew in from Vancouver the next day and bought them all. He wanted to know where I got them so that he could get the others, and I gave him Drecker's address. He was very excited.'

'Do you know why? Collector's mania?'

'No.' MacLeod savoured what he was about to say. 'He said he knew the man who once owned them.'

'Did he?' Salter said, digesting this bit. 'Did he, indeed?'

'I asked him how Drecker had got hold of them and he said that was what he wanted to know, too. I asked him if the prints had been stolen and he said, perhaps, but he didn't think so. That was the last I saw of him. When I heard about Drecker, I called Gene's store in Vancouver, but they told me he was in Toronto, had been here a week. I thought that was a bit strange because he always calls on me. We are sort of friends now.'

'Could you describe him, Mr MacLeod?'

'About seventy-five, conservatively dressed, umbrella – the whole old Japanese gentleman bit.'

'Accent?'

'Oh no. He's a Canadian. He was born here, I'm sure – a nisei, at least.'

Salter formulated a question that was puzzling him.

'Prints, Mr MacLeod. I know they number prints nowadays when they run off a limited edition, but I thought that was a recent practice. Were these prints numbered? If not, how did Tanabe recognize them?'

'Do you know anything about Japanese art, Inspector?'

Salter shook his head. Or Canadian, or any other kind.

MacLeod opened a thick volume like a catalogue of wallpaper samples. Each page was a plastic envelope containing a picture. 'Let me give you a short course,' he said. 'Here we have a print by one of the best-known of the Ukiyo-e artists, Kuniyoshi, printed about 1840. It's a print of characters in a Kabuki drama. Now, look, here. These marks were not on the original print, they are seals put on by collectors who owned the picture.' He pointed to some oriental-looking signs on the corner of the print.

'You mean you guys stamp every print?'

MacLeod's eyes glazed. 'No, no,' he said. 'These marks were only added by Japanese collectors of the past – the practice is frowned on now – not by every Tom, Dick and Harry over here. Let me get on. We can generally identify a print by its markings, then, but look at this, too.' He turned to a block of photographs. 'Here are six impressions of the same picture. You see how they differ? The results vary so much in light and shade that they are virtually all different pictures, and we can identify them as such.' MacLeod started to leaf through the book. 'Let me find two I can show you by way of comparison,' he said.

Salter said, 'There's an interesting one.' It was a picture of a couple enjoying each other in a position Angus would have recognized from the magazines he had been studying. Behind the couple, two ladies were seated on the floor. They seemed to be either applauding or praying. 'Nothing new under the sun,' Salter said. 'How much is that?'

MacLeod seemed surprised. 'You want to buy it?' he asked. 'Seven hundred and fifty.' He looked at Salter curiously.

'No, no, just joking,' Salter said, realizing what MacLeod must be wondering.

MacLeod closed the book and waited for Salter's next question.

'So Drecker sold you some prints, Tanabe came to

town and bought them off you, claiming he recognized them, and disappeared. Right? How many prints were there altogether, and why didn't you buy them all?'

'They were a mixed lot. None of them was very valuable, but the ones I bought were by far the best – a Hiroshige, a couple of Shunko hosoban – '

'Could you write those down for me?' Salter interrupted.

MacLeod scribbled on a piece of paper. 'And three others,' he continued. 'You want their names?'

Salter nodded. 'What about the ones you didn't buy?'

'There were about ten more, but they were all in pretty poor condition.'

'Where would Drecker have got rid of them?'

'He *might* have sent them to an auction house. And a lot of antique stores carry a few Japanese prints.'

Salter thought about his next question. 'Was there anything to connect these prints? With each other, I mean.'

'You are asking me to speculate about them? About whether they were a collection?'

'Yes,' Salter said. 'That's what I would like you to do. Speculate about them for me.'

'They all had the same collector's seals on the back,' MacLeod offered.

'What does that mean?'

'It means they all passed through the same collector's hands. But not necessarily at the same time.'

'Nothing else struck you about them, as a group.'

'Like what?'

Salter shook his head. 'I don't know, Mr MacLeod.'

He did, though. A bit of Sherlock Holmes stuff from MacLeod, like: 'These prints must have been assembled in a suburb of Yokohama in 1913, by a woman who had served at court . . .'

MacLeod waited patiently.

'Did he offer you anything other than prints?' Salter searched his mind for the word 'netsuke' but was unsure how to pronounce it.

'No.'

Now Salter had run out of questions. He stood up. 'That was the only time you saw Tanabe, then? And you have no Toronto address for him?'

'That's right and he hasn't been home for a week.'

'If he appears, would you let me know right away? You can tell him I'm looking for him,' he added, to get MacLeod off the hook of being disloyal to his friend.

'I don't think Gene could have anything to do with Drecker's store burning down. I'd vouch for him.'

'All I'm trying to do is find out what Drecker was up to lately, and with whom. Anyone who has dealt with him, like you, might be able to give me a lead.'

Now, Salter thought, as he walked to his car, I have another one who might have a grudge against Drecker: Gene Tanabe.

He made one more call, on the interior decorator. This one specialized, as he said, in 'tarting up old town houses', and he often included the garden in his design. Drecker routinely sold him any stone or concrete ornaments that he picked up.

Salter thanked him and checked his watch. He had begun a second, expensive half-hour in the parking lot, so he decided to treat himself to a bowl of goulash soup in the Coffee Mill, for Salter's taste, the best food in the area. While he ate, he listened to four American tourists taking the weekend off from being mugged in Detroit, enthusing about how clean Toronto was. Toronto the Clean, he thought. It's not much, but am improvement on Toronto the Good.

'Frank,' he said, back at the office, 'call the Vancouver cops and ask them if they know of a Gene Tanabe, pronounced "Tarnarbay". Here's his address. And call the pawn squad and see if anything is known about Drecker. And I want you to check up on this list of dealers – all of them did business with Drecker in the last three months. Leave those two, I've just seen those, but find out if any of the others had any unfinished business with Drecker. Do it yourself. Take the day tomorrow and work out a little story about having to wind up Drecker's legal affairs or some such horseshit, and watch for any funny reactions, all right?'

'I'll enjoy that, Charlie. I'll tell them I've got 'em on a list. I'll tell them I found the list in Drecker's safe-deposit box with crosses against some of the names.'

Salter laughed. 'Don't fuck around too much, Frank. You don't look the part for the heavy brigade. Just see if you can smell anything.'

'Right you are. Can I have a car?'

'Okay.' Salter made out a requisition.

Gatenby grinned with glee. 'Just like the TV. "Gatenby here, Homicide." This is great. I haven't been outside for months on a job. Should I pack a rod?'

The pawn squad called back in five minutes with the information that Drecker was licensed, that nothing was known about him, and that he had registered a box containing assorted knick-knacks and pictures, value (estimated) $200, six weeks before, offered to him by a casual vendor.

Well, well, Salter thought. Does that put Drecker in the clear in whatever was going on? Not necessarily. Nelson had emphasized that Drecker was a careful man, careful enough to cover himself if something went wrong.

He spent the rest of the afternoon writing up his report, but before he went home he called on a colleague in the Homicide department, a man who had offered him a hand on his last case. Harry Wycke seemed pleased to see him and put to one side the paper he was working on.

'What's it these days, Charlie?' he asked. 'Another Montreal murder? You'll be doing us out of business.'

His tone was friendly, and it crossed Salter's mind that he had meant to invite Wycke and his wife to the house after their last chat but he had put it off too long, until the detective would have been surprised by it. He told Wycke first of the case he was on, then, self-mockingly, of the trouble he was having with the screen door, and finally about Angus. This last problem made him feel that he was lacking something, that if he were a proper father he would know what to do without going around asking people.

Wycke reassured him immediately. 'I don't know, Charlie. Raising kids, relating to them or whatever the bullshit term is nowadays, is bloody hard. Every

Christly magazine has got an article on it, all different, but if you look around, it's gotta be mostly luck. I've got girls, so Shirley worries about all that. I'm the father figure; I just have to be careful they don't catch penis envy off me. But with boys I think the big risk would be trying to avoid all the wrong things that were done to you, you know what I mean? But how can you tell? I mean, look at Wilcott's kids. He did nothing for them – nothing. I don't think he even likes them. Straight A students, both of them, one's going to be a doctor and the other one's studying architecture. Then there's Joe Loomis's kids. You remember how Joe used to bore the ass off us in the canteen about how he was raising them? No, you wouldn't. You never ate there. Well, Joe started with Spock and bought a new book every year. Taught them all about liking themselves, stuff like that. So what happens? Poor old Joe is pinning all his hopes on the youngest one now – the other two have gone off to find themselves. They didn't finish school, can't hold a job – nothing. It's all in a play we did at school about a salesman who committed suicide. Nothing's changed. I don't think it matters a fuck what you do.'

'I need to try, Harry. Gatenby said I should take him fishing.' Salter watched Wycke for any trace of a smile.

'You like fishing? I never thought of you in the great outdoors, Charlie. A real townie, I figured.'

'I am. I don't spend my leaves canoeing the great Nottawasaga, but I like fishing and I never get to go. Got any suggestions? For a place, I mean. I think I'll go for a weekend.'

Wycke leaned back in his chair. 'I've got a place,' he said. 'You know that.'

'I didn't know that, Harry,' Salter said, embarrassed. 'I didn't come here on the scrounge.'

'Well, I have. You can have it if you want.' Wycke's voice was neutral, uneager.

A silence had opened between them, but once raised, the subject had to be discussed.

'What kind of place is it? Do you ever rent it out?'

'No, I plead with people to use it, *if* they know what they are doing. I built the place myself, and it's not a cottage, it's a cabin. It's mosquito-proof, waterproof, and it has a Coleman stove for cooking, two Coleman lamps, and four bunks. No power, no water, just a shelter. But I'm careful who I let have it. You'd be surprised how many people think it sounds romantic, but when they get up there they are afraid to use the outhouse in case there's a bear hiding down below.'

Salter laughed. 'I'm not worried about bears snapping at my ass,' he said.

'So you can have it. But look, Charlie, don't come back and tell me you couldn't find the hot-water tap, will you? You get your water out of the river in a bucket. There are mice, spiders, big hairy bugs with two hundred legs, and at night it gets as cold as a witch's tit because it isn't insulated. There's a wood stove, but at this time of the year you'll wake up at four in the morning and see your breath. It doesn't have the woman's touch because my family don't like it. I do, though.'

Salter said, 'I worked at a fishing camp once on the English River near Kenora. We lived in cabins like that from April to October. I know how they work. Can I have it? I'll be able to show Angus how resourceful his old man is. Make up for not taking him to baseball and football games.'

'When? When do you want it?'

'The weekend after next if I can?'

'It's yours. Here.' Wycke opened a drawer. 'Map; list of instructions; I'll call the marina so they will let you have the boat; a picture of the cabin so you'll recognize it; and the key. There's one good rod up there, but you'll need to take up another one for the boy.'

'I appreciate it, Harry. Nice of you to let me have it.'

'No it isn't. The more people use it, the less chance it will become derelict. People get to know when a cabin isn't being used and start nosing around. Enjoy yourself and bring back a list of stuff that's missing or needs repairing.' He consulted a piece of paper. 'According to the last guy, you'll need naphtha, salt and toilet paper. There's a store at the marina.' He looked at Salter. 'Maybe if you like it we could go up together some time.'

'All right. Let's talk about it when I get back.'

Salter left, wondering if he would have been as generous in the same position.

On the way home, he made another attempt to get a wheel for the screen door at a hardware store on Yonge Street run by three New Zealanders. Usually resourceful, they were unable to help.

'All I can tell you is that you aren't alone,' the owner said. 'The last guy who broke his screen door decided to sell his house rather than try to get it fixed.' They all roared with laughter.

'I thought you might like to go fishing with me one weekend,' Salter said after supper.

Angus looked as startled as if Salter had proposed sky-diving together. 'With you?' he asked. 'We've never been before. I don't know how.'

'I do. Want to give it a try?'

Annie was looking at Angus so eagerly that he flinched. 'All right,' he said. 'When?'

'Next week. We'll go up Friday night and come back late on Sunday. This place is north of Parry Sound but we should get almost two days there.'

'What do I have to get ready?'

'I'll look after it all. There is some tackle up there and I can pick up the rest. We'll need some food.'

'I'll make chili and freeze it, and some hamburger patties – I'll freeze them, too, then all you have to do is cook them as they defrost. What do you want for breakfasts?' Annie asked.

Salter looked at her and she shut up, but she continued to look pleased.

When the dishes were done, Salter got out his notebook. 'What's a nisei?' he asked.

'A second-generation Japanese Canadian. Why?'

Salter told her.

'I know the gallery,' she said. 'He has some wonderful things. Now you tell me one. Where can I get some gnomes?'

'What?'

'Gnomes. You know, those plaster gnomes people

used to have in their gardens. They are "in" again and I have to dress up a fashionable garden for some stills tomorrow.'

Salter consulted his notebook. 'Try Inigo Robinson on Davenport,' he said. 'He specializes in gnomes.'

'How do you know?'

'It's just one of the things I know about,' Salter said. 'Now, about this weekend. You think I'm doing the right thing?'

'Oh yes, Charlie. You've never taken Angus or Seth away on their own. Don't worry about me. I need a weekend just to catch up.'

'Washing? Ironing?' Salter asked, surprised.

'No, at the studio. There's about six things going on and I'd like to get ahead of it if I can.'

'What will you do with Seth?'

'He's got a standing invitation to sleep over with his pal. Robbie. If not, I'll think of something. Now, did you get anywhere with the screen door yet?'

Salter picked up the paper. 'I'll phone Fred Staver. If he can't fix it, we may have to put the house up for sale.'

Annie recognized this for what it was, not an answer, but a flung gauntlet, and declined to pick it up.

Chapter Three

He had arranged to interview Drecker's girlfriend, Julia Costa, at work since she was alone there in the mornings. The shop was called Mary Lightfoot Interiors without punctuation, and it specialized in 'collections'. There was an Indian collection along one wall, a collection of glass furniture that Drecker's assistant would have approved of filled the centre of the room, and the back of the shop was devoted to a bamboo collection. Five or six smaller collections were grouped about the store, including one from the west, of chairs in the shape of saddles, and an 'Old Ontario' collection of iron and copper fireplace implements grouped around a pine mantel. The idea, as far as Salter could see, was for the customer to have a different collection in every room of the house. The prices were all in units of a hundred dollars, written out in script.

The woman who came forward as Salter entered was in her middle thirties. She wore a denim skirt and a top made of knitted string. She seemed to have glass slippers through which her feet showed, but Salter presumed they were plastic. She was tall, with a slightly Irish look about her face and hair – a very pale skin with what Salter thought of as greenery-yallery eyes and a lot of dark hair twisted into a rough bunch behind.

Salter showed her his identification and she took

him into a back room, leaving the door open so she could watch for customers.

'You want to know where Dennis was when the store burned down,' she said. 'He was with me.'

'You've been talking to him, of course.'

'Sure. He phoned last night. Shouldn't he have?'

'It doesn't matter.'

'Oh, I see. We could be in a conspiracy, of course.'

She seems nervous, Salter thought, but who doesn't when the inspector calls. 'But you aren't?' he asked.

'No. I think it was an accident, anyway.'

'Why?'

'Have you checked on Cy?'

'In what way?'

'You'll find out he's got a record. His last store burned down, too.'

'The Insurance Protection Bureau will come up with that one. You think he set this up?'

'I think it's likely and somehow he didn't get out of the way in time.'

Salter said nothing. The details of Drecker's death did not fit her idea, and yet she sounded genuinely convinced of it herself. He said, 'Let's get back to Dennis Nelson. Can you swear he was with you from one-fifteen onwards?'

'Yes, I can.' She leaned back and crossed her legs, looking at Salter.

Salter persisted. 'If he were sleeping on a sofa in the living-room – you have a sofa? – you wouldn't have known if he disappeared for a couple of hours, would you?'

'He wasn't on the sofa, he was in my bed, and I

would have known. As a matter of fact he kept me awake for two hours talking about Jake, his boyfriend, before we went to sleep.'

'Miss Costa, Nelson says he's bisexual. Are you lovers, like?' Salter tried his friendly bumpkin voice.

'No. It would have been OK with me, but that's neither here nor there. We've never made love. He says it would spoil our relationship – silly twit. He's a sweetheart and I love him and it's not the first time we've spent the night together when he's been upset. But, no, we aren't lovers. He may be the best friend I've got, though. I don't think he *is* bisexual, more's the pity.'

'It doesn't make for a very strong alibi, does it?'

'I've just thought of something. Dennis came in a cab. Find the driver and you'll know he arrived at my place, won't you?'

'That seems to cover Nelson. What about you?'

'How do you mean?'

'I'm looking for motives, Miss Costa. I'm told you were connected with Drecker.'

'Who told you that?' she said sharply. 'Not Dennis?'

'No. You for one, when you called him Cy. And Mrs Drecker.'

'So; all right, we were connected.'

'His mistress?'

She didn't answer for a few minutes. Then: 'What's a mistress, Inspector?'

If this was a game, then Salter had a few minutes to play. 'The regular sexual partner of a man who is married?' he offered.

'Not bad. He doesn't have to be married, though,

does he?' she said. 'What's the difference between a mistress and a lover?'

'Money, I guess.' It was now clear that Julia Costa was involved in some metaphorical throat-clearing.

'Then what's the difference between a mistress and a whore?' she asked, just before Salter got to this one himself.

'Not much. They both peddle it for money, but the whore works a lot harder.'

'Choose your term, then. I had sex with Drecker about once every two weeks.'

'For money?'

'He gave me money, yes.'

'It sounds very businesslike. Did you like him?'

'Does it? Yes, I did, He was a handsome man, Inspector. Has anyone told you that? He looked like Clark Gable with wavy hair. And he enjoyed himself. He reminded me of a guy I knew in Saskatoon, a guy called Big Red. Big Red owned six cabs and he lost them one night in a crap game, but he didn't shoot himself. He just laughed and went back to driving one of his own cabs, with a little pimping on the side. For Saskatoon, that's style. Cy was like that. He was a bit of a crook, maybe, but he enjoyed himself. He liked winning on a deal, but he could lose, too. He liked women, and in Toronto that isn't all that common.'

'You mean that everyone you know here is gay?' Salter asked incredulously.

'No, just the opposite. The gays I know like women, but the others, the disco crowd I've met, don't seem to. They want you, of course, but when they get you they don't seem to enjoy it much. They

frighten easy, too. Cy didn't. He liked me.' She
moved both hands up to adjust her hair at the back,
lifting her breasts within the string vest. The gesture
reminded Salter of a colleague in Homicide who liked
to stand with one hand on his hip, holding back his
jacket just enough so that the customers could see the
butt of his gun.

'His wife doesn't share your opinion,' he said.

'His wife doesn't like sex,' Julia Costa said. 'They
found that out early, back in the days when you had
to get married to find out. But even *that* Cy didn't
turn into a big deal. I think he married her because
she held out on him, and when he realized what she
was like, he just took the loss and found other women.
She didn't care, and they got along well together. He
said she was a smart businesswoman.'

'I see.' Salter the more-or-less contented husband
had been appalled in his soul at the emptiness of
Drecker's flat, the lack of food, warmth or sex, but as
Julia Costa explained it, it sounded plausible that
Drecker would not have cared. Another world.

'What about Nelson?' he asked. 'Drecker was
pretty unpleasant to him, wasn't he?' He was having
trouble with the image of Cyril Drecker, the salt of
the earth.

'Not really. He teased him, is all. He liked Dennis,
I think, but for Cy, Dennis was someone to have fun
with. I'm not defending Cy, but he wasn't mean or
vicious. If Dennis had laughed back and teased Cy
about – oh, I don't know – something – he would
have loved it. He was a rough diamond, if you like,
but no sadist.'

'If you are Dennis Nelson it must be hard to tell

the difference,' Salter said, realizing that he was 'relating' to Nelson.

'I know,' she sighed. 'Poor Dennis. The only taboo subject we had was what I saw in Drecker.'

'What about his enemies – Drecker, I mean? Did you know of any?'

She shook her head. 'A lot of people didn't like him, but setting fire to his store would be too much. No.'

'Okay, Miss Costa. Now the rest of your story. You were by yourself until Nelson arrived?'

'Yes, I was. I was in bed when he arrived.'

'Did you get any phone calls during the evening?'

'Yes, I did. I got one about twelve-thirty.'

'Who from?'

'A man named Raymond Darling. He's married, by the way, so you might question him at his work.' Now she looked embarrassed. 'He *is* my lover. Nobody gets paid.'

'Where can I find him?'

'He has a little showroom on Church Street. He's a bathroom remodeller – a plumber, really.'

Salter noted the number. Darling, Julia Costa's lover, had remodelled the bathroom in Drecker's store. Afterwards, according to Dennis Nelson, Darling and Drecker had had a swearing match. Julia Costa must have heard of it. Save some for later, when she isn't ready for it, and list Darling as suspect number three.

'May I ask you where you met Raymond Darling, Miss Costa?'

'Through the trade,' she said promptly. 'I used to work in a store off Queen Street West, and Raymond was in and out all the time. He's interested in antiques.'

'Did you introduce him to Drecker?'

'Yes, I did.' She looked at Salter. 'That's *all* I did, Inspector. I told Drecker I knew a plumber, and I told Raymond that Drecker needed a bathroom fixed. After that they were on their own.'

Salter considered his next question carefully. 'Was there any chance,' he asked, 'that either man knew of your relationship with the other?'

'None. None at all. No way. Drecker knew I didn't belong to him exclusively. Raymond thinks I do – he wouldn't like the idea of sharing me. But they both knew that one word about me to anyone else and I would have made their life bloody hell. That was clear from the start – no confessions to wives – nothing. My life is private.'

'But it is possible that Darling, by chance, could have heard of your relationship with Drecker and taken action, become jealous, like?' He was goading her now.

'No. The only one who could have told him was Drecker himself. And Cy didn't need to boast.'

'Dennis Nelson knew about you and Drecker.'

She laughed. 'Don't you worry about Dennis, Inspector. He may not like Raymond, but he doesn't have a nasty bone in his body. My private life is a sacred trust with him.'

'One last thing, Miss Costa. When you and Drecker got together, where was it usually?'

'Above the store, always. He liked that arrangement.'

'That's how Nelson knew of it?'

'No. Drecker told him. He liked to tease Dennis.'

Salter got up to go and she accompanied him to the door. As he was leaving, she said, 'One thing, Inspector. I need a favour.'

'I can guess. I won't talk to your boyfriend about you and Drecker if it isn't necessary.'

'Thanks.' She pushed the door open for him without looking at him. 'I still think it was an accident,' she said.

Salter put another quarter in the parking meter and walked through to The Cakemaster for coffee and a cheese Danish. On Saturdays Annie bought croissants here and they ate them heated up for breakfast on Sundays. For a special treat she bought cheese Danish, and Salter had become addicted to it. Whenever he was in the area (and working on his own) he tried to squeeze in a coffee break at The Cakemaster.

He gobbled one of the pastries and wiped the crumbs off his face and hands, and got out his notebook. He had now questioned all the main people in his list. The obvious suspects all had alibis, except for Raymond Darling who would have, he was sure, and that ended round one. Nobody with singed eyebrows had appeared, and no one was missing except Jake Hauser, Nelson's boyfriend, and the Japanese collector. Unless one of these was his man, it looked like a long and maybe hopeless case, a killing by person or persons unknown. Round two was a matter of endless patient questioning, of the neighbours again, of the suspects, and of anyone else even faintly connected with the dead man. There were searches to be done – of Drecker's store and his apartment. Someone would be assigned to watch the store to see if any strangers took an unusual interest in it. In all of this Salter would play second fiddle to the experts in Homicide, to the well-known team of Munnings and Hutter.

Salter let the waitress refill his cup. He had lots of time to see Darling before his squash game, and then he would let the Superintendent, Orliff, decide. Through the window of the café he saw a fleet of tow-trucks assemble to haul away illegally-parked cars on Cumberland Street. Already the policeman in charge was arguing with an owner who had appeared just as his car was being hoisted off its front wheels, ready to go to the pound, where it would cost the owner a small fortune to get it back. Salter watched the officer keeping his patience as the citizen, red in the face, danced about on the sidewalk, demanding his car back; but once the tow-truck was hitched up, the full fine and fees had to be paid.

'Dickens,' said a fat, smoothly-groomed man standing next to Salter.

It was Browne, the chairman of the English Department at Douglas College, the scene of a recent case Salter had been involved in.

'Hullo, Professor,' Salter said. 'What's Dickens got to do with tow-trucks?'

'*Our Mutual Friend*, Inspector. In Dickens's time, some watermen made a living scavenging bodies from the Thames and picking the pockets before they turned the corpses over to the authorities, who paid them a bounty. When bodies were in short supply, these ghouls were not above hiring murderers to supply them. Those tow-truck operators out there are the ghouls of our time.'

'Somebody has to be the scavenger. We don't enjoy it much either,' Salter said.

'Of course, of course. I was just getting off a nice literary analogy. I don't drive, myself. Nice to see you, Inspector.' He picked up his bill. 'I have to buy some Florentines for my daughter.'

Salter watched the girl pick out a dozen large, brown cookies, and hand them to the Professor.

'Try some,' Browne called from the cash register. 'They're *delicious*.'

All right, thought Salter, guessing from what he knew of Browne that you could trust him on cookies.

'I'll have a dozen of those,' he said, when he came to pay his bill. The girl put them in a bag and added up the tab.

'Twenty-five twelve,' she said.

Salter stared at her. 'Two dollars a *cookie?*' he asked.

'Two dollars a Florentine,' she corrected.

Salter put away the five-dollar bill and gave the girl two twenties. Bought a treat today, Annie, he rehearsed. A few cookies. Twenty-five dollars worth. Jesus Christ. Who says I'm tight?

The window of Darling's plumbing shop displayed a small badly-made cardboard model of a bathroom; inside the store were several coloured bathroom fixtures, and the counter held advertising displays of faucets that could be installed by the home handyman. It looked as if Darling still needed to bring in the day-to-day cash while he moved up-market.

The man sitting behind the counter, reading the
business section of *Globe and Mail*, was about forty
years old, handsome, with a slight tan and fair, curly
hair. His dark leather pants looked, to Salter's eye,
several sizes too small, and his brown silk shirt (more
like a blouse, the policeman thought) was open to
show his chest and a large gold key on a chain. And
this is what Annie and Jenny want me to look like?
Salter inquired of himself.

'Raymond Darling.' he asked.

'That's me, friend,' the man said, and laid down his
paper. He smiled to show a full set of white teeth
with a large gap in the centre of the top row.

'You know who I am?'

'I can guess.'

'You don't have to, though, do you? Your girlfriend
just phoned you.'

They were sparring. Darling was matching his man-
of-the-world 'cool' with Salter's tweed jacket and short
haircut.

Salter let him have his hour. 'I understand, Mr
Darling, that the night before last you telephoned
Miss Costa, at her apartment. Could you tell me the
time of the call? Just a routine check.' There. The
flat-footed cop to the life.

Darling rose like a hungry bass. 'I called Miss Costa
at twelve-thirty from a friend's house,' he said, the
words uninflected as they would be under cross-
examination.

'You are close friends with Miss Costa?'

'Very close.' Darling smiled around the court-
room.

'Lovers, I understand.'

Darling smiled again.

Then Salter, still playing the flat-foot, let him have it. 'I understand that you and Cyril Drecker got into an argument last week. You were shouting threatening remarks, I believe. What was that all about, could you tell me?'

'Nelson told you that, did he?'

Salter waited. Just answer the question, Mr Darling.

'It was nothing at all. I did some work for Drecker, and he didn't want to pay for it. He was a bit of a shafter. Has anyone told you that?'

'I see.' Salter pretended to write it all down. This is fun, he thought. 'A disagreement over a bill?'

'Right.'

'That looks after Miss Costa, then.' Salter wrote away busily.

'Good.' Darling shook out his paper again.

'What was the job you did for Mr Drecker?' Salter asked, licking his thumb and turning to a fresh page of his notebook.

'I put in the bathroom on the second floor of his store, designed it for him. I'm a qualified plumber, but I do a lot of design work now. Some friends, a lawyer and a doctor friend of mind, want to put up the money for me to expand as soon as I find a better location. But I knew Drecker as a dealer, too. I do a bit of dealing myself. Here.' He came round the counter and led the way into a back area, formerly a plumbing workshop. Now most of the space was taken up with furniture that was being stripped. 'I know a fair bit about antiques,' he said.

Salter looked at a collection of bits and pieces of

rubbish that even Drecker might have been ashamed of. 'Very interesting. Now where were you that night.'

'Me? I was at a poker game with some friends. It's a regular game. Mostly professional people.'

'I see. What time did you get home?'

'About half past one.'

'Your wife could confirm this?'

'I think so.' Now Darling looked smug. 'You want to ask her? Here.' He gave Salter a card printed with 'Raymond Darling – Bathroom and Kitchen Designs'. 'My home address is on the back.'

Salter took the card and prepared to leave.

'Oh, Inspector,' Darling said, 'I'd be grateful if you didn't tell my wife about the phone call.' He put a hand on Salter's arm. 'She'd be upset by Julia.'

'Nothing to do with us, Mr Darling,' Salter said, the bumpkin again. 'I just want to confirm the movements of everyone who might have had reason to commit the crime.'

'Good. Thanks. Must be a rotten job yours, sometimes.' The decline from braggart to chumminess, via defensiveness, was complete.

Salter nodded stolidly and left. Darling had impressed him as almost fitting Julia Costa's description of Cyril Drecker: Tom Jones with his wits about him. Was it a type she attracted or did she go looking for this kind of man?

Darling's house was in Cabbagetown, the new, fashionable Cabbagetown that was taking over the old working-class district. No. 23 was in the process of having its porch removed and its front yard cobbled.

Salter knocked and waited. Just as he was about to
knock again, a small dark haired woman wheeling a
baby carriage turned into the yard. She was in her
mid-thirties, with a hard-looking little body dressed
in a sweat-shirt and jeans which showed the muscles
of her thighs. Her face was cheerful with the look of
someone who enjoyed a joke, and she crackled with
energy as she manouevred the carriage into the front
yard and leaped back in mock surprise at seeing Salter
on the doorstep. 'Don't tell me,' she cried. 'You're
selling aluminium siding. Right?'

'No, ma'am.'

'Roofing?'

Salter shook his head.

'Real estate. You want to list the house?'

'I'm from the police, ma'am,' Salter said. 'May I
come in?'

'Oh Jesus, yes. What have I done?.'

'Nothing that I know of. I want to ask a few
questions about your husband's acquaintances. He's
done nothing either,' he added quickly. Across the
street, five bums from the old Cabbagetown were
watching him from the broken-down porch of an
unreconstructed hovel. *They* had certainly smelt him
for what he was. Mrs Darling lifted her baby out of
its carriage and unlocked the door, and they went
into the living-room. Here Darling's avocation was
everywhere apparent. The room was a junk heap of
bits and pieces of furniture. There were three rock-
ing-chairs, a grandfather clock, and a huge wardrobe
without doors, as well as assorted tables and ornaments.

'Mrs Darling, I have to confirm the movements of

everyone who might have been involved in an incident that happened the night before last.'

Mrs Darling laid the baby on one of the chairs and stared at Salter, with her hand flat on her breast, over-reacting as she seemed to do to everything.

'Your husband isn't involved, but he has confirmed the whereabouts of a couple of people and we want to get the times straight.'

'The people he was playing poker with? They are all professional people,' she said, echoing the husband.

Salter ignored this. 'Can you confirm the time your husband came home?'

'Just a minute, Officer. This little bugger has done it again. Let me change him and I'll be with you.' With expert bustle she stripped the baby of his wet diaper and folded a clean one. The baby waved his legs in the air and shouted happily at her. 'Now watch it, you little bastard,' she cried, tickling him. She turned to Salter. 'When I was changing him this morning, the little bugger pee'd straight in my eye,' she explained. She finished changing him, gave a final tickle, and put the baby on the floor.

'Now,' she said, sitting down in the chair herself. She looked hard at Salter, seeming to suppress a laugh. 'Twenty past one,' she said.

'Can you be certain?'

'You betcha. We have a clock beside the bed. Raymond pointed out the time, the way he always does.'

'You mean he announces the time every night when he gets into bed?'

'No,' she giggled. 'Afterwards.' She whooped and covered her mouth in mock seriousness.

'After what?' Salter asked cautiously, knowing the answer.

'After we do it.' She watched Salter's face joyfully.

'I see. You mean you woke up when he came in and – made love?'

'We always do when he wins. He gets very excited when he wins and it calms him down,' she said, grinning again.

'I see. He came home and woke you up, you made love, and then you checked the time. Which was?'

'Quarter to two.' Another whoop. 'He was proud of himself. He said we had been doing it for twenty-five minutes.'

Salter was absorbed. I must remember to tell Annie about this, he thought. 'Did he always time himself?' he asked.

'It was a joke he started when we were first married.'

Salter resisted the temptation to ask what Darling's best time was. 'Well, that's that, then,' he said.

'Good,' replied a voice from behind him. It was Darling. 'Found out what you wanted to know?' He winked at his wife.

'Yes, thanks. I won't be troubling you again,' Salter said, touching his forehead with his finger.

'Care for a beer, Inspector, before you go? I've got some Stella Artois in the fridge.'

'No, thanks. I must be getting back,' Salter said, and started to leave. The Darlings followed him, grinning, to the door.

Stella Artois, for Christ's sake, he thought. What

was that? Some Greek beer professional people
drink?

But, to his ear, Darling's wife was telling the naked,
vulgar truth, which confirmed the alibis of the two
people closest to Drecker, his mistress and his
assistant.

When Salter returned to his office, Gatenby was
already waiting to report. 'I did the list,' the Sergeant
said. 'Some of these places – you should have seen
them! Fagin would be ashamed to own them. I asked
them all what they knew about Drecker, what dealings they had with him, but I couldn't smell anything
fishy. All the same story: the high class ones bought
the odd things from Drecker to sell again, and the
real grungy ones that were full of old toot . . .' He
pronounced the word to rhyme with 'put'.

'Old what?'

'Old toot. What my old mum used to call it.
Rubbish.'

'Go on.'

'They used to sell their rubbish to him if he thought
he could make something on it.'

'So that's that, then.'

'Ah no. No. Something very interesting cropped
up. About half of these shops, mostly the good ones,
told me about an old Japanese chap who'd been
looking for anything they had recently bought from
Drecker.' Gatenby sat, shining, waiting to be prodded on.

'You mean after you'd asked them about Drecker,
half of these people said, "There was an old Japanese
in here last week asking after him?"' Salter said
patiently.

'No, no. It happened with the first one, a dealer in pine on Avenue Road. He told me about the Japanese fella. So I asked the next one, and he'd had this guy in, too. I knew you'd be interested so after that I asked them all. Eight of the fourteen confirmed they'd had a Japanese inquiring about anything Drecker sold them.' Gatenby paused.

Salter waited to be sure the story was over, then said, 'So what do you think, Frank? Have we got a Maltese Falcon on our hands?'

'What, in Toronto?' Gatenby gaped.

'I'm joking,' Salter said. 'But who is this old guy?'

'Ah,' Gatenby said. 'I'm not finished yet. Vancouver phoned. They haven't found Gene Tanabe and there's no one been fished out of the harbour lately, but they had something else to tell us. Seems your Japanese friend was inquiring himself about three weeks ago after someone else, someone called George Kemp that he knew forty years ago in Vancouver.'

'Did they know him? This Kemp?'

'No. But I asked them to check up on him for *us* if they could. They'll phone us back.'

'You've been busy, Frank. Anything else?'

'The chief wants to see you.'

'Okay. Anything else? Maybe I can hold the chief off until you've got this one all wrapped up.'

Gatenby grinned. 'Better not. He's called down twice. I'll proceed with inquiries, as they say, while you keep him happy.'

'That's it, then? No bumf today?'

'Lots, but I sent it all back. They wanted you to talk to the cadets about police administration. Then there's that programme where the schoolkids take over a station for the day – could you organize that? I told them, no. And – oh yes – would you be available to brief the new members of the Police Commission about our work. I said we were too busy right now, and to tell the commissioners to come back next year. A lot of little stuff, too, but I took care of it.'

'You're a treasure, Frank. I have a feeling we'll be a few more days yet, so keep them at bay. I'll go and see Orliff.'

The Superintendent was in his office, and Salter gave him what he had so far.

'Couldn't have been an accident?'

'The Fire Marshal doesn't think so.'

'Orliff made a note. 'So far, then, you've got six possibilities: the assistant, his friend, the girlfriend, the wife, this Darling character, and the old Japanese. The assistant and the girlfriend could have done it together, couldn't they? They sound like a flakey pair.'

'She had nothing against Drecker that I know of.'

'What do you make of her, though, and the assistant?'

'Nothing much. The assistant is all right. He's uptight but he's quarrelling with his boyfriend. There might be something there, when I find the boyfriend. The woman is nervous about something, but she didn't seem like a killer to me. If you want *my* preference, it would be for this guy Darling.'

'Why?'

'He's a cocky bastard, and I think Drecker might have swindled him. Darling wouldn't like that.'

'But he's got an alibi, Charlie, as good as any of the others.'

'I guess so.' Salter shrugged.

Orliff looked at Salter for a long minute until Salter looked away.

'So what are you going to do now?' Orliff asked.

'Talk to this lot again. See if I can smell anything else. Find Nelson's boyfriend, and the Japanese. It could be I haven't picked up anything real yet.'

'That's what I was thinking. You haven't got much in the way of motives, have you? What about the wife? She takes over the store, and I guess there's insurance. Could she have hired someone to do it?'

Salter shrugged again. 'I can't figure her out. She could be the head guard in a women's concentration camp, or one of those people who don't kill mosquitoes because all life is sacred. Her relationship with Drecker was pretty strange, and I couldn't get much idea of her life away from him, except that she spends a lot of time on yoga and bridge.'

Orliff made another note. 'Okay, stay with it next week. After that we'll let the Homicide people have it. Let Munnings and Hutter beat their brains out. All right, Charlie. No real suspects, no motives, no clues. Don't make yourself ill. Something will turn up.' Orliff nodded in dismissal. Just then his telephone rang. Salter got up to go but Orliff signalled him back. 'It's for you,' he said.

It was Gatenby. 'Vancouver on the phone,' he said immediately. 'Do you want to talk to them?'

'Yes. What extension?'

'Two-o-five.'

Salter pressed the button. 'Salter here. Who am I talking to?'

'Sergeant don't-make-any-jokes Renfrew. We've found your man.'

'Tanabe?'

'No. Kemp.'

'Christ, that's quick. I thought he'd left town forty years ago.'

'You know how it is sometimes. This country's just one big village strung out along the forty-ninth parallel. We called the union hall – your man was a steam-fitter – and they asked around among the old-timers and someone remembered him. He lived in Victoria until six months ago – they even knew his address – and the local post office gave us his forwarding address. He lives in Woodstock, Ontario, now. Here's the address.'

'Great. Many thanks. No sign of Tanabe?'

'No, He owns an antique store on Pandora Street here in town. His assistant – a gorgeous Japanese piece, by the way – is very worried about him. He called her from Toronto last week, but since then they've heard nothing.'

'Family?'

'He doesn't have one. Parents dead. No brothers or sisters. Not married.'

'Anything known?'

'Nothing. Totally clean.'

'Right. Thanks again.' Salter hung up and turned to Orliff.

'The old Japanese is still missing, but we've got a lead on the guy *he* was looking for.'

'Something to do, anyway, Charlie,' Orliff said equably. 'Lotsa luck.'

Back in his office, Salter phoned the town police at Woodstock and told them who he was looking for. A car was despatched, the neighbours were talked to, and in half an hour the Woodstock police were calling him back.

'He doesn't live here any more,' the sergeant reported. 'He moved last month to Toronto.' He gave an address in the Beaches district. 'The neighbours think he's living with his daughter there. By the way, there's something else a little strange. The neighbours told us that another guy was in town last week trying to find Kemp . . .'

'. . . An old Japanese?'

'I guess so. They said Chinese, but all they know is oriental. You know about him?'

'I keep crossing his trail, as the mounties say. He's the one I'm really looking for.'

'Is he, though? Well, good luck. I expect that completes the Woodstock phase of your investigation, Inspector?'

Salter laughed and hung up. He looked at his watch. 'I'm going out to get a sandwich, Frank', he said. 'Then I'm going over to find this guy Kemp. He might lead me to Tanabe. We are missing two guys – Tanabe and Nelson's boyfriend, Hauser. If either of them comes by, put him on a hook until I get back. I'll call in after I've seen this Kemp, but I won't come back unless there's something to do here. I have to go to the hospital this afternoon.'

'Again? What for?'

'I don't know.' Salter jerked at his tie. 'If I ask them

they won't tell me. "X-rays," they said. "What for?" I
asked. "To establish a diagnosis for the probable cause
of microscopic hæmaturia," they said. "What's that?"
I said? "You are peeing blood," they said. That's
where I started.'

'That's what they do nowadays. They give you tests,
look up the results on a computer and tell you what
you've got. If they're wrong, they tell you the computer malfunctioned. I'm sure it's nothing.'

'It sure drags on, though,' Salter said as he left to
find George Kemp.

Kemp's daughter lived in the Beaches, an area in the
east end where the city and the lake meet in a way
that makes it possible for the local citizens to enjoy
Toronto's only natural amenity. There is a park here,
beside the lake, and a boardwalk that runs along the
shore, and in July, if the wind is in the right direction
so that it doesn't bring in waves from the permanently
frigid waters in the centre of Lake Ontario – waters
so cold that there is a legend that sailors who drown
never come to the surface – it is possible to swim, for
a week or two, anyway.

Like a lot of Toronto people, Salter was sentimental
about the Beaches. He had grown up nearby and
spent large parts of his school holidays on the beach.
His father still lived in the area, in a small flat not far
from the streetcar barns where he had worked all his
life, and Salter was always glad when his route took
him through the area.

Since Salter's boyhood, other parts of the lakefront
had been made accessible to the population. 'Har-
bourfront' had been born, a centre of cultural and

social activity drawing crowds year round, especially on sweltering summer nights. But the Beaches is a real district, where people live, the most human quarter of the city.

Salter drove down Jarvis Street and eastwards along Queen to the race track, then south and east again to run along the edge of the park until he came to Melita Street. He cruised slowly, looking for the number he wanted, noting that while the street was still apparently intact, with the same small family homes, many of them owned or rented by the kind of people Salter had grown up with, some brightly-painted verandas testified to the arrival of new immigrants from the Mediterranean. Here and there, too, the white-painters had appeared, sandblasting their way across the city in the name of restoration.

Salter found his house, parked, and knocked on the door. A small, fat, frizzy-haired woman in her forties opened it. Over her shoulder Salter could see down the hall into the kitchen where a man of the same age was reading a paper.

'Mrs Murdrick?'

'Yes?' the woman said in a no-thank-you tone.

Salter showed his identification. 'I'd like to talk to you about your father,' he said.

'Oh, I don't know. What about? Phil!' she called to her husband over her shoulder, keeping her eye on Salter.

Her husband looked up. 'What?' he shouted in a don't-keep-bothering-me voice.

'There's a policeman here asking about Dad.'

'You'd better ask him in then, hadn't you?'

Salter stepped into the hallway.

'What's the trouble?' Murdrick asked, a man who knew his rights.

'No trouble. I'm looking for George Kemp,' Salter said.

'Well, yez've found him,' a voice said from the top of the stairs. An old man stood on the landing, short, barrel-chested with stubby legs and long arms. His face was brick-red and shiny, and his lower jaw was thrust forward, giving him an aggressive look. A pair of old-fashioned steel-rimmed glasses had worn a groove in the bridge of his nose.

Slowly, rolling from side to side, he descended the stairs until he came face to face with Salter. 'George Kemp,' he said.

'I'm making inquiries about a Mr Gene Tanabe,' Salter said. 'I think you know him.'

'Ah,' Kemp said. He cleared his throat with a sound like a drain being unplugged, blew his nose in a large khaki handkerchief, adjusted his glasses, and waited.

For a few moments no one spoke or moved. Then Kemp turned and started to walk back up the stairs. 'You'd better come up here,' he said.

Salter looked at Mr and Mrs Murdrick, who said nothing, so he followed the old man up the stairs and into his room. Kemp was already seated in an arm-chair by the window.

'Close the door,' he said. 'We 'ave no particler need to let his majesty – ,' he pointed with a stumpy finger to the floor – 'know all our business.'

Salter closed the door and sat down in the other chair.

Kemp said, 'I take me meals with me daughter, but I spend me time up here when I'm at home. I can make meself a cup of tea, and it avoids too much argumenting.' His accent Salter had now placed as Newfoundland – round Irish vowels drained of their music, and a slightly ornate syntax.

'I don't know where Gene is to be found at this particler moment,' Kemp began. 'But I do know him, yes. I've known him ever since I first came to Canada.'

'You aren't Canadian?' Salter asked, puzzled.

'I am, mister, but I was born in Newfoundland, and in them days we wasn't part of Canada. When I left in nineteen hundred and forty-two we still wasn't. But before I tell the whole history, would yez like a cup of tea? Yez'll have to take it bare-legged, because I'm not allowed to drink milk, the doctor says.'

Salter declined and looked around while the old man made himself a cup of black tea. The room was furnished so that a single person could look after himself. There was a washbasin in one corner, a two-burner hotplate on a small metal table, a single bed, a bureau, and several well-worn rugs.

Kemp organized himself in his armchair and began again.

'I met him first in nineteen forty-two in Vancouver, where I was working on a government contract.'

'You were a steam-fitter?'

'I was and am a Master Steam-Fitter and a Master Plumber,' Kemp said. 'When I took me apprenticeship in Newfoundland, you got your papers for both.' He stopped, inviting Salter to question or comment on the story so far.

Salter recognized that Kemp was one of those people who could not tell a story simply, but required

to be prodded along each step of the way. A tedious
business.

'And you went to Vancouver when you got your
papers?' he asked, trying for a small leapfrog.

But Kemp wasn't to be abbreviated. 'Not right
away, I didn't,' he said. 'I had me own business in St
John's at first. I borryed a bit of money from the bank,
d'ye see, and bought out old Murdoch McElway's
shop. It was going downhill and I got it cheap.'

A long pause. Salter started to get a little fed up.
He waited forever – two minutes? three? – and
opened his mouth to speak some words of encourage-
ment. But the ancient plumber was now fully
embarked on his tale, and the story came in larger
chunks.

'When the war came, business fell off, so I went to
work for the government, in Canada. I'd never been
west of Halifax, and I took a chance and went out to
Vancouver. I says to the wife, we might never get the
opportunity again, and she agreed. So the finish was
that I installed heating plants in about half the army
camps in British Columbia. After the war I went up
north to the D.E.W. Line, Distant Early Warning
Line, that was, and after that I went to work for the
oil companies all over Alberta. I'm known in the trade
everywhere west of Winnipeg and east of Halifax, and
the only province I've never set foot in is Quebec. I
never bothered with this part of the country until me
wife died two years ago. I was in Victoria then, and I
stayed there about a year and then packed up and
came down east to be near to me daughter and him
as she's married to.' Once again Kemp pointed with

contempt to the floor where the sound of the Murdricks' quarrelling could be heard through the floor-
boards.

'You moved to Woodstock?'

'Ah. That was near enough to be able to see her
occasionally. I was retired, of course, but I bought a
little house and started to do a few odd jobs, working
for the hardware store nearby. Pretty soon I was as
busy as a one-armed paperhanger. These Ontario
fellas don't seem to know how to put a bit of glass in
a window, nor a washer on a tap. A man who's built
his own house can always make a livin'. I never went
short of something to do once they found out about
me. I've always kept me licence and me truck, though
I never thought I'd end up as a hobbler.'

I wonder if he can fix a screen door, thought Salter.
Just then, there was a timid tap at the door and
Kemp's face split into a huge smile.

'Come in, young fella!' he called.

The door opened and Salter gaped at a tiny George
Kemp who stood in the doorway holding on to the
doorknob which was almost level with his eye. Salter
looked close and saw a small boy, five or six years old,
dressed in a miniature version of Kemp's coveralls,
with a small lunch-pail in his hand. Even the tiny
steel-rimmed glasses were the same. Behind them,
though, was a pale, diffident face which stared shyly
at Salter.

'Come in and meet the polis,' Kemp said, accenting
the first syllable

The boy edged forward.

'Inspector,' Kemp said, 'this is me helper, George,
named after me. Me grandson,' he added proudly.

'George, this is Inspector Salter. Shake hands with him like I showed you. I'm teaching him some manners,' he added to Salter.

And driving your daughter up the wall, Salter thought, as he solemnly shook hands with the boy.

'George comes out on me rounds,' Kemp said, his red face glowing. 'It didn't take me long to find a hardware store here with a use for me services, and this young man and I have a few calls to make today. Now, young fella, you've got your lunch, have you? He allus brings his lunch to eat in the truck with me, he said to Salter. 'Well, I won't be long. You go down and wait in the truck and I'll be right down.'

He watched as the child obediently left the room, carefully closing the door with his eyes on Kemp to see if he was noticing how well he did it.

'That's the main reason I stay here,' Kemp said, when the door was shut. 'The lad needs me to teach him a few things.'

After a respectful pause, Salter prompted him to continue his story. 'What happened after Woodstock?' he asked.

'I took sick. I incurred an infarction of me heart,' the old man said. 'They thought I was going to die, but they was wrong shipped on that one. I pulled through. But then me daughter insisted I come up here to be with her because the doctors said I shouldn't be left to meself. Three weeks I was on the critical list.' He paused to give weight to his next words. 'And that is why you are talking to me at this moment now,' he said.

Salter waited. After another pause, he asked, 'Why is that, Mr Kemp?'

'Because *that* was when Gene's box went.'

At last, Gene Tanabe's box. 'How?' Salter asked. 'How did it go?'

'That is the bloody mystery I'd like *you* to get to the bottom of, mister. I'd had that box for forty years, and when I come out of hospital it was gone.'

'Why? Why did you have it?'

'I had it because Gene Tanabe trusted me with it. I looked after it for forty years and when I got sick for the first time in me life, it went.' The old man spoke with a solemn passion, as though he had been over the words again and again in his mind, learning them by heart.

'Gene Tanabe was a friend of yours?'

'He was and is. I never let him down. He knows that. At least he knows the box went unbeknownst to me.'

Salter tried again. Each end of the story was important. 'Could we go back to the beginning, Mr Kemp? Why did he leave the box with you?'

'Because you fellas, the polis, come for him and took him away. You thought he was a dangerous enemy alien. He wouldn't hurt a bloody fly, mister.'

'He was interned?' Salter asked, ignoring Kemp's detour into Tanabe's innocence.

'They all was. Interned. Shipped away. It was no place to be Japanese in nineteen forty-two, Vancouver wasn't.'

'So he trusted you with a box of his possessions?'

'That's right. We was neighbours. He was a woodworker, did you know? He could do anything with wood. He made me a tool-box you could bury a baby in – beautiful bit of work – but the nicest thing he

made that I saw was a doll's house for me little girl.
She's still got it. I'm pretty handy with metal meself,
and when we got to know each other we used to swap
little jobs. I did all the plumbing around his house
and the odd bit of solderin' and such, and he did all
the joinery I needed doing. He was a lovely fella.
When they told him he had to move, he come to me
and says would I look after this box for him. A good
thing, too, because he lost everything else in the
finish, commandeered by the local patriots. I was glad
to help out. It was a privilege, mister, to do something for him.'

'Then what happened? After the war he came back
to look for you?' Salter asked, still keeping his distance from Mr Kemp's belligerent sentimentalism.

'That's right. But we was gone. There was a fire at
our house, d'ye see, and we had to move. When he
come back to look for me, I was gone. He tells me
now he figured that the box went in the fire. It didn't,
you know. I still had it with me, but he stopped
looking then.'

'Why didn't you try and find him?'

'Do you think I bloody didn't?' Kemp shouted
suddenly, angry at being accused of leaving a stone
unturned. 'I went back to the district dozens of times
after the war, but he never came back from Ontario
until nineteen forty-seven or 'eight, and by that time
I'd given up traipsin' around looking for him. I told
Gene I'd keep the box safe, and safe it was, with me.'
Then in a conversational tone, he added, 'Tell you
the truth, I thought he might be a goner by then.'

'But you kept the box. Did you know what was in
it?'

'I kept the box, yes, and no, I did not know what was in it until last week. It wasn't none of my business.'

'Last week?' Now the other end of the story was coming into sight.

'Ah. When Gene come back here. He'd tracked me down, d'ye see, found out where I was and knocked on the door. I didn't recognize him at first. Then, when I did realize it was Gene, the first thing I thought, o'course, was how I didn't have his box. It wasn't like it was supposed to be.'

'Did he think you still had the box?'

Kemp shook his head. 'No, mister, he knew I didn't. He'd found his box by then as well as some of his pictures. He said he just couldn't understand how they'd appeared like that, sudden-like, but he knew there would be a good reason and he only wanted to find out what it was. He trusted me from start to finish. And so he should. If I hadn't gone into hospital, I would have his box safe still.'

'But he wouldn't know that, would he, Mr Kemp?'

'Mebbe not. I would, though,' Kemp said. He took his glasses off, blew his nose, and wiped his face off before putting his glasses back on.

'What *did* he think?' Salter asked.

'Nothing. He didn't jump to conclusions, just waited to hear my story. After he heard about how the box disappeared while I was in hospital, he didn't care any more. Or p'raps I should say that he was so pleased to find I hadn't let him down after forty years that the box didn't interfere with our enjoyments if you understand me.'

Salter nodded.

'We went out for a bit of supper then,' Kemp
continued. 'He took me to a place downtown – we
went by taxicab – where we had a slap-up Japanese
dinner.' Kemp's manner became diffident. 'You ever
had a Japanese dinner?' he asked.

Salter shook his head.

'A bit peculiar,' Kemp said. 'Very *interestin*,' but
not quite my cup of tea. Nice for a change, though,
and they didn't make me sit cross-legged. They had a
few proper tables. And Japanese beer is all right, so
we had a few jars and got caught up. Old Gene has
done wonderful well since I saw him last, and I've not
done so bad either. I tell you, mister, that evening
with Gene was the best thing that's happened to me
since I moved down east.' Kemp blew his nose again.

Salter waited a moment, and said, 'That was it,
then? He found out it wasn't your fault, and that's the
last you saw of him?'

'Not quite. He came back once more to say he'd
got most of his pictures back. I came in one day and
found him talking to me son-in-law in the kitchen.
The four of us had a drink together then, me and
Gene and me daughter and that nunny-fudger she's
married to, and that's the last I saw of him. He had to
pay a terrible price to get his pictures, but he's a
pretty rich man by all accounts, so no doubt he's
happy on balance. Now, mister. I know how youse
fellas' minds run so don't be thinking that Gene set
fire to that shop out of revenge or something. It just
isn't in him to do a thing like that'.

'Why has he disappeared, then?'

'How the hell do I know? P'raps he's afraid of you
fellas – he has reason to be. But Gene Tanabe never

hurt another human being in his life. You'll track him down eventually, I suppose, but I won't hold me breath waiting.'

Salter put away his notebook. 'Thanks, Mr Kemp. Can I find you here if I need you?'

'At mealtimes, I'm down below. The rest of the time, I'm here, or out doin' jobs. Now you can go down and confirm me account with me daughter.' Kemp stared triumphantly at Salter to show he knew how the police worked.

Salter stood up and then remembered. 'You haven't told me yet how the box disappeared,' he said.

'Ah, right. When I was in hospital with me infarction, me daughter sold me house and everything in it except for one or two bits she kept for this room here. They had a garage sale, d'ye see, and though she was particler to keep the box back, it went during the sale – lost, stolen, or strayed'.

'Do you think it might have been sold by mistake?'

'No. Me son-in-law conducted the sale.'

Salter waited, but there was no more forthcoming. Kemp sat, finished, staring out of the window.

On his way down, Salter passed the grandson sitting on the stairs, his lunch-pail at the ready, waiting for the policeman to let his playmate go.

Downstairs, Salter asked the Murdricks to confirm the essential points of Kemp's story.

'That's right. We think it must have been lifted during the sale,' the husband said. He sounded edgy, and his wife's next comment accounted for it.

'Forty years Dad kept that box. And as soon as his back was turned it was gone,' she said, giving her husband a look. It was evidently a line she had used before.

'It wasn't my bloody fault,' Murdrick answered. 'It was there the night before and then it was gone. I didn't sell it. It was lifted, I tell you.'

Salter waited for an explanation.

'Phil was supposed to set aside the stuff Dad might want to keep, any mementoes, like, including the box, but when we went to pick them up after the sale, the box was gone,' she said.

'So you think someone stole it during the sale?'

'Must have,' Murdrick said. 'Must have. I was collecting the money, but I couldn't be everywhere, could I. Someone walked off with it.'

'Forty years,' his wife repeated.

'For Christ's sake don't keep on about it,' Murdrick said. 'The bloody thing wasn't worth a pinch of coon-shit.'

'Was anything in it?' Salter asked.

'Rubbish,' Murdrick said. 'Jap rubbish. Fans and pictures – all rubbish.'

'You don't know that, Phil.'

'I bloody well *do* know that,' he shouted. 'You had a look at the stuff. A pile of crap.'

'Was it locked?' Salter asked.

The wife blushed.

'Yes, it was,' Murdrick said. 'We opened it to find out if there was a name inside. I took the screws off. I closed it up again, and we didn't touch anything.'

'I saw to that,' Mrs Murdrick said.

'Did you know why your father kept it?'

'He said he'd promised to keep it until Mr Tanabe returned.'

'Not likely after forty years, was it?' Salter said comfortingly, addressing himself to Murdrick. 'And yet he did. What a pity he didn't get there a bit sooner.'

'That's what I told him,' Mrs Murdrick agreed.

'When was it he came here?' Salter asked.

'Last week. He knew we didn't have the box any more, but he wanted to hear what happened. Funny, though, he didn't seem upset. More interested in talking to Dad, he was.'

'That was the only time you saw him?'

'No. He came back once more. He wanted to speak to Phil.'

'He was still nagging away about his bloody box,' Murdrick said. 'I told him to stop bothering us.'

'You were terrible to him,' his wife said, continuing the old row between them. 'There was no need to speak to him like that.'

'We did have a few words about it,' Murdrick said to Salter. 'But we all had a drink before he left.'

'He was a friend of Dad's and there was no need for you to treat him like that,' she said directly to her husband. They were ignoring Salter now.

'We fought those bastards during the war and I don't like them,' Murdrick shouted.

'Not you, you didn't. You didn't fight anyone. Anyway, no one had to fight Mr Tanabe. They put him in a concentration camp.'

Salter watched them argue.

'You keep on,' Murdrick threatened, 'and I'll do the same thing I did last time.'

'Go out and get –' she paused and looked at Salter – 'pissed.'

'Go somewhere for some peace,' Murdrick corrected. The two sat there simmering, and Salter judged that he had heard everything of any use to him. 'If you hear from him again, let me know, will you?' he said mildly.

There was no reply.

Salter added, 'And if I have any more questions, I suppose I can find you here, can I?' He looked inquiringly at Murdrick. What was he doing home at this time on a working day?

'My wife is always here. I might be out on a job but she'll take a message.'

'Where do you work, Mr Murdrick?'

'I work for myself. I'm a tiler.'

'Roofer?'

'No. *Not* a bloody roofer. Ceramics, mosaics – floors, bathrooms, fireplaces, I do all kinds of work, all quality work.'

'And you use this as your business phone?'

'That's right,' Murdrick said. 'It's legal. You can find me here.'

Salter got up to go and Mrs Murdrick led him out of the hall. 'I'm sorry about Mr Tanabe's box,' she said as she opened the front door for him. 'It's a shame after forty years.'

As she closed the door, Salter heard her husband shouting at her again from the kitchen.

'Slip this on, Mr Salter, and wait until we call you. Leave your clothes in the cubicle there and keep your shoes on.' A young Lena Horne imitating a nursing aide showed Salter to a changing booth where he did as he was told. He emerged in a white shroud that stopped at his knees and was missing the ties that held it together. Clutching it over his nakedness, he shuffled to the bench in his unlaced shoes like an inmate in a Dickensian madhouse. Two other men his own age were already sitting there, but the three men ignored each other for fear, in Salter's case, of learning what they were in for.

This was a hospital, so Salter had prepared himself for a wait of anything up to three hours by bringing a book, but he was surprised after a few minutes by the return of Lena Horne.

'Come with me, please,' she ordered, and led him down a long corridor to a small room with an X-ray table. 'Use the step and lie down on that,' she said. 'The technician will be here in a moment.'

Lena Horne gave way to Doris Day. 'Hi there,' she said. 'Let's have a look at you.'

Salter sat up and started to take off his shroud, and she leaped to stop him. 'That's all right,' she said. 'We can manage with that on.'

Salter lay back. He had so nerved himself up to the probable necessity of displaying his parts to all the female staff that he was now slightly disappointed. Once he had thought his fear of exposure in hospitals private and aberrant, but a sergeant of detectives had told him years before that if ever he, the sergeant, needed any kind of surgery below the neck he would announce on entering the hospital that he would shave himself, thanks, and remind every shift of it until the operation was due.

'Could you move down a fraction – a bit more – that's it. Comfortable?'

'No.' A steel bar creased Salter's calf muscles

instead of supporting his feet. Doris jiggled the support, moving it an inch.

'Better?' she asked.

'No,' he said. 'It hurts.' He had decided that this time he would not lie around smiling and uncomplaining until someone happened to notice that he was dying. He would be one of those surly bastards who survived.

'There isn't much I can do,' Doris Day said. 'You're pretty big.'

'I'm five feet ten and a half and I weigh a hundred and sixty-five pounds. About average. I can't lie with this thing under my legs for more than two minutes. How long do the X-rays take?'

'The doctor will be along shortly,' she said. 'Perhaps I could wrap a towel around it.'

'You do that,' Salter said.

She disappeared, and Salter heard her complaining about him to Lena Horne, but when she returned she was carrying a thing like a head-rest on two small rods. She removed the bar under his legs and replaced it with the padded rest. It was evidently designed for the job.

'All right, now?' she asked, as if she had laid Salter on a bed of swansdown but still expected him to complain.

'Perfect,' Salter said. 'Now if you'd turn on that light, I'll read until the doctor comes.'

'He'll be here *very* shortly,' she said.

'Good. When he comes, I'll stop reading.'

Reluctantly she turned on the light and went for the doctor. Once again Salter settled down for a long wait, and arranged himself so that he was not touching any of the icy chromium bars. Once again the technique worked, and Doris Day reappeared, accompanied by Richard Chamberlain, in need of a shave.

'This is Dr Tannenbaum,' she said.

The doctor nodded to him and fiddled with a hypodermic. 'This injection I'm going to give you will make you feel very cold, then very hot.' He paused. 'That's normal. But you could have an abnormal reaction. Are you allergic to anything?'

'Penicillin and euromycin,' Salter said. Simultaneously the doctor said something to the technician and she started swabbing his arm.

He didn't hear me, thought Salter. I am going to die.

'Now,' the doctor said, when he had the hypodermic dribbling to his satisfaction. 'One of several things could happen. You could break out in a rash. That's no problem. You could develop low blood pressure. That's more of a problem. Occasionally, perhaps one case in fifty thousand results in death.' He looked at Salter. 'Okay?' He moved out of Salter's vision.

'Why are you telling me this?' asked Salter.

'We have to under the law, so that you can refuse the injection if you like.'

'But then you couldn't take the X-rays.' Salter wished he could see the man at least.

'That's right.'

I have three seconds to decide, Salter thought. Exit one policeman with an infarction of the heart. The hell with it, let him stick the needle in himself. I'm going home.

'Go ahead,' he said.

The doctor shoved the needle into his arm and

looked deep into his eyes. He loves me after all,
Salter thought.

'All right. If anything were going to happen, it
would have shown up by now,' the doctor remarked
to the technician, and left.

After that it was just chilly and boring, and twenty
minutes later Salter shuffled along the corridor and
got dressed.

'So what did they say?' Annie asked.

'Nothing.'

'Didn't you ask?'

'They said they'd send a report to the specialist. I
have to see him again on Tuesday.'

'For God's sake find out what's going on, will you,
Charlie? It's you it's happening to. You won't lose
face by asking.'

The evening was spent beginning the preparations for
the trip. Angus was still avoiding his father, and Seth
was out collecting the money from his paper-route.
Salter watched Annie fuss around, accumulating a
pile of warm clothes in the middle of the living-room
floor. Salter was slightly irritated at her keen encour-
agement of this first attempt of his to be his own son's
Big Brother, and he made no attempt to help beyond
pointing out that everything had to go into one bag.
He took time off to telephone Fred Staver, the man
who had installed the screen door, to ask if he
remembered where the door had been bought, and
he was moderately encouraged when Staver, after
hearing the problem, promised to look around himself
for a wheel. Fred Staver, in their experience, could

fix anything. Eventually it was bedtime, and Annie,
who had refused to rise to Salter's surliness, slid
naked under the duvet.

Salter tried to keep his distance. 'It's not that warm
yet,' he grunted, but she scratched his belly in
invitation and he gave in. A little later he looked at
the bedside clock.

'Fifteen minutes, nearly,' he said.

'To what?'

'From the beginning.'

'You timing us now?'

'Just curious. Not bad, though, is it, at my age?'

'Wonderful,' she said. 'Practice makes perfect, or
better, anyway.'

'What do you mean by that?'

'When we first got married you would have needed
a stopwatch.'

'I was a raw, inexperienced youth then.'

'Was that it? I thought it was me. Hotter than a fire
cracker. Anyway, you were twenty-eight.'

'I was a late bloomer. Now shut up. All this talk is
getting me going again, and I need a little nap
between rounds.'

'Poor old man.' She stroked his belly again, but just
to say good-night. 'Soon be time to put the clocks
back,' she murmured, fitting herself, spoon-like, into
his shape.

Salter dozed, letting daylight-saving time take him
into the end of fall and on into the winter. If I live
that long, he thought. First though, some fishing. He
reached out and pulled Annie closer into him. Fifteen
minutes wasn't bad, he told himself. Darling was
probably bragging.

Chapter Four

On Monday morning Fred Staver phoned before
Salter left for work. 'Appen you've found yon widget?'
he asked. Staver had immigrated thirty years before
from the north of England but he still spoke in a
dialect so thick you could hear the batter pudding
cooling on the doorstep.

'I haven't found a plastic wheel yet, Fred, no,'
Salter said.

'Aye. Well, nobbut a smell of one at Tunney's, lad,
and if Tunney's havena' one, no booger 'as. But I
found out t'bloke 'oo makes 'em. 'Appen you've got a
bit o' pencil or summat?'

'Aye,' Salter said.

'Aye. Well then. It's Graberg Doors out at Weston.
A little factory, like.'

Weston. A factory in an industrial park on the edge
of the city which would take an hour to get to and
another hour to find when you got there. 'What's the
street address, Fred?'

''Ere it is, then. Eight, got that, eight, that's right,
eight, seven, two, one. Eight, seven, two, one – big
number 'nt it? Ryle Boulevard.'

'Spell it, would you, Fred?'

'Aye. R-I-E-L – Ryle.'

'It's pronounced Ree-el, Fred. Riel was a famous
rebel. They hanged him.'

'Aye, well, they named a boulevard after him, too.

Ah've never been to t'place meself but 'appen you'll find it easy enough.'

'Thanks, Fred. Thanks for your trouble.'

'No trouble, mate, but listen, listen. If you do find t'place, buy a couple for me, eh? I might 'ave a need for one. No point in wasting a journey is there? Ta-ta.'

Before he went to the office, Salter called in at the Canadian Tire store and bought a cheap rod and reel for Angus, some mosquito repellent, and a gallon of camp fuel. Then he moved on to Ziggy's where he picked up a dozen Mars bars and a giant can of mixed nuts. When Salter went fishing he liked to eat Mars bars and drink beer while he was waiting for a bite. In the evenings, in the cabin, he liked nuts with his beer. He never ate chocolate or nuts at any other time. He tucked the goodies into a corner of his truck so that Annie wouldn't see them and make fun of him.

At the office, for something to do, he phoned the dealer who had sold Tanabe the prints. 'Mr Mac-Leod,' he asked, 'we'd like to talk to Mr Tanabe more than ever. Are you sure you have no Toronto address for him, a hotel or something he used on one of his visits?'

'No. I'll ask Hajime when he comes in, but Gene used to give me a cheque and disappear. I never knew where he stayed. Have you tried his store in Vancouver?'

'Yes, he's gone missing from there, too. If he comes back or calls, get hold of me right away will you?'

'Of course. I hope nothing has happened to him.'

'Probably not. I don't think we're dealing with gangsters. Thanks, Mr MacLeod.' Salter hung up.

It was time for another chat with Nelson.

He found the assistant at home, and once more in a very distressed state. He let Salter in to the living-room and stood waiting for him to speak.

'Can I sit down?' Salter asked.

'If you want.' Nelson took the chair farthest from Salter and continued to stare at him.

'Something wrong?' Salter asked.

'Nothing to do with you, Inspector. Just a lover's quarrel.'

Again. 'Hauser has been here?'

'No. He phoned. We're finished. I won't have him checking up on me.'

Salter was out of his depth. 'What was he checking up on you for?'

Nelson stood up and began walking round the room, like an actor expressing agitation, although his distress was very real. 'The same thing you were. Where was I the night of the fire? I told him I went home to my parents, so he went over to see them with an excuse about me wanting him to pick up a jacket I'd left there that night. Naturally they thought there was a mistake; they told him they hadn't seen me for two weeks. So he made a scene about how I was being unfaithful to him. My parents live in Oakville! There were neighbours in for bridge! They have been extremely supportive ever since I told them about myself, but my father was very upset when he phoned. Then this morning Jake phoned, pleading with me, but I've made up my mind. He says he'll kill himself, but I'm not giving in to blackmail, either.'

'Mr Nelson, perhaps if we talked about my problem, it might help you to forget yours for a minute.'

'I'm sorry, Inspector. I'm sorry.' Nelson took a breath and returned to his chair.

Just then the telephone rang and Nelson lifted it, listened for a moment, then laid the receiver on the coffee table, where it beeped for a few moments to let him know what he had done, then was silent.

'Right,' Nelson said again, determinedly. 'Go ahead.'

'I've checked up on everyone Drecker dealt with in the last few months from the list you gave me. Nothing very unusual, except for the old Japanese gentleman who was interested in something Drecker sold. Do you remember anything more about him.'

'No more than I told you. He was in several times. He bought a box from us, a sort of cabinet about the size of an attaché case, with a fitted tray inside, with a lovely glossy finish. He asked me where it came from but I didn't know. Drecker just appeared with it one day the way he often did, and I thought it was from a garage sale. He wasn't in when I sold the box so the man came back next day. He and Drecker spent a long time in the back room, and when they came out Drecker looked a bit uptight. I remember him saying something like, "I can't tell you any more. I bought it, box and contents, from a man who walked in the shop. I get a lot of stuff off the street that way. I don't know who he was." The old man came back once more a day or so later, and Drecker wouldn't even talk to him. Told him to stop bothering him.

When the old man left, Drecker told me if he ever came back I was to say Drecker was out. I didn't think anything of it at the time, except that he had probably swindled someone else.'

'It sounds to me as if the contents of the box might have been worth a few bucks.'

'Yes? As I say, I never saw what was in it. When it appeared in the store it was empty. It just had a label on the side "To be held until called for". Drecker had me take that off.'

'And that was that?'

'Yes. Except that after the old man left I heard Drecker shouting at someone on the phone, I'm fairly sure that it was about the box. After he'd finished talking, though, he seemed a lot calmer as if whoever it was had satisfied him. Why, do you think there was some kind of Japanese Maltese Falcon in the box?'

'Don't be silly,' Salter said, embarrassed that Nelson was toying with the same melodramatic fancy that he had entertained. 'I think it's more likely the old man was trying to establish the – what do you call it – the provenance of the box. We know who he is. He's a dealer himself.'

'Ah. The genuine antique Japanese box turned out to be made in Taiwan. Could be. We sold it "as is", though.'

'Another question, Mr Nelson. Who had access to the store? Who had keys?'

Nelson now looked nervous. 'Drecker, of course,' he began. 'His wife, I think. She is part owner and she goes down on Sundays sometimes to look the stock over. She never comes near during normal hours.'

'Anyone else?' Salter watched with interest as Nelson's face turned dark red.

'Yes. Me.'

'You?'

'Yes. I had keys to the doors. I worked late sometimes, and Drecker let me use the workroom to refinish things I wanted to sell.'

'Did you ever spend the night there?'

'Sometimes. There were always a couple of couches or settees to sleep on.'

'Why?' Salter looked around the elegant apartment. 'Why would you sleep there? It's not far away.'

'It was a place to go if I wanted to be alone.'

'Not with anyone?'

'No, never. To get away from someone.'

'I see. Your room-mate.'

'Yes. This isn't the first fight we've had, though I swear it will be the last.'

Salter pondered this. 'Mr Nelson,' he asked. 'Did you ever leave the keys around anywhere? Where are they now, for example?'

Again Nelson looked very agitated. 'I don't know. I lost them.'

'You lost them? When?'

'The day before the fire.'

'Christ Almighty. You don't know where, of course. In here?'

'No. I'm sure I didn't leave them around here. I don't remember handling them after I left the store. They are probably in the store somewhere.'

'Did you look around for them, the next day?'

'Yes, I did. I couldn't find them.'

'What did they look like? Two or three keys on a ring?'

'No. That's what I don't understand. There were four of them – both the doors had two locks – and they weighed a ton. They's why I tried to leave them in the store most of the time.'

'And if you brought them home, what did you do with them?'

'If I took them out of my pocket, I put them on the bureau in my bedroom.'

'I see. And did you? That night?'

'I don't remember. When I came home Jake was in a difficult mood and we started quarrelling right away. As I told you, it went on and on – we didn't even have any dinner. Then I got sick of it and left.'

'So you didn't change. What were you wearing?'

'My suede jacket. Oh, for God's sake, Inspector, do you think Jake stole them?'

'Maybe he thought you went back to the store.'

'And followed me and burned the place down? He isn't a *killer*.' Nelson was shouting now.

'He did have access to the keys, though, didn't he?' Nelson refused to answer.

'I think I'd better find him,' Salter said. 'Any ideas where he might be? We've tried all the obvious places.'

'I told you I don't know where he is.' Nelson was breaking down again.

'All right, Mr Nelson. He's probably just – ' Salter nearly said 'sulking' – 'hiding out somewhere. We'll find him. If he gets in touch with you, let me know, will you?' Salter let himself out of the apartment. He knew what Superintendent Orliff would say: 'A lovers' quarrel, revenge, and then flight when he realized what he'd done.' It seemed obvious. But Salter's hunch was growing stronger.

There was nothing to do until Hauser was found, or the mysterious Japanese turned up, but he needed to think, and he didn't want to be questioned by Gatenby or Orliff, especially Orliff. So he drove home, put the broken screen door in the trunk of his car and drove out to Weston to find the factory. As he expected, it took him nearly an hour to find the place, but when he finally located it he got a pleasant surprise. It was a one-man operation – a kind of carpenter's shop except that the material was aluminium. The owner-manufacturer listened carefully to Salter's problem, then looked at the door. Without a word he turned back to the workshop and led Salter to a huge box of plastic wheels. 'How many?' he asked.

Salter gaped. 'Give me six.' he said.

'Six dollars,' the man said, and dropped the wheels into Salter's hand.

'Will I be able to put them on myself?' Salter asked.

'Sure. There are two little prongs. Open the prongs with a screwdriver or something, and the broken wheel will drop out. Then you drop your new wheel in. No problem.'

'Don't I have to unscrew the corner?' The corner of the frame was held in place by a metal screw.

'Don't unscrew the corner. Don'ᵗ touch the corner. Leave the corner alone. Just open the prongs and drop the wheel in.'

'Can you show me?'

'Mister, you want me to repair the door? I charge a

minimum of thirty-eight dollars for service. Do it yourself. Just open the prongs. Okay?'

'Right,' Salter said, briskly. But he knew when he came to do it there would be one other small thing the man had not mentioned as being too obvious, like 'Put the wheel in the right way round, dull side up.' Ah shit, he thought. After I've broken three wheels I ought to know everything there is to know. He drove home and put the door back on the third floor deck, leaving the wheels on his wife's dressing-table. Later, he thought. Later.

Tuesday was a lost day, except that he found out early that he had some years to live. He reported to the hospital at eight o'clock and was led into an examination room and asked to take his clothes off and lie down on a piece of apparatus that supported him with his legs apart and his feet in the air. A medical aide chatted continuously about how the examination was a bit personal but not painful.

The doctor appeared, the same specialist who had looked at him the first time, nodded to Salter and went to work. Speaking from somewhere below Salter's feet, he said, 'You will feel this pass over the membrane. When it does, tell me.'

Salter ignored him. Very soon he felt something sliding through his vitals on its way over the membrane. After that nothing happened for a few minutes while the doctor searched in Salter's innards. He looked up once and said to Salter, 'How old are you?'

'Forty-seven.' He's appalled by my bladder, Salter thought, which looks like that of ninety-year-old syphilitic.

The doctor grunted, and soon thereafter an icy sliding sensation began again as the instrument was withdrawn. He lay waiting for the verdict.

'You have a slightly enlarged prostrate,' the doctor said.

That's what de Gaulle died of, Salter thought.

'Not too abnormal for your age. The X-rays showed nothing, and the other tests are negative, too. I can't find anything wrong with you. Drink lots of liquids.'

'Thanks. Will I be able to work today?'

'What do you do?'

'I'm a police inspector.'

'Mainly sitting down? You will be all right. You'll want to urinate more frequently, and you may find a trace of blood in your urine. Nothing to stop you working.'

'Thank you. I'm all right then?'

'As far as I'm concerned, yes.'

Of course I may have eleven other diseases that do not come under your speciality, but for you I'm fine. 'Thank you,' he said again.

The doctor left and Salter got dressed, turning his back on the aide to examine himself. He looked normal, but much smaller than he remembered.

At the office he phoned Vancouver again, but Tanabe had not turned up. Another check showed that Jake Hauser was still missing. But he had little time to brood about his collection of dead ends. Very shortly he became acutely uncomfortable and he made a dive for the washroom. When he came back to the office he prepared to start work on some kind of report for Orliff, but within ten minutes he was off to the washroom again. He stayed in the office for an hour during which time he visited the washroom six times, until he got sick of the sympathetic clucking of his sergeant. At noon he said, 'I'm going home where I can pee in peace. If anything interesting happens, call me there. Tomorrow I'm going to hand over this case to Munnings and Hutter.'

He drove home and let himself into the house, looking for aid and comfort, before he remembered that Annie had a job and the house was empty. Supposing the news at the hospital had been bad, he thought. I might be lying here with three months to live and she's off looking for the props for a beer commercial. He lay on the bed, waiting for the next false call of nature, and the phone rang. It was Annie.

'What did he say?' she asked.

'Who?'

'Charlie, please. I've been waiting for you to call all day. I just called your office and they said you had gone home. What did the doctor say?'

'He said I'm all right.'

'Oh, Charlie.' Her breath poured out in a huge sigh. You don't sound very happy about it.'

'Well, you know how it is. You find out everything is all right, then five minutes later you are back in the world looking for something to worry about. Were *you* very worried?'

'Not until Blostein said it might be serious.'

'You talked to Blostein about me?'

'Yes. I'm sorry. I wanted to know.'

It didn't matter now. Salter decided on a joke. 'I'll tell you what,' he said. 'If I become impotent, don't discuss it with Jenny, will you?'

'Why? You still think if she played her cards right she could win you?'

He laughed. 'Hang up now,' he said. 'I've got a problem.'

'What?'

He told her.

Now it was her turn to laugh. 'Want me to come home and take your mind off it?'

'How? Oh Jesus, no. My guess is that I'll be sleeping in the spare room for about a month, trying to keep a low profile. Goodbye now, I've got to go.'

For the rest of the day Salter read, trotted, and wondered at specialists who regarded his condition as not interfering with his work. Once he made an attempt to fix the screen door, but he was unable to concentrate with the ferocity the job required, so he did no more than establish that there were no prongs visible to the naked eye; the instructions had broken down at the first step. He was not much cheered by the increase in the number of wasps on the deck. They seemed to be hiving, or whatever wasps did, and there were seven or eight round him all the time. They made the deck unusable, and because the glass door had to be kept closed until the screen was fixed, the third floor of the house was ten degrees warmer than the rest. Things were shaping for a crisis.

Next morning Salter tested his condition by staying home until ten o'clock. The house was empty. He lay on the bed, letting his mind wander. What I should do, he said to himself, is to systematically review all the possibilities, eliminate the ones that don't work, and proceed from there. Right. How to start? Pretend

you're talking to Gatenby. Right. Here we go, then.
We have several possibilities, Sergeant. One:
Drecker stole the box at the garage sale. Unlikely.
Drecker from all accounts was a chiseller, not a thief.
Two: Drecker bought the box at the garage sale, and
Murdrick, in charge of the sale, pocketed the money
and told his wife the box had disappeared. No,
because if that were the case why had Drecker
refused to tell Tanabe where he got it? Three:
Drecker and Murdrick were in league, and Drecker
then was covering for himself in case the box was hot.
Possibly Murdrick had found his wife's guardianship
of the box ridiculous after forty years and felt safe in
stealing it. Possibly Murdrick had thought the old
man would die. Now, Frank, who set fire to Drecker's
store? One: Tanabe, in revenge after he had tracked
the box down. Possible, if we could figure out a way
the old man could have got into the basement. Two:
Murdrick. The two thieves had fallen out over the
price of the box. The most likely. He's shifty, mean
and possibly capable of it, especially if slightly drunk.
But how did *he* get in? Three: Nelson, the assistant.
Possible, if Julia Costa was covering for him, although
he didn't seem violent. But he loathed Drecker, he
had a set of keys, and there might be some other
reason not yet apparent. Four: Nelson's lover,
Hauser. After the quarrel he might have chased over
to the store, having stolen Nelson's keys. But if he
stole Nelson's keys he would know that Nelson was
not in the store. But a wanton bit of arson was still
possible. Five: the mistress, Costa. Drecker might
have given her a key for their assignations (nice word,
that, Frank). But, like Nelson, she had an alibi, and

there was no good reason that we know of. Six: the
wife. Possible. She had a set of keys and a lot to gain.
But she had also been in Alberta that night, Charlie.
She could have hired someone, Frank. In Toronto it
is possible to hire the services of a killer or an arsonist,
or just a leg-breaker, but you have to be well-
connected and on these grounds Mrs Drecker seems
out of it. Seven: Darling, because Drecker had swindled him. How, though?

Salter sighed. It is, of course, possible, Frank, that
this is one of those nice old-fashioned mysteries, in
which Nelson will turn out to be apparently gay,
while all the time a practising closet heterosexual in
love with Drecker's wife, and the two of them had
planned it together to get the insurance and live
happily ever after, doing yoga on an annuity. In that
case, Nelson's lover doesn't exist, and Nelson is using
him as a cover to screw around with the wife, the
mistress, the lady across the hall, and even Mrs
Murdrick, like in a play I saw once at Stratford
(Ontario) of which all I can remember is that the hero
was named Horney and all the other men thought he
was impotent and trusted him with their wives.
Maybe they are all in it together, and they have
invented Tanabe (really a clever out-of-work male
impersontor aged twenty-two with fair hair)?

Screw this, thought Salter. I'd better get back to
work. He could check on at least one of the theories
right away. He called the office and told Gatenby to
expect him at noon. Then he drove to Queen Street,
turned right along Murdrick's street and parked on
the corner where he made a phone call from the
telephone booth. He went back to his car and waited

an hour, and eventually Murdrick emerged alone and drove off in a panel truck to estimate the non-existent job Salter had invented. Salter waited another five minutes, then knocked on the door.

'It's all right, Mrs Murdrick,' Salter said heartily. 'No problem. I forgot to check on something. Just routine. I have to establish the movements of anyone I talk to in connection with last week's incident. Can you tell where you were on Monday night last week?'

'Sure,' she said promptly, looking relieved. 'In Montreal. I have a sister there, and since Phil didn't have a job on I asked him if we could go down for a couple of days. It was her birthday and they had a big party. We stayed overnight. Her name is Carrier. She lives at sixty Colwood Road in St Henri.'

And there were ninety-five witnesses, thought Salter.

'Thanks, Mrs Murdrick. One last thing. Is your husband around?'

'No. He just got called out to estimate a job.'

'I just wanted to ask him how long Drecker's bathroom took him. Him and Darling, I mean.'

At first there was no bite. 'He didn't work on that job,' she said. 'He's been with some Italian company doing a mall in the West End for the last six weeks. Unless it was before then, was it?'

But Salter was trying to establish something else. 'No,' he said. 'He won't be able to help me, then. Pity. He usually does work with Darling, doesn't he, when Darling needs a tiler?'

'Oh yes. He does all Raymond's work when he can. Why?'

There must be some technique, thought Salter, for

finding out what you need to know without stumbling
around like this. What I've done now is made sure
that as soon as Murdrick comes back he will hear I've
been checking up on Darling. 'It's just that I need to
know who has been in Drecker's store lately. I've
already talked to Mr Darling, but I forgot to ask him
who his helper was. I will. Thanks.' Salter smiled to
show that the matter was of no importance, and left.
Clumsy, but he had got the connection he wanted
between Murdrick and Darling.

Salter drove back down Queen Street to where his
father lived. The two men had little in common any
more, but Salter tried to visit whenever he was in the
neighbourhood.

The old man opened the door of the upper duplex
and expressed surprise, but not a lot of pleasure, at
his visitor. 'Hello, stranger,' he said. 'Lost your way?'

'I was here last week Dad,' Salter said, 'And the
week before that you had dinner with us.'

He followed his father upstairs and greeted May,
his father's girlfriend, who was sitting drinking coffee
in the tiny living-room. She smiled at him and
disappeared into the kitchen. In the five months
Salter had known her she had said only about three
words. She was a stout, mushroom-coloured lady with
wig-like hair and a contented expression. Salter's
father had taken up with her after being a widower
for years when her husband, an old buddy of his, had
died. The effect had been to change the old man from
a misanthropic bigot, grinding slowly and sourly
through his retirement, into an old lecher who never
failed in Salter's company to hint at the sexual capers

he and May got up to. The change was an improvement because it relieved Salter and Annie of the sole
responsibility for the old man's emotional welfare,
with all the attendant dutiful and difficult visits and
invitations. It was true that they thought of him less
often now, a fact the old man was quick to notice.

Now he said, 'What are you up to, son? Caught any
drug smugglers lately?'

'I'm not on the Drug Squad, Dad.'

'That's right, I forgot. You're a dogsbody these
days. What are you doing, then?'

For lack of any other topic, Salter told him something of the case. The old man listened judiciously.

'Ten to one it's the old Jap,' he said. 'Scheming lot,
they are.'

When, thought Salter, have you ever spoken ten
words in your life to a Japanese? To change the
subject, he told his father about Annie's job.

'You want to watch that, son,' his father said
immediately. 'When they start getting restless, the
trouble's usually in there.' He pointed with a thumb
to the bedroom. Then he looked around to make sure
May was out of hearing, and leaned forward confiden-
tially. 'Itchy pants,' he explained. 'You been up to the
mark lately? Keep an eye on her.'

Salter had been raised by this man in an atmos-
phere of Anglo-Saxon puritanism, but now late-
blooming lust had released in his father a powerful
strain of dirty-mindedness that Salter found difficult
to cope with. This, combined with an awareness that
the same idea had crossed his own mind, made him
change the subject again. 'I'm taking Angus fishing
next week,' he said.

'He's the oldest one, isn't he?' His father insisted on confusing the two boys in spite of having seen them at least once a month all their lives. 'Is he keen on fishing, then?'

'Not as far as I know.'

'Ah. Doesn't surprise me.'

'Why?' Salter asked, thinking: This is silly, what do I care what he thinks? But now he was irritated enough to be looking for a quarrel.

'Well, he's not very typical, is he? I mean, not really a man's boy, is he?'

'What the hell are you talking about?'

'Don't get uptight, son. I've watched that boy. He's a bit off the mark, if you ask me. Too much of his mother's hand. What's he interested in?'

'He wants to be an actor.'

'Ah. There you are then. What did I tell you?'

'You don't have to be abnormal to be an actor, for Christ's sake.'

'Watch your language, son. May's in the kitchen. No. But a lot of them are. Fruits, I mean.'

'We caught him with some skin books last week. What do you make of that?'

'He's trying to repress it, see. But it's bound to come out. Never mind. The other one seems all right.' His father never spoke the boys' names, finding them affected, even though they had been used in Annie's family for generations.

Salter stood up. 'Worry about yourself, will you,' he said noisily. 'Let *us* worry about Angus.'

'Don't lose your temper, son. Don't forget, I've had more experience than you've had. I knew a *mechanic* who was a fruit, once, believe it or not. When are you coming back?'

'You are supposed to be coming for supper next week. Annie called you.'

'That's right. I got a message. Oh, son, see if you can stop her from giving us any of her chowder muck. I don't like it, and nor does May. Make it a proper dinner, or we might as well stay at home.' A proper dinner, for Salter's father, meant meat, potatoes, peas and carrots, all with a lot of gravy, followed by something soaked in custard.

'Annie hasn't served you chowder for ten years, but I'll remind her,' Salter said, and slammed the door behind him.

That afternoon he sat down with the telephone and tried seriously to find a suspect with a flaw, or a flaw in his suspect. He began by phoning the Montreal police, asking for Sergeant Henri O'Brien who owed him a favour. O'Brien was delighted to hear from him.

'Charlie,' he shouted, 'what can I do for you? When are we going to the races again?' O'Brien had introduced Salter to harness-racing while they were cooperating on a case.

'Soon, Onree. Soon. Come to Prince Edward Island for your holidays this year and we'll go to Charlottetown races every night.'

'Sounds terrific, Charlie. I've got a cousin with a farm in St Louis. Is that nearby?'

'Not really. We stay with my wife's family near Cavendish. But I can get away. Every night.'

'Ah. Sure.' There was a delicate pause. O'Brien continued. 'So what's the problem, Charlie?'

Salter explained. A routine check that the Murdricks were at a party in St Henri on the previous
Monday.

'It's a pleasure,' O'Brien said. 'I'll call you back.'

Next he called Mrs Drecker. 'We are looking into
the possibility that your husband may have stumbled
across something valuable which someone else
wanted,' he said. Like the goddam Maltese Falcon.
'Can you remember as far back as June? Did you and
he, or just he alone, go to a garage sale in Woodstock?'
He held the phone a foot away from his ear, waiting
for her reply.

'Where's Woodstock?'

'It's about ninety miles away. On Highway Four-o-
one.'

'No,' she said promptly. 'Never. Cyril wouldn't go
out of town. He said it wasn't worth it. When we
went picking we always did three or four sales, and in
a place like Woodstock you would only have one in a
day. It wasn't worth the trip, according to Cyril.'

'You're sure? Not even for something special?'

'Just a minute. What day?'

'The fourteenth.'

'Hold on. I'll look up my book. Whenever Cyril
wanted me along I put it in my engagement book. It
was usually on a Saturday; then, if I had a free day I
could plan a little outing on my own. Hold on.' She
put the phone down, and Salter could hear her
walking along the hall. When she returned, she said,
'On June fourteen we went to three sales in the
morning and two in the afternoon. All in Toronto.
Got quite a bit of stuff, too.'

'Thanks.'

'Oh, Inspector. When do you think this will be cleared up? I'd like to get going again, now the funeral's over.'

'What do you mean?'

'I've been thinking. I might take the store over myself. I enjoy the trade, and all I'd need is someone to run the shop.'

'You might try that assistant, Nelson,' Salter said. Your fellow conspirator is one of my fancier theories.

'I was thinking of him. When would I be able to open up, do you think?'

'That depends on the insurance people, Mrs Drecker. When they are satisfied, you'll get your money.' Unless I catch you doing headstands with Nelson.

'I'll give them a ring. Any luck yet?' She sounded about as concerned as someone inquiring after a lost wallet, Salter thought.

'Nothing firm, Mrs Drecker. We have a number of leads. I'll let you know.'

Next he called the assistant, Nelson. He described Murdrick to him and asked him if he had seen anyone like him around the store or heard his name.

'No, never,' the assistant said, after a moment. 'Never heard of him, and I don't remember seeing him. But we do get a lot of casual trade. He might have been in.'

'Thanks. No news of Hauser?'

'I was going to ask you that.'

'We're looking, Mr Nelson. We'll let you know.'

The telephone rang. It was O'Brien, from Montreal.

'Already, Onree? I only spoke to you ten minutes

ago. I know. There's no such street as Colwood in St
Henri, and there's no one named Carrier in the
Montreal phone book. So I have a suspect with a
phoney alibi and the case is closed. Something nice
like that, is it, Onree?'

'No such luck, Charlie. We didn't have to check.
One of the men here is related to this Carrier. He
was at the party, and he remembers the Murdricks.
Worse yet, Charlie. There is a picture of the happy
feast someone took that night. My man had a copy,
and I'm looking at it now. He says Murdrick is right
in the middle. Sorry.'

'Thanks, anyway, Onree. I'll see you in Charlottetown.'

'Look at it this way, Charlie. It is sometimes nearly
as helpful if you know which horse *can't* win a race as
to know who the winner will be. It helps with the
triactor, anyway.'

'Right now, Onree, I've got eight horses and
they've all broken stride.'

'Then you'll have to start again. That's what they
do at Greenwood.'

'We're beating this metaphor or whatever it is to
death. I'll talk to you later.'

'There's a call for you on the other line when you've
finished with Interpol,' Gatenby said. 'That art dealer
in Yorkville.'

Salter pressed a button. 'Mr MacLeod? Salter here.'

'We've found an address for Mr Tanabe,' MacLeod
said without preamble. 'Gene forgot his briefcase
here one day, and he was so concerned about it I sent
Hajime over in a cab. He just reminded me. Here it
is.' He gave an address in Forest Hill, a district of

upper-class homes in mid-town Toronto, and a name to go with it, Jacob Harz.

Salter looked up the name and dialled. 'Mr Harz? Inspector Salter here, Metro Police. I am inquiring into the whereabouts of a Mr Gene Tanabe and I am informed that he visited you recently. Do you have any idea where Mr Tanabe is now?'

There was a long pause, followed by a theatrical sigh. 'I'm afraid not, Inspector.' An old man; a comfortable, easy voice with a slight accent.

'You know Mr Tanabe?'

'Sure I know Gene.' The voice sounded surprised. 'But you want to talk to him, right?'

'I want to find him.'

There was another long silence. 'I don't know about that. Look, Inspector, can you come by the house? Not now. Tonight. I'm upstairs right now and my daughter won't let me on the stairs unless someone is with me, and the housekeeper's out for a little while. Can you do that? After work. I'll tell you a story.'

'I'm investigating a serious case, Mr Harz. Can you tell me over the phone? Now?'

'This story goes back forty years, Inspector. Can a few hours make any difference?'

'Right. I'll be there at seven.'

'Sure. Any time. I'll tell you a story about Gene Tanabe. I figured I'd be hearing from you, one way or the other. See you tonight, then. Take care.' The old man hung up.

Gatenby put his head round the door. 'Your wife called,' he said. 'She said she's going to be working late. Can you take the boys out for a hamburger.'

Salter dialled his wife's number. 'Gatenby told me you're working late.'

'That's right, I told you I might be. We have a location shot in Markham Village. I have to get a car into the courtyard of a restaurant for a shot of beautiful people dining out. It has to be a night shot.'

'Do the beautiful people drive their cars right into restaurants, now?'

'In the ad they do.'

'What time will you be home?'

'I don't know for sure. You can come and watch if you like.' Annie named the restaurant.

'I'd look a real horse's arse, wouldn't I, hanging about keeping tabs on you.'

'Is that what you would be doing, Charlie? You don't have to.'

'Ten o'clock?' Salter asked. 'Eleven?'

'I don't *know*, Charlie. We may have a drink afterwards. Can you take the boys to McDonald's?'

'I hate McDonald's,' Salter said, who had never set foot in it. 'I'll feed them something.'

'I'll tell you if the plans change. Things happen quickly around here.'

'Don't call after eight. I won't be there.'

'Why not?'

'I'll be working,' Salter said. 'I have to see a guy in Forest Hill.'

'See you in bed, then. 'Bye, Charlie.'

It was three o'clock. Salter sat with his head in his hands and stared at the wall. Tonight, he thought, I will hear a story about how an old Japanese art dealer finally found some pictures he thought he had lost. It will be an interesting story but it will have nothing to do with the case because on the night of the fire the old Japanese will be able to show that he was in Tokyo, visiting relatives. Too many people had testified that Gene Tanabe was not the kind of man to go around burning down buildings for Salter to have much hope. On the other hand he didn't have anything better to do.

'Tea?' Gatenby asked.

Salter looked through his sergeant. 'What haven't I done?' he asked himself.

'I don't know, do I?' There was a note of reproach in Gatenby's voice. 'You haven't told me all of it yet.'

'Sorry. I thought you were picking it up as we went along. You want to go over it? I'll tell you the whole story and you can tell me what I haven't thought of.'

'Like Holmes and Watson!' Gatenby cried. 'But I get to be Holmes, right? Okay, go ahead. Let me pour the tea first.'

'Shut the door if you are going to horse around. I don't want Orliff listening.'

'Right. Go ahead, my dear Watson.'

Salter began with the fire. He outlined all the facts and then concluded, 'So it seems likely that someone set the fire and then let himself out the front door. So somebody had a key and the obvious one is Nelson. Failing him, his boyfriend, Hauser.' Carefully, as he had done for two days, Salter tried to remain objective and let the evidence accumulate, but nothing he could do would prevent his hunch from growing more and more into a certainty.

'But Nelson's got a good alibi.'

'Yes, and anyway, I don't get any smell off him. But he took the keys home and that is the last time he remembers having them. It seems obvious, then, that Hauser picked up the keys after Nelson left, drove over to the store where he thought Nelson was spending the night, and set fire to it.'

'But if Nelson left keys behind, then Hauser knew he wasn't in the store.'

'Right. So Hauser didn't do it. Good.'

There was silence for a while.

'Well, that's the end of that one,' Gatenby said. 'Any other possibilities? Suppose Nelson didn't leave the keys behind?'

'Then Hauser is more likely to have gone to the store, right?'

'I was thinking more of where Nelson *did* leave the keys.'

'They weren't in the store. We checked.'

'So he still had them on him when he got to Julia Costa's apartment. Unless he dropped them somewhere.'

'Well, Costa didn't do it because Nelson was with her the rest of the night. We'd better not get too buried in this. Nelson could have just lost the keys, and anyway, someone else, someone we don't know about, could have picked the lock. The door wasn't barred.'

'Could anyone else have had a key?'

After a while Salter said, 'Julia Costa. But we've ruled her out already.'

'If we keep ruling everybody out, we won't get anywhere. Maybe this Costa woman did it with Nelson – they've given each other an alibi, haven't they.'

Salter shook his head. 'Nelson wasn't lying. The

woman across the hall heard the row, and he did go straight over to Costa's. But you've given me an idea. I don't know if Julia Costa had a key. If she did, maybe others did, too. Nelson said that Drecker often had more than one woman. We may have to look right outside this gang. But let's find out first if Costa did have a key. Come on, let's go and see her now.'

'Me, too?'

'Sure. Stay quiet and watch. Put your new raincoat on. With that hair of yours they'll think you're the Deputy Chief checking up on *me*. I'll just say you're a colleague.'

'Okay, Charlie. I'll just get a match to chew on and we'll be all set.'

They found Julia Costa alone in the store arranging a collection of Mexican furniture made of straw and leather and grey wood. Salter introduced his sergeant as 'Mr Gatenby', and the sergeant sat on the arm of a chair to watch his man at work. Salter explained about the possibility of an extra key and Julia Costa stopped him before he could put the question.

'I have a key, Inspector,' she said. 'It's in my purse. Two, actually, one for each lock. You want me to get them?'

Salter looked at Gatenby who nodded solemnly back to Salter who then nodded to Costa. She disappeared into the back room and reappeared holding a ring with two large brass keys.

Salter took them from her. 'What were your arrangements with Drecker?' Salter asked.

'Usually he was waiting for me,' she said. She

jerked a thumb at Gatenby. 'Does he know the whole story?'

Gatenby looked away as Salter nodded.

'Yes. Well, then. We would arrange to meet in the flat in the evening after dinner. If he got held up I could let myself in and wait for him.'

'Did anyone know you had these keys? Nelson, for instance?'

She shook her head. 'Dennis knew I slept with Drecker, but we never talked about it. It wouldn't have been – tasteful?'

'Good. Now I have a delicate question for you, Miss Costa. Is it possible that someone else, someone like you, could also have had a key?'

'One of his other women? You don't have to be too delicate, Inspector. I know what Cyril was like. No. For the last couple of months I've been seeing a lot more of him and I'm pretty sure there was no other woman. In fact, I know there wasn't. He said so, and the way we were, he didn't need to lie.'

'But in the past he might have given someone a set of keys and never got them back, mightn't he?'

'No. Maybe, but – no. He would get them back, I'm sure.'

Just then the door opened behind Salter, and Julia Costa's face went still. Salter looked around as Raymond Darling came in.

'Hello, hello, hello,' Darling said noisily. 'The fuzz is back, with reinforcements. What's the problem now, Inspector?'

There had been time for Salter to gather his wits and interpret the panic on Julia Costa's face as a fear that Salter would let slip her connection with Drecker.

'Just checking again, Mr Darling. We're trying to locate all possible acquaintances of the dead man. Miss Costa told us before that she knew him slightly through the trade, and I wondered if she could tell us of anyone else who might know him.'

'That's how I met him,' Darling agreed. 'Julia put me on to him when I got interested in antiques. And I did his bathroom, as I told you.'

Out of the corner of his eye, Salter could see Gatenby staring at his inspector in surprise, a sergeant again. Salter fixed him with a stony glare and turned back to listen to Darling, who was still speaking.

'I don't know why you're pestering Julia,' he said. 'I hear the queer's boyfriend has disappeared. Looks pretty obvious, doesn't it? By the way, I thought you were supposed to warn people of their rights before you questioned them?'

Salter said, 'We can talk to anyone we like in the course of an investigation, Mr Darling. If we suspect them, we warn them; then we can use what they say in evidence against them, see?'

'You've been watching too much television,' Gatenby said, trying to get back into his role.

Darling began to look angry.

'Maybe you can help us, sir,' Salter said quickly. 'From what you knew of Drecker, would he be likely to give anyone a set of keys for the store?'

Darling reacted immediately. 'Never,' he said. 'Never. He was too cute for that. No, that assistant had the only keys.'

The accusation hung in the air.

'Oh, don't be so stupid, Raymond. Dennis wouldn't hurt a fly,' Julia Costa said.

'How do you know? Maybe Drecker made a pass at him? You don't know what Drecker was like. What the hell was that apartment of his all about?'

Salter looked at his notes, Julia Costa rummaged in her purse and Gatenby stared with an open mouth from one to the other.

Salter broke the hush. 'That's it, then, I think?' he asked inquiringly of Gatenby, who nodded firmly and stood up. The two policemen paired themselves near the door.

'If any other names occur to you, Miss Costa, or you, too, Mr Darling, call me at the station, will you?' Salter asked.

'What the hell was that all about?' Gatenby asked when they were in the car. 'Who was he?'

'Raymond Darling. Her boyfriend. Her *real* boyfriend. He doesn't know that she screwed Drecker. He wouldn't like that. Not so easy-come, easy-go as Drecker, but otherwise the same type, I would think. You remember, he's the stud who times himself.'

'My, my. Reminds me of you a bit,' Gatenby said. 'Oh, not the *looks*,' he added quickly, as Salter reacted. 'He's got your build and he walks like you. If you ever disguised yourself as a swinger, that's what you'd look like.'

'Thanks. Remind me to request a transfer to the uniformed branch tomorrow.'

'What are you going to do now, Charlie?' Gatenby asked when they were back at the station.

'I don't know yet. I'd better get something written
to show Orliff before I go see this guy in Forest Hill.
Then I'll see.'

He assembled the story in something like orderly
fashion and began to write. When he came to Drecker's involvement, he stuck. There was a firm possibility that the Japanese box was at the bottom of all
this; on the other hand, he still had not found Hauser,
another firm possibility; the third firm possibility was
a person or persons unknown. At this stage the report
required that he give full and accurate details of all
the possibilities. He dialled the pawn squad.

'The box that Cyril Drecker registered with you
on – ' he gave the date – 'did he sell it eventually? If
so, do you know the date and who to?'

'No. After the full fifteen days he could do what he
liked.'

'That means that no one reported the box stolen,
right?'

'Right. Not in Metro, anyway. It might have been
pinched in Timbuctoo, but we don't use Interpol for
stuff like this. One of these days everything will be
on computer, they tell me, and we'll just be able to
punch up a record of everything that's happened,
everywhere in the world, but right now we limit
ourselves to Toronto.' The sergeant's voice was
breezy and jokey.

'So the box appeared in Drecker's store; he covered
himself by listing it with you as sold to him by an
anonymous stranger, then waited fifteen days, and
that's the end of your interest. Right?'

'Not anonymous, Inspector. There is a name listed,

but if the box was hot, the name will be phoney.' He told Salter the name.

The inspector felt an excitement like that of a winner at a race-track. 'Say that again,' he asked, unnecessarily, and heard the sergeant repeat it. 'Thanks,' he said. 'Thanks.'

'As to our interest,' the jokey sergeant continued, 'it tends to fade long before that. It usually lasts about as long as it takes me to write the name in the book.' He chuckled merrily.

'I think you are confusing "disinterested" with "uninterested", Sergeant. You've been out of the court-room too long. 'Bye.'

Salter put the phone down, pleased with his erudition and thrilled with his discovery. 'We've got him, Frank,' he said. 'We've got him, we've got him, we've got him. Now what's that thing that O.P.P. guy is always saying at conferences – "Softlee, softlee, catchee monkey," – that's me now, Charlee the monkee-catcher.' He pulled his papers together.

'You going to tell me, Charlie?'

'Nope.' Salter rubbed his hands together. 'No, Frank, I might spoil it if I say it out loud. You'll be the first to know, though. Now. Let's put it all together.' Salter began to write; after half an hour he came to the details of the fire and checked once more with the Fire Marshal. 'Tell me again, Mr Hayes,' he said, 'why the fire must have been started from inside.'

The investigator went over the details patiently. 'Most of all,' he concluded, 'there was no trail.'

'Trail?'

'Fuse. You'd expect to find some kind of fuse in a

job like this, so that the guy igniting the fire would be safe. That place was a hell of a mess but we didn't find any evidence of a fuse. He just poured it out and set fire to it. And he must have been in the room because he only had a few seconds before the mixture would be too dangerous to be near.'

'So someone poured this stuff around, lit it, and got right out.'

'That's about the size of it.'

'You think he might have been trying to make it look accidental, like a spill?'

'I don't know. Why wouldn't he leave the can behind, then? You found it in the lane, didn't you?' A yearning for Munnings or Hutter surfaced in the Fire Marshal's voice.

But Salter didn't mind now. 'Yes,' he said. 'The Forensic lab confirms the can contained camp fuel, which is right for the job, and there were no prints on it which means the guy was being very careful. He didn't have to be an outdoors type, did he? A lot of people use this stuff for all kinds of things, don't they?' Salter's voice was slightly pleading. He had the solution to this case, so long as there were no difficulties he hadn't seen.

'That's right. Even plumbers use it or they used to. I use it myself in a torch I keep for odd jobs.'

'A blow-torch?' Now Salter was getting a bonus prize to go with the jackpot. 'The kind with the little pump?'

'Right. You know the kind?'

'I've seen pictures, Mr Hayes. Thanks.' Salter put the phone down carefully in case it caught fire and melted what he had just heard.

Careful now, Charlie. Make sure of every possibility. Stay cool.

It was very hard to do. Salter wrote steadily all afternoon.

Chapter Five

'Your mother's working late,' he said to the boys when he got home. 'So we're going out to eat.'

'Can we go to McDonald's?' Seth asked immediately.

'No. I'm going to take us to the best hamburgers in Toronto.'

'Where is that?'

'A place called Hart's.'

'McDonald's is pretty good,' Seth, the arch-conservative, offered.

'Hart's is better. C'mon.'

'It won't have blue cheese and stuff on it, will it?'

He sounds like my father, Salter thought. 'No,' he said.

Angus joined in. 'C'mon, Seth. Dad has a special place. I want to see it. We can go to McDonald's any time.' Lately, between silences, Angus had been Charlie's staunchest ally in the house, hoping, Salter thought, to begin a new life.

They drove down Yonge Street past two McDonald's which Seth pointed out wistfully, and turned on to Church Street. As they were approaching Gerrard Street, the traffic obliged them to stop, and Seth pointed excitedly through the window. 'Could we go there, Dad? It looks real neat.'

'Across the street was a restaurant that had been converted from a gas station, and it used the old

station as its motif. The only time Salter had been in
the place he had been taken there by a young girl, a
student from whom he had been seeking information.
For a short time Salter had experienced the classic
middle-age intrigue with youth to the extent of letting
the girl buy him a record of some country music that
was playing at the restaurant. Taking the record
home, and pretending to have bought it himself, had
precipitated a giant row when Annie produced the
identical record, one of a number owned by Angus
that Salter regularly complained about. It had taken
Annie two seconds to guess that her husband was
under a small spell, and although the end result had
been better relationships all round, the incident
brought back several different emotions – nostalgia,
guilt, and nervousness among them. Now, blocked
by traffic, he swung across the road to the restaurant's
parking lot.

Inside, the music of the age thumped and twanged.
Around the walls, chromium-plated hub-caps and
fenders hung like sculptures.

'Terrific,' Seth said, and picked up the menu.

Salter ordered a beer and two cokes while they
were making up their minds.

'I want an "Eighteen-wheeler",' Seth said.

'I think I'll have a "Tail-pipe",' Angus decided.
'What about you Dad?'

'I don't know. I can't make up my mind between
an "Oil-change" and a "Gear-box". No, I'll have an
"Eighteen-wheeler", too.'

When the waitress came over, Salter ordered two
hamburgers and a hot-dog.

'Why didn't you tell her the proper names, Dad?'
Seth asked, disappointed.

'Because I'd feel silly.'

The two boys looked at him in sympathy. Poor self-
conscious old man, their faces said. It must be rotten
to be like that.

Salter drove them back, conscious of having given
Seth, at least, a big night out. He made sure that they
had what they needed to get them through the
evening and into bed, and set off for Forest Hill on
foot.

The rich are different from us, thought Salter; they
live in Forest Hill. Not all of them, because there are
several quarters in Toronto where prices are out of
the reach of all but the successful dentist class, but
Forest Hill is more than a row of gaudy châteaux like
Old Post Road; nor are the houses being discreetly
converted into flats as in Rosedale, the original High
Anglican quarter.

The village stands at the top of Spadina Road which
has been one of the great caravan routes of upwardly
mobile immigrants since the nineteenth century. At
the bottom end of Spadina Avenue, near the lake, the
garment trade still flourishes. The best delicatessens
are still here, and the Kensington Market is still
called the Old Jewish Market by a previous generation, although the produce is now mostly Portuguese
and West Indian. As Spadina Avenue crosses Bloor
Street, it becomes Spadina Road and passes through
an area inhabited mainly by respectable transients –
students, "singles" setting up house for the first time
– then it climbs north through a middle-class district
until it crosses St Clair Avenue and becomes for a

mile or two the main street of Forest Hill Village.
The village is synonymous in Toronto minds with the
Jewish Establishment, although it was originally created by successful Anglos and still honours Protestant
thrift in the shape of Timothy Eaton United Church,
a cathedral blessed by the money of the successful
shopkeeper to whom the church is dedicated, and it
still contains Upper Canada College where the Canadian Establishment (including Salter, because it was
a tradition in Annie's family) sends its sons.

Salter lived slightly to the east of Forest Hill and
he figured it would be no more than a fifteen-minute
walk to the Harz residence. He walked south to
Upper Canada College, then west into a network of
quiet, tree-lined streets, with large, thick-walled
houses and hardly any pedestrians. As the noise from
the traffic on Parkway faded, Salter took the time to
enjoy the quiet lushness of the area. Autumn was at
its peak, and there were leaves everywhere, enough
on the trees to canopy the sidewalks, and still piled
in brown ad gold heaps along the sides of the road.
The grass was green again after its battle with the
summer sun, and the gardens still had enough bloom
to make a worthy climax to the season. Some of the
houses were surrounded by simple lawns, usually set
with two or three trees, or clumps of white and yellow
birches like the one outside Salter's bedroom
window. Others tried for more elaborate effects; one
house was enclosed on two sides with a superb if
slightly incongruous English rose-garden. Annie was
a good gardener, and the Salters had spent a lot of
summer evenings, when the children were small,
walking these streets, while Annie worked out what

she wanted to do with their own patch of yard behind the house.

The houses were becoming bigger and the grounds larger. The address Salter was looking for turned out to be an immense house surrounded by a high fence which was itself set farther back from the street than Salter's front yard. He walked across the grass and pressed a button beside the gate, setting off a bell somewhere inside the house. The gate unlatched itself with a clicking noise, and he walked through. Now he got another surprise. Between him and the front door, a space of about two hundred feet, lay what even to Salter's eye was a very carefully made Japanese garden. There were rocks, a tiny stream, a variety of shrubs and small trees and a couple of large stones all woven into an elaborate three-dimensional tapestry that forced his eye to work in order to try to take it in. To someone used to roses and coloured borders, it looked strange, deserted and slightly arid. Salter looked at it for a long time, feeling the human hand in its composition, but unable to see the design.

'Nice, isn't it?' a voice said from the door of the house. An old man was standing in the doorway watching him. 'Come in and sit down,' he said.

Salter walked through the garden still unable to take his eyes off it, until he was shaking hands with his host.

'Gene built that,' the old man said. 'That's how he paid his rent. I'm Jacob Harz. Come in, come on in.' He led the way slowly into the house, where a woman of about fifty was sitting in a straight chair.

'Good evening, Inspector,' she said.

'My daughter, Esther,' Harz said.

Salter shook hands. He looked around and picked up a quick impression of a lot of old European furniture, thick rugs, and more pictures than he was used to, most of them individually lit.

'A cup of coffee?' Esther asked.

- 'A cup of coffee would be nice, yes,' Salter said, feeling as if he was in a drawing-room play set in Vienna in 1910. He waited for the next line. Harz waited, too, until his daughter returned with the coffee. He had a narrow dark face and a mass of curly white hair. His hands looked as if every bone had been broken and badly set – arthritis, Salter guessed. He was wearing a dark blue woollen sports shirt, buttoned to the throat, the bottom half of a grey track suit, and carpet slippers.

Esther returned and they all sipped their coffee. Harz settled in his chair and spoke first. 'Now,' he said. 'Gene Tanabe. You're looking for him. Right?' He hasn't done anything, you know.'

Salter said nothing. He was concentrating on being a policeman, on not being charmed by these people.

'But you'd like to talk to him – what do you call it? – you want him to help you in your inquiries. Right?' The old man smiled.

Salter got out his notebook. 'That's right. I'm investigating a case of arson. Mr Tanabe had some dealings with the owner of the store that burned down. I'm talking to everyone who can, or might be able to, help me. That's all. Do you know where I can find him?'

Harz sipped his coffee. 'I can tell him you're looking for him,' he offered.

'How will you do that?' Salter felt himself falling into the old man's style.

'He gets in touch with me regularly. Every day. I'll tell him.'

'I see. Good. When might that be?'

'Tonight. Tonight, Esther?' Harz looked at his daughter to confirm his reply.

'He gets in touch every day,' she said.

'Should I wait?'

Harz shook his head. 'No. I'll make him get in touch with you. He's a bit frightened.'

'What of?'

'That's a thing you should ask him yourself, Inspector, when you see him.'

'All right. Would you tell him it is an official inquiry? If he doesn't present himself to us he'll be committing an offence.' Salter got up, not so much to leave, but to assert that this was *his* interview, not Jacob Harz's.

'No need. Please sit down, Inspector. I said I'll tell you a story. Would you like to hear how I knew Gene?'

'If it helps.'

'It might. Sit down.'

Salter sat down again. In the presence of this old man he felt about thirteen years old.

'During the war,' Harz began, 'they took Gene's house away and put him in a concentration camp.'

'Who did?'

'You people. The Canadian government. The police. Gene spent a year in a camp.'

'I don't think they could have been concentration camps, Mr Harz. Not in Canada.'

'Sorry. The word slipped out. I just missed one myself in Germany. What did you call them over here?'

'Internment camps. But go ahead. It was wartime. There was a spy scare on.'

'Sure. I know. With us they just didn't want us to live any more. Anyway, after a year in a camp, Gene got permission to live outside, so long as he didn't go near the west coast. If he stayed away from Vancouver he could live, so he came to Toronto. Just in time. Did you know they passed an ordinance in this city saying only seven hundred Japanese would be allowed to live in Toronto? City council did that. Where was I? Oh yes, I had a little antique business then, the same one Esther's got now, but I did some furniture restoring too. After the war I got back into the art business and did well – ' he waved a hand at the house and garden – 'but during the war I was just getting by. I was happy to be alive, though, in a free country. Well, Gene came to me for work. I had no work and he wasn't allowed to work except as a domestic, but no one else would have him and he came back and so I let him help me out. I paid him fifty cents an hour, all I could afford and not so bad in those days. He worked like a slave. Some weeks, though, I just didn't have the work and I couldn't pay him the full twenty dollars. But I couldn't lay him off, could I? So we made an accommodation. He moved in with us – officially he was a domestic, anyway – we had a little room, so if I couldn't pay him he wouldn't go hungry. Esther, there, thought he was her uncle, didn't you, pet?'

His daughter spoke now for the first time. 'Inspector, we're worried about him. He's too old to wander about on his own.'

'You say he was staying here, in this house?' Salter pressed.

'He always stays here,' Harz said. 'I look forward to it every year. He's family to us. He's my friend.'

Salter waited for a minute, then asked, 'When did he leave?'

'Two days after the fire. The day your sergeant talked to my daughter. She told Gene your sergeant had been in the store and he got very upset and left that night. He told me not to worry, he would keep in touch. And he has. I know how he feels. Once upon a time if I saw a policeman coming to the front door I went out the back, quick.'

'Mr Harz. If you are any judge, Mr Tanabe is running away from nothing. But he might be able to help me. Will you tell him that? And will you tell him that unless he comes forward on his own we will charge him with obstructing the police when we do find him. Which we will. Now, did he tell you why he was in Drecker's store? I have heard that he thought Drecker had some things that belonged to him.'

'Inspector, ask him yourself when you see him. I would get it all wrong. It was something about a friend who betrayed him and I didn't want to know because it made Gene upset, all right? I don't want to know about things like that about people. I've had enough of it.'

'All right, Mr Harz.' Salter again prepared to leave,

but the old man put his hand up in a gesture to stop him.

'I didn't tell you about the garden,' he said. 'After the war, Gene went back to Vancouver and started his own business. He comes to stay with us once a year on his buying trips – did I tell you that already? – and one year when he came I had been doing well and we had moved in here. He said he wanted to give us a house gift, for what we did for him during the war, and he asked us if we would let him plan the garden. I said, sure. Look at it. He designed it himself and we had a landscape company working here for a month. I've had twenty years of pleasure from that garden. Each time I look at it, it seems a little bit different, or I see something new. It's peaceful.' The old man fell silent, and Salter left.

Now the streets were completely deserted, and Salter walked north, heading for Eglinton Avenue. A yellow patrol car drew up alongside, then pulled away and turned right at the next corner. On an impulse, Salter turned right after the car and almost immediately it appeared behind him and the driver called to Salter to come over to the car.

'You live in the district?' the constable asked.

They are just doing their job, Salter told himself, and showed his identification.

'Right, sir, sorry. We had a couple of calls this evening about a stranger wandering round looking at the houses.'

'That was me. I was looking for a number of a friend's house.'

The constable saluted and the car pulled away.

How do yellow cars make old Jews feel, or old Japanese, he wondered. Secure? Nervous? Anyway, not nostalgic.

At the house Annie was not yet home and Seth was in bed. Angus was watching television and offered to make Salter some tea.

'No, thanks, Angus. Did your mother call?'

'Not while I've been home.'

Salter picked up the paper, but after a while he became aware that Angus was still around. I wish we had something to talk about, Salter thought. Maybe when he's twenty we can start again.

But Angus had something to say. He cleared his throat several times for Salter to look up, then broached his topic. 'Can I ask you something Dad?'

'About life, yes. About my life, no,' Salter said, guessing that this was heart-to-heart.

'We never talked about those skin books I had. You know what I was reading them for?'

'The crossword?'

'No,' Angus said, breaking into giggles and trying to stay serious at the same time. 'I thought I might be gay.'

Salter stared at him. 'You *what!*'

'I thought I might be gay. You know – queer. The way some of the guys talked, I felt kind of left out.' He was still laughing in spurts at his father's joke.

'And?'

'I'm not. I'm not queer.' Angus made a face and left the room.

Annie came in at that point and Salter was too

amazed at what he had heard to greet her. He told her what Angus had said and asked her what it meant.

'Just what you think it means, Charlie. Now you'll *have* to have a talk with him.

'You know, at his age I was still throwing snowballs at little Mabel Tucker, hoping she'd notice and throw one back at me.'

'Oh, I know that,' Annie said.

'How? How do you know that?'

'Oh, Charlie. We've been married for eighteen years. It's one of the things you know about people. Let's go to bed. I'm exhausted.'

Salter's last thought as he looked at the little plastic wheels on his wife's dressing-table was to wonder if people in Forest Hill had as much trouble with screen doors as he did.

'Okay, Charlie. I admit it sounds good. Darling picked up the box from Murdrick at the sale and sold it to Drecker. Drecker swindled Darling, or Darling *thinks* he did, and Darling got hold of the keys and set fire to the store. You figure Darling got the keys while he was working on Drecker's bathroom; maybe Drecker let him have a set so he could work when the store was closed. You also think Darling could have another motive – if he'd found out about Drecker and his girlfriend. So what about Darling's alibi?'

Orliff was leading Salter through his report.

'I'll break it,' Salter said.

'So go and ask Darling why Drecker listed the box as being sold by him.'

'No. I don't want to move until I can hit Darling with everything. I want to drown him. Right now he thinks he's totally in the clear. If I can hit him with a packet all at once, he'll break down. The alibi is phoney. He cooked it up with his wife.'

Orliff looked back through his notes. 'Did Darling's wife seem to be lying when she spoke to you?'

'No,' Salter admitted. 'But it's a phoney alibi, I know it.'

'Interesting,' Orliff said. 'This box. It sounds like an old movie I saw on television the other night. You know the one? With Humphrey Bogart?'

Salter shook his head. 'No,' he said, thinking: Christ Almighty.

'Had that fat guy, Sidney Greenstreet, in it.'

'No.'

'And that sinister little guy, Peter Lorre. What was it called?'

'I don't know. I've never seen it,' Salter said doggedly.

'I'll remember it in a minute. Probably all bullshit, though.' Orliff paused and looked over Salter's report. 'There's one thing I don't like about all this, Charlie. You don't like Darling, do you?'

'No, I don't. What's that got to do with it?'

'Don't get tunnel vision, that's what. Darling is a suspect, right. So is this pansy, Hauser. When you find him don't be surprised if he's still covered in soot. And the old Japanese, too. Keep your options open. Investigate the case, all of it. Look, some of the heat is off the Homicide Squad now – they've found that rapist. We could give it back to them – the whole case – in pretty good shape. Why don't I do that?'

'Oh no, for Christ's sake!' Salter saw his chance slipping away. 'It's *my* case. If I can nail Darling it will do me some good.'

'That's right, it would. But don't make a goddam fool of yourself, okay? Take a couple more days, go see Tanabe, but keep an open mind, do you hear?'

Salter said nothing. Orliff was right and he was offering protective advice, not threats. But Salter was certain of himself and eager to get on with it. Two days would have to be enough.

'All right,' Orliff said. 'Keep me in touch.' He nodded to dismiss Salter and clipped the report to the neat stack he was accumulating on the case, after making the inevitable little note that Salter couldn't see.

When Salter got back to his office, Gatenby was waiting for him in a state of excitement. 'An anonymous call, Charlie,' he said. 'Someone saw a silver Jeep drive away from the scene just before the fire started. And they've found Hauser. He's in Toronto General in bad shape. He got beaten up last night. And someone called Harz phoned, very urgent.'

Salter looked at the sergeant for a moment, then smiled.

'Okay. Put a guard on Hauser. What's Harz's number again?'

Gatenby gave it to him and Salter dialled.

'He's coming here, tomorrow,' Jacob Harz said. 'You want to come over? He's a little bit afraid, so take it easy, will you?'

Like all policemen, Salter had had his share of being regarded as the Establishment thug, but it hurt to hear Jacob Harz slip into the assumption, and, in his slightly edgy condition, he reacted badly. He said, 'I had planned to bring my sergeant over, Mr Harz. He likes interrogating people, especially if they don't confess too quickly. He's lost a couple of cases, though, before we got what we wanted. You got a basement we can use, and a chair? I'll bring the matches.'

On the other side of the room Gatenby had paused in his tea-making activities. His glasses had slipped to the end of his nose and his mouth hung open as he stared at Salter.

'Please, Inspector,' the old man said. 'No jokes. These things happen.'

'So do arson, murder, rape, and beating children to death. Every day. I'll be over late this afternoon.' He hung up the phone. 'Frank,' he said, 'have you ever in your entire career hit anyone?'

'Only once.' Gatenby smiled at the memory. 'I was trying to separate a couple of winos, old chaps they were, who were fighting in that little park at Church and Queen. They were making a lot of noise and it was late, but they were too far gone to hurt each other. Hysterical they were, really. I tried to talk them down but they couldn't hear me, so I gave each of them a little slap round the face. It did the trick. They both started to cry and I made them shake hands.'

Headline, thought Salter: METRO POLICEMAN BRU-TALLY ASSAULTS DERELICTS. POLICE COMMISSION PROMISES FULL INQUIRY. CONSTABLE GATENBY SUS-PENDED. 'Then what?' he asked.

'I left them alone. The last I saw of them they were sitting on the bench, crying their eyes out. When I came back, about half an hour later, they were gone. I could have been reported if anyone was watching, but I didn't *hurt* them.'

POLICEMAN ABANDONS WOUNDED PRISONERS. CIT-IZENS' COMMITTEE DEMANDS SUSPENSION.'

'I'm going to talk to these people, Frank. I probably won't be back today, but I'll call in.'

'Watch out for the old man, boss. Make sure he doesn't try any Tae Kwon Do on you.'

'He's nearly eighty, Frank.'

'They keep themselves in shape, those people. Eat a lot of raw fish.' Gatenby chuckled away to himself at his own wit.

First, Salter drove over to Washington Avenue, and found, as he was half afraid he would, a silver Jeep parked in the street outside Nelson's apartment. Nelson let him in silently and Salter came to the point quickly.

'Mr Nelson, on the night of the fire, you took a cab to Julia Costa's apartment, right?'

'Yes.' Nelson looked exhausted and ill. All the brightness had disappeared.

'Do you own a car, Mr Nelson?'

'Yes, I do.'

'Why didn't you drive it?'

'I wasn't sure where it was parked. Sometimes we have to park on Spadina when this street is crowded.'

'But why wouldn't you know where it was?'

'Because Jake was driving it that day.' The statement came out slowly and painfully.

'What kind of car is it?'

'A Jeep.'

'The one on the street now?'

'Yes.'

'When did you drive it again?'

'The next day, when Jake brought it back. He tried to kill me, didn't he?'

'You know him better than anyone. Would he do that?'

'He had the Jeep that night, didn't he? He went to the store. Now he's disappeared.'

'We've found him.'

'Where? *Where?*'

'I'll let you know after I've talked to him. When did you realize all this?'

'Right away. That was why I didn't want to see him again.'

'So you've known all along that Hauser might be our man.'

Nelson looked at Salter and his face twisted as he fought with his misery.

'I thought so, yes. But I didn't want to see him in prison for life. I talked to Julia about it and she agreed that the best thing was to try and forget about it and hope Jake was gone for good.' There were no tears, but his throat was jerking with the pain of holding them in.

'Did she? When did you talk to her?'

'All the time. She's the only one I can talk to.'

'Did you accuse your friend of trying to kill you?'

'Yes. The next day. He swore he didn't, of course, but he would, wouldn't he, especially after we knew Drecker was dead?'

Clocks were chiming in Salter's head. 'I'm going to see him now,' he said. 'I'll call you later and tell you if you can see him.'

'Don't hurt him, will you.'

Twice in one day was too much. 'For Christ's sake,' Salter shouted, really angry. 'We don't spend all our time beating up people like you for fun.' Then he was

sorry at the effect of his words as Nelson crumpled
into his chair. Against his better judgement Salter
continued. 'Look, Mr Nelson, right now I think you
talk to other people too much when you should be
talking to me. I'd like your word that you will not talk
to anyone about this case, including your friend Julia,
until I say okay. Then I'll tell you something.'

Nelson nodded two or three times as he wiped his
face with his hands.

'Good. Right, then. Here it is. I do not believe
your friend set fire to Drecker's store. I think I know
who might have killed Drecker, but I don't know why
or how. When I can figure those two out, I'll be able
to do something. I may have the answers this
afternoon.'

Now the look of relief on Nelson's face was harder
to take, if possible, than the misery. 'I won't say a
word, Inspector. I'll take the phone off the hook and
lock the door,' he said. 'When can I see Jake?'

'I'll let you know,' Salter said, and left to drive to
the hospital.

Hauser was in a private room to make guarding him
simpler. Salter walked along the corridor until he
came to the constable reading a magazine outside the
door. He showed his identification and the policeman
let him in. 'Not much to guard,' the officer said. 'He's
not going anywhere.'

Hauser was lying back on his pillow, watching the
door. Both eyes were black, and bandages covered
his throat. His lips were swollen and bruised, and his
hair had been shaved on the front of his scalp where
another wound had been dressed. According to the

report, he had three broken ribs and severe bruising on the abdomen where he had been kicked.

'What happened?' Salter asked.

Hauser reached beside his pillow for a pair of steel rimmed glasses. 'Who are you?' he asked.

He was a wretched sight. His skin was mud-coloured and greasy, and his hair was scanty and dying. At his best he could not have been handsome, and the ugly glasses suggested he was indifferent to his looks. Now, swollen and bruised, he would be a real test of charity for any Samaritan, Salter thought. But Nelson loved him, which was no more or less mysterious than the attraction of some married couples to each other. The policeman identified himself. 'What happened?' he repeated.

'I was lonely. I went to a bar for some company and met a couple of queer-bashers. I've already described them, but you won't catch them. You never do.'

'We might,' Salter said. 'But I'm more interested in something else right now.'

'Drecker. I didn't kill him. I know Dennis thinks I did, but I didn't.'

'You were there about the time the fire was set,' Salter asserted.

'I guess I must have been. But I didn't set it.'

'Tell me what you did that night. In detail.'

'Dennis and I had a fight. You know that. Then he left, and I thought he went to the store, so I followed him there.'

'In the Jeep?'

'Yes. But he wasn't there when I arrived and I could see Drecker's truck parked out back, so I went back to Washington Avenue to wait for him. I waited all night, but he never showed up. Finally, I took off and came back next day. That's when Dennis decided I had tried to kill him.'

'So why did you disappear?'

'If Dennis believed it, you would. How could I prove I didn't? I was terrified.'

'Let's get back to the night. You drove to the store. Where did you park, on Bloor Street?'

'No. I went around the back to the laneway. I thought there would be parking space behind. But Drecker's truck was there, so I waited in the lane for about five minutes in case I had beaten Dennis to the store. Then I went back to Washington.'

'How? What route?'

'I went along the lane to the end, and then I went north for a block, then east for another block, then north again, then east – you know how all those one-way streets won't let you go where you want until you get to a major street?'

'Did you come out at Bloor?'

Hauser shook his head. 'You can't get out to Bloor from that lane. I had to go all round the Annex before I could get back on to Spadina first.'

'How long did it take you?'

'About ten minutes. There was no traffic at that time. Why?'

'It's important. To you. Did you see anyone else, any other car, parked with anyone in it?'

'No. It would be nice, wouldn't it? But I didn't notice anything strange.'

'All right, Mr Hauser.' Salter stood up. 'I'll get back to you as soon as I can.'

'I didn't kill him, Inspector.'

'No. I know you didn't. But it looks bad, and I'll have to leave the guard on you for a little longer.'

'You mean that? You believe me?'

'Let's say I don't disbelieve you, and I hope I'm right.'

Hauser looked down at the bed. 'How is Dennis?' he asked, his voice a croak now.

'Upset. And asking after you, so the sooner I get on with this the better. Do you need anything?'

Hauser shook his head. 'Thank you,' he said.

From the pay-phone in the vestibule he called Sergeant Gatenby.

'Tell me again exactly what that anonymous caller said,' he asked.

'He said,' Gatenby began, reading his notes, 'I saw a Jeep, a silver one with the word RENEGADE on the side tearing off along Bloor Street right after the fire.'

'West or east?'

There was a long pause.

'He said towards Spadina. That's east.'

'What sort of voice?'

'Male. Over thirty – not a kid, anyway. Sure of himself. Actually he sounded familiar, but I couldn't say why.'

I can. 'Okay, Frank. That's what I wanted. He won't call again, but if he does, get all the details you can. You know, play along with him.'

'Right you are. On to something, are you?'

'I think so, Frank. I think so. I'll call you later.'

Next Salter drove up Mount Pleasant Road to the American Motor's showroom. There he wandered

around the cars parked outside until he found a Jeep,
and crossed the road to look at it from the other side.
He looked at it from all angles and various distances
until he was satisfied. Two of the salesmen from the
showroom watched him closely. 'I'm in advertising,'
Salter explained to them. 'Just trying out angles for a
visual.' Darling, he thought, you've trapped yourself,
you clever bastard. Now I've just got to figure out
how to jump you.

He drove back down to the Metro Library on
Yonge Street and spent an hour reading up the history
of the Japanese in Canada, especially the wartime
years. Finally he was ready to meet Gene Tanabe.

Jacob Harz opened the door himself and showed him
into the living-room where a Japanese gentlemen
dressed in a grey flannel suit and wearing an open-
necked white shirt was waiting for him.

'Mr Tanabe?'

The old man looked at Jacob Harz for guidance.

'Sit down, Inspector. We'll have some tea, then
Gene can tell you his story.'

A woman in an apron brought in the tea-things,
and Harz poured them all a cup, while Salter got a
good look at Tanabe. Where old age had given Harz
a broken, knobbly look, it had had the effect of drying
and preserving the Japanese. His hands were large,
with heavy, flat fingertips, but the rest of him had
withered gently so that he reminded Salter (and here
the policeman realized where his mind was leading
him) of an old grasshopper, and a legend he had
heard from a Grade Twelve English teacher.

Salter left his notebook in his pocket. Story first,

questions afterwards. 'Now, Mr Tanabe. What is your connection with Cyril Drecker?'

'I killed him, Inspector,' Tanabe said, quietly, impersonally, with a little smile.

'No, you didn't,' Harz said. 'He didn't, Inspector. Gene, tell the man your story, for God's sake.'

'Mr Harz,' Salter said. 'Why don't I listen to Mr Tanabe. Then later on you can comment.'

'Shut up, you mean?'

'That's right.'

'I won't let Gene hang himself.'

'Neither will I. Okay?'

'Okay,' Harz said. 'But Gene wants me to stay with him.'

'So do I. Now, Mr Tanabe. Your story.'

'The whole thing?' Tanabe's manner seemed to suggest a thousand years of history.

'Yes, please.'

'It starts in nineteen forty-two.'

'Start there, then. We've got all afternoon.'

The old man looked again at Harz, who nodded at him. He began. 'In nineteen forty-two I was living in Vancouver on Pandora Street. I was a cabinet maker and furniture restorer. Then the police came and told me I had to move inland. I had nowhere to go. Fortunately I had no family, no wife or children, so I went to a place, a sort of ghost town they were sending people like me to, in the interior of the province. I had a lot of furniture in stock but they would not let me sell it because the local dealers complained it would depress the market, so I put it in storage. When I came back after the war it had all gone – stolen, I suppose. I took only some clothes and my tools so I could work.' The old man paused, and Harz fussed about him, refilling his teacup.

'I had a few personal things from the old country, although I was born in Canada, like you, Inspector.' A small rustle of life appeared in the quiet tale, a hint of passion.

'He's a nisei,' Harz explained. 'That means second-generation Japanese.'

Salter looked at Harz, who shrugged and picked up his teacup.

Tanabe cleared his throat. 'My parents were dead and I had no other family. These few things I put in a box and asked a friend to keep them for me.'

'George Kemp?'

'Yes. George was a good friend, and he was sorry for what was happening to me so he offered to look after anything I wanted to leave with him. I left him my box.'

'Did he know what was in it?'

'No. So I went off to this town and stayed there for a year. Then they moved me to a camp in Ontario, farther away from the coast. After another six months they said I could live on the outside if I stayed away from Vancouver. I wanted to work at my trade again.'

'That's when he came to me,' Harz said.

'Jacob took me in, and I worked for him and lived with his family until the war was over. As soon as I could I went back to Vancouver to start my business again. I became a dealer, now, though, as well, especially in Japanese art.'

'Gene is one of the best known in the business,' Harz said.

Whenever Harz spoke, Tanabe waited, smiling.

'When I returned I went immediately to my
friend's house, but it was gone. Burned down, the
neighbours said, soon after I left. No one knew where
George was. He and his wife and baby had left the
district. The neighbours told me that there was very
little saved from the fire, so I forgot about my box. I
never saw or heard of George again, but about a
month ago I found some of my prints on sale.'

'At MacLeod's gallery?'

'Yes. I often buy things from him. He told me
where these had come from and I called on the man.
I bought my prints back from Mr MacLeod first.'

'You are sure they were yours?'

'Oh yes. Do you know anything about Japanese
prints, Inspector?'

'Something, yes. I know they can be identified. So
what did Drecker say?'

'First, I found my box on sale in the shop.'

'Do you still have it here, in Toronto?' Salter held
his breath. A varnished box in storage for forty years.
It should yield perfect fingerprints – Drecker's, Nelson's, Murdrick's, Tanabe's, and Darling's. 'May I see
it?'

'Of course. It is in the basement.' Tanabe got up
without any of the awkwardness of age, and moved to
the door. Harz waved them on. 'You go ahead, Gene.
I can't run up and down the stairs.'

Tanabe led Salter down the stairs into the huge
basement. A small part of the room was taken up with
a furnace, and along one wall were ranged the usual
laundry machines and tubs, but a corner of the room
was evidently a workshop where Harz could still

dabble at his old trade. There, on the main bench, was the box, glowing with a rich shine.

'You cleaned it up?' Salter asked.

'Yes. Beautiful, isn't it? I had very little to do so I completely refinished it. I want to keep it to remind me.' Tanabe took out a handkerchief and rubbed the lid softly.

So much for fingerprints. After Salter had sufficiently admired Tanabe's work, the two men returned upstairs.

Tanabe continued his story. 'Drecker was not at the store that first day. When I came back he was very unpleasant. He said the box had turned up as part of a lot brought in by a picker, and he had bought it for cash. He did not know who had sold it to him, he said. There was no more to be done. He would not even tell me who had bought the rest of my things. Why? But I felt Drecker was dishonest, and I wanted to find out why the box had turned up after forty years. I bought it back from Drecker. I knew it was mine but there was no point in arguing. I really wanted to find out if my old friend had sold it. In Vancouver, in nineteen forty-two, he was very good to me, and I trusted him. I had a happy memory of George.'

'So you went to look for him?'

'Yes. It wasn't very hard. I soon found out about his daughter, Mrs Murdrick, who lives in Toronto. And then I found out about my box. George had saved it from the fire and he had kept it for me all those years in case I came back. He didn't let me down, not at all.' Tanabe looked happily at Salter.

'But his daughter did?'

'I don't think so. Did you talk to her?'

'Yes. She told me the box had been stolen from a garage sale they had after Kemp got sick.'

'Yes, that is what she thinks.'

'You believed her?'

'Yes. I believed she was telling the truth. She told me her father had kept it all those years and she was very upset that it was gone. Yes, I believed her. But I did not believe her husband, who seemed to be lying and angry with me. I did not believe Drecker, either, so I thought that Murdrick had sold the box to Drecker and told him that he had told his wife it was stolen.' Tanabe paused to allow Salter to speak.

'You couldn't prove it though, could you? It might just as easily have been as they said. Someone stole it and sold it to Drecker.'

'Then why did Drecker act so strange, so hostile?' Tanabe was teaching Salter now, leading him through a dialogue.

'All right. So what could you do?'

'Nothing for myself. But I decided to take a little revenge. I thought that with these people they would all try to cheat each other. Some of my prints have become quite valuable . . .'

'I know what MacLeod paid Drecker, and what you paid to get them back.' Salter interrupted.

'Yes? Well, I thought that maybe Drecker would have cheated Murdrick. So I went back to say good-bye to George and pretended to sympathize with Murdrick over losing "our" box. I told him how valuable the prints were. I exaggerated a little. I told him how happy I was to get them back even though I had had to pay so much for them. I told him Drecker probably got five thousand for them. Lucky Drecker, I said. That's how I killed him.'

'How?'

'Because my shot in the dark was right. I think that two days later Murdrick burned down Drecker's store because he had been cheated.'

Salter shook his head. 'Murdrick was in Montreal that night.'

Tanabe let out a sigh. 'Then it was an accident? Good. But it might have been my fault.'

'What did you expect to happen?'

'I thought Murdrick would perhaps demand some money from Drecker, perhaps assault him a little. But when I heard that Drecker was dead I got frightened. These people were more violent than I thought.'

'So you disappeared.'

'Yes.'

'Where did you go? We searched this town pretty carefully.'

'To Buffalo. I have some friends there. I was frightened to stay in Canada.'

'We serve and protect, Mr Tanabe. That's our motto. We would have looked out for you. But what, specifically, were you frightened of?'

'I thought if Murdrick would kill a man who was cheating him, he might kill me for exaggerating, if he found out.'

It was hard to believe. To do so, thought Salter, you had to get inside the skin of an old Japanese gentleman who had been made timid by his experience.

There was a long pause while the three races drank tea. Then Salter said, 'Murdrick didn't kill Drecker.'

Tanabe said, 'So you say. But I have just thought. You can hire people to do these things.'

'You need influence and money for that. Murdrick had neither. Someone did kill Drecker and I think I know who it was. Up until now I didn't know why. Now I think I know why, though from the start I figured it was a case of thieves falling out. I still can't prove it because there is a very good alibi to break, so what I'd like to do is to take a shot in the dark, like you did, Mr Tanabe. If it works, as I think yours did, then we'll catch him. Will you make another phone call to Murdrick, and tell him something?' Salter outlined the story he wanted told.

'Mr Salter, I am not interested in these people and I do not want anything more to do with them. I don't care who killed Drecker. You will have to find out by yourself.'

Harz said, 'The man is doing his job, Gene. What's there to say no to? Do what he asks.'

Salter stayed silent while Harz urged Tanabe to cooperate. He saw that his request had made Tanabe angry, or, perhaps, revealed the anger he always carried, and he felt the danger of saying the wrong word. Gradually Tanabe relaxed under Harz's pleading and finally agreed to make the call.

'Now?' he asked.

'No. We'll catch him at home, this evening. I'll have to set it up first, so I'll leave you now and come back at eight. Okay?'

'Why go away?' Harz said. 'Eat supper with us, Inspector. It's the sabbath. Please.'

What would a Jewish sabbath meal with a Japanese guest be like? Raw fish or rye? Bagels and seaweed?

'Thanks,' Salter agreed. 'I'd like that. One thing before we leave your story, Mr Tanabe. Why did Kemp make so little attempt to find *you* after the war, instead of carrying the box around for forty years. He didn't seem to try very hard.'

Tanabe looked embarrassed. 'That's what you and I would have done, Inspector, but I think George *liked* looking after the box for me. His daughter said that he told everyone about the box, and how he was keeping it for me. If he inquired after me, and perhaps found I was dead, (and I'm sure people suggested that to him) he might be able to sell the box, but his life would not be so interesting without it. George is a good man, and he isn't stupid, but he is not sophisticated, I think. The box was a sacred trust – it represented his honesty, our friendship, and the time when he went against mob opinion. Of course, he wanted me to come back and claim the box, but the next best thing to that was having the box beside him, not selling it for a few dollars. Am I making any sense? I have often thought about it.'

It made a great deal of sense to Salter as he remembered his own impression of Kemp, the independent old Newfie who regarded Canada as another country, and his son-in-law, Murdrick the twister, as a typical Canadian. ('I gave me word to Gene, d'ye'see, and where I come from you can trust a fella's word.') Salter felt himself surrounded by honourable old men from another age, and he was surprised by the quick flash of an old adolescent regret that his own father did not inspire the same feeling.

No one said anything for a few moments. Then

Salter asked to use the phone and called home. Angus answered.

'Mom phoned, too, Dad. She's working late. Don't worry. I'll take Seth out to McDonald's,' he said, one man to another. 'I'll use my own money. You can pay me back, and it's OK about the fishing. We'll go next weekend.'

Salter then called his office, telling Gatenby to wait for a later call, and to have two cars and four men standing by.

'Can I come?' Gatenby asked.

Salter laughed. 'You can direct field operations, Frank,' he said, and hung up.

While they were waiting for supper, Esther served them more tea, and Harz and Tanabe took the opportunity of a new audience to reminisce about the wartime days in Toronto when the two outsiders lived together. At one point Harz asked Salter if he would like some whisky. 'We have whisky, don't we, Esther, for the Inspector? No? Brandy then. Have some brandy. Esther give the man some brandy.' Again Salter refused. Harz and his daughter then began discussing the various other liquors they could offer the policeman, and Tanabe said, 'They have a little folksong, Mr Salter . . .'

Harz cut him off quickly. 'No, no, no,' he protested. 'My mother used to say that, a long time ago. Now I know as many drunks as Mr Salter does. You shouldn't say things like that.' He was very embarrassed, but Tanabe smiled like an ancient schoolboy. The old grasshopper could still chirp.

Salter suspected that the exchange was something to do with the way gentiles drank.

Esther announced dinner, and they sat down. It was back to Grade Six for Salter, sitting still and watching his manners. Would they put on little hats?

First the daughter lit two candles and recited something formal.

'That is the blessing,' Tanabe said.

The first course seemed to be some kind of fish balls. Tanabe passed him a dish of something red. 'Horse-radish,' he explained. 'You eat it with the fish.'

Probably a compromise, Salter thought, because of Tanabe. One Japanese dish (raw fish) and one Jewish. My old dad should be here for this. He tried some of the fish and horse-radish, and while it was not bad, it was not wonderful, either.

'Did you invent this combination, Miss Harz?' he asked.

'No,' she said. 'Horse-radish is traditional with gefilte fish.'

'Maybe the Inspector would like some beer,' the ever courteous Harz suggested. 'Esther, get Mr Salter some beer. We got some during the summer. It's in the basement.'

Salter stopped them, insisting he did not want any, and Esther served them some chicken soup. This was delicious; it was followed by chicken stew with dumplings. Salter asked if this dish was traditional, also.

'This is a Reform household,' Tanabe said. 'But what we are having is a traditional Friday night meal. Jacob quit going to the synagogue during the war, and raised Esther as an agnostic. Now she is more orthodox than he ever was. She would like him to observe all the rituals.' Tanabe seemed to be teasing

Esther slightly. The daughter said nothing, but smiled tolerantly at him.

Finally Esther served some fruit salad without any ice-cream, and afterwards they went back to the living-room for more tea. Salter, slightly more relaxed, paused to look at a tapestry on the wall.

'That's very old,' Harz said. 'It portrays God's love of the universe.'

'Hebrew?' Salter asked.

'It came from Persia,' Harz said.

Salter gave up, and just concentrated on keeping his eyes and ears open for stories to tell Annie. When he finished his tea he went to work, calling his office and explaining to Gatenby what he wanted. 'Two men at the back, two in front, all of them in plain cars and out of sight, and a car following in case I'm wrong. Okay. In an hour. At seven-thirty. Right.'

While they waited Harz prodded Tanabe to tell Salter the story of his treatment in the war, but Salter had spent time in the library and he grew slightly restive at Tanabe's continual reference to the police forces who moved the Japanese out of their homes.

'Mr Tanabe,' he said. 'The mounties didn't make the decision to move you. That was a political decision. The federal government, the provincial government and the local council. One local MP was particularly active – a guy with a Scots name.'

'They all looked alike to us, Inspector,' Tanabe said.

'Maybe, but things might have been even rougher if one of the senior mounties hadn't dragged his feet, trying to stop what was going on. He knew the Japanese were no threat and he said so.'

'The effect was the same to us.' Tanabe's tone was uninterested. Salter was having no effect.

'Yes,' he said, 'but behind the cops were the politicians, looking for votes. It's usually that way.'

'Why don't we talk about something else?' Harz pleaded.

There was an embarrassed silence for a while, until Harz asked Salter to tell them how he had learned about Tanabe, and the talk turned to MacLeod's gallery and Japanese prints.

Finally it was time, and Tanabe got ready to dial the number Salter had given him. 'Do you really think he will believe this, Mr Salter? If he thinks about it, surely he will suspect something.'

'Murdrick is not a thinker, Mr Tanabe. We are trying to make him panic. If it doesn't work, I'll have to go at it another way, but if it does work it will save me a hell of a lot of trouble.'

Tanabe dialled the number and waited. Then, 'Mr Murdrick, this is Gene Tanabe. Do not hang up. Listen. This is very important to you. Please. Listen. The police have the box, my box. They have been questioning me all day and now they have just taken it away for testing. I told them I do not care now who stole the box, if it *was* stolen, but they are very interested in whoever had the box lately. I don't know why. I am calling you just in case. Because your wife and her father looked after it for so long. I thought maybe you did sell the box, and I am phoning to tell you that I want to forgive and forget. But the police are being very persistent.' Here Tanabe paused, and the other men could hear Murdrick shouting. 'Then you have nothing to worry about, Mr Murdrick. I am

very glad. Please give my regards to your wife and
your father-in-law. Goodbye, Mr Murdrick.' Tanabe
broke the connection immediately and put down the
receiver.

'Very nice, Mr Tanabe.' Salter said. 'That should
be it.'

'What if Murdrick just phones, Inspector? You got
his line tapped?' Harz inquired.

Salter shook his head. 'He won't phone in front of
his wife. And if we've scared him, he'll want to talk to
Darling right away.'

The phone rang again, and Salter answered it.
'Right,' he said. 'We're on our way.' He stood up.
'Murdrick is getting into his truck,' he said. 'I'll see
you later.'

Salter raced along Chaplin Crescent, slowing slightly
at all the new stop signs, crossed Yonge Street and
drove along Davisville Avenue to Mount Pleasant
Road, where he turned towards downtown.

The radio spoke. 'Suspect travelling west on Queen
Street.'

Salter was now travelling south on Jarvis and he
continued on to Queen and turned east into Cabbagetown.

The radio spoke again. 'Suspect now travelling
north on Parliament.'

Now they were right behind the police car. Salter
turned north on Parliament and saw the car about a
block ahead. In front of it was Murdrick's truck,
paused at a stop-light. He spoke into the radio. 'Take
it easy. I've got the house staked out, and I can see

him. When he stops just keep circling the block until we need you.'

Murdrick turned left and Salter followed. When the truck stopped, Salter parked fifty feet away. Murdrick ran up to the door and banged on it with his fist until he was let in.

Salter spoke into the radio. 'Give them five minutes, exactly. I'll take us in the front door. I want them separated right away and taken down to the station. Then we'll search the house.'

Five minutes later Salter knocked at the door. When the door opened, he said, 'Mr Darling? I'd like a word with you.' Darling tried to close the door, but two policemen carried him with them as they moved into the house. There was a small scuffle when Murdrick tried to get through the back door, but the two men were soon installed in the police cars and taken away.

Chapter Six

Murdrick and Darling were being held in adjoining rooms. Salter began with Murdrick and it took him very little time to uncover the tiler's involvement. He had arranged for Darling to take the box on the day of the yard sale, and Darling had delivered it to Drecker. That much he admitted to in a rush in order to deny any involvement in the fire, which he could not have been involved in anyway, as he pointed out, six or seven times, belligerently, pleadingly, and finally in a continuous whine, because he was in Montreal.

'But you knew Darling could have set the fire,' Salter pointed out.

'He could have; he might have; I don't know anything about that,' Murdrick repeated over and over again, abandoning Darling immediately.

'So you stole the box and profited from the theft? Right?' Salter asked, adopting a quasi-legal tone.

'I got two hundred dollars for it,' shouted Murdrick. 'Two fucking hundred.'

'Darling swindled you, then.'

'I guess so. No. I don't *know*. He says he only got four hundred from Drecker,' Murdrick said, shouting still in frustration and fear.

'Why did you go over to Darling's tonight, then?'

'To warn him. Because I didn't know *what* was going on, and when that old Jap told me how much Drecker had got and then called me to tell me you fellas were on to the box, I figured I'd better let Darling know.'

'You didn't want to let your old pal down?' Salter jeered. 'Or you figured we could nail you as an accessory after the fact to arson and murder?'

'I didn't have nothing to do with the fire.'

'But you thought Darling might have, didn't you?'

'Yes, I bloody did.'

'Why?'

'Because of the state he got into when he found out how much the stuff in the box was worth.'

'What did he say?'

'I don't remember.'

'Threats? Promises to get Drecker?'

'I don't remember. All I remember is he was in a bloody rage.'

They went round it for an hour. Salter had got what he wanted in the first five minutes, but he pressed Murdrick to the limit before he got him to sign a statement about the theft and Darling's involvement. Then he told Murdrick he was holding him for theft and for further questioning about the arson, and had him locked up for the night.

Before he moved on to Darling he went over the case with Gatenby to clear his mind, and got a useful suggestion from the sergeant. He took Murdrick's statement into Darling and read it to him while Gatenby sat by, taking notes.

'So, Mr Darling, we have you, on the evidence of the box itself, and on Murdrick's statement, on a charge of theft over two hundred dollars. Looks as though you are going to need one of your professional friends pretty soon.'

'Drecker set it up,' Darling said immediately. 'He was the fence, and he's dead.'

Salter smiled. 'He'd covered himself,' he said. 'He listed the box with us when you brought it in to him, in case it was stolen. Said it had been sold to him by a casual vendor. You. R. Darling of Church Street. I've known that for a week.'

'That cunning bastard,' Darling cried, as he realized how careful Drecker had been.

'Now let's move on. When did you decide to burn down Drecker's store?'

Darling exploded. 'What the hell are you bastards up to?' he shouted. 'Sure I stole the box with Murdrick, but I'm not a bloody arsonist, mister, and you know it. My wife and the people I was playing cards with that night can testify as to where I was. You won't get me on that one. I'm covered.'

Salter pressed the point in several ways and watched Darling's confidence build as the policeman found no new chink to probe. Then he said, 'Do you read detective stories, Mr Darling?'

'What's that got to do with anything?'

'I'm just asking. You don't have to answer.'

'Sometimes. Sure.'

Salter nodded. 'Do you know what a cliché is?' A recent case had taken Salter into the academic world where he had heard a lot about clichés from the experts.

'Of course I know what a cliché is,' Darling responded, offended and arrogant.

'Well, let me tell you then that you've been reading too many stories. Your alibi is a cliché, Mr Darling, one of the oldest in the trade.'

'What the hell are you talking about?' Darling responded, frightened but still noisy.

'The trick of putting the clocks back.' Salter pretended to consult his notebook. 'According to you *and* your wife, on the night of the fire you woke her up, pointed out the time.' Salter searched for the right word. 'Did your stud act, pointed out the time *again*, and went back to sleep. Right?'

'That's right.'

'I'll tell you what really happened, shall I? You went down to Drecker's store from your card game – I've talked to the professional people you played with and they confirm your story – set fire to it, drove home, put the clock back an hour, showed your wife the time, performed, pointed out the time again, waited until she was asleep, then put the clock forward. As I say, a cliché, typical of a clever-dick mind.'

Darling went white. 'Jesus Christ. You bastard. You *are* trying to frame me.'

'I'm trying to get you to make it simple for me.'

'Never, you sonofabitch. No way.'

Salter hardened his pose. 'I mean, save me a lot of trouble. Let me tell you something. It's very tough to get out of a fire clean. You always take something with you. We will pick your house and shop apart until we find something you took away from Drecker's that night. A bit of dust from his basement floor on your shoe; a fleck of paint from the wall. It'll be there, and we'll find it. But it may take us a long time. You could save us a lot of trouble.'

To his dismay, Salter saw some of the tension go out of Darling.

'You can search all you want, but I wasn't there, so you won't find anything you haven't planted. I wasn't there.'

Salter brought up his last gun. 'Then why did you try and frame Jake Hauser?'

Once more Darling went pale, but this time there was real fright in his voice, as he said, 'What the fuck are you talking about?'

'I'm talking about the phone call you made about the silver Jeep you saw leaving the fire.'

'What phone call? What Jeep? What are you talking about?'

Now Salter felt sure of himself. 'We have a voice-print of the call,' he said (this was Gatenby's suggestion) 'and we can match it as easily as we can match your fingerprints on the box. So why did you try and frame Hauser?'

Darling looked for a way out, then accepted the charge.

'Well, he did it, didn't he?'

'Did he?'

'Sure he did. Those two queers had a fight so Nelson's pal tried to kill him. It's bloody obvious, except to you.'

'Who told you? Julia Costa?'

Darling was silent.

Salter nodded. Even Nelson thought so, and he shared all his thoughts with Julia Costa. 'So you wanted to help us out, like a good citizen, like your professional friends would have done,' Salter said. 'Instead of reporting your suspicions to us, you made up a nice little story to wrap it all up for us, right? You might be interested to know that your story was so bloody silly that I was able to prove Hauser couldn't have done it just by checking your story. So now, why the phone call? I know the answer, of course. To divert suspicion, as they say in those stories of yours.'

'No, it goddam wasn't,' Darling roared. 'I didn't set fire to the goddam store. All I was worried about was getting nabbed for stealing the lousy box. Sure Drecker swindled me . . .'

'And you swindled Murdrick.'

'I took more risks than he did. But *I didn't set fire to his store.* But you were so hung up on that box I figured you might find out eventually how it got stolen, and I figured that if you got Hauser first, you'd be happy and forget about the box. Christ, it looked obvious to me.'

'Just like you do to me.'

'Never, mister. Never. I didn't kill him, I tell you.'

And there they stuck. Salter tried all the tricks, including getting a colleague to play Mutt to his Jeff, but Darling was immovable. He was badly frightened as he saw the case against him, but he found a certainty from somewhere to hang on to and nothing would shift him.

At midnight Salter gave up. He charged Darling formally with the same offences as Murdrick, and went home to bed, where he lay awake for most of the night, replaying the mental tape of Darling's interview.

'Are you going to have another go at him now?' Orliff asked him the next morning. He was in the office

when Salter arrived and the two men had gone over
the case together.

'I guess so. Then we'll take his house apart.'

'You certain of yourself, Charlie?'

'Yesterday I was, but last night I got a feeling from
Darling that there's something I haven't thought of.'

Orliff stiffened. 'I told you, leave the feelings and
the hunches to Sherlock Holmes. Just get all the facts
and see what they add up to. Now, do you think he
did it from what you've found out so far, or not?'

Salter looked out the window. 'I think I do,' he
said.

'Then go and get him. By the way, whose idea was
it to tell him we had a voice-print. That was cute.'

'Gatenby,' Salter said, still brooding.

'Sly bastard. And this clock stuff. Cliché or not, it
sounds okay to me. It'll make you look pretty at the
trial if you can nail him.'

'If I'm right, I'll nail him,' Salter said, and picked
up his notes to go back to questioning his two
suspects.

But Salter was wrong. He had spent ten more minutes with Murdrick, trying to get him to recall every
word Darling had ever spoken, when Gatenby poked
his head round the door.

'Something funny here, sir,' he said. 'You should
look at it.'

It was a report from the Fire Marshal's office:
someone had set fire to Darling's store the night
before. Salter stared at the report, sensing that his
whole case against Darling was coming to pieces.

'Does this screw it all up?' Gatenby asked gently.

Salter picked up a pencil and started listing. 'Murdrick and Darling are in jail; Tanabe is in the clear;
Hauser is in hospital. So who have we got?'

'Maybe a coincidence,' Gatenby offered. 'Or a good
way to give Darling an alibi.'

'Right, Frank, right,' Salter said immediately. 'That
must be it. Who then? Not Nelson, that's for sure.
Julia Costa? Mrs Drecker? One of the wives? Darling's wife, maybe, not Murdrick's.' Salter thrashed
around, looking for an accomplice of Darling's. He
pulled the phone towards him and dialled the Fire
Marshal's office, asking to speak to the investigator of
the fire.

'Smudge-pots,' he cried, after listening for a few
moments. He listened for a few more moments.
'Okay. Thanks.' He put the phone down. 'Somebody
put smudge-pots in Darling's store last night while
Darling was here. Smudge-pots are what construction
workers use in the bush to keep off mosquitoes. No
damage, just smoke. What the fuck.' Salter gazed out
the window.

Five minutes later Gatenby spoke, but Salter
waved him to silence. After a good ten minutes he
slumped in his chair and began to scratch the top of
his head with both hands. Then he put his hands over
his ears, and shut his eyes.

Gatenby looked at him worriedly. 'Okay, sir?' he
asked.

Salter got up. 'I'm okay, Frank. Put your coat on.
We've got a call to make.'

In the car he explained to the sergeant exactly what
had happened. 'Stay downstairs when we get there,'

he said. 'I won't need any help inside. This is not going to be much fun.'

He parked alongside the house with his wheels up on the sidewalk. When he knocked on the door, Mrs Murdrick answered immediately, her face muddy with lack of sleep. 'What do you want now?' she wailed in misery, when she recognized Salter. 'You've got my husband in jail.'

From the top of the stairs George Kemp spoke. 'I think it's meself he's after,' he said. 'Come on up, Inspector, while I put me coat on.' He stood majestically on his short legs, holding open the door of his room in invitation.

Salter climbed the stairs and entered the old man's room. Kemp closed the door and the two men sat down. They waited for a minute, then Salter spoke.

'I have to warn you . . .' he began.

The old man waved his hand slowly. 'You can forget all that,' he said. 'I did it; I'm not sorry I did it; I'm sorry for the fella who died, but that was no part of me intentions. I just wanted that bunch of twisters to pay for stealing the box I had kept safe for forty years. Now Gene will know how I felt about it, anyway.'

'How did you know it was Drecker and Darling? Your son-in-law never told you, surely?'

'I've bin follerin' the case step by step from the beginning,' Kemp said. 'Listen.'

Downstairs the phone was ringing. The two men listened while Mrs Murdrick answered a call for her husband and told the caller that Murdrick had gone away for a few days. Every word came clearly through the floor.

'They built these houses of plywood,' Kemp said.

'So you knew that Darling took the box and passed it to Drecker?'

'I had me suspicions from the first, but when Gene came and told me he'd found it, I assumed then that it had got into Drecker's hands by accident. But then the twister downstairs got a bit nervous and started making phone calls while I listened in.' He pointed to the floor. Now his face was definitely splitting; his mouth was open a little wider at one side than the other and a wedge-shaped gleam of yellow teeth showed through. 'Then I heard Gene telling him about the money Drecker had got for them pictures, and after Gene left he waited until me daughter went out shopping and then all bloody hell broke loose downstairs. Shoutin' at Darling on the phone he was – you didn't need any extension.'

'So you drove out to Drecker's store and set fire to it. How? Where did you get the keys?'

'I didn't need any keys. Just a length of half-inch copper pipe, a funnel and a drop of white gas. They are all in me truck still. You'll need them for evidence.'

Salter found it hard to believe. 'You stuck a pipe through the window, poured gas down it, and then lit it?'

'That's right. One of the windows was covered over with a bit of plastic. It was easy as stealing pennies from a blind man.'

'What did you use for a fuse? We didn't find anything.'

Kemp beamed. 'Fooled you there, did I? Well, I'll tell yez. The week before, I'd taken the little lad over to Centre Island to one of them picnics. They had a lot of fireworks there, and they come to mind when I was looking for a fuse. You know them sparklers we used to have as kids? You can still buy them in Chinatown and I bought a packet on the Saturday. I chucked one in first and let the gas reach it. Made a dandy fuse, that did.'

'Jesus Christ,' Salter said. 'You could have blown yourself up, you know that?'

'I've been using naphtha for sixty years, mister, and I'm still here.'

'But didn't you think that we might have suspected your son-in-law?'

'Ah. That's why I did it when he was in Montreal. I drove him to the station meself before I went over to Drecker's. I thought of it, right enough.'

Salter thought to himself: That's it. When Mrs Murdrick had told him of the family outing to Montreal, he had assumed it included Kemp. He never checked, though. Just forgot about them all after that. Jesus Christ.

'We were bound to track you down eventually,' Salter said, to keep the old man talking.

Kemp cleared his throat and sniffed, twisting his face to open up all the passages. 'I don't know about that, Mister. Some of the polis I've known in this country couldn't track a wounded elephant through six feet of snow. Anyway, youse are forgettin', I didn't plan to kill that fella; I just wanted to set the cat among the pigeons, d'ye see? I thought if there was a little fire in Drecker's basement, and me son-in-law away in Montreal, then Drecker would jump to the conclusion that Darling had done it, and those two would have a go at each other. That's all I planned. A little back payment to the whole gang of them for taking Gene's box away. A little bit of a frame-up, like.'

A little bit of a frame-up. Just like Tanabe. A little bit of revenge. 'Your son-in-law and Darling and Drecker were all in it together,' Salter said. 'Why take it out on Drecker?'

'Well, me son-in-law is stupid, d'ye see, so Darling and Drecker swindled him easy enough, and then Drecker swindled Darling – gave him four hundred dollars for stuff worth thousands, he was the only one really profitin' – Drecker, I mean. I figured that if I could make him pay, then I'd be satisfied. As I say, I didn't mean to kill him.'

'You're a hard man, George,' Salter said eventually.

'He made me let down me friend,' Kemp said. 'After forty years.'

There was nothing left, except, 'How did you ketch on to me in the end?' Kemp asked. 'That was smart of you,' he added generously.

'After last night it wasn't hard. All I needed was to find a plumber who wasn't in jail, someone who knew about white gas and smudge-pots.'

'How's that?'

'Smudge-pots. The kind steam-fitters and plumbers use up north. You keep *them* in your truck, too?'

'There's a couple left still.'

'But why smudge-pots? They wouldn't set fire to anything, would they?'

'Haven't you figured that out yet? One – ' here Kemp stubbed a finger like a banana into his palm – 'I wanted to cause a lot of smoke damage. Two: I didn't want anyone hurt this time. Three: smudge-pots or no, I heard me son-in-law phoning Darling last night, after he got a call from Gene, d'ye see. I can put two and two together and I knew it might look pretty bad for Darling. I've killed one man, hangashore that he was, and I wanted to rightify it. I didn't want another going to prison for me act, so I figured if Darling's place caught fire while you was having at him with your billy knockers, he'd be in the clear.'

Salter stood up. 'We'd better go,' he said.

Kemp put on his jacket and a flat cloth cap, and preceded Salter down the stairs. His daughter stood in the hall, silent and terrified. Kemp gave her an awkward kiss on the cheek. 'I'm going down to the cop-shop to help them with their inquiries,' he said. 'Don't upset yourself.'

From upstairs came the sound of a toilet flushing and a child's voice calling for his grandfather.

'Let's go before the little fella sees us,' Kemp said quickly.

Inside the car, he settled himself down and addressed Gatenby. 'How are you, Officer?' he asked.

'Fine,' Gatenby said, nonplussed. 'How are you, Mr Kemp?'

'Not bad, considering,' Kemp said. Then: 'How much do you think I'll get for this little lot?' he asked.

It was a question that had occurred to Salter. 'I don't know, George, I don't now,' he said eventually.

'Well, as the man said, I'll do as much as I can, but me infarction will probably take care of most of it.' And he laughed.

*　*　*

Before Salter went home he had a personal call to make, in Forest Hill. Harz and Tanabe were both at home, and Harz greeted him enthusiastically.

'All wrapped up, Inspector?'

'Yes, it is.' And Salter told the story. As he got to the point of his discovery of Kemp's involvement, Tanabe anticipated him and made a sighing noise, a tiny cry of misery.

'George?' he asked. 'My friend George? He did it?' He felt for a chair behind him and sat down.

Harz moved over to him. Salter explained how, and as far as he knew, why, Kemp had done it.

Tanabe stared at Salter, but turned to Harz when he spoke. 'It was my fault,' he said. 'George did it for me.'

'No, no, Gene,' Harz said. 'George did it for himself. Right, Inspector?'

Salter grabbed at this. 'I'm sure of it, Mr Harz.'

'How is George?' Harz asked.

'He seems fine, Mr Harz. I'll arrange for you to see him as soon as possible. I'll call you.'

'Good, good,' Harz said. 'I'll call my lawyer now.'

Salter got up to go. 'Goodbye, Mr Harz,' he said. 'Mr Tanabe.'

Harz came forward to show him to the door, but Tanabe just sat there looking at his hands for help.

There was enough distraction at home to keep Salter occupied until the evening, but by nine o'clock Annie was watching television and he was staring at the wall. She kept her eye on him until they went to bed, then slowly she got him talking. After a while Salter stopped justifying himself and began to speak calmly

about his prejudice against people like Darling, to
treat it objectively. When he started yawning, Annie
shut up and concentrated on staying awake until he
began to snore.

'Plumbers,' Salter said to Orliff later. 'I got stuck on
the idea that we were looking for a plumber, and all
the rest fell into place, the wrong place. I might have
sent Darling up, you know that?'

'Don't sweat about it, Charlie. I warned you about
tunnel vision, but you got there in the end. If you
hadn't figured out that Darling made that phone call
you wouldn't have pulled him in, and the old man
might never have acted. Sounds to me like the old
fella would have come forward anyway if we'd charged
anyone else. Nice old guy. And you couldn't have
found any evidence on Darling.'

'The only one with the know-how and no alibi. I
assumed he was in Montreal with the rest of the
family, but he only went as far as Union Station. Not
very bright, was it?'

'I told you, don't sweat about it. Next time, though,
don't let any little hunches get into the act. If you
hadn't liked Kemp so much, maybe you'd have
checked up on him earlier. And the same goes for
Darling. You didn't like him, did you? What happened to the two gays, by the way?'

'Nelson is taking over the shop, in partnership with
Mrs Drecker.'

'And his friend?'

'He and Nelson have split up. Nelson *did* think
that Hauser tried to kill him, and Hauser finds that
hard to forgive.'

'That's too bad.' Orliff made a final note. 'And this Julia Costa? The friendly neighbourhood tart? She outside it all?'

'Oh yes. She's had it with plumbers, though.'

Orliff laughed. 'Now Charlie, listen to this. The Deputy wants to know if you want back in administration. While you are thinking about that, think about staying here with me. Special assignment. The old man is agreeable and I like having you around. I get everything that doesn't fit the regular squads, and I help out during the rush periods. What do you say?'

Salter considered. Orliff was in many ways an ideal boss, without affection, malice, envy or fear. He did his job scrupulously and well, and watched the politicians on the Force manoeuvre and strain for position while he sat still, moving upwards into the spaces created by the internecine struggles in the organization, all the while looking after his own men.

'I'll stay here,' Salter said.

Orliff nodded. 'What about old Frank? We'll shift him out, eh? Get you a real sergeant. Who would you like?'

Salter shook his head. 'No. I'll keep Frank. I think he likes working with me and I'm used to him now. Besides – ' here Salter the paranoiac confessed his real need – 'I can trust him.'

'Right. You tell him, will you?' Orliff nodded to show the interview was over.

Wednesday evening. Annie had taken the boys to a movie, and Salter was in the back yard, looking at one of Angus's magazines which he had found at the bottom of the pile of old newspapers waiting to be put out for garbage.

Then, first one, then two wasps appeared, until a little swarm had materialized around him.

Right, he thought. He finished the rest of his beer, put the magazines in the garbage can, and climbed the stairs to the third floor. There he sat and looked at the screen door for a long time, then got out the magnifying-glass that came with the dictionary they had received for joining the book club. Through this he could see, as clearly as anything, the prongs that held the broken wheel. On his wife's dressing-table he found a nail file and a pair of eyebrow tweezers. With these he opened the prongs, lifted out the wheel, and dropped in the new wheel, easy as pie. He lifted the door on to its track, using the nail file to depress the wheel on the top of the door, and the door slid neatly into its grooves. He tested it gently, then firmly, and the door rolled smoothly in its track, just as if it had never been broken.

His family arrived home a few minutes later, and Salter just had time to get settled in front of the television with a fresh beer before they walked in.

When the boys had been hustled off to bed, Annie said, 'Look what I bought today.' She showed him a can of 'Hornet Death'. 'All you have to do is spray this stuff on the nest and it's guaranteed to kill all the inhabitants in thirty seconds.'

Salter nodded approvingly. 'I've fixed the door,' he said, over his shoulder. 'No problem.'

'Wow!' Annie said. 'I should go out more often. Oh, I've got a bit of news for you.' This in her 'by-the-way' voice. 'I overheard Angus and Seth talking about sex tonight.'

'Seth!' Salter yelled. 'He's eleven, for God's sake.'

'Think back, Charlie.'

'What was Angus telling him?'

'He was telling him not to worry. It was all normal, what was happening.'

Salter gaped at her. Then he smiled. 'So, I don't have to take Angus fishing,' he said.

'Oh, Charlie. You were supposed to go *last* weekend.'

'Okay, okay. I was just joking. Don't worry. We're going.'

'Good,' she said. 'You never know. You might even enjoy it.'

Epilogue

They fished for two hours, catching a few small pickerel and some bass, and then Angus reeled in. 'I think I'll just sit here for a bit,' he said.

He's bored, Salter thought. Huckleberry Finn would have been as happy as if he'd been on salary, but my son is bored stiff. Salter got out the lunch of sandwiches he had made, and after they had eaten he started moving them upstream again, towards the cabin. The afternoon wore on slowly until Angus said, 'How long do you usually stay out, Dad?' and Salter gave up. He was now in an ugly mood, and yet aware enough of Annie's voice in his ear to try and blame himself for it. They docked at the cabin at five, and Angus disappeared inside. By the time Salter had tidied up the boat and joined him in the cabin, the boy was once again sitting on his bunk looking at a magazine.

'Start the fire, will you?' Salter asked him.

'How?'

'With paper, and little sticks, then bigger sticks and then logs,' Salter said.

'Where can I find any wood?'

Salter pointed through the window. 'Out there,' he said.

Angus went outside and came back a few minutes later with two sticks in his hand. 'This is all I could find,' he said.

Salter led him to the window. 'Out there,' he said,
'is maybe two hundred square miles of virgin forest
with maybe twenty dead and fallen trees to the acre.
Now get the hatchet and go out and bring back some
wood.'

Angus went out again and eventually returned with
an armload of wood, some of which was dry enough
to be useful, and Salter showed him how to lay the
fire in the stove. Angus moved to this task while
Salter started the Coleman stove in the kitchen. In a
few minutes the cabin was full of smoke. Salter
opened the damper in the stove chimney, and then
opened all the windows.

'Can I go for a swim now?' the boy asked, not
looking at his father.

'Of course you can. But go and get some more
wood first. The fire is almost out already.'

Angus ran out and brought back another armful of
wood which he dumped by the stove, then changed
quickly into his trunks and disappeared. Salter waited
for a minute, then walked out to the porch in time to
see the boy dive in and start to swim across the river.
At least he can swim, Salter thought. Better than I
can.

By the time the chili was hot, Angus had returned
and dried himself, and they ate supper in silence.
Suddenly Angus said, 'Why did you become a policeman, Dad?'

Salter considered his reply. He knew, or thought
he knew, that he was becoming a slight embarrassment to Angus, surrounded as he was at his posh
school by the sons of surgeons and stockbrokers. He

said, 'Because I needed a job and it seemed like a good idea.'

'Do you still like it?'

Again Salter considered.

'Yes, I do,' he said. 'That's what I am, a policeman, the way other people are sailors and farmers, and even dentists, I guess. Why? Does it bother you?'

'No. Mum said you got very depressed by your last case.'

'Did she? Well she's right, I did, but I'll get over it.'

'Did you mess it up?'

Salter considered the question while Angus watched him closely. 'I went after the wrong guy, maybe because I didn't like him. I did like the guy who did it,' he said eventually.

'Mum said you got the right guy in the end.'

'Eventually, yes.'

'You're usually right, aren't you?'

Salter excused this piece of blatant flattery, and said nothing, wondering what Angus was working up to.

There was silence for a few moments. Then Angus said, 'I don't want to be a cop.'

'Good. What *do* you want?' At least they were talking.

'I don't know.'

'No ideas at all?'

The boy was silent for a while. Then: 'An actor maybe.' He looked cautiously at his father.

'So I hear. On the stage?'

'Sure. Did Mum tell you?'

'She mentioned something, yes. It's a hard life,' Salter said, who knew nothing about it.

'I don't care. Mum said she didn't mind.'

Did she? Salter thought. 'I don't mind either, son. I don't care what you do. Why didn't you tell me before?'

'I thought you might make fun of me, like you do with cricket and stuff.'

Salter was silent, feeling slightly sick.

'Well, I wouldn't,' he said. More was needed, though.

'You know why your mother doesn't mind? Because she loves you and wants you to do whatever will be satisfying for you. I feel the same way.' There. Nearly.

'Could we play some Scrabble?' Angus asked suddenly.

Salter loved playing Scrabble, but Angus had never shown any interest. Warily he asked, 'You don't like the game much do you?'

'No, but Mum said I should ask you.'

'Did she?' Salter shook his head. 'No, it's no fun unless you're a maniac for it like me and your mother. No, let's clean up, get some more wood, and just read. This is the best reading place I know. A fishing cabin, I mean.'

'Okay. Can I have a beer?'

'No.'

'Why not?'

'It's against the law at your age, and you really are too young.'

'I've drunk beer before.'

'I know. And you've read skin books, too. So now you know about drinking and fucking.' I sound just like Gatenby's father, he thought. 'But you're still too young and you can wait a while for the big time. In the meantime, don't ask me for beer and don't bring skin books into the house. If you want to know anything, I'll try and tell you unless you get too personal.'

Angus gave a lop-sided grin, and that was that. They washed the dishes and settled down to read.

The next morning, either Angus had drawn strength from the tiny bond they had created, or the bond had disappeared. When Salter had the boat organized, he told Angus to hurry up.

Angus shook his head. 'I don't want to go fishing. Do you mind?'

'Why? Something wrong?'

'No. I just don't like it.'

'We could fish just around here. You could come in any time you want.'

'I JUST DON'T WANT TO GO FISHING. I DON'T WANT TO SIT IN THAT FUCKING BOAT ALL DAY.'

'All right, all right. So what are you going to do? I'm going fishing.'

'I'll be okay. There's stuff I can do. You go ahead.'

'You want to go home?'

'NO! You go fishing. Go on! I'll be fine.'

Salter looked at the boy who had once more picked up a magazine. Right, he thought, I will. 'Don't go swimming until I get back,' he said.

'All right.'

Salter turned upstream this time to a falls about three miles away. He had a perfect day. He found a shoal of pickerel that lasted for two hours, then he fished the shoreline for the rest of the day, looking for bass, eating Mars bars and drinking beer. Eventually he came in sight of the cabin again and saw Angus sitting on the dock in his bathing trunks. As he approached, the boy watched him calmly, then caught the prow of the boat and tied it up.

'Catch any?' he asked.

'Enough,' Salter said. 'Have you been sunbathing all day?' He didn't want to get into an argument, but he couldn't keep the irritation out of his voice.

'Nope,' the boy said. 'I've been working.' Salter looked more closely at him and saw that his hands and arms were covered in superficial cuts. There were scratches on his legs and even one or two on his face.

'Doing what?' Salter asked.

'I'll show you. Right now. I'm dying for a swim. Okay.'

'Okay.'

'Stay here, then. On the dock. Don't go up to the cabin.'

Salter waited wonderingly as the boy dived in, swam out halfway, then raced back and pulled himself on to the dock.

They walked back to the cabin, and Angus said, 'There!'

'Where?'

'The wall.'

Salter looked again. Under the front of the cabin, in the gap between the supporting corner foundations, was a rock wall which had been taken apart and entirely rebuilt. They approached the cabin and Salter inspected the wall closely. One of the bottom boulders must have weighed a hundred pounds. 'How did you shift that?' Salter asked.

'With a crowbar.'

'And you lifted the others on? How long did it take you?'

'I started right after you left and finished about two o'clock.'

'Jesus Christ.'

But there was more to come. They walked round to the back door and Angus pointed up the slope to the outhouse. There was now a neat path through the brush four feet wide between the outhouse and the cabin.

'Jesus Christ,' Salter said again. He walked back to look at the rock wall with Angus following. He stared at Angus, who looked back, smug and smiling, sure of himself. He must have been working like a slave the whole day, Salter thought. Any second now we are going to do that scene where Pa Walton embraces John-Boy, both crying. We might even kiss.

'You can have that beer now,' he said.

They drove back in near silence. Angus, naturally, slept; Salter had trouble containing the urge to sing.

Annie was waiting for them with soup and a hopeful look in her eye; the two men answered her questions over the shoulder while they unloaded the car.

'How was it?' she asked.

'Fine,' Salter said. 'I went fishing and Angus read eleven Maclean's magazines.'

'Didn't you go fishing, Angus?' she cried.

'I tried it. I didn't like it,' Angus said. The two men exchanged cheery looks.

'So what happened?'

'Nothing. I told you. I fished. He read.'

'Did you have a fight?'

'Fight? Us? What about?'

'Oh, bugger you,' she said, exasperated.

'We had a good time, didn't we, Angus?'

Angus giggled. 'Yeah. Never again, though.'

Salter laughed.

Annie looked from one to the other, understanding that she had got what she wanted. Later, when they stopped being male with each other, she could find out how it happened.

DEATH IN THE OLD COUNTRY

For Maurice Elliott

Part One

LIFE IN THE OLD COUNTRY

At three o'clock on a rainy afternoon in early May, Charlie Salter was driving in heavy two-way traffic on a narrow country road, keeping plenty of space between him and the car in front, happy that for once the conditions were so bad that no one was trying to overtake him as he led a procession of cars at a safe speed across the middle of England. He was enjoying himself, pleased with his miniature rented car, and very nearly comfortable with being on the wrong side of the road. Beside him, his wife, Annie, was reading a guide-book.

Before long they would have to choose where they were going to stay the night, a problem that could generate enough tension between them to last well into the evening, especially if the dinner was bad. The Salters were Canadian, used to travelling on a continent of standardized motels with restaurants attached which provided standardized meals from dawn to midnight. In England, they had discovered, you could find yourself at five o'clock in the afternoon in a village where the teashop was closed and there was no room at the inn; this was a land where the natives did not set foot out of doors without an exchange of stamped, addressed envelopes reserving their accommodation months in advance. On several afternoons already they had agonized as they tried to guess whether there might not be somewhere more inviting 'just round the next bend', passing up the 'Bed and Breakfast' sign outside the local Wuthering Heights as they searched for an inn with mullioned windows, a fire roaring in the hearth, and a jolly host waiting with a steaming bowl of bishop for his damp and weary guests.

Annie's instinct was always to stop, unless they had had a bad experience the night before, when she became single-minded in the pursuit of comfort, determined on a five-star hotel at a hundred guineas a night, if necessary. Salter tended to drive on, 'just to the next town', not even checking anything that looked less than perfect. And so they beat on (since he was usually driving), getting more irritated as they became more worried. If, after an hour of this, they did stumble on somewhere good, the relief was so enormous that they heaped credit on each other for finding the place; if they settled in despair on somewhere bad, the best they could manage was an elaborate politeness as each rose selflessly above the desire to blame the other.

All this was an hour away, however, and Salter gave himself up to meditating contentedly about the rain. How many words did the English have for it? 'Spitting', 'drizzling', 'a few drops', 'damp out'—these were a few of them. And it *was* different. Salter was used to rain, real rain, that had been forecast, that had a beginning and an ending and then left you alone for a few weeks. This rain, though, did not so much fall as hang in the air, silently enveloping the world and soaking it to the skin.

The road curved to the left following a high stone wall which protected the local stately home from being looked at by tourists in rented cars. As they chugged along in their little sealed chamber, daydreaming in the quiet time when the stationary world is having a nice nap, the road straightened, and Salter heard, first, the sound of a woman screaming, then saw, through the mist, a motorcycle and sidecar combination coming at him out of control on his side of the road. The woman was riding on the pillion, and the driver, a small hunched figure in a black overcoat and a green helmet, was trying to point his wheel out of the skid. Salter had all the time in the world to pull in as close to the wall as he could and come to a dead stop before the sidecar smashed into him with a noise of splintering wood.

Salter unbuckled and stepped out into the rain as the motorcyclist disentangled himself. Gradually the woman's screams wound down as she realized she was alive, and she fell silent. Three small boys clambered from the wreckage of the sidecar, a do-it-yourself contraption of plywood and two-by-fours, and all parties tested themselves for injuries. No one seemed to be hurt, so Salter and the motorcyclist began to square off.

A woman with a coat over her head ran towards them across the fields on the right. 'Oi seed it all,' she cried as she ran. 'Oi seed it all. Oi've already notified the police and the ambularances.' She arrived at the car breathless, and repeated her message. Salter broke off his conversation with the motorcyclist, who was shaking his head and saying, 'Coming at a fair lick, wasn't you? A fair lick?' as he established his opening defence.

The traffic was stopped for some distance in both directions and Salter approached the driver of the car behind him.

'Did you see what happened?' he asked the man. His car had been glued in Salter's rear-view mirror for the last five miles.

'No, not properly,' the man said. 'Like, not to be sure, I mean.'

'Oh, you did see it, Les, didn't you,' his wife said. 'I mean, you can't deny it. You did see it all. It wasn't this gentleman's fault. I mean, you did see it, didn't you.'

'Oh, bloody hell,' the man said. 'All right. Here's my name and address. I can't give evidence, though, not in person. I'm on me 'olidays.'

'Still,' his wife said, 'you did see it.'

Salter looked around for more witnesses, but the other drivers were back in their cars, avoiding his eye.

Two police constables appeared: one, dark-haired and dapper with a moustache, the other fair and clean-shaven.

They quickly began the process of sorting out the scene. The accident was so clear-cut—the motorcycle had been trying to overtake a stream of traffic on a blind curve—that Salter could see the concern of the police shift quickly from establishing responsibility to deciding whether to lay a charge against the motorcyclist. It was time to pull rank. He approached the dark-haired constable and showed him a second piece of identification and suggested that while the motorcyclist was obviously at fault, it really was an accident. 'Besides,' he added, 'I'm on my holidays.'

The constable called to his colleague and showed him Salter's identification. 'Ah well, then,' the colleague said. 'We'll have this sorted out in no time then, won't we, Inspector?'

The motorcyclist turned to his wife. 'He's a bleedin' copper,' he said. 'Just our luck.'

Annie, who had been standing by the car under an umbrella, appeared beside them. 'What's happening, Charlie?' she asked. 'Those poor people are getting soaked.' She motioned to the motorcyclist's family who were huddled together by the wreck of their vehicle. 'Get into our car while they sort this out,' she said to the woman. 'At least you and the children.'

'Oh no! We'll make your car all wet!' the woman cried.

'It's wet now. Please get in,' Annie insisted.

'Yes, well, all right, then. If you are sure your husband won't mind,' the woman said, and squeezed herself and the three boys into the back of the car. Two breakdown trucks arrived, and the whole group was transported to a garage in the local town, where hot tea was provided while they assessed the damage. For such a slight collision, the damage turned out to be considerable. 'I think you've bent the frame,' the garage proprietor said. 'Take us two weeks. Easy.'

Salter arranged for a fresh car to be delivered from the rental agency the next day, feeling fat with the knowledge that he had paid an extra two pounds a day to insure himself to the hilt. 'Now,' he said to the two policemen. 'We need a place to stay. Any suggestions?'

'P'raps we might go down to the station,' the dark-haired constable suggested. 'My inspector would like to meet you, I'm sure, and he'll know the best places.'

'Right,' Salter said. 'What about them?' He indicated the motorcyclist and his family, now sitting in a row on a bench against the wall, each with a bag of potato crisps.

'We'll look after them,' the constable replied. 'They're Londoners. They'll have to go on by rail, and there's no train until seven. Got no money, of course, but we'll take care of them one way or another.'

'Where are we, by the way?' Salter asked. 'What town, I mean?'

'This is Tokesbury Mallett, sir,' the constable said, surprised. 'Now, if you and your wife will come with me—oh yes, luggage—right you are, then. We'll be off. See you later, Robbo,' he called to the fair constable who was filling in forms with the proprietor.

Tokesbury Mallett was made entirely of the local yellow stone, and the buildings in the high street might have existed for five hundred years. The entrance to the police station was at the end of a row of shops, through an arch over the cobbled driveway of a large inn. Apart from the discreet blue lamp over the door, the station was indistinguishable from its olde worlde neighbours. The constable led them inside and introduced them to a sergeant sitting behind a counter, who shook hands with Salter and nodded to the constable to take them through to an inner office which overlooked the high street. Here, a thin, flat-haired man in a tweed suit with a handkerchief in his breast pocket sat writing at a desk.

The room smelled strongly of furniture polish. On one wall, an ordnance survey map of the area was decorated in military fashion with little flags and coloured pins. Beside it was a chart on graph paper on which a line ended in mid-air. It was too far away for Salter to read what was being charted. Rainfall? Behind the desk another large board displayed some kind of duty roster carefully picked out in three colours of ink. The highly polished desk sported a silver inkstand with two small crystal bottles of ink, one red, one green, an IN-tray and an OUT-tray, and a blotting-pad with edges of gold-embossed leather.

'This is Inspector Churcher, sir,' the constable said, 'and *this* is Inspector Salter, sir, from the Toronto police. In Canada, sir. He was in a head-on collision on the Oxford road, nobody hurt, other party liable.'

'And his wife, I assume,' Churcher said, rising to shake hands with Salter and smile at Annie. 'Please sit down.' He waited until Annie was in contact with her chair and sat down himself. 'A bit grubby, I'm afraid—a working office. Nasty thing to happen on holiday, Inspector, but I am very glad to have the opportunity to meet a colonial colleague. What can we do to make up for your trouble? Cup of tea?'

'No, thanks. Tell us where to find a bed,' Salter said. 'And where to get something to eat, later.'

Churcher ran a smoothing hand over his neat haircut, and sat at attention. His hands moved to settle his tie in the centre of his shirt-front and to equalize the exposed portion of his shirt-cuffs. He screwed his fountain-pen together and laid it in the tray of the inkstand.

'Now, I'm a bit new here,' he said. 'But, we do boast a two-star establishment, the Swan. Then there's the Jolly Alderman. And there are any number of smaller places. Hang on a second. Sergeant!' he called, through the open door. 'Come and join us for a moment. Sergeant Robey is a local man,' he explained to Salter. 'Ah, Sergeant. This is Inspector Salter, a colleague from the Dominions, and his wife. They need lodgings for the night. What do you suggest?' He looked keenly, first at the sergeant, then at Salter, then back at the sergeant.

'I want somewhere dry and warm with a decent bed and lots of hot water,' Salter said.

'And no restrictions on the use of the bathroom,' said Annie, whose teeth were starting to chatter. 'We don't care if there's no television, and we've got our own whisky so it doesn't have to be licensed, but it would be nice if they would give us something to eat so that we don't have to go out again in this weather.'

'You want Boomewood, ma'am,' the sergeant said.

'Oh, surely not, Sergeant,' Churcher protested. 'I don't think it's even rated, is it? Hardly appropriate.' He smiled at Salter and Annie.

'Binks, who runs the Swan, is on the fiddle, especially with foreigners,' the sergeant replied. 'And I wouldn't serve the food at the Jolly Alderman to my dog.' He turned to Salter. 'Frozen faggotts and peas,' he said. 'And tinned rice pudd'n for afters.'

Salter, not sure he had heard right, nevertheless felt himself in good hands. 'Boomewood it is, then,' he said. 'Anything wrong with it that you know of, Inspector?' he asked politely.

Churcher, irritated at the immediate understanding that had sprung up between Salter and his sergeant, shrugged. 'Don't let me put you off,' he said. 'But I think we'd better give him fair warning, Sergeant, don't you?'

'I was going to, sir.' The sergeant turned again to the Salters. 'There's been a report there's been a prowler there, sir. An Indian lady staying there a few days ago complained that someone woke her up in the night. This prowler was tickling her foot, saying "wakey-wakey". She sat up and he did a bunk, sir. She never screamed or nothing, very collected she was. She was sharing the room with her daughter, you see. They were on a motoring holiday before the daughter went to college, and the Indian lady didn't want to alarm her daughter, but she went to the landlord and told him. The next day she came to us because she thought the landlord wasn't taking it serious enough. We investigated, of course, but it was a waste of time. In my opinion a couple of the other guests had arranged a bit of slap and tickle—excuse me, ma'am—and he'd got the room number wrong. You know what I mean? But it's a nice place, and the locals say they've got good grub, if you like Italian. I do,' he added.

'Oh God, Charlie,' Annie exclaimed. 'Let's go.'

'Right you are, then,' Churcher said, attempting to take over. 'And if anyone grabs you by the ankle in the night, apart from your wife, I mean, hang on to him until we get there, will you?' He laughed to show he was joking. 'I'll get Potter to drive you.'

'I'll take them, sir,' Sergeant Robey offered. 'I'm just going off duty.'

'Right you are, then,' Churcher said again. He shook hands with Salter. 'Do come in tomorrow morning before you leave. I'd enjoy a little chat with a colleague from the New World. Now take this poor lady off and find her a nice hot bath, Sergeant. I'll telephone Boomewood to expect you.'

Salter said, 'Would you mind not mentioning that I'm a colleague of yours? From the New World. It makes people nervous. I'm calling myself a maintenance supervisor from the Toronto Transit Commission.'

'Ha, ha, ha. Your cover, eh?' Churcher said. 'Right you are, then. Mum's the word.'

And bob's your uncle, thought Salter. And keep your pecker up. And cheery-bye, then. 'Thanks,' he said.

In the car, the sergeant said, 'I spoke up because the inspector's a bit new to the district, sir. He doesn't know what a rotten hole the Swan is. Now.' He turned a corner and stopped the car with the engine running. 'If it ever stops raining and you feel like a walk, there's the best pub in the town.' He pointed across the street to a sign, the Eagle and Child, above the door. A single lighted window, as from a cottage, was the only other evidence of life. 'It's warm, cosy, *and* the beer's good.'

'Sergeant,' Annie called from the back seat. 'How far is Boomewood?'

'Half a mile, ma'am.' He looked round and registered a white, pinched face. 'Sorry, ma'am,' he said. 'You're cold. I'll have you there in a jiffy.'

He turned right, down a street lined with shops, past an intersection, and pulled up by a row of large attached houses with square windows and doors that opened directly on to the pavement. At one time, Salter guessed, these were residences for fops in wigs. Now, most of them had been taken over by auctioneers and chartered surveyors, but outside one a discreet plate announced that it was 'Boomewood—Private Hotel'.

'What does "Private" mean?' Salter asked.

'It means they don't have a public bar,' the sergeant said. 'They do have drinks, though, for the guests, and wine in the dining-room.'

He helped them carry their luggage into the narrow hallway where they were met by a slightly plump woman who was evidently not English, though Salter was not sure why he thought so. She was in her late thirties: dark, creamy complexion; brown hair pulled back and held behind her head; dark woollen dress with a cardigan round her shoulders; and elegant, nearly non-existent shoes that made her feet look nice and were the opposite of sensible. It was the shoes, Salter decided, that gave her away.

'Hello, Sergeant,' she said, touching him on the arm. 'No problems for you today.' She laughed as if she had made a good joke. Her accent was Italian.

Robey looked pleased with himself. 'This is Mr and Mrs Salter,' he said. 'The inspector called, did he, Mrs Dillon?'

She nodded and smiled. 'We are waiting for you,' she said. 'A double with a bathroom.' She moved forward to bring her arm around Annie and make her the centre of the group. 'If you would sign the register, Mr Salter, I will show your wife the room,' she said, leading Annie away and up the stairs.

'I'll be off, then, sir,' the sergeant said. 'You'll call in tomorrow, will you? The inspector would like it if you would. He's very keen on exchanging ideas.' The sergeant's face was bland.

'I'm just a layman,' Salter reminded him clearly. 'But I'll be happy to let him know that I think his policemen are wonderful.'

'That's it, sir. That's the sort of thing he likes to hear.'

Thus, with no more than a couple of inflections, did the sergeant confirm Salter's impression that Inspector Churcher was not only new, but zealous, uncertain of himself, and perhaps a trifle silly. Poor bugger, thought Salter.

'This way, please,' Mrs Dillon called.

Salter's hopes rose as they climbed the stairs which were lined with ancient photographs of sunny foreign landscapes. They rose further when he saw the room: a huge, solid-looking bed, two armchairs, a view of the rain-soaked hills from the window, and heat coming from the radiators. The bathroom, also, was heated, and it contained a giant's bath, a shower, a shaving light, and at least six—count 'em, he thought, six—thick-looking towels. One more test. Salter switched on one of the bedside lamps and a light bright enough to read by came on. They wouldn't need the hundred-watt bulb they carried around with them on the advice of a friend experienced in English hotels.

'This'll do,' he said to the waiting woman.

'Our best *camera matrimoniale*,' she said.

'What?'

'Double room.' She smiled, and left.

Salter took off his shoes and sat on the bed to test it. 'You think we've been asking for the right thing?' he called out to Annie, who was already running the bath. '*Camera matrimoniale* is what we wanted. You think they are all like this in Italy?'

'Don't be silly, Charlie.' Annie stepped into the túb and slid under the surface, whimpering with pleasure. After a few seconds she adjusted herself so that the water came to her chin. 'We just got lucky, that's all. Pour me a drink.'

Salter, now half-undressed himself, dug out the bottle of Scotch that their experienced friend had advised them to carry with them at all times in England, found two tooth-glasses, and measured out the drinks. He took off the rest of his clothes and sat on a towel on the edge of the bathtub with his feet in the water.

'I wish I smoked,' Annie said. 'Then I could have it all.'

'There's room for me in there,' Salter said, pointing to the nearly half of the tub which lay beyond Annie's feet.

'No, there isn't. Wait your turn.' She sipped her drink. 'Can we have dinner here? Should we?'

'The sergeant said they cook. All the evidence says we should try it.' He reached into the water, pulled out one of her feet, and began using the toes for counter. 'One, it's warm. Two, there's hot water—lots of it. Three, the bed has a proper mattress. Four, you can read in bed. Five, the owner, Mrs Whatever, looks well-fed, and has an Italian accent.'

She pulled her foot away as he tickled first her ankle, then behind her knee. 'Six,' she said, 'it's pouring with rain. Seven, I can smell garlic.' She stood up. 'Your turn,' she said.

Salter topped the bath with more hot water and lowered himself in. 'Ah-ah-ah-ah-' he said.

When he had soaked enough, he dried himself slowly and moved into the bedroom, where he found Annie with a towel wrapped around her head, fast asleep under the eiderdown. He poured himself another drink, draped himself in one of

the enormous bath-towels (don't bother with dressing-
gowns, their experienced friend had said, use your raincoats;
so far he was batting about five hundred) and sat in an
armchair, gazing out across the roofs to the fields and hills
of the home of his fathers.

They had been travelling for a week, the first of a planned
four-week holiday touring England and Scotland. After a
long, cold, Toronto winter, and a bad patch in their marriage, the Salters had decided on a major change of scene
and rhythm. They had both been working hard, Annie
especially, absorbed in her new career in an advertising
agency. Salter had been slow to adjust to the new pattern
demanded by her job, a life of more restaurant meals than
usual, occasional dinners assembled at a delicatessen by
Annie on her way home, and even more occasionally, Salter,
alone, cooking grilled cheese sandwiches for himself and the
two boys. Several times on a Saturday Annie had been
involved in setting up a 'shoot', and Salter had been left
to mooch about by himself. The intervals between their
love-making lengthened because of tiredness and because
an irritation between them had turned into a wall when
they retired. Then, in February, Annie had decided to finish
with child-bearing. She was approaching forty, the boys
were ten and fourteen, and they agreed it was now too late
for another child. All this made sense to Salter, but he
nevertheless endured a small sadness because of it. He loved
his sons, but he got on with them less well than Annie did.
Father and sons were wary of each other. When he looked
at colleagues with daughters, he envied slightly what looked
like a much simpler relationship, and he thought he would
have liked a little girl around. But he did not crave another
son, and besides, the timing had never been right. When
Annie came back from hospital after the operation, he
imagined a new fragility about her that created another
barrier. Salter, typically, tried to ignore the problem that
seemed to be developing but when Annie's job was secure,

she carved a gap in her schedule and suggested a holiday. He concurred, and asked his superintendent for the necessary leave.

It was natural to think of England, 'the old country', where they both claimed roots. They asked Annie's mother to come and stay with the boys, arranged for a rented car to be at the airport, and landed at Heathrow in the rain in the second week in May. The idea was to travel, staying at places that offered bed and breakfast, in the south first, then on up to the Lake District.

Their first experience was in a two-star hotel in a resort on the coast of Dorset which they reached on the first night, groggy from jet-lag. There the landlord showed them a huge, dank bedroom with two double beds and two cots.

'It's a family room,' the owner said. A small pot-bellied man with an RAF moustache, cavalry twill trousers, and egg-stains on his checkered waistcoat. 'You can have it for the price of a double.'

'I only need one bed,' Salter said, looking around at the chipped paint on the floor-boards, and glancing at the hand-written notices by the light switches, limiting the hours of enjoyment of everything from taking baths to eating in bed.

'I would normally put a family in here. Full board, four people,' the host said. 'Still.'

'How much?' Salter asked. Take your time, he thought, as he watched the man add up their 'American' accents, the pouring rain, and Annie's weariness as he arrived at his price.

'Twenty-six pounds,' the man said. 'That includes breakfast.'

'I know,' Salter said. He did a mental sum. 'Fifty dollars,' he said to Annie, who just shrugged. Salter looked around the room again. Perhaps, he thought, with one small extra effort we could find one of those hotels in the British Airways pamphlets, with Robert Morley as the host.

'If you take dinner, I could let you have it for twenty-one,' the host said, watching him.

'How much is dinner?'

'Nine pounds fifty. Inclusive, of course. Say forty pounds altogether.'

'Oh, Charlie, let's take it,' Annie said, sitting on the edge of one of the beds.

'Right you are, then,' the host said. 'No need for a deposit, of course.' He moved to the door. 'I'll bring your bags up if you'll give me your keys. I think I know your car.'

While they were waiting, Annie tried each of the two double beds. One of them sloped heavily into a pit in the centre: the other one was oddly hard, and when Salter lifted the mattress, which seemed to be stuffed with old teddy-bears, he found the sagging frames of two single cots lashed together so that where they met an iron ridge ran down the centre of the bed. Salter moved to the window and watched his host in the parking lot below examine their baggage labels and peer into the glove compartment of their car. When he arrived with the bags at the bedroom door, he had one more message. He pointed to the notice on the door of the bathroom across the hall. 'We ask you not to take baths before dinner, or after ten o'clock or during the breakfast hours,' he said. 'Enjoy your stay.'

It went on like that. Dinner was a five course affair, if you counted the half grapefruit at the beginning and the triangle of processed cheese, still in its tinfoil, at the end. The soup was 'Potage Maison', a gelatinous suspension of bits of parsley. The entrée was a flat disc of grey meat, accompanied by serving dishes of carrots, potatoes, cabbage stalks and diced turnips, all served in small pools of the water they had been boiled in.

Picking their way wondrously through all this, the Salters drank a bottle of wine and ate some bread. 'Dessert,' Annie said, 'will be tapioca pudding and custard.' But she was wrong. Before Salter could ask her what tapioca was, they were served some crusts of bread soaked in milk in which some raisins were floating. 'What's this?' Salter asked, long past anger and despair, and now merely curious. 'Bread and butter pudding,' the waiter said.

Instant coffee was served in the sun lounge, a chilly glass-enclosed annexe furnished in broken rattan. 'It's probably quite nice here in hot weather,' Annie said, hugging herself against the chill. They had a drink in the empty bar and retired for the night, dirty, insufficiently fed, and cold. Then a turnaround occurred. As they crawled into the hollow bed ('It's just damp, not wet,' Annie assured him), Annie started to giggle, and Salter, picking up her mood, expanded it into some horseplay which brushed aside their new diffidence and turned into a happy, uncomplicated tumble that dissolved most of their problems of the last three months. They were so cheerful in the morning that not even the single cold fried egg they were served for breakfast, or the additional charge for VAT ('only the dinner was inclusive, sir') could upset them, and they drove off early in the rain in case some redeeming feature should spoil the squalor of their first night in England.

'What are we going to do?' Salter asked.

'We are going to be very, very careful,' Annie said. 'We will start looking for a place to stay at three in the afternoon, and we are going to buy some guidebooks.'

They drove along the coast road to Torbay through the lush green countryside while Annie, an avid gardener, exclaimed steadily at the profligacy of the English spring. 'They pack so much in,' she said. 'They must spend all their time gardening.'

'When it's not raining,' Salter said. He was having to concentrate hard to follow the road through the mist. In Torbay they bought every guide to good food and accommodation they could find, and spent an hour in a pub matching up recommendations. They settled for their second night on an inn on the other coast near Clovelly, telephoned to make a

reservation, and headed inland, exchanging primrose-filled
lanes for lonely, gloom-haunted moorlands. Salter detoured
slightly in order to have a look at the prison, but the
thickening mist soon sent him scurrying back to the main
road before they could come within sight of it. All afternoon
they picked their way across the peninsula, concentrating
on not getting lost.

They had decided to take up their reservation only if the
place looked inviting, and at five o'clock they approached
it warily. Salter pulled up on the highway, a few yards short
of the inn.

'The grass is cut,' Annie said. The experience of the night
before might have been avoided if they had paid careful
attention to the signs of decay on the outside of the hotel.

'Flowers are nice,' Salter said, pointing to a bed of gilly-
flowers in the centre of the grass. They got out of the car
and walked forward.

'Smells good,' Annie said, putting her head in the door.
They ought to have noticed the smell of cabbage yesterday.
'Let's do it,' she said.

A pleasant-looking woman in young middle-age was behind the desk, and Salter asked for a double room. The
woman laid a card in front of him which listed the amenities
of the hotel, and the precise charges, which were nearly
identical to those they had paid the night before.

But nothing else was the same. The room, part of a new
extension tucked in behind the hotel, was warm, well-
furnished, and cunningly fitted with everything they looked
for, including a television set concealed in a cupboard which
could be switched on and off from the bed. When they asked
where the bathroom was and if it would be all right to have
a bath, the woman looked surprised and opened the door to
an adjoining bathroom which a Swiss hotelier would have
admired. The water was boiling.

Dinner began with game pâté, followed by roast lamb so
tender they had to gobble it before it melted, and a choice

of desserts from which they selected one made with grapes and sour cream which had Annie nearly crying with pleasure. Again coffee was served in the lounge, but this time the lounge was a small library full of armchairs, with a fire blazing in the hearth.

There was one other resident, a middle-aged man pouring himself coffee who, as they sat down, offered to pour some for them. A gent with a private income who lives here year-round on his income from his rubber plantation, thought Salter, noting the expensive thorn-proof clothes, the manicured hands, the handkerchief up the sleeve, and the mild, weathered look, probably acquired hunting and fishing.

'On holiday?' the man inquired.

'Yes,' Salter said. 'You?'

The man shook his head. 'I don't work, so I'm never on holiday,' he said. 'I live here during this part of the year. You are Canadian?'

'Yes. Is it that obvious?'

'If you know the signs. Canadians have none of the American brashness or the English preoccupation with class and manners which would have had you circling the room for five minutes before you decided you wanted to be spoken to by me.'

'A perfect blend of the best of both?' Annie asked. 'Lovely us?'

'On the other hand, though, some of you combine the unattractive national characteristics of both. Canadians, in short, can be positive mongrels or negative ones.'

Christ, thought Salter, we've only been here three minutes. But Annie took to eccentric situations like Alice.

'You've thought about this a lot?' she asked.

'That's what I do, dear lady. I have lots of time.'

'My husband only said two words,' Annie said. 'We might have been Australians. How did you know we weren't, just by looking at us?'

'Because the landlady told me.' He uncrossed his legs and leaned forward with a little giggle. 'I don't think I can keep this rubbish up any more,' he said. 'Let's have a drink and you tell me what you've seen so far.'

Annie laughed. Salter, who had been nearly taken in, was relieved to find it was a little game, and he launched into an account of the differences between the two identically priced hotels they had stayed at so far. The brandy arrived while he was talking, and the man's face began to take on the charged air of a television set warming up. When Salter finished, he was ready.

'Now *that*,' he said, 'is something I can tell you about. What you've stumbled on is the English pairing system. You'll find it works throughout the service industry here.' He rose an inch in his chair with the joy of a really good story to tell. 'Everybody who has to deal with the public in this country has a double,' he began. 'I'll call them Tweedledum and Tweedledee. Now Tweedledum is entirely benevolent—friendly, courteous, eager to serve—thoroughly wonderful in all the ways his job allows. Tweedledee, on the other hand, if your wife will pardon me, is a prize pig. As Tweedledum enjoys serving people, so, conversely, Tweedledee gets his pleasure from being surly, swindling and bloody-minded. No, no, let me go on. I am convinced that Tweedledum and Tweedledee are aware of each other, *know* each other, actually pair up, so that at some hoteliers' conference in the past, the owners of this hostel met the owners of your last night's horror show and they decided which would be which. Hang on a minute. It works, in my experience, everywhere—bus-drivers, policemen—struck a chord, have I?—shop assistants—every Tweedledum has a Tweedledee. And they *know* each other. Further, I have found out that they sometimes switch roles. Not long ago, I was in a ticket queue at Waterloo station and became aware as my queue shuffled forward that we had a grade one pig behind the window. He was sneering at old ladies, contemptuous of foreigners—generally performing his role to the hilt. Now at the other window —yes, another brandy would be nice—was a real Sunny Jim. Couldn't be more helpful; suggesting cheaper ways of travelling, telling people the best part of the train to get on for their purpose, cheerfully changing fifty-pound notes. Tweedledum and Tweedledee. Don't interrupt. I'm nearly there. Now, a very strange thing happened. As I approached the window, very nervous because I had several questions I wanted to ask, the two ticket sellers went to the back of the room and had a little conversation. When they returned to their cages, my man smiled at me and asked me what he could do for me. He was positively servile as we worked our way through my problems. At the same time, I could hear the seller in the next window—the former nice chap, you remember—shouting at a child for daring to try to pay for her ticket with a handful of tenpenny pieces, as snotty as a French museum attendant. You see? I am convinced that they were dum-ing and dee-ing in shifts, one hour as Tweedledum and one hour as Tweedledee. Now, here is my worry. I am terrified that this place will end its Tweedledum period any day now and we shall all be faced at dinner with Brown Windsor Soup and frozen cod and Brussels sprouts, with prunes and custard for pudding.' The man finished his brandy with a flourish and stood up.

'That,' Salter said, 'is the most terrific load of balls I've ever heard in my life.'

'All true, though,' the man said. 'All true. You'll see.' He left the room in triumph.

Salter looked at Annie. 'You think there's anything in it?' he asked.

'It accounts for the facts, which is what matters. Now let's go to bed before someone ordinary comes along.'

For the next four days they steered their way through the minefield of English hospitality, never finding anything as bad as their first night or as good as their second, until they came, by accident, to Boomewood, which had all the markings of a genuine Tweedledum.

A knock at the door was followed by a voice saying that dinner would be ready in ten minutes. Salter woke up Annie, and they presented themselves in the dining-room which was already nearly full. An excessively handsome, dark-haired waiter took them to a table set for two and said, 'Dinner?'

'Could we see a menu?' Annie asked.

'No menu,' the waiter said. 'Dinner?'

A woman at the next table leaned over. 'Trust them,' she said, from behind very thick glasses. The man with her nodded.

The soup was delicious and it was followed by cross-sections of a calf's leg, accompanied by slightly sticky yellow rice.

'*Osso buco*,' Bottle Glasses said. 'Veal shanks. And risotto.'

The Salters tucked in happily. The dessert was a water-ice. 'Yum yum,' Annie said happily.

Once more they were invited to take coffee in the residents' lounge, which they assumed would be packed like the dining-room, but only the lady in the thick glasses and her husband followed them in. The coffee was espresso.

'Want to know what you've stumbled into?' their new companion asked when they were seated with their coffee. 'This is the best food, for the price, in the Midlands, if you like Florentine cooking.' She flashed her lenses at them. 'They only serve one menu—it's pot luck, but by God, what a pot. Last night they had *spaghetti carbonara* and veal kidneys cooked in Marsala. I thought my husband was going to faint, didn't I, Henry?'

Henry nodded. 'That's right,' he said.

'And a chocolate thing for dessert that made the backs of my knees damp as it went down. Didn't it, Henry?'

'That's right,' Henry said, and made as if to speak again.

She cut him off. 'Breakfast is a giant cup of *caffè latte* and fresh rolls if you like. If you want sausages and fried bread you should leave tonight and good riddance to you.'

Salter wondered if he was going to spend the evenings of the next three weeks being entertained by garrulous eccentrics in residents' lounges. It was not an unpleasant prospect.

'Where is everybody?' he asked, more to keep Bottle Glasses going than because he cared. From the nose down, she was an attractive woman, about forty, in a dark red woollen dress and matching shoes, with jaunty breasts and thin, muscular legs. Only the glasses and the difficulty of making eye contact with her made the initial social skirmishing awkward.

'There are very few guests at the moment,' she said. 'Just us and an American girl. Oh, and a Canadian woman, a Miss Rundstedt, at least I think she's Canadian. I've been trying to find out. All the rest are local people, attracted by the food. They don't take reservations for the dining-room, so every night there's a line-up outside the door at seven. First come, first served. Only one sitting.'

'Have you been staying here long?' Annie asked.

'A week. We stumbled on it last year, like you, and we came back this year just to eat for a couple of weeks after a winter of the *haute cuisine* at Watford, where we live. You're not English, are you?'

'No.'

'American?'

'No.

'I didn't think so.'

There was a pause.

'We're Canadian.'

'Ah. Well, that's a bit of a conversation stopper, isn't it? But let me tell you about this place. It's run by a man about whom I have my doubts, don't I, Henry? He has a very curious accent, which he believes is upper, but is really the sort of accent that ships' pursers and masters of ceremonies at holiday camps have: very put-on, but I can't be sure what he's putting off. He may be Australian. His wife, whom you met (I was in the lounge here when you arrived), is Italian, and her brother speaks no English and waited at table tonight.'

Nobody said anything for a few moments. Then: 'Haven't you been able to find out more than that?' Salter asked.

'Your husband is being ironical,' the woman said to Annie. 'But I don't mind. I'm a very nosey woman; it's my chief pleasure in life. Isn't it, Henry?'

'What are your other pleasures?' Annie asked. 'By the way, would you like to know who we are?' She introduced them to the other couple.

'I'm Maud Beresford,' the woman said. 'And this is my husband, Henry. Henry's a doctor, aren't you, Henry, but he spends all his time in a laboratory playing with rats.'

'I'm a psychologist,' Henry said.

'He's summing you up right now,' Maud said. 'But he never lets on what he knows. Not like me.'

Henry lit a pipe. He was dressed for survival in a thick pair of trousers, a tweed jacket over a hairy pullover, a khaki shirt, a woollen Paisley tie, and shoes with leather laces and double soles. 'I'm on holiday, dear,' he said, pinching out sparks as they landed on his trousers. 'Besides, I'm interested in typical behaviour. I'm not a psychiatrist.'

'And what do you do?' Maud asked Salter, cutting Henry off.

'I'm a maintenance supervisor for the Toronto Transit Commission,' he said. 'The bus company,' he explained.

'I don't believe a word of it. What about you, Annie?'

'Me? I'm a housewife.'

Maud looked at them both in turn. 'I suspect you are both running away from your respective spouses,' she said. 'Never mind. If you stay here for two days I'll find out all about you. Come along, Henry. Let's go to bed. It's been a dreary day except for the *osso buco* and the mysterious Salters. See you at breakfast.'

Henry winked and followed her out.

'What do you think?' Salter asked when the door had closed. 'Shall we check out now or wait until the morning?'

'Why, Charlie? I enjoyed them, didn't you?'

'Oh, sure. But it will only take her about five minutes to blow my cover. Then she'll tell everyone else.'

'You'd better practise getting your story straight, hadn't you? Make a change for you, being on the other side.' She laughed. 'I feel very cheered up, so let's go to bed.'

The day seemed to deserve a nightcap which they drank as they were getting undressed. The conversation with Maud had left Salter in an absurd mood, and when he finished his drink, he took off his clothes and stood over Annie who was already under the covers.

'Nancy,' he said in what he imagined was the voice of his favourite fictional character, Bill Sikes, as played by Robert Newton, 'Nancy, I wants yer body.'

'Shshsh,' Annie said.

Salter, surprised, stopped dead. Annie pointed to the window, where the curtain was drawn tight, and put a finger to her lips.

'Nancy,' Salter growled again. 'I'm a-coming for yer,' then stopped again as he heard it, a giggle from outside. They were being overheard. He started to speak again, but this time he moved towards the window as he spoke. 'You've been avoiding me all day, Nancy,' he said, 'and I'm claiming me rights, see. You know what I like before I go out on a burgle, so let's 'ave yer.' He jumped for the window and pulled back the curtain in time to see a shadow disappear around the corner of the house. 'Christ,' he said. 'A genuine Peeping Tom. I'd better tell the landlord. Tomorrow.' He closed the curtains and made sure the door was locked, and came back to the bed in his own character. 'Do you think it might be Maud?' he asked as he gathered Annie to him.

In the morning it turned out that Maud had exaggerated slightly. There was indeed *caffè latte* for breakfast, but there was bacon and eggs, too, and Salter ordered some of every-thing. The Beresfords joined them at a table for four, and Maud resumed her inquiries.

'Do maintenance supervisors for the bus company get four weeks' holiday every year?' she asked, when she had cleared the ground with a few preliminary questions.

'We save them up,' Salter said. 'You can add your over-time to your regular vacation allowance.'

Maud's eyes travelled lightly over Annie, pricing her shoes and her jewellery. 'Hmmmm,' she said. 'What are your plans for today? Not moving on immediately, I hope?'

It was something they had talked about in the bedroom that morning. For nearly a week now they had been locked in the car in the rain, and Annie wanted to stop. The skies were still slate-coloured, but no rain was actually falling, and she suggested that they take advantage of their luck and stay at Boomewood for a few days, exploring the countryside in daily outings. Salter was agreeable. Now that they were in England, Annie, who had done her homework, had a lot of gardens, houses and castles she wanted to see. But Salter did not know what he wanted to do. Or rather, he did know; he wanted to do nothing, hang about the pubs and live the life, chatting up the natives while Annie went sightseeing. In a nutshell, he wanted to wander around Soho while Annie visited the Royal Academy. So long as it was raining there was no conflict, but now Annie was dusting off her guidebooks again. When they took possession of their new car, she had plans.

Annie said, 'If they have room, I think we'll be staying here for a while.'

'Good,' Maud said. 'What are your plans for today?'

They explained about the car, and Annie mentioned her desire to see some famous gardens in the neighbourhood.

'Why don't you let us take you?' Maud cried. 'Let *him* worry about the car.' She pointed to Salter. 'We want to see the gardens, too, but we need a guide, don't we, Henry? Do you know anything about flowers? I just know daffodils and geraniums, but I love smelling them. Henry does, too. Let's the three of us go and leave the maintenance supervisor to haggle with the garage.'

Salter and Annie exchanged three or four glances and conveyed between them that it sounded like a good plan, and that Maud, at least, was an entertaining companion in spite of or including her compulsive nosiness, so they agreed. The Beresfords would drop Salter off, and the other three would go on to the gardens. They would return to Boomewood sometime during the afternoon and Salter could do what he liked, including following them if the car had arrived. It was perfect. Tokesbury Mallett looked just big enough for a couple of hours' walkabout, and that plus a pub lunch would do him nicely.

They were interrupted by the approach of the waiter, a fair youth of about seventeen.

'Ah,' Maud said. '"The Smarmy Boy."'

'Here we are, then, ladies and gentlemen. I *am* sorry to keep you waiting. Bacon and eggs for you, sir, careful with the plate, it's very hot. *Caffè latte* all round. Don't spill any on your nice suit, ma'am; and rolls, nice and hot. Butter. Oh, I'm sorry, I'll be back in a jiffy. Here, I'll give you the butter on this table. Anything else, anybody? Marmalade? Jam? Ketchup, sir? I know you Americans like it on most things. Worcester sauce, sir? No? I'll leave you to it, then. Just call out, won't you. I'm in the kitchen.'

It was Uriah Heep being played against type by Michael York: a handsome youth from whom unctuousness in a local accent oozed like treacle.

'Who is that?' Annie asked Maud automatically.

'Gregory,' Maud said. 'Gregory is an apprentice electrician who lives in a room over the garage and pays for his keep by helping out with odd jobs, including waiting at table, when electrical work is slow. Our landlady took pity on him when his mother went off somewhere a year ago, probably to shake off Gregory. Only a foreigner would not see that such ingratiating manners in an English youth today are not normal.'

'Probably a Tweedledum who has overbalanced backwards,' Annie said.

'A what?'

Annie explained.

'What a lovely theory. Quite true, too, Isn't it, Henry?'

Henry, who had been trying surreptitiously to read the paper, looked up. 'I told you dear, Gregory is probably an extreme case of Wanker's Self-Doubt,' Henry said.

'What?' asked Annie and Salter.

Maud for the first time looked discomposed. 'Henry retreats into psychological jargon sometimes,' she said, 'Ah, look. Our American friend.'

The girl who seated herself at a table for one would have looked at home on any American campus during the last twenty-five years: black turtleneck sweater, kilt-type skirt, black woollen stockings and penny loafers—almost the same costume as that worn by the first girl Salter had wooed during his brief college career. They watched her dispose of Gregory's attempt to get her to smile at him while ordering her breakfast.

'She's in love with Mario,' Maud said. 'Last night's waiter. He gets his pick of the girls, I would think. And now here comes Miss Rundstedt, your compatriot.'

A woman of about forty entered the room with the delicate steps of a young girl. She had a tiny face topped with frizzy red hair which fanned out from the top of her head at a forty-five-degree angle, in an Egyptian style. She had very large breasts which she rested on her arms while she talked to Gregory.

'A bit mysterious, like you,' Maud said. 'On holiday, apparently, but I've seen her about town on very friendly terms with mysterious strangers in pubs.'

'But not with you, dear,' Henry said.

'No,' Maud agreed. 'I'd say she dodges me.'

'That it, then?' Salter asked. 'Can we go now?'

While they separated to pick up raincoats and cameras, Salter went in search of the host. He found him in a dark little office at the end of the downstairs hallway, a man in his late fifties with a large grey beard and hornrimmed glasses, wearing a heavily striped shirt and a club tie under a woollen cardigan.

'Everything satisfactory, sir?' he asked, when Salter had introduced himself.

'Perfect,' Salter said and went on to explain the purpose of his visit.

'Peeping Tom, eh? We've never had a complaint like that before. Couldn't have been mistaken, sir?'

'No,' Salter said, registering the man's lie. An automatic defence of the establishment's virtue?

'We'll keep an eye open, then,' the host said and waited for Salter to go.

'Would you like me to mention it to the police at Tokesbury?' Salter suggested. 'I'm calling in on the inspector this morning.'

'No need, no need. Leave it to me. You have official business with the police, do you, sir?'

'No, I don't,' Salter said, surprised at the directness of the question. He explained about the accident.

'Yes, of course. Maria told me. Rotten luck, that. Never mind. Insured, of course?'

Salter nodded.

'Good,' the man said, and turned back to his desk.

Salter was mildly intrigued by his landlord, who seemed to prefer this cave at the end of the hall to the hotel's public rooms. His manner to Salter was polite, but not expansive: there was not enough ebullience there to run a successful bar. But if you've got an attractive Italian wife, twenty years younger than yourself, you can leave her to keep the public happy, thought Salter. Especially if she can cook like that.

The rest of the party was assembled in the hall and they drove Salter into the town and left him outside the police station, where Inspector Churcher was waiting for him in his immaculately tidy office, looking himself as if he had attended to the items of his personal appearance with a check-list.

'I was waiting for you to join me for coffee, Inspector,' Churcher said. 'You will have some, I hope?' When Salter nodded, Churcher asked, 'White or black?'

Coffee-coloured, thought Salter, wondering which of the dozen varieties of drink the English called coffee he was going to get. 'White,' he said aloud in case it came out of a bottle.

Churcher called the request through the doorway and Sergeant Robey brought in two cups of a milky grey liquid.

Churcher shot his cuffs and started in.

'You play golf?' he asked.

'No,' Salter lied instinctively.

'Pity,' Churcher said. 'I didn't before I came here, but I think that community relations are very important, so I've joined the local golf and tennis clubs. Quite enjoy it, too. I've been urging my men to get involved. Not at golf, of course, but at their own level.'

What would that be—skittles for constables, lawn-bowling for sergeants? 'Don't they live here?' Salter asked.

'Ah yes, I take your point,' Churcher said. 'But I think they could easily become detached, once they join the Force. Don't you agree? What sort of activities do your people encourage?'

'Various things, Inspector. Boxing clubs, that kind of thing. And we are putting more men back on the beat.'

'Very wise. By the way, my name is Charles. Charles Churcher. C.C. My father wanted a carbon copy of himself.'

He chuckled and looked invitingly at Salter.

After a struggle, Salter said, 'Charlie.'

Churcher's mouth opened into a huge smile. 'Really.' he said. 'Really. How extraordinary. Tell me, Charles, do your men get any special training in crowd control. I was just looking at a report on the French methods. Very interesting.'

Salter looked through the window at two old men rioting on the bench by the bus-stop. There was no one else in sight. How long does a little chat go on, he wondered. 'It's part of our general training,' he said. And then: 'By the way, there's a Peeping Tom at Boomewood.' He told Churcher the story of the previous night.

'The Prowler, eh? Sergeant!' he called. When the sergeant of the night before appeared, Churcher said, 'Come in. Close the door. Now, Charles, I'd like you to repeat your story if you would. Just as you told it to me.'

Jesus Christ, thought Salter, but he did as he was asked.

'Now. What do you think, Sergeant?' Churcher said, as if he were giving the sergeant a little test.

'I think someone was listening outside the inspector's window,' the sergeant said, after consideration.

'Surely more than *that*, Sergeant. This is the second incident, remember.'

'They may not be connected, sir. One is listening, as the inspector tells it, and the other is tickling feet, saying "wakey-wakey". They might be quite different types of people.' The sergeant said this with the air of a man exposing a serious flaw in a complex theory.

He's going too far, thought Salter, as he watched to see if Churcher would react to this tiny pull on his leg.

'Of course, they both seem to have a common basis in sexual motivation, sir,' the sergeant offered.

Churcher brushed away any doubts. 'I think they *must* be connected, Sergeant. Look into it, will you?'

'Right, sir,' the sergeant said, his glance barely touching Salter as he made his exit.

Salter stood up. 'Thanks for the coffee,' he said. 'Now I think I'll go for a stroll around town.'

'Would you like a guide, Charles?' Churcher offered.

'No, thanks. If you are known in the community, they might wonder who I am,' Salter said. Especially if Maud sees us. 'I'm still a maintenance supervisor for the Toronto bus company, on holiday.'

'Of course. I understand. Well, drop in again, won't you. I enjoyed our little talk.' Churcher put out his hand, and Salter left.

He was joined on the steps of the station house by Sergeant Robey. 'We have our share of Peeping Tom reports,' the sergeant said. 'But I'll tell the boys to keep a watch out.'

'Have fun, Sergeant. What do you know about the staff at Boomewood,' he asked.

'Why, sir? Something fishy about them?'

'No, no. But it's an unusual place to find in the middle of England. Who's the owner? Where's he from?'

'Somewhere in the south, sir. London way, I should think. We did a bit of homework on him after the prowler incident. He came into the district two years ago and bought Boome-wood, which was a dump at the time, and, well, you can see what he's done with it. He opened up at the end of the season and last year was his first full year. He's a bit of an odd one. No record or nothing. He met his wife in Italy, apparently, and brought her back here. The waiter is her brother. Came over on a work permit a couple of months ago to learn English. That's it, except for Mrs Peabody, their daily, and that kid Gregory. They must work hard.'

'They do,' Salter said. 'It's paying off, too. Now, Sergeant. Point me to that pub you mentioned yesterday.'

'The Eagle and Child, sir? Down there, first turning on the left, sir. Try their ham. He cures it himself.'

'Okay. Now what else should I see around here?'

'Well, sir, there's Broodleigh Castle which was built by one of James the First's favourites,' the Sergeant began.

Salter cut him off. 'I was thinking of something a bit livelier,' he said. 'Like a sheep-shearing contest.'

'If you stay till Saturday there's the annual shin-kicking contest over at Chipping Camden, sir. A bit of a drive, but very nice when the sun's out.'

'That sounds more like it,' Salter said. 'But what about today?'

'If I were off-duty, I'd be at the races,' the sergeant said, looking nowhere in particular.

'That's it. Where?'

'Right here, sir. About two miles down that road. We have a little meeting three times a year. Over the sticks.'

'Sticks?'

'Fences, sir. Steeplechasing.'

'Just my meat. What time?'

'I believe the first race is at two o'clock. If you do go, try a few bob on Joe's Folly in the third. Napper Marston trains him. He's a local lad we've taken an interest in once or twice. He mentioned yesterday they were having a go with this one.'

'Joe's Folly. Right. Thanks.'

'Good luck, sir. Might win your holiday money, eh, sir?'

Salter set off in the direction of the Eagle and Child, and then, since it was still only eleven-thirty, took a wide detour to look at the market street. He stopped at a street trader, attracted by a beautiful display of polished apples, and asked for a pound, pointing to the ones he wanted. The assistant turned his back and picked out three from under his feet and weighed them up, swung the bag expertly tight, and offered it to Salter.

'I want those three,' Salter said, pointing to the display. A little queue was forming behind him.

'Can't pick and choose, guv. Take the rough with the smooth,' the assistant said. ''Ere. Forty pee.'

'Sure I can. I want those,' Salter insisted. Behind him the queue started mumbling.

''Oo does he think he is?' one woman said.

'I don't know about that,' replied a huge, black-haired woman in a pinafore and carpet-slippers. 'Time somebody said somethink.'

'You want them or not, squire?' the assistant demanded.

'No,' Salter said.

'Right. Next!' The assistant emptied the bag into the container at his feet. 'Bleedin' Americans,' he said.

Salter moved a few yards down the street to another barrow. 'I'd like those three apples,' he said loudly. '*Those* three.'

'Certainly, guv, which ones? That one and that one and *that* one? Right. Forty-eight pee, please. Cheers. Now then, darlin', what can I do for you?'

Salter went on his way, wondering.

The Eagle and Child served a good lunch of ham rolls and pickles, and he found a place at the bar and tucked in.

'On holiday, sir?' the barman asked.

Salter nodded.

'Staying in the area?'

They really are a nosey lot, thought Salter. It's just that Maud is more honest. He nodded again.

'At the Swan, I presume?'

'No. At Boomewood, as a matter of fact.'

Two yards along the counter, a man in a hacking jacket with a bushy moustache caught his attention. 'Like it?' he asked. 'Boomewood, I mean. Thought I might try it myself. I hear it's pretty good.'

'It's good,' Salter said. 'I'd recommend it.'

The man nodded. 'Just touring, are you? From Canada?'

'Yes,' Salter said, faintly irritated. Did he smell of maple syrup? 'How did you know?' he asked.

'I lived there for a bit.'

'Oh? Whereabouts?'

'Here and there. Where are you from?'

'Toronto. I work for the bus company.'

'I spent most of my time in Winnipeg. Do you know it?'

'I've been there. A long time ago. I don't know it now.'

'It hasn't changed much. Not like Toronto. What do you have on the agenda today? Stately homes?'

'No. I'm going to the races.'

'Oh, really? I'm going there myself. You follow racing here?'

'I've never been to a steeplechase in my life. The only racing I know anything about is harness-racing.'

'Greenwood, eh?' The man smiled companionably. 'Like some company? I'll show you the ropes.'

While they were talking, Salter had been trying to get a fix on his companion. He had taken in the man's brand-new clothes and watched him pay for a drink with a healthy wad of bills which he kept in a money clip. There was a smell of sharpness about the man; a hint of the con man brushed the policeman's antennae. Would he try to set Salter up? Introduce him to three friends a__ _ _ack of cards? Salter was intrigued.

'All right,' he said. 'When do we leave? I'll see if my car's ready.' He explained what had happened to him.

'Leave it here. We'll go in mine. Finish your beer and we'll be off.'

And so it was arranged. Twenty minutes later they were in a light stream of traffic heading towards the racecourse.

'My name's Parrott. Jeremy Parrott,' the man said when they were under way.

'Charlie Salter. What did you do in Winnipeg?'

'Worked for the government. Public works. I supervised government building contracts.'

'Are you retired now?' The man was in his early fifties.

'Temporarily. The NDP got back into power and they put their own people in. Spoils of office. But they won't last.'

It was a familiar story in Canadian politics. Salter's background in the working class district of Cabbagetown in

Toronto had made him incapable of supporting either of the major parties had he been able to distinguish between them, at the same time as he recognized the possible truth in the assumption of the worldly-wise that the New Democratic Party had kept its virtue intact because no one had yet offered anything for it. Nevertheless, he remained a closet socialist until such time as an honest man appeared elsewhere. His new companion had just revealed his affiliation with the Conservatives, so Salter shut up.

The stream of traffic turned down a narrow lane, through what looked like a space in a hedge, into a field. Some of the cars parked here, but Parrott drove across the field to a gap in a rail fence which turned out to be the track itself. Here an attendant took some money from them and waved them across the track. They drove on to the centre of the course and turned to park by one of the brushwood fences the horses had to jump.

'This is the public enclosure,' Parrott said. 'We'll watch most of it from those stands over there, but I like to watch one right by the fence. I like to see them jump. If we park here we can sit in the car if it rains, and be ready to take off after the last race. Now let me show you round.'

They walked down the course to where a small crowd was gathered around some bookmakers who were beginning to call the odds. Salter was stunned by the squalor. His only experience of racing in Toronto, where even the cheapest seats are under cover and only the horses brave the elements, had not prepared him for this. The public enclosure was an open field, now a swamp, in the centre of which stood a ramshackle wooden shed with a corrugated iron roof. Inside this hut a small crowd was drinking tea and beer. By the rail a dozen bookmakers were gathered under huge umbrellas. Everyone else stood in the open, soaking up the rain.

His companion explained what was happening, and Salter decided to bet. He picked a horse at random and walked up to the nearest bookmaker, a small cheerful-looking man whose board proclaimed that he was Jack Edwards from Nottingham, 50p Minimum, E.W. taken.

'I'd like to place a bet of two pounds to win on Mitcham Lane in the first race,' Salter said.

'And so you shall, my old darlin',' Jack Edwards said. He took a printed card from a pack he was holding and spoke to the ancient tramp beside him who was holding a ledger. 'The gentleman wishes to wager two sovereigns on Mitcham Lane in the first race, Frederick.' He said, 'Shall we accept his offer at odds of seven to two?'

The nearby bookies laughed. Salter took the card from the grinning Edwards and stepped back to see why he had made a fool of himself.

'Just say "Two pounds, Mitcham Lane,"' his companion suggested. 'It's easier.'

Mitcham Lane fell over half way round the course, out of sight of the public enclosure, and Salter threw away his ticket. They had agreed to cross the track for most of the races, to watch them from the stands, but before they reached the rail, there was a commotion down the track where two men in red coats on horseback were surrounded by a pack of dogs. Then the voice of the Queen came over the loudspeakers.

'Good afternoon, everyone,' the Queen said. 'Welcome to the third meeting of the season, sponsored today by your local Hunt. My name is Alison Lamprey and I am secretary of the Tokesbury Mallett pack. I won't detain you for more than a moment, but we are here to make an appeal to you, the local sportsmen, who love horses and for whom National Hunt Racing is so important. We of the Tokesbury Mallett Hunt ask you to support us in resisting the efforts of some outside groups who are trying to interfere with the tra-ditional English sport of hunting. I won't bore you with the reasons why hunting is *not* a cruel sport, and *not* in any way harmful to the agricultural interests among you—you know all that—but I would just like to say to you that hunting is the backbone, the lifeblood, of the sport you are gathered here today to enjoy. Without us, without hunting, there would be very few horses for steeplechasing and the sport would very quickly die. So, please, write to your local newspaper, and to the national papers, to show your support for us. And now we thought that you would like to see some of the colour and drama of a hunt in full chase so we have brought you the Tokesbury pack, who will run down the course, accompanied by Mr Simnel and Viscount Oates, the joint masters of the hunt. When you are ready, gentlemen?'

There was the sound of a horn, and down the course came the dogs, followed by the two riders in red coats. When the pack was opposite the crowd, one of the riders turned his head sideways and made a sound like a coyote barking. When the pack reached the end of the course, they turned and ran back, and this time the rider howled into the stands.

'Thank you all,' said the Queen.

Salter looked around at the crowd, expecting cheers, or hoots of derision, but there was nothing. A small silence was broken by Jack Edwards, shouting, 'Right, lads. 'Oo wants a bet? Come on, support your local bloodsport. Seven to one, bar one.' Otherwise the event had caused no more commotion or interest than a low-flying aeroplane.

'You think that'll help?' he asked Parrott.

'Can you see this lot writing to *The Times*?' Parrott replied.

'Do they *believe* it?'

'They didn't even hear it. They came here to bet.'

'So did I.'

They paid some more money to cross the course and enter a large shed where the well-heeled patrons were keeping dry. From here he had the satisfaction of seeing his choice in the next race unseat his rider and gallop off down the course alone.

'I've got a tip on the next one,' Salter said, and told his companion what it was.

'It's ten to one,' Parrott noted. 'I should get on now if I were you.'

'Fiver. Joe's Folly,' Salter said to the bookmaker out of the corner of his mouth.

Before the race began, the odds had shortened to six to one.

'They've come for it,' Parrott said.

The horse was ridden by the trainer's son. When the starter's flag went down, it set off at a fast gallop and by the end of two miles it was three furlongs clear. Salter's money was as good as in the bank. Then the others set off in pursuit and started to close the gap. With two furlongs left, Joe's Folly was still fifty yards in front, but staggering badly. Behind it, four fresher-looking horses were making a grim charge. Joe's Folly cleared three more fences and there was one left, but by now the horse was weaving from side to side. The four other horses swept by it and rushed for the last fence, and then, just as Salter got ready to throw his ticket away, the leader stumbled and fell as he landed over the last fence, bringing down two of his companions. Joe's Folly chose a broken spot in the fence to crawl through behind the only other horse, who looked certain to win now, but as the crowd roared them home, the rider on the leading horse began to slip sideways. He clung desperately to the neck of his horse for a few yards, but the horse shook him off and Joe's Folly tottered alone past the winning post.

'Well done,' Parrott said. 'I wouldn't back him again, though.'

A man on Salter's other side spoke. 'It oughta be stopped,' he cried. 'Puttin' bleedin' cripples on good 'orses. Did you see him? Couldn't even stay on the bleeder at a canter. Gawd bloody 'ell. What won it? Bleeding Joe's Folly. A fucking fiddle. 'Oo'd back that thing?' He was beside himself with rage.

'I did,' Salter said.

'*You* did? *You* did? 'Ere, Alf.' He turned away from Salter. 'Bloke 'ere says he backed that sodding 'orse. Backed it to win!' He glared at Salter, then turned back to Alf. 'Come on. Let's go and 'ave a cuppa tea,' he said in disgust.

A few minutes later when Salter and Parrott entered the refreshment shed in search of a drink, he heard the man's voice behind him from a corner of the room.

'That's 'im, Alf. That's the bleeder 'oo backed that soddin' 'orse.'

Salter stayed in the tea line with his back to the voice, listening hard.

'That's 'im all right,' the voice continued. 'There.'

Another voice spoke. Alf. 'You know what, Des,' the voice said, 'I bet he didn't do it at all. I think he was just trying to upset you.' And Alf laughed.

Salter won no more races. As promised, they watched the last race from the rail by the first fence, and Salter got a worm's eye view of three tons of horses as they rose into the air and smashed down on the other side. Watching the previous races from the insulating distance of the stands had not prepared him for the assault on his senses that this close-up provided. The horses themselves were an astonishing and beautiful sight (the nearest one was only six feet away), huge masses of shifting muscle sailing through the air, but the most vivid impression was of the enormous risks the jockeys took at each fence as they shouted from high in the air at their horses and each other, fighting for a safe and advantageous landing. To Salter, it looked like the most exciting and dangerous sport he had ever seen and he thought later, when he had gathered his senses together, that he would have liked, just once, to ride the safest horse in the world over one little fence just to see what it was like, even though he had never been on a horse in his life.

Walking to the car, he said, 'And one of them was a *girl!*' He was still, in spirit, by the fence.

'What?' Parrot asked. 'Oh, the jockeys. Yes. Women have been riding for a few years, I think. Going to try your luck tomorrow, or will you be moving on?'

Salter looked around and found himself on a racecourse. 'We are staying here for a few days. I'll be back tomorrow, all right. What about you?'

'I don't make any plans,' Parrot said. 'I might see you here. Depends.' Twenty minutes later he pulled up at the garage where Salter was to collect his car.

'Thanks,' Salter said, still in a slight daze. 'I enjoyed that.'

'Cheers,' Parrott said, and drove off.

Back at Boomewood Annie was having a bath after a happy day of sniffing flowers. Maud Beresford had suggested another expedition for the following day which Annie was keen to go on, and Salter saw his opportunity. He described his day at the races as enjoyable enough, carefully keeping back too much enthusiasm.

Annie said, 'Do you want to do something else tomorrow? I don't have to go with Maud.'

'No, no,' he protested. 'You go. I'll amuse myself around here.'

Annie said, 'You could go to the races again tomorrow, couldn't you?'

'I might, yes. Yes, maybe I'll do that.'

'Good,' she said. 'Ask Henry. He looked a bit bored today.'

'All right.'

'Got what you wanted, Charlie? Good. So have I.' She turned on the hand shower to wash her hair. Salter reached over her back and turned the cold water tap on to full and left her yelping.

When she emerged he was sorting out his pockets and disposing of his betting tickets.

'We'll need some money tomorrow, Charlie,' she said.

'You'd better cash a traveller's cheque at the desk here.'

Salter reached into the wardrobe to find the spare jacket where he kept his passport and traveller's cheques. He took out the cheques, and paused. 'My passport's gone,' he said.

Annie moved over to him and patted the pockets of the jacket, reached inside and drew out the passport.

'It's in the wrong pocket,' he said.

He explained. The left-hand inside pocket was the deep wallet pocket where he kept his passport, traveller's cheques, airline tickets, etc. The right-hand pocket was smaller and too high up for comfort. A passport in that pocket would dig into his armpit.

'But if you changed while it was hanging up . . . ?' Annie suggested.

Salter sat on the bed and reconstructed the sequence of events when he undressed the night before. 'No,' he said. 'I put it in the left-hand pocket and then took it off. Someone's been in here.'

'Have we lost anything?'

They went over their possessions quickly. Nothing was missing. Even a wad of Canadian money was still there in the top of the suitcase.

'You must be wrong,' Annie said.

'No, I'm not,' Salter said. 'But if you don't believe me, no one else will. Okay. Put all this stuff together and I'll give it to the hotel to look after.'

Downstairs he found the landlord in his office and handed over his valuables to be put in the safe. On the spur of the moment he asked, 'Does anyone have access to the room when we're out?'

'How do you mean, sir?' Then: 'Something missing?'

'No, no. I just wondered.'

'Your room is perfectly safe, Mr Salter. The cleaning lady, Mrs Peabody, is totally reliable. Do you have any reason to think someone has been in? Apart from Mrs Peabody?'

'My passport was in the wrong place. But we are pretty careless. I probably forgot where I put it. I wouldn't want to lose anything, though.'

'You won't. One of us is around all the time. Here's a receipt for the valuables. Dinner tonight?'

'Yes, please. And every night we are here.'

'How long would that be?'

'A few days, I think. My wife likes it here.'

'Good.' He nodded to dismiss Salter.

All right, Salter thought. But you took that a bit calmly. No noisy defence of the hotel's honesty. Now we have a prowler, a peeper (or rather, a listener), and someone going through the room. All standard items in English country life?

Dinner was again superb. During it, Henry jumped at the chance of a day at the races, and Maud and Annie planned their next day's outing. The Canadian woman took her usual place, but Maud was more interested in the progress of Mario, the waiter, with the American girl. They were getting along well.

'Have you ever been picked up by a waiter?' Maud asked Annie.

'No. I was a waitress once and I got picked up by a customer. Him,' she said pointing at Salter. This was a slightly inaccurate version of how Salter had found her when she was helping to manage a resort hotel in Prince Edward Island, owned along with a lot of other enterprises, by her family, one of the leading families on the Island.

'Really,' Maud said. 'How romantic. Henry found me in a library. He came in every day for three months and then put in a request for me on a call slip. Look, I think he's propositioning her.'

They all looked around covertly. The American girl was nodding to the waiter and looking at her watch as she stood up. The waiter moved to another table, looking pleased.

'I wonder what language they use,' Annie said. 'He doesn't speak much English.'

'Italian,' Maud said promptly. 'She's a graduate student, studying romance languages. I got chatting to her before dinner in the bar.'

'You interrogated her,' Henry said. 'She's twenty-two, unmarried, studying at Cornell, and her home is in Ithaca. New York, that is.'

Later, in bed, Annie said, 'How long do you think before Maud finds out you are a copper? This is getting a bit of a strain.'

'No, it isn't. It's fun. I told her this morning what a wonderful safety record we have. The bus company, I mean. She's nearly convinced, or defeated, which is the same thing. I thought I'd send her a card from the office when we get home. An official one. Her first failure. Now let's give that Listening Tom his money's worth.'

Two new arrivals appeared at breakfast the following day, a man and a woman in their thirties dressed as twins in identical blue jeans and windbreakers.

'They're not English,' Maud said. 'They look too much at home, and they aren't taking any notice of the rest of us. Perhaps more of your compatriots, Charlie.'

Breakfast was served by the Smarmy Boy, and Maud put the question to him.

'Australians, I think, madam. I'll find out for sure.'

Miss Rundstedt arrived, and Maud pointed out to Annie that she was either divorced or widowed.

'How can you tell?' Salter asked.

'It's a matter of rings, Charlie,' Annie said, slightly embarrassed. Mario put his head around the door and exchanged signals with the American girl, who got up quickly and left the room.

'Well, that's that,' Maud said. 'We might as well go now.

We'll take our car and Henry and Charlie can go in yours.'

Salter went into the lounge to read the racing page of *The Times* while he waited for Henry, and watched, through the window, the American girl and Mario leave in her car. After ten minutes, when Henry still had not appeared, Salter went up to his room to organize his own needs for the day. He considered putting a hair across the door of the wardrobe, but when he tried he was unable to get it to stay in place. He tried spit and scotch tape until the area around the invisible hair began to look slightly wrecked, and he abandoned the idea, wiped the door clean and joined Henry.

The two men had a lot of time to kill so Salter fabricated an excuse and dropped Henry off at a bookshop while he 'did some errands'. He strolled casually into the police station, made a feeble inquiry about directions, and left. The sergeant joined him on the steps.

'You did it, did you, sir?' he asked, looking thoughtfully down the street.

'Yes. Got one for today?'

The sergeant's eyebrows went up. 'You are a sportsman, sir. But if you insist, yes. Try Licensed Guide. Should be good odds. First time out this year. My nephew's a stable lad there.'

'Right. By the way, Sergeant, when you were looking into the background of my host, did you find out where he learned Italian? And anything about what he was doing before he came here? What did he do for a living?'

'No, to both, sir. Why? Something fishy about him?'

'Just curious. Nothing to bother your inspector about but he seems to keep well out of the way.'

'I understand, sir. I'll have another peek at the file. Best of luck now, sir. Think you can remember it?'

'Licensed Guide. I'll write it down. Keep your fingers crossed.'

After a short stroll around the town, Salter bought all the other morning papers and settled down to ham rolls in the

Eagle and Child, where he had arranged to meet Henry. He read the papers carefully, underlining his selections as he had seen others do. He looked for horses with omens in their names, like Annie's Choice, and he found plenty; his real difficulty was that he could find significant omens in about half the horses in each race. He sat at the short end of the L-shaped bar, and when he looked up he was surprised to see the Canadian woman at the far end of the room. He considered speaking, decided against it, and leaned into the corner of the bar where he was shielded from view by a row of mugs hanging down from a rail above the bar. He was watching her composedly drinking when the door opened behind her and his racing acquaintance of the day before entered. Parrott looked around the bar and Salter very nearly came out of hiding when the man caught the woman's eye and walked over to her table. She smiled at him and he sat down.

'Make a lovely-couple don't they, sir,' a voice in his ear said. It was the barman, polishing glasses and looking at Salter in ironic complicity. 'Very sociable type, she is,' the barman said.

'I know her,' Salter said to cut him off. 'She's staying at the same place I am.'

'Boomewood, sir? I wouldn't be surprised if she moves a little closer to the centre, soon.' He looked pointedly across the room, and Salter, following his gaze, watched Parrott pat her knee.

'They come in here a lot, sir.'

'Do they?' Salter said. He guessed, like the barman, that she got patted a lot, but his reaction was to feel a small dislike for the barman for not keeping his observations to himself. And after all, the woman was a Canadian.

He shook out his paper and tried once more to make sense of English racing jargon. Henry appeared and ate his lunch and it was time for them to go.

Henry drove, and Salter carefully guided him over the route that Parrott had taken him the day before, right down to the rail by the first fence. He explained about watching the horses jump one fence, and how they would see the rest of the races from the stands.

'You've really got your feet under the table,' Henry said. 'Now show me about bookies. You know, I've never been to the races before.'

They crossed the course into the stands and Salter showed Henry how to bet, and where. Licensed Guide was in the second race and had no trouble romping home at odds of six to one. After the fourth race, they were joined for a while by Parrott. Salter had noticed his car parked near their own, and noticed, also, the Canadian woman who stayed in the car throughout the afternoon, but some small delicacy concerning what Maud would certainly make of it had held him back from pointing her out to Henry.

Now Parrott appeared at his elbow. 'Getting the hang of it?' he asked.

'Hullo,' said Salter, and introduced Henry. The three men chatted until it was time to bet and Salter moved off to find a bookmaker. The race began while he was still putting on his bet and he walked down to the rail to watch the horses sweep by for the first circuit. When he got back to Henry, Parrott was just leaving. No one had picked the winner.

Salter found two more winners, and the only flaw in the afternoon was that Henry, at the first race-meeting of his life, picked a winner in the third race with his first try and became an instant expert, explaining to Salter how to pick them out. Happily, when he had no more luck he shut up, and Salter could enjoy himself.

On the way home Henry said, 'What does your friend do for a living?'

'He's a building inspector, or some such. Why?'

'I just wondered. He certainly wanted to know all about you.'

'He's lonely, Henry. He's lived in Canada. I'm the first white man he's met around here. Old home week.'

'Yes? He sounded to me as if he was pumping me.'

'What did you tell him?'

'I told him you were probably a CIA agent, posing as a bus conductor.'

'For the last time, Henry, I'm a Canadian. The CIA is American. Anyway, he doesn't look mysterious to me. Just lonely.'

'Really? You forget I'm married to an expert interrogator, Charlie.'

'Yes, and it's made you pretty good at it, Henry. And now I'll tell you what you talked about, shall I? *You* asked *him* if I seemed like a maintenance supervisor, didn't you? So what did he tell you?'

Henry blushed. 'I just like to do Maud in the eye sometimes, Charlie. As a matter of fact he said you seemed to be just the type.' Henry paused. 'But I tell you he *was* pumping me.'

Salter considered this. He was certain that he had never met Parrott before, but a lonely man on holiday will scrape an acquaintance wherever he can, and the policeman guessed that if he had lunch at the Eagle and Child the next day the man would be there, eager to be invited to the races again.

Part Two

DEATH IN TOKESBURY MALLETT

At breakfast next morning the dining-room exploded. The Salters were late down and Maud and Henry had given their orders to the Smarmy Boy. He brought the Beresfords their eggs and took orders from the Salters. 'I'll do my best, sir and ma'am,' he said. 'But there's trouble in the kitchen —would you like some marmalade, Mrs Beresford?—so I can't promise anything.' He smiled at the Salters, then at the Beresfords, and left.

'Trouble in the kitchen?' Maude asked. 'Our hostess *is* the kitchen. We are lost without her. Hullo, here's the answer.'

Mario, the handsome waiter, had appeared in the door-way in street clothes with a suitcase in his hand, looking around the room. He spotted the American girl and walked over to her table and began a long conversation in a whisper. The girl rose to her feet in evident distress and responded in Italian.

'This is maddening,' Maud observed.

Soon the waiter was shaking his head and the girl burst into tears. Dillon appeared in the doorway and said something sharply to Mario, who responded angrily. Then the American girl seemed to be arguing with Dillon. Mrs Dillon appeared from the kitchen and joined the girl in pleading with her husband while Mario stayed silent. Suddenly Mario turned on the host and shouted at him for about a minute, pointing to the Canadian woman, at which Mrs Dillon turned on her husband and began cursing him. The

American girl ran out of the room in tears, followed by Mario, leaving the landlord and his wife arguing and pointing to Miss Rundstedt, who was now staring at them. Next the host grabbed his wife and pushed her out of the room, still shouting. There was a silence like the end of an artillery duel.

'I think we should leave,' Annie said.

'Are you out of your mind?' Maud cried, lenses flashing. 'Gregory,' she called. 'Come here. What's going on? Everything, please.'

Gregory was full of it. 'As far as I can tell, ma'am, Mr Dillon has just given Mario the sack because he says he won't have his hotel made into a—excuse me, ma'am—knocking shop. The American lady says it was her fault and quite innocent—I'm sure it was—so it's not fair that Mario should have to lose his job. Poor old Mario. He's only got a work permit for this place, you see. He'll have to go back to Italy now. But the boss is insisting. He suspects Mario of ending up in one or two other beds in the past.'

The Prowler, thought Salter.

'What about the other bit? What was all that between our landlord and his wife?' Maud demanded.

Before Gregory could answer, the landlady appeared and slapped a piece of paper on the table in front of Miss Rundstedt and folded her arms aggressively across her bosom. 'You want to know why this is?' she screamed. But Miss Rundstedt grabbed the paper and rushed past the hostess out of the room.

Gregory returned. 'Carry on,' Maud said.

'Poor old Mario, he didn't like being fired,' Gregory said, 'So he accused the boss of being a hypocrite. Said he's been having it off with Miss Rundstedt. He's seen the boss coming out of her room more than once. He didn't say anything before because he didn't want to upset his sister, but I suppose it just slipped out now. A pity, really. These things are best left unsaid, don't you think so, ma'am?'

But he was talking to the wrong person. 'More,' Maud demanded.

'Well, the boss's wife has just told Miss Rundstedt to pack her bags, and the boss is having a terrible argument with his wife now in the kitchen. I'm afraid your eggs are spoilt, sir. Shall I get you some more bread?'

Salter nodded. Maud stopped the boy as he was leaving. 'What will this do to our dinner?' she wanted to know.

'I'll find out, ma'am,' he said. He returned almost immediately. 'No dinner tonight, I'm afraid,' he said. 'Now Mrs Dillon is packing her bags. Such a shame, really.'

The two Australians came over to their table. 'Fill us in, would you, mate?' the man said. 'What's up?'

Salter deferred to Maud, who supplied an already-polished account of the last twenty minutes.

'Christ!' the Australian said. 'And we were just thanking our stars for finding this place. I suppose we might as well shove off, too.'

Annie had been considering this. 'I wouldn't,' she said. 'This place without dinner is still better than most places with it.' She looked at Maud interrogatively, who nodded. 'We'll stay and see what happens.'

Suits me, thought Salter. One more day over the sticks.

'Right, Jilly?' the Australian asked his wife, who smiled her agreement. 'See you later, then,' he said to the table.

'Hang on a moment,' Maud said. 'Have you met our landlord? Is he Australian? We can't place his accent.' Thus incorporating the whole table in her nosiness.

'We thought he was a Yank,' the man said.

'That's it,' Annie said. 'He sounds like one of those English actors on television trying to do an American accent.'

'Well, well, well,' Maud said. 'No dinner, but what a lovely breakfast. Would you have thought it of our host? One never saw him above stairs until this morning but he hardly looks the type. I'm surprised at Miss Rundstedt, too.

We saw her in town with another man and they certainly looked like an item. What a lot of pigs you men are,' she added irrelevantly. 'Ah, well. I've never understood adultery. No óne ever gives me the chance. Come on, Henry. See you outside, Annie.'

Salter had been granted his wish for one more day at the races, and Henry had chosen to accompány the women again, so he went off to read the papers while everyone else got ready to leave. From the lounge he heard the argument in the kitchen continuing, but quieter now, and at ten o'clock Mrs Dillon appeared without her coat and Salter assumed she had been persuaded to stay. He watched the departure of all the other guests and witnessed one last kiss between Mario and the American girl before she drove off with her luggage.

He decided that the local police ought to know about this morning's events because they were probably, in one way or another, connected with the prowler or the listener. He also wanted to have a word with the sergeant.

'Hullo, again, Charles,' Churcher greeted him. 'I was mentioning you to my wife last night, and we were wondering if you and your wife would care to have a bit of dinner with us while you're here.'

'That would be nice,' Salter said. 'I'll ask my wife what our plans are. I dropped by to tell you that I think you can close your file on the Boomewood Prowler.' He told Churcher the story of the morning's excitement; the inspector wrote it all down on a pad of foolscap paper.

'Hmm,' he said, ticking off the sentences as he re-read them. 'You think, then, that our Italian lad got into the wrong bedroom?'

'I did at first. But it's possible that the landlord may be the one.'

'I see. You think this Cànadian woman may be one among many, do you? Our landlord exercising a sort of *droit de seigneur* over his unattached female guests?'

'She may be the only one; she was staying there last week.'

'Right, I see,' Churcher said again. He considered for a few moments. 'Which, do you think?'

'I would say the landlord, on the evidence of the phrase "wakey-wakey". That's not an Italian expression.'

'True. But you know sometimes these fellows pick up the slang first. There was an Italian waiter at a little place we used to go to when I was courting my wife who began half his sentences with "Cor bloody blimey". We would order something and he would say, "Cor bloody blimey, signor, the veal isa the besta thing tonight." '

Salter laughed. 'Either way, it's probably an inside job. Now I've got to go. I'll ask my wife about dinner, but don't be offended if we leave tomorrow. She's very changeable.'

'Not at all. A woman's privilege. Keep in touch, though.'

Salter nodded to the sergeant on the way out and waited to be joined on the steps.

'What's the word for today, Sergeant?' he asked without preamble.

'Monkey's Paw looks good in the first, sir. What did you get about Licensed Guide.'

'Sixes,' Salter said.

'Ah,' the sergeant sighed. 'That's the advantage of being there, isn't it? It went off at fours. Cheers.' He disappeared inside the station, and Salter headed for the pub.

The bar was empty, and Salter ordered his beer and looked for Monkey's Paw among the runners.

'I hear there was a bit of bother at your place this morning, sir,' the barman said. 'The lady left in a bit of a rush, like.'

Salter felt a growing dislike for his confidant, and decided to risk the lunch at another pub in future. 'I heard the landlord made a pass at her,' he said. 'Not her fault, was it?'

'I see, sir. Defending her honour, was she?'

Salter sighed. By now the whole town was probably in on

458

the gossip, but he felt sorry for the woman and a need to dissociate himself from the nudging matiness of the tapster. He said nothing, but picked up his paper to try to read what Our Newmarket Correspondent had to say. The barman took the hint and moved away, and when a small flurry of people came in, Salter left the remains of his beer and headed for the parking lot.

Monkey's Paw won and in four other races Salter picked the horse that came second, so that while he lost money he was pleased with his performance.

When the four of them assembled at Boomewood they learned that although Mrs Dillon was still in residence, she was taking the evening off and the dining-room was closed. They dined at the Swan, chewing the edges of some braised ox liver and turnips followed by cubes of a cake-like substance called cabinet pudding. Even Maud was too dispirited to make more than one bright remark about the alternative dessert, which was called 'Spotted Dick'. 'Ah,' she said. 'Dead Man's Leg in a Bandage.'

The waiter, a huge, toothless fellow of the type used to open the front door in gothic films, was surly because they had not taken his suggestions about the menu. 'I told you to 'ave the 'ot-pot,' he growled, as he cleared away the nearly untouched liver. 'You wouldn't listen!'

Afterwards they had drinks in the 'American Bar' where the barman tried to sell them his special.

'I think,' Annie said, without consulting Salter, 'that we might as well push on tomorrow.'

'Oh, give it a day,' Maud cried. 'Wait and see if Maria goes back to her kitchen. And if she is still sulking, there must be a Tweedledum to eat at somewhere.'

Annie looked at Salter. He was hers to dispose of, and he could see she was tempted. As she became familiar with the area, she became more and more interested in it and wanted to dig deeper. If they left now they would simply drive through the rain to another hotel, and so on the next day. Salter wondered if the police sergeant would know of somewhere in the same class as Boomewood. 'I'll ask around tomorrow,' he said. 'There must be somewhere.'

'You know people here?' the ever-alert Maud asked.

'I know a barman at a pub,' Salter parried. 'I'll ask him.'

So they decided to give Boomewood one more night and make a decision the next day.

In the event, the decision to leave Boomewood was made for them. In the early hours of the morning, Salter was awakened by a banging on the door from a dream in which he was eating a boiled sheepshead. He put on his raincoat and opened the door to the sergeant from Tokesbury Mallett. Outside there was the noise of cars arriving, doors opening, and voices in the hall.

'The Prowler?' Salter asked.

'A bit more serious than that, sir. Your landlord. He's dead. His wife stabbed him. Would you mind coming downstairs, sir, and making a statement?'

'Good Christ!' Salter said. 'You want my wife, too?'

'Yes, please, sir. In the residents' lounge, please.' He moved along the hall to wake up the other guests.

They put on some clothes and descended to the lounge where the Beresfords and the Australians were already waiting. The only other person present was Gregory, who was offering to make everyone a cup of tea. Inspector Churcher had taken charge. As Salter arrived, he greeted him loudly. 'Charles,' he said. 'A bit of a busman's holiday for you, but I don't think I'll need any help. I'll brief you later, but right now I'd like to get a statement from everybody as to where you all were last night, what time you went to bed, whether you heard anything unusual, that sort of thing. I'd like you to do it one by one, please. The constable is waiting in the dining-room, so if you'd go in first, sir.' He nodded to the Australian.

Salter was very conscious of Maud's glasses trained on him and he turned to look at her.

'I'd have found out eventually,' she said. 'I never believed that bus company rubbish.'

Salter acknowledged the remark with a small inclination of the head, and Annie grinned. But now that someone had been killed, Salter felt less interested in larking about with Maud Beresford. He felt as if he had been acting in a brightly coloured travelogue, moving through the gentle, if rain-soaked, English countryside without really believing in it or taking the inhabitants seriously. A murder changed that: the film was black and white again, familiar and real.

Annie, watching him watching the proceedings, said, 'It's nothing to do with you, Charlie.'

'I know that,' Salter said. 'I'm just interested to see how they do it.'

He was the last to make a statement, and then Churcher sent everyone else back to bed with instructions to let him know before they left the district.

'I'll follow you up,' Salter said to Annie.

'Soon,' she said warningly.

The photographer left, along with the doctor and the ambulance men. Salter settled down at Churcher's invitation to another cup of tea with the inspector and the sergeant.

'Here's the story,' Churcher said. 'Quite clear-cut. Mrs Dillon was picked up about an hour ago driving erratically on the Oxford Road. The patrol car suspected she was drunk, but when he got a good look at her he saw blood on her clothes and her hands. She seemed hysterical, so they took her into custody and brought her back to us. Take over, Sergeant.'

'The constable on duty called me,' the sergeant said, 'and I had a little chat with her, calmed her down a bit, and then she told me she'd killed her husband. Just like that. So I called the inspector—I didn't really believe her—and we came up and found him.'

'Where? How?'

'The old pro, eh, Charles?' Churcher said. 'He was in his office along the hall. He was dead all right. The surgeon said he'd been stabbed seven or eight times. There was a lot of blood about.'

'What with? Does she carry a knife?'

'No. She used one that Dillon kept in a drawer, it seems. A memento of the war.'

'Where is it?'

'We haven't got it. She said she threw it away. She doesn't remember where, she says. We'll have a bit of a search, of course, but it might be anywhere. She was ten miles away when they stopped her. Of course, the weapon isn't really necessary, with her confession. A fairly simple matter, really.'

'Have you got a proper statement from her?'

'Not yet. We'll get that now, eh, Sergeant?'

'It's the next thing, sir, according to procedure.'

'Right. Well, Charles, a little story for you to take back to Toronto. But I imagine you get a lot of this with such a high percentage of foreigners.'

'Yes, it's the interesting English-type murders we miss. The ones where some railway clerk has fourteen middle-aged women buried in the basement.'

Churcher chuckled. 'Yes. Well, I must be off,' he said.

'Can I come by in the morning?' Salter asked. 'I'd like to hear her version of why she did it.'

'Oh, I think we all know the motive, Charles. Sexual jealousy, of course. All the people here witnessed that little scene the other morning. Yesterday, wasn't it?'

Salter nodded. 'You'll have to confirm that with the Rundstedt woman. We all got the same version from the Smarmy Boy and he was translating from the Italian.'

'From who?'

'Sorry. Gregory. The lad who made our tea.'

'Do we have Miss Rundstedt's address, Sergeant?'

'She's staying at one of the hotels in town, sir. She should be easy to find.'

'Right. Let's go, then, Sergeant. Busy day ahead.'

Churcher walked down the hall to the front door; Salter held the sergeant for a moment.

'This place will be closed after tonight,' he said. 'Where can we stay? Most of all, where can we get a decent meal?'

'Plain or fancy?' the sergeant asked.

'Plain.' 'Fancy', they had already learned, meant imitation French.

'The Plough,' Sergeant Robey said promptly. 'In Wartlock. About two miles down the road towards Marstonbury Edge. Roast beef, apple tart, their own eggs. And they have Hunter's bitter, sir.'

Churcher reappeared in the doorway looking for his sergeant.

'Thanks, Sergeant,' Salter said. To the inspector, he said, 'We'll need a place to stay. I was just asking the sergeant if he knew of anywhere. Can you recommend a place, Charles?'

Churcher posed thoughtfully, then shook his head. 'No, I suppose Sergeant Robey is your best man on that. Cheers, then.'

Poor bugger, thought Salter again. Nobody asks him anything.

In the morning they found a constable in charge of the hotel. Gregory made everyone tea, and the Australians left. Salter told the Beresfords about the Plough and they all agreed to try it for a night. The bill was easy to calculate and Gregory solemnly gave them all receipts, apologizing for the inconvenience of the murder. Annie and Maud had become addicted to a little book of 'walks' in the district and had decided on a long one that would take them most of the day.

Henry wanted to 'nip back to Watford and look at my rats for an hour', and Salter, declining an offer to accompany the women, assured everyone that he would be quite happy mooching about the town.

The exterior of the Plough looked promising. It was built of grey stone, and the name was spelled out along the front of the hotel in fresh gold paint, a combination of colours that reminded Salter of the clock tower of Hart House in Toronto. The hotel faced the village green, and Salter guessed that the management took some responsibility for maintaining the green, a piece of pure Merrie England with a pond, ducks, and what looked like a monument to those who fell at Agincourt. The green sward blended perfectly with the grey and gold of the hotel, so perfectly that Salter decided that if he ever owned a racehorse, these would be his racing colours.

He led the way through the door, stumbled and tripped down two stone steps, and recovered to smash his head against a giant beam that served as a lintel over the inner door. The other three waited while he staggered about, then joined him in the lobby.

'Heeazeard abeuve, heeazeard beleough,' a voice said from inside the lobby.

'What was that?' Salter asked, his head ringing.

The owner of the voice stepped forward. A dapper little man in a blazer and brilliantly polished shoes. 'Heeazeard abeuve, heeazeard beleough,' he said again, pointing first at the lintel, then at the step. He executed a manœuvre with his feet that turned him sideways to them and pointed across the lobby at the desk.

'Ah,' Salter said and looked inquiringly at Maud. 'Sandhurst Oxbridge,' she whispered in his ear. 'The accent peculiar to army officers who have to shout.'

The landlady, behind the desk, smiled a welcome. A pleasant-looking, fat little lady, she signed them in, organized their luggage and showed them to their rooms, all the while her husband stood guard by the door.

As they learned later, she cooked the meals, kept the place shining, and generally made life agreeable for the guests, while her husband looked after the outside of the hotel and the bar. His accent, however, intensified as the day went on and in the late evening Salter and Annie needed Maud to translate for them. He had one other habit that was especially disconcerting when he was away from the bar. He preferred to conduct all conversations with a rigid back at a two-hundred and seventy degree angle from his guests; occasionally he veered around until he was virtually back to back, and talking to him was like playing a stylized scene in a comedy of the Thirties. Otherwise, it turned out, there was everything to recommend the place.

By ten o'clock that morning, Salter was once more chatting to Churcher in his office.

'She had gone to see *Romeo and Juliet*,' Churcher said. 'When she got back, quite late, I gather, though she doesn't know the time, she and Dillon got into an argument again, over the Rundstedt woman, and one thing led to another and she stabbed him. A bit operatic, but these people are not like us, are they?'

'And then she decided to run away? Why the Oxford road?'

'It joins in with the London road. She said she was going back home to Italy.'

Salter said, 'There were six of us and the Smarmy Boy around. Maybe we were all asleep but nobody heard anything. There couldn't have been much of a row.'

Churcher shrugged. 'I think that just goes to show. When you know who the culprit is, and they confess, you don't have to worry about all the odd little bits, do you? She has signed a statement, after proper warning, of course.'

'Have you talked to Rundstedt yet?'

'Of course. She confirmed the row. Says that Dillon did visit her in her room a couple of times. She didn't see any harm in it, she says. Not on holiday.'

'I see. Where is she now?'

'Staying at the Swan. Why?'

'On her own?'

Churcher looked at Salter in surprise, and with a touch of embarrassment. 'She is now,' he said. 'But when we spoke to her there was someone else with her.'

'A man named Jeremy Parrott?'

'Yes. Apparently a one-night stand. He left this morning. You seem very interested in her, Charles. Fancy her yourself?' Churcher arranged a knowing leer on his face.

It was a silly remark, and Salter forgave him for it. It must be irritating to have some smart-aleck 'colonial' copper anticipate you. 'Not really,' Salter said. 'She gets around too much.' He had a thought. 'I suppose there's no chance I could talk to Mrs Dillon, or watch you talk to her.'

' "No" to both. I remember you asked about that last night, but it's against the proper form and besides she isn't here. We've transferred her to the regional headquarters where they have proper facilities for women prisoners.'

'So that's that, then.'

'Yes,' Churcher said. 'My first murder in this posting. My first real murder, as a matter of fact. Nice to have it all tickety-boo. No credit to me, of course, but it looks well. At the end of the day, that's what counts, isn't it.'

I hope so, for your sake, Salter thought. It was, of course, like nine out of ten homicides in its typical motive, its 'in-house' suspect, and the lack of any real mystery, but Salter was troubled by it. What bothered him was the apparent lack of any detail or witness that would confirm Mrs Dillon's account. And there was a very big disparity between the angry woman they had seen the day before, the woman who had kicked out Miss Rundstedt, and a killer who inflicts seven or eight stab wounds. But she had confessed, and if Churcher had done a solid job on her statement, there was no point in going behind it. Churcher had a right to feel pleased.

'May they all be like this,' Salter said, and stood up.

There being no racing he was in no hurry for lunch, but the pubs were open and habit took him into the Eagle and Child. He regretted his choice as soon as he saw the barman, who welcomed him as a regular.

'Lots of excitement at your place last night, sir,' the barman said.

'Oh? What do you hear?' Salter asked.

'I hear your landlady did in her old man, sir.'

'That's what you heard, is it?' Salter asked politely.

'That's what they tell me. Trouble over a lady, I hear,' he said.

'You hear a lot,' Salter said, and stared at the barman. He got his effect as the barman went back to polishing his glasses and moved away. Salter went back to his beer in silence. He left the bar and walked over to the Swan for lunch, where the 'ploughman's lunch' consisted of a bun and a piece of cracked orange cheese accompanied by a stick of celery. While he nibbled on these, he inquired casually of the barman if he knew if Miss Rundstedt was still at the hotel, saying he wanted to look her up. He saw the barman go wary and knew that the whole town knew the story. 'She's still here, sir,' the barman said. 'In there, having lunch.' He pointed through the glass doors to the dining-room where Miss Rundstedt could be seen at a table not twenty feet away.

'I won't bother her now,' Salter said. 'I'll surprise her later.'

The barman nodded and moved away. When Salter left the bar, he felt the man's eyes on his back, and knew that the barman would have an extra detail to tell anyone who cared to listen. On the other hand, he thought it was unlikely that anyone in this town would keep Churcher in touch with the local gossip, so that the knowledge that 'some American' was snooping around would probably die before it reached the inspector's office.

Salter drove back to the Plough where he tried to make up for his disturbed night with a little nap. He woke up at four and went down to the residents' lounge in search of a cup of tea or coffee, and had an agreeably absurd conversation back to back with his host. When Henry and the women returned they all had a pint of Hunter's bitter and an early dinner of steak pie and apple tart and cream which made them happy to have found a home again.

'Been sleuthing, Charlie?' Maud asked, over some more beer.

'You think they'd let me poke my nose in?' Salter asked.

'I just wondered,' Maud said. 'Of course, you may not be a policeman at all. That may be one of your many disguises. I must say Annie is extremely well got up for a policeman's wife.'

'Oh, Maud. I told you. I have my own job.'

Salter turned the conversation around. 'I'll show you my passport in the morning,' he said. 'And my official identification, if you like.'

'She'll say it's just a clever piece of cover,' Henry said.

'It's so hard with you colonials,' Maud said. 'You can't tell a thing from the accent—at least, I can't.'

Salter thought about something Maud had said to him two days before. 'What sort of accent did our host at Boomewood have, under the American act?' he asked. 'Upper, middle, lower, or one of the eleven in between. See, I'm learning.'

Maud laughed. 'Aren't you, though. My guess would be that he was a grammar school boy. He wore all the old school tie gear, but it was all a bit wobbly, like his accent. There was something else about the way he spoke too. He used a lot of out-of-date phrases, like a Rip Van Winkle. Or like one of those German spies during the war who mugged up their English from old Bulldog Drummond stories.'

'Did he seem like a lecher to you?'

'Nobody makes passes at me, Charlie, I told you. Though if they came at me when I didn't have my glasses on I'd be helpless. But that's an odd thing. I can usually tell who would and who wouldn't—we all can, can't we, Annie?—and I was quite surprised when the row blew up over the Rundstedt woman. Weren't you, Annie?'

'I never saw the man except during the row,' Annie said. 'Now, knock it off, Charlie. I want to talk about tomorrow. If we stay here I want to do some shopping for the boys, and I want you to come with me.'

'All right. Where do you want to go?'

'Cheltenham,' Annie said. 'It's a long drive but we missed it on the way through and I hear they have good shops there.'

'What's the forecast?' Salter asked. 'Sunny with cloudy periods, or cloudy with sunny periods?'

'It's going to piss down,' Henry said. 'You might as well go shopping.'

'Are we going to spend the rest of our time here with Maud and Henry?' Salter asked as they tramped around Cheltenham in a steady drizzle. 'We seem to have become a foursome.'

'They like us, Charlie, and I like them,' Annie said. 'We can take off anytime we want, but there's no need to be wary of them.'

'It's a bit un-English, isn't it?' Salter grumbled. 'I thought they were supposed to be stand-offish.'

'Haven't you noticed, Charlie? The English are either very stand-offish or friendly as hell. There are two kinds, you see—'

'Oh, don't start that, again. Come on. Let's buy Angus that Swiss army knife and get out of here. The main street in that village we went through is about ten feet wide and

I want to be through there before the rush-hour starts when the shepherds quit.'

'But you can get Swiss army knives in Toronto!'

'I know. Probably cheaper, too. But he hasn't got one, has he?'

Down came the rain. At dinner that night even Maud was slightly depressed. The forecast was glum but there was still no point in driving north to sit in another hotel. On the other hand, while Maud and Annie had uncovered a huge layer of interesting activities in the neighbourhood—market days, horse fairs, and such—nothing was very much fun in the rain.

'Let's go up to town,' Maud suggested.

'Where's that?' Salter asked.

'London, idiot.'

The prospect of having a look at London while the women shopped would normally have pleased Salter, but he had developed new priorities. In Cheltenham, he had picked up a racing diary and discovered that while racing was over at Tokesbury Mallett, it was just beginning at Burford. By comparing the diary with a map, he had uncovered the wonderful information that the authorities had so arranged things that there was a race meeting somewhere every day within a reasonable drive. And he had come to enjoy standing up to his ankles in mud, with the rain trickling down his neck, trying to find the bookie with the best odds.

'You go,' he said. 'I might watch *Pot the Black*. One of our boys looks like winning it.'

Annie looked at him thoughtfully. Salter had never played pool in his life to her knowledge, and spending the afternoon watching anything on television was completely out of character. Salter returned her gaze blandly.

'All right,' she said at last. So it was agreed.

'What are you up to?' she asked, when they were in bed.

'Who, me? Nothing?'

'Don't get addicted,' she said. 'As long as it's raining, I'm glad the racing is keeping you cheerful, but when the sun comes out, I want us to start having a holiday together.'

But Salter did not go to the races. When he called in at the police station the next morning for a tip from the sergeant, and to thank him for recommending the Plough, he found Churcher looking glum.

'Area headquarters are getting involved,' he told Salter. 'Apparently they don't like the woman's statement. They've raised a number of questions.'

'What's wrong with it? Did they say?'

'Inconsistencies, they said.' He looked at Salter worriedly. 'They think the confession may be false. As a matter of fact they've released her.'

Salter said nothing. He felt sorry for Churcher.

'I'm expecting someone this afternoon, a Superintendent Hamilton. Would you mind coming in to meet him? He'll be here at three o'clock. You may be able to tell him something I've missed. I seem to have missed a lot.' Churcher looked at his hands.

'Sure,' Salter said. 'He'll probably tell me to get my ass out of here, though. I would if I were him.'

'Did you have any inkling that the Dillon woman might be lying? I mean, why the hell should she?'

'I never spoke to her, did I?' Salter said. Should he tell Churcher that he had smelt something wrong from the start? No. 'What next?' he asked, standing up.

Churcher shrugged and avoided Salter's gaze. 'It's out of my hands now.'

'I'll see you this afternoon,' Salter said.

There was no point in talking to the sergeant now, and Salter headed directly for the Eagle and Child, risking the barman's confidences for the sake of the food.

'All alone today, sir,' the barman said as he brought his beer.

'I always am,' Salter said, surprised.

'No, sir. I mean in here.' Salter looked around. The bar was empty.

'She left about an hour ago, sir,' the barman confided. 'I saw her drive off from the Swan as I was getting some change from the bank.'

To ask 'who' would have been pointless. Salter grunted and sipped his beer.

'I expect things are a bit quiet for her at the Swan,' the barman offered. 'She seems to like a lot of action.'

Suddenly Salter had had enough. 'Why don't you keep your goddam observations to yourself,' he suggested. 'Or save them for your memoirs.' For a moment the barman looked as if he was going to respond in kind, and Salter picked up his beer and waited. But the arrival of another customer gave the barman reason for breaking away, and he stayed at the far end of the bar, contenting himself with casting sour glances along the bar from time to time.

Superintendent Hamilton was seated at Churcher's desk when Salter walked in. Churcher was standing beside the desk with his hands clasped behind him.

He was perhaps sixty, with a ragged ginger-and-grey fringe of hair around a weatherbeaten bald head. His face was like a piece of rock, patchily coloured as if the sun had not penetrated all the crevices. His eyes were small and very close together, which should have made him look devious but because of their piercing quality created a shotgun effect. He fixed Salter in his sights. 'The Toronto copper, eh?' he said. 'Salter? My name is Hamilton, Wylie Hamilton. Take a chair and tell me what you think of all this. Bugger orf for a bit, would you, Churcher? You've heard all this before, and besides, you might intimidate Salter here.' He twisted his mouth to show he was joking, and stared at Churcher until the inspector left.

What class said 'orf' instead of 'off', Salter wondered. Hamilton looked and acted like a squire, but he must have been a constable at some point or could you start above the ranks in this mob, if you had the right background and said 'orf' instead of 'off'?

'Your man has handled this thing very well,' Salter offered. 'I was impressed by . . .'

Hamilton cut him off. 'I don't want to know what you think of Churcher,' he said. 'Tell me what you saw and heard. *Then* you can tell me what to think.'

Salter went over the events from his point of view, from the row over Miss Rundstedt to the death of Dillon. 'It looks pretty clear to me, as it did to Churcher,' he finished.

'It's a balls-up and you know it,' Hamilton snarled. 'If you had handled anything like this, Orliff would have kicked your arse through your hat.'

Orliff was Salter's superior in Toronto. Salter tried not to react immediately. 'You know him?' he asked, appearing to register the name only casually.

'I've had dealings with him,' Hamilton said.

'And you've been in touch with him?'

'I phoned him this morning. Got him out of bed. Apparently it was five o'clock in the morning, eskimo time.' Hamilton smiled briefly. Then he said, 'He told me you're not a complete bloody fool.'

'Did he also tell you that I am on holiday?'

'The people at the Plough told me you are staying for the next two days. I don't need your help, Salter, but it would be nice to have someone to talk to.' Hamilton's reference was clear. 'All right?' he asked.

'Sure.' Salter shrugged. 'So what's happened? Has Mrs Dillon retracted her statement?'

'Her what? Retracted her what? What bloody statement? Have you seen it?'

Salter shook his head. It was clear that whatever Hamilton's natural manner was, he was now very angry.

'The bloody statement broke down at the first sentence. You wouldn't need a lawyer from London. One of the local toss-pots could do it. Here.' He tossed the statement across the desk.

'Now,' he said. 'I don't know how they do it in Saskatchewan . . .'

'Ontario,' Salter said.

'Wherever. But in this country when a hysterical woman confesses to murdering her husband—immediately, mind you, not under questioning or anything, in pidgin English —we try to make sure she's telling the truth.'

'She was caught running away,' Salter pointed out. 'Covered in blood.'

'From what, eh? From what? Churcher!' he shouted. 'Bring us some tea, will you?'

When the tea arrived, and Churcher had been dismissed, Hamilton resumed.

'We took her over her statement,' he said, 'And every time it came out differently. First she said they quarrelled right away. Then she said they had a long talk, maybe an hour, before they quarrelled. Then she said she stabbed him as he was sitting in the chair. Then she said she stabbed him in the back. And the knife!' Hamilton squinted at the statement. 'He kept a knife in his bedroom. First she says she ran upstairs and got it and came back down to kill him with it. So I asked her why she locked the bedroom door after her. We tripped her up on every single, sodding, sentence.'

'You think she's lying, then?'

'I know she's lying, laddie. I know she's lying. But why?'

'Did she go to the play?'

'Oh, she went to the play all right. We found a pal she went with. An Italian woman. And you know what? Her husband was killed when Romeo was getting his in the tomb.'

'How do you know?'

'We asked the surgeon, laddie. We asked the bloody surgeon to establish the time of death. Dillon was killed

while you lot were roistering in the Swan. Churcher did not
even bother to check the surgeon's report. They hardly
exchanged two words! Christ Almighty!'

To divert him from his fury, Salter said, 'She's covering
for someone, obviously.'

'Obviously. Obviously. Obviously. Who?'

'Her brother?'

'Ah. Got there, have we?'

Screw you, thought Salter. Up until now he had been
intrigued by Hamilton, but he had no intention of trotting
alongside the Englishman's stirrup, being catechized.

'Well?' Hamilton barked.

Salter shrugged. 'So find the brother,' he said.

'He's disappeared. We have an all points bulletin out—
is that what you call it? Any other suggestions?'

'Italy.'

Hamilton shook his head. 'We've tried that. He hasn't
gone home, or he's not there yet.'

'Ask his sister. She might know.'

'Of course she knows, but she won't tell us. She says she
has no idea.'

'So keep asking her. Churcher tells me you've released
her. You had some charges that would stick; she's your
only lead to her brother. Why take the chance that she'll
disappear, too?'

'You underestimate my enormous cunning, old son. I'm
not taking any chances on that one. I have installed a
bright young constable in the ditch outside her hotel with
instructions to follow the lady wherever she goes. He's got
a big picture of her brother in his pocket, too, so that he can
check up on any visitors that may call. The idea is, you see,
that if she thinks we are no longer interested in her, she
might just lead us to the brother. Not fearfully subtle but a
bit better than what you give me credit for. Any other
suggestions?'

'The American girl.'

'Who?'

'The American girl. Her name is in the register. She and the brother were lovers, or something. Very close, anyway. He may have told her where he was going. I saw them kissing goodbye in the parking lot.'

'And right now she's somewhere in England, or Scotland, or buggered orf altogether, I suppose.'

'You have her car licence number from the register at Boomewood—Dillon was fussy about that—she rented from the same company I'm using, so they could give you a complete description.' All these little cars look alike to me.'

Hamilton mused. 'That's a bit of help. I'll put a trace on her. Put her on the fucking computer.'

Salter looked at his watch. 'Hold on. Can I borrow your phone for a minute?'

Hamilton pushed the instrument across the desk. Salter dialled Information and got the phone number of the Plough, then dialled again. He was answered immediately. 'Hyelleough?' the voice said.

'Mr Stiles? Charlie Salter here. Do you know if my wife is back from London yet?'

'All here present and correct, swilling tea,' Stiles shouted. 'You'd like a word with your CO?'

Salter worked out what Stiles had said. 'No,' he said. 'Let me speak to Maud Beresford if she's there.' He looked up at Hamilton who was ringing his ear furiously with his index finger. 'Ah, Maud. You remember the American girl? Mario's girlfriend? Yeah. Do you know where she headed for when she left that morning? Good. Hang on.'

Hamilton took his finger out and pushed a pad of paper across the desk at Salter.

'Okay,' Salter resumed. 'Cranmer House, Gosforth, Seascale, Cumberland. And the name? c/o Gush. Thanks.' He put the phone down. 'You'll find her here,' he said to Hamilton. 'Staying with some people called Gush.' Good old Maud.

'You keep track of everybody?' Hamilton asked, impressed.

'She gave her address to a woman who is staying at the Plough with us.'

'Huh.' Hamilton transcribed Salter's note into a form he could pass on. The door opened as he was writing and a man in his thirties in plain clothes entered.

'Ah, Woodiwiss,' Hamilton said. 'Inspector Salter of the Toronto police. Detective-Sergeant Woodiwiss.'

Woodiwiss glanced at Salter and nodded. 'We've completed the search, ' he said. 'We found this.' He threw an envelope on to the table.

Hamilton opened the envelope and drew out a thick wad of twenty-pound notes. 'How many would you say?' he asked.

'Fifty, sir.'

'Skimming, was he?'

The sergeant shrugged. It was not up to him to speculate and maybe get skewered for it by Hamilton.

'All right.' Hamilton nodded. 'I think that's it, Salter, until we get hold of Miss America. If you have any more thoughts, share them with me, will you? I'm at the Swan.'

Good, thought Salter maliciously. Enjoy the 'ot-pot. He left the office and was intercepted by a slightly forlorn-looking Churcher who was putting on a show of activity at the front desk.

'Fierce old devil, isn't he?' Churcher said. 'I hear he's like that with everybody. Can't take offence, eh?'

'He's a type,' Salter said comfortingly. 'Don't let him bother you.' After Salter's twenty minutes with Hamilton, Churcher seemed to have a slight cockney accent. At any rate he was now sure that 'orf' was upper.

'Thanks, Maud,' Salter said at dinner. 'Your professional curiosity was very helpful. Made me look good.'

Maud said, 'Don't be rude. It wasn't pure nosiness this time. The girl was very miserable and I was just trying to be helpful. Now what's on the agenda for tomorrow?'

'I'll just tag along with you two,' Annie said. 'Charlie's on a case.'

'Knock it off, Annie. I just happen to be a copper and these people feel more comfortable asking me whether it was raining on the night of whatever-it-was. That's all.'

Annie said nothing.

'How far is Coventry?' Henry asked, interrupting the silence. 'I'd like to see the cathedral.'

They consulted the landlord. More than an hour, less than two, Maud translated, because the road zigzagged across country. Maud and Henry decided to go, and Annie asked to be allowed to join them. Salter said nothing, his desire to stay in touch with Hamilton overcoming the need to be nice to Annie.

The next morning, when Salter was alone after breakfast, he was interrupted in his attempt to answer a single clue in *The Times* crossword puzzle by Hamilton on the telephone. 'We've found Miss America,' Hamilton said, 'and she's driving down immediately. She's heard the news and thinks we are jumping to conclusions, I gather.'

'We don't want to do that, do we?' Salter said, enjoying the opportunity to be flippant to a senior officer. 'What are we going to do now?'

'Sit here and scratch my bum. Come and talk to me, unless you plan to be funny.'

Salter arrived at the station in time for coffee, and Churcher brought him a cup, hanging about the office until Hamilton thanked him pointedly. I'll have to accept that dinner invitation, Salter thought.

'I've been looking at this hotel register,' Hamilton said. 'How long were you there?'

'Two days.'

'Hmm. What about that nosey-parker you phoned yesterday?'

'Maud Beresford? She'd been there over a week, I think.'

'Have her look at this register, will you? We will probably have to check them all the way back through March, but she might remember something from her stay that would save us some trouble. Here. Show it to her, will you?' Hamilton threw the vital piece of evidence across the desk.

'What are we looking for?' Salter asked.

'She is trying to remember anything funny about the people who stayed there while she was around. Especially any rough-looking fellows who threatened our host.' Hamilton bared his teeth, and pulled another document to him. 'I'm not joking entirely. I've been looking over the history of our dead friend. It's interesting. We have no idea what he was doing from 1944 until 1978. Just his word as reported to us. According to the statement he gave to the War Office, in 1944 he was in a village in Tuscany, hiding out from the Germans. Apparently he had found himself behind the lines at some previous point and gone into hiding. When Jerry started to pull back and our people arrived, he came out of hiding and fiddled himself a psychological wound—loss of memory, shell shock—and got back to Blighty, where he disappeared. He was listed as "Missing, Presumed Dead", and certified as such in the records when no trace of him emerged. He gave himself a false identity and went underground, living on his wits, he said. An amnesty on deserters was declared after the war but he didn't come forward until 1978, when he was tried, given a conviction without penalty and formally discharged. Then he popped up here. He had obviously made a pisspotful of money because he bought Boomewood and spent a lot on it.'

'That accounts for the fact that he could speak Italian. Did he meet his wife there during the war?'

'No. She would have been a nipper, then. No. After he got his dry-cleaning job he took a sentimental journey

back to—' here Hamilton consulted the document again—
'Valdottavo to see if he could find the people who had helped
him during the war. That's when he met his wife. Swept
her orf her feet, apparently. Brought her back to England
and opened an Italian pensione. Was the food good?'

'Terrific.'

'Really? Do you know what I got at the Swan last night?
Toad-in-the-hole.'

'What the hell is that?'

'Sausages in batter pudding. Yorkshire pudding to you.
It can be good. This tasted like rancid lava-crust. But I'm
getting off the point. This spring Mrs Dillon sent for her
brother to help out. That's the story.'

'What was Dillon doing for thirty years?'

'The most likely thing is something crooked. He had no
papers, though God knows, you can get some easily enough,
so he probably worked the black economy. His wife knows
nothing about it—he was in business, he told her—and the
War Office didn't go behind his story; when the police tried
to, he said he worked for day wages in the street markets.
He probably did something of the sort, maybe in London.
They say that on Sunday mornings along Petticoat Lane
you can get your watch stolen at one end of the street and
buy it back at the other, but I heard that story when I was
in nursery school. It's true, though, that a lot of stolen goods
find their way to the street markets and plenty of wide boys
make a good living along the way.'

'It's possible, then, that he was still receiving, and hence
the envelope you found.'

'Anything's possible, Salter, and I shall have to ask
around to see if we can pick up a whisper. The thing is that
Boomewood was doing well, he was respectable now, and
something in his past may have caught up with him.'

'Blackmail?'

'Possible. Some villain with a grudge who got done when
Dillon didn't. You see, the scope of this investigation is

unlimited.' Hamilton spoke the word bitterly. 'A pity Churcher wasn't right in the first place,' he said.

'Maybe the brother will provide a quick and dirty solution.'

'Ah yes, Romeo. He's still our best bet.'

'There is also the possibility of a jealous husband or boyfriend,' Salter pointed out.

'Right. According to the Rundstedt woman, he was a bit of a ram when the right guest came along. That may be all bullshit, of course, in her own defence. She seems to have regarded him as attractive, but I have my doubts about how many would agree with her. According to the people here, there wasn't the slightest gossip on that score before. Still, he does seem to have thrown a leg over your compatriot.'

'She could be the only one. She seems to have trouble saying no to anyone.'

'So I gather. Anyway, there's nothing to be done until Miss America arrives.' Hamilton pulled all the documents together into a bundle and stuffed them into a drawer. 'Do you play squash?' he asked suddenly. 'I haven't had a game for two days because of this.'

Salter considered the question. He was at least ten years younger than Hamilton; he had been playing squash for more than a year, and he was holding his own among the middle-aged crowd at the Simcoe Squash Club.

'I don't have a racquet,' he said. 'And I'm not much good.'

Hamilton frowned and pulled the phone towards him. He dialled a number he found in his wallet. 'Derek,' he said. 'Got a court free? Eleven o'clock? Got an extra racquet there?' He put his hand over the receiver. 'Kit?' he asked Salter. Salter shook his head. 'Shoe size?' Hamilton asked. Salter told him. 'Got any extra togs, Derek? Shoe size nine. Good. We'll be along.' He put the phone down.

Three-quarters of an hour later and twenty miles away, Salter was being introduced to the custodian of a ramshackle wooden building in the middle of some sodden playing fields. 'Heart of England Police Athletic Club,' Hamilton said.

They changed in a room more dilapidated than any Salter had seen outside Cabbagetown, the slum of his boyhood, with a corrugated iron cubicle at one end. 'The shower,' Hamilton said.

The court had been preserved intact since the Twenties, although the larger cracks had been recently filled in with cement.

Hamilton served. After three minutes, he said, 'You really aren't much good, are you?'

'I told you that,' Salter said.

'But you said you *played* the bloody game. All right. I'll give you a lesson. First. Hold your racquet like this. Now. *Hit* it.'

He instructed Salter for twenty minutes and then they had a little knock-up. Afterwards they washed themselves off in the trickle of tepid rusty water that came out of the iron pipe in the wall of the cubicle.

'Toronto is the squash capital of the world, I heard,' Hamilton said as they were driving back.

'I live in the suburbs,' Salter said. 'Do you play golf?'

Hamilton laughed. 'Got your goat, have I? No, I've been out, of course, but there's too much chat involved for me. Try Churcher.'

The two men were still together when the American girl arrived after lunch.

'Now, Miss Kryst,' Hamilton began. 'There was no need for you to come back. The local police could have taken a statement.'

'You think Mario killed Dillon, don't you? You're wrong. He wouldn't do anything like that. I came back to help him. He's not a killer, for God's sake. He's not.' She began to cry.

Hamilton leaned back in his chair. 'He's a witness, at least, and we can't find him,' he said. 'We thought you might be able to help. Nobody's in court yet.'

'But you think he's run away,' she cried. 'He hasn't anywhere to go. He can't work in England now that he's been fired by that dirty-minded swine.'

'Mr Dillon is dead,' Hamilton said.

'That doesn't change him.' She started to cry again.

'Where is Mario? He's not in Italy yet.'

'I don't know. He talked about finding some friends, getting some part-time work while he tried to get a new permit. Here. I've got a letter from him.' She held out an envelope.

Hamilton took out the paper inside and raised his eyebrows.

'It's in Italian, of course,' the girl said. 'But all it says is that he will let me know when he has a permanent address, and some stuff about us.'

'Written yesterday,' Hamilton said.

'Yes. I got it this morning. He wouldn't be able to write that if he was frightened, would be?'

'No address.' Hamilton turned the letter over again. 'Postmarked Oxford. Thank you, Miss Kryst,' he said. 'That's all we need to know right now. Please enjoy the rest of your holiday.'

'I'm staying here,' she said. 'I'm going to see that Mario's all right.'

Hamilton raised his eyebrows again and looked around the office.

'If you need a place to say, Miss Kryst, my wife and I have found a good hotel,' Salter said.

'Who are you?'

'I was staying at Boomewood. I'm on holiday,' Salter said. 'Passing the time. Do you want me to phone?'

She nodded through her handkerchief, and waited for Salter to telephone the Plough and confirm they had a room for her. Salter gave her directions. She ignored their goodbyes silently, putting away her handkerchief and buttoning her raincoat, keeping a determined distance from the two men.

When she had gone, Hamilton said, 'That's it, then, for the moment. What do you make of her?'

'She doesn't seem silly,' Salter said. 'And she sounds very sure of that waiter.'

'She's certainly going to a lot of trouble for him,' Hamilton agreed. 'Not everyone would want to get involved. But let's not piss about gossiping. Don't forget to have Mrs Nosey-Parker look over the register. What have you got on for this afternoon?'

'What time is it?'

'One-thirty.'

There was just time, he figured, to catch the last four races at Burford. 'I have to meet my wife,' he said. 'I'll drop by first thing in the morning.'

On the last race Salter decided to have a small bet on an outsider. Handing the bookie a twenty-pound note, he said, 'Two on Valerie's Choice.'

'Two tenners, Valerie's Choice,' the bookie called, and Salter let it stand.

Valerie's Choice won at ten to one and Salter, driving back to his hotel, reflected that there was nothing, absolutely nothing, quite as nice as a pocketful of money won by gambling.

At the hotel Salter found Maud drinking tea with Bonnie Kryst. She signalled him to stay away and he went upstairs to flush his betting slips down the toilet and tidy up. There was no sign of Annie, so he went downstairs again, where he found Maud now alone.

'Don't press her too hard, Maud,' Salter said when she had poured him a cup of tea. 'She's very upset.'

Maud looked at Salter for several moments. 'There's a

bit more sensitivity in me than meets your eye, Charlie Salter. Or should I say ear. I haven't been pumping her, as you seem to think, but consoling her as best I can. Would you like to hear her story, as I got it?'

Salter nodded and put down a half-eaten chocolate cream biscuit, feeling a sudden longing for a butter tart.

'She's not in love with Mario, I think,' Maud began, 'but she's his most loyal defender. This may be a bit subtle for a thick-skinned bobby, but I'll try and give it to you properly. Bonnie has been travelling around Europe for the past two months and she hasn't had a very good time. She was nearly raped in Paris—Paris was the worst, I gather. She said just walking along the street got her down because of the propositions—and in Munich, in a tram, a man put his hand up her skirt and wouldn't take it down until she screamed. Nobody came to her rescue. She was fondled in Stockholm, pinched in Brussels, and in Cannes an Arab taxi-driver exposed himself to her while she was trying to find the right change. She travels alone, you see, and she has that friendly air which must be the result of all that health food. Mind you, these things can happen to any of us. The creepy element just require that you be female.'

'It can happen in Boston, or New York, or Toronto if she walks slowly enough. Annie encountered a flasher on the Avenue Road bus last year,' Salter said, unimpressed.

'But European men seem to think that American girls are fair game. They assume that they have come over because they have heard of the prowess of the men here. They assume that a girl who travels alone is thus saying that she's available.'

'You don't think she's neurotic, then?'

'No, I don't. Now listen to the rest. The only country she had no trouble in was Italy, which I'd always heard was the worst.'

'There are lots of Italians in Boston. Maybe she knows

how to read the signs with them. Besides, she speaks Italian.'

'Maybe. Whatever the reason, Bonnie loves Italy and all things Italian, and when she came to Boomewood her prejudices were confirmed.'

'By Mario?'

'By Mario. Take that look off your face and let me finish. Mario offered to show her London on his day off. She was wary, she says, but he gave her the nicest day she's had in the whole two months she's been here. They walked in Hyde Park, rode on sightseeing buses and ate fish and chips at Manzi's in Leicester Street. On the way home they stopped off at a pub and drank Amaretto.'

'Holding hands?'

'Probably, Charlie. What's that supposed to mean? Let me finish. The end of the story is the important bit. They went dutch all day, and she gave Mario her wallet so that she wouldn't have to carry a handbag. When they got back, he took her to her door and kissed her good night, thanking her for a lovely day. She says it was the nicest kiss she's ever had. And that was it. You see the point? She had laid down the ground rules in the morning and by the end of the day she was quite willing to change them, but he accepted them and stuck to them.'

'Maybe Mario's impotent,' Salter suggested.

'Oh, you prick, Charlie.'

'Sorry. So tell me about the wallet.'

'Yes, that's important. Next morning before breakfast Mario came to her room and she let him in so that no one would see them talking in the doorway. He had just come to bring back her wallet. Dillon saw him as he left the room and you know the rest.'

Salter waited. Then he asked. 'Why is this important, Maud?'

'Because if the girl is any judge at all, then Mario is no killer. It just isn't in him.'

'It wouldn't even convince a jury of romantics, Maud.

She's hardly an unprejudiced character witness, is she? Do you believe it?'

'Yes, I do, Charlie. Nothing like that has ever happened to me, but I'm sure Mario is all right.'

'I'll tell them down at the station. They may laugh me out of the place, though. Now, they need your help.' He produced the Boomewood register. 'Look over the names of the people here, all the ones you saw around. Do you remember if any of them was in any way odd or unusual?'

Maud scanned the pages showly. 'They've become a bit blurred now,' she said. 'No. Nothing.' She thumbed the pages back and forth, idly. 'I don't remember this one,' she said. 'A bit of an odd entry.' She turned the book around so that Salter could see. A week previously an entry appeared with a blank space between it and the previous entry, drawing attention to itself. There was no name, just 'Greetings from Valdottavo' scrawled in big letters. There was no address and no date.

'You remember someone from Italy?'

'No, I don't. But I don't remember some of the others, either, so maybe I was having an off-day.'

Salter put a little tick by the entry. 'Okay,' he said. 'Let's have a drink. I'm sorry if I upset you, Maud. It's a nice story.'

Maud grimaced and stood up. 'You can make up for it by buying this old bag a gin and tonic. It's a bit early for Amaretto, or I'd have that.'

'Any sign of the brother?' he asked Hamilton next morning.

'Not yet. We'll catch him, though.'

In spite of himself, Salter had been impressed by Maud's conviction, and he told Hamilton the story as tonelessly as he could.

'What if he turns up with a knife in his boot?' Hamilton asked. But he too had listened to the story carefully.

Salter shrugged. He produced the Boomewood register.

'Maud Beresford was no help on this, I'm afraid. She couldn't remember anything strange about any of these people. She pointed this out, though.' He showed Hamilton the entry from Italy.

'Pity. I circulated Dillon's picture. We may turn up someone who knew him when he was underground. If we can fill in some of his past someone might come forward with a suggestion. In the meantime, let's go out to Boomewood. Maybe Mrs Dillon will have something more to tell us. She's calmed down now, but she is obviously terrified we'll find her brother.'

'What's her story now?'

'It's the same in the beginning. She went to *Romeo and Juliet* and got home sometime after midnight. She saw the light on in the office and went in and found Dillon stabbed on the floor. She was afraid immediately that it was her brother's doing and she panicked. She drove off to Oxford because she thought she knew where he might go—we checked it, he isn't there—and her idea was to protect him somehow, get him away, perhaps.'

'And the knife?'

'There was no knife that she remembers. She never touched one, anyway. Come and talk to her yourself.'

They were interrupted by Churcher. 'I thought you'd like to know, Charles, that we have found your Peeping Tom,' he said. 'Constable Dakin caught him last night outside the motel at the roundabout.'

'What's that?' Hamilton asked.

Salter explained. 'How do you know it's the same one?' he asked Churcher.

'Not much doubt, I think, when you see him,' Churcher said, triumphant and mysterious. 'Shall I bring him in?'

Hamilton was looking amused. 'Certainly,' he said. 'Perhaps he'll tell us what he heard. Unless *Charles* would rather not.'

'Constable,' Churcher called. 'In here, please, with the accused.'

A uniformed constable entered, holding Gregory. But there was nothing left of the Smarmy Boy in the frightened youth looking for pity in the faces of the policemen around the room.

'I don't know what came over me,' he began immediately. 'I heard these people talking as I stopped for a minute and the constable, quite understandably, of course, got hold of me and brought me here.'

'What makes you think he was eavesdropping, Officer?' Hamilton said.

'He was in a state of acute sexual excitement, sir,' the constable said. ''Orrible little bleeder.'

'I was caught short, sir,' Gregory pleaded. 'I was having a slash.'

'Constable?'

'No, sir. He was enjoyin' 'isself.'

'All right. Leave us now, would you, Officer. Don't go far away in case this fiend gets out of control.' He bared his teeth at the pathetic Gregory. 'Have a chair, Churcher, while we interrogate him. It's your case.'

Churcher sat down, looking surprised and pleased. Gregory looked around for a chair for himself.

'Stand still, laddie,' Hamilton shouted. 'How old are you?'

'Eighteen, sir. Just turned.'

'Right. You're a man. You know the penalty for indecent exposure?'

'No, sir.'

'And trespass? And invasion of privacy?'

'No, sir.'

'You will be finished around here, laddie. Now, you also listened outside Mr Salter's window when he was staying at Boomewood, didn't you?'

'No, sir.'

'Yes, sir,' Hamilton corrected him. 'In fact you spent a lot of time listening around the bedrooms at Boomewood, didn't you?'

'No, sir.'

'Yes, sir,' Hamilton corrected him again. 'You heard a lot of things you'd like to tell us about, wouldn't you?'

'No, sir.'

'Yes, sir. I want you to think hard, laddie. Because you may be in possession of vital evidence, vital to us, of whose significance you may not be aware. You have heard of turning Queen's evidence, have you? It means that in return for your cooperation we do our best to see that you get regarded favourably when your own case comes forward.'

Salter, in spite of feeling some pity for Gregory, nearly laughed. He could see the headlines, FLASHER TURNS INFORMER. He caught Hamilton's eye and composed himself.

'Right,' Hamilton said, when Gregory had had time to think. 'You did listen outside the bedroom windows at Boomewood, didn't you?'

'Sometimes I would hear things as I was passing on my way to bed, sir. My room was over the garage.'

'That's the idea. You did hear Mr Salter here one night, did you?'

'I heard something, sir, yes.'

'What?'

'Hey!' Salter protested.

Hamilton ignored him. 'I don't want to know the filthy details, laddie,' he continued. 'I just want to know if you could hear words. Don't tell me what they were.'

'More than that, sir.' Here Gregory looked at Salter. 'I heard the voice of another man in your room, sir.'

'You what!'

'Yes, sir. Another man with a funny accent, talking to someone called Nancy.'

Hamilton looked at Salter.

Salter said, 'Take my word for it, he heard right. I'll explain later, or maybe not. Go on.'

'All right, my boy, let's forget about the shenanigans in Mr Salter's room, and empty your mind of any other filth you may have heard, and tell us of anything, anything at all, that you heard which you think we should know about. Most of all about your former employer, Mr Dillon. Did you, in your travels, hear him in Miss Rundstedt's room?'

'Yes, sir.'

'I see. He made her his mistress while she was there, did he?'

'I don't know about that, sir. Mostly they seemed to talk and talk, and I couldn't hear much of what they were talking about but it didn't seem to be love talk, sir.'

Salter, who was beginning to get over his early embarrassment, found himself blushing again, but no one was looking at him.

Gregory continued. 'And he wasn't the only one, sir, in her room. I heard her with another man one night and with him she *was* having it off.'

'Mario,' Hamilton said.

'No, sir. I'd have recognized Mario's voice. I didn't know this man but he wasn't Italian. English, I think.'

'A guest?'

'Not one I recognized, sir.'

'And you heard nothing else lately?'

'No, sir.'

'Think hard, laddie. The night before the row, when Mario got thrown out. Did you hear anything from any of the rooms?'

'You mean Miss Kryst's room, sir? No, I didn't. But they might have been very quiet. He was in her room next morning, wasn't he?'

'Was he? I understand he wasn't, at least not in a way to interest eavesdroppers. All right. Now I want you to look over this register. You waited at table in the mornings sometimes. Can you remember noticing anything unusual about any of these people? Or overhearing anything?'

Gregory looked carefully over the list of names. 'No, sir,' he said.

'What about this one,' Hamilton asked, pointing to the 'Valdottavo' entry. 'Do you remember any Italians recently?'

'No, sir. No one came from Italy lately that I know of.' It was obvious that Gregory was desperately eager to please Hamilton and scouring his memory for any scraps that would help, as he felt a tiny pulse of hope in Hamilton's manner. Although his face was still white, he was nearly in control of himself.

'All right, laddie. Inspector Churcher will deal with you. Off you go.'

The boy tried to smile at Hamilton and walked through the door. As Churcher got up to follow, Hamilton said, 'It's your case, Churcher, but I'd be pleased if you'd find some way of dealing with the brat without charging him. If he comes up before your local bench, old Beldin will be very hard on him. It won't help the boy.'

'It's a serious business, sir. A very nasty case,' Churcher protested.

'Yes, of course. But right now it's much more serious for him than it is for you. No one is laying a complaint against him, are you, Salter? I think it's our duty to help as well as punish, don't you, Inspector? Word will get around. They'll call him the Tokesbury Wanker. Isn't that enough?'

'Yes, sir. I'll inquire what counselling services are available to help people like him. Perhaps advise him to move.'

'Very wise, Churcher. Besides, if we keep him on a leash he may remember something else.'

The door closed. 'Let's go and have that chat with Mrs Dillon,' Hamilton said.

'Hang on a minute,' Salter said. 'Bring that kid back.'

When Churcher returned with Gregory, Salter said, 'This

is important, Gregory. Nothing is missing, nothing is stolen, but I want to know if you ever went into the guests' bedrooms. Mine, for instance.'

'No, sir, never,' Gregory said promptly. 'Mr Dillon was very strict about that. He told us if he ever caught anyone except Mrs Peabody in any of the rooms he would give us the sack without any references. But I just remembered something else about you, sir. Mr Dillon knew you were a policeman. I heard him on the phone once mention the Toronto copper. That would be you, sir.'

'All right, laddie, off you go,' Hamilton said, and turned to stare interrogatively at Salter.

'Someone was in my room looking at my passport,' Salter said.

'Dillon?'

Salter shrugged. Hamilton brooded for a few moments, then picked up his coat off a chair beside the desk. It was an enormous, shapeless thing of many pockets that looked as if it was made out of tarpaulin. Hamilton saw Salter staring at it, and grinned. 'My wife claims I stole it off a dead poacher,' he said. 'Not true. I found it at Oxfam.'

Hamilton parked his car near the hotel and guided Salter into a coffee bar in the middle of the block opposite Boomewood. They joined a young workman who was reading a paper at a table by the window.

'Elevenses?' Hamilton asked the young man.

'That's right, sir. You don't often get a convenient spot for a cup of tea on these jobs. Usually I have to bring a Thermos flask.'

'So tell us what you've seen this morning.'

'Mrs Dillon is still in the hotel. No sign of her this morning. But she's got a visitor. Girl arrived about half an hour ago, with luggage. That's her car across the street, illegally parked.'

'Bonnie Kryst,' Salter said.

'That's handy,' Hamilton said. 'Saves me a man.'

'Yes, sir. Hayes followed her here, of course. Then we tossed for it and he went off duty. He had to take his mum to the clinic, about her legs.'

'Okay, son. We're going over to have a little chat with Mrs Dillon now. We'll see you later.'

'Right you are, sir. While you're in there, could I pop round to the station and get a pullover? It's very cold on the corner there.'

'You can have fifteen minutes. All right?'

'Thank you, sir.'

Outside the coffee bar, Salter asked, 'You are keeping tabs on everybody?'

'I'm looking for Mario, Salter. I told you why I released Mrs Dillon. If Mario is our boy, there is a chance that he'll contact her or the Kryst girl—is already in touch with one of them. See?'

Salter wondered how much more was going on off-stage, and modified his impression that Hamilton was sitting in his office, waiting for something to happen.

The door was opened by Bonnie Kryst, who let the two policemen into the hall and waited for them to speak with the air of someone who now belonged at the hotel.

'We'd like your help, Miss Kryst,' Hamilton said. 'Mrs Dillon doesn't speak enough English and I need an interpreter.'

'Maria doesn't know where her brother is and nor do I,' Miss Kryst said, making no attempt to lead them further inside.

'I'm not here about her brother. I just want to ask Mrs Dillon some questions about the last few days.'

Bonnie Kryst turned away and walked down the hall into the kitchen. She returned in a few minutes and led them to where Mrs Dillon was sitting at a table, looking apprehensive. She spoke a few words of Italian to the American girl who replied soothingly.

'May we sit down?' Hamilton asked.

The girl translated, and when Mrs Dillon nodded she pointed to two chairs at the table, and sat down herself. Hamilton smiled at Mrs Dillon who was biting her nails compulsively and turned to the girl.

'First of all, Miss Kryst, I want to know if Mrs Dillon can tell us anything at all about her husband's life since 1944. It's a tall order, I know, but if we assume her brother is innocent—' Hamilton paused at the word—'then we have to assume that someone killed her husband for reasons we don't know about. We think he may have been expecting the man or woman who killed him, and that they talked for some time before Mr Dillon was killed. We know he was a deserter and that he managed without proper papers for thirty years, but what had he been doing?' Hamilton sat back and waited while the girl translated.

Mrs Dillon started shaking her head immediately and then spoke for some time. Bonnie Kryst translated. 'She only met him two years ago. He was in Valdottavo during the war—one or two of the older people remembered him being there. When he came back on a visit to Valdottavo he ate every day at the restaurant in Lucca where Maria worked and he began to court her. He went away for a little while, then returned and asked her to marry him and come to England. Except for her brother, she was all alone. Her husband was dead. So she accepted. He brought her here and they opened this place. Then he arranged for her little brother—' here Bonnie Kryst blushed slightly—'to come over to help out and to learn English. They were very happy until now. She wants to stay here, she says, but the police will probably not let her.'

'Tell her the police cannot stop her. She is a British citizen now.'

Mrs Dillon reacted to this news with another question.

'And her brother? Can he stay?'

'If he is not connected with this case, I think he can. I'll find out, but my guess is that Mrs Dillon can sponsor him as her husband did.'

Mrs Dillon stopped biting her nails and spoke rapidly and eagerly to Bonnie Kryst, who smiled and touched her shoulder.

They returned to Hamilton's original question. After a speech from Mrs Dillon, Bonnie Kryst said, 'She cannot remember if her husband ever mentioned any enemies. She doesn't know what he did before he turned up in Lucca. He told her he had been in business. She says he was a good man. There is a will leaving everything to her, and she is already a joint owner of the hotel. He was good to her brother, too, until this happened.'

Mrs Dillon spoke briefly and passionately.

'She says Dillon worshipped her and never looked at another woman. But lately he has gone a little crazy and she thought this Rundstedt woman must be the reason. She says Rundstedt must be a whore.'

'Why did he fire Mario?'

'She says her husband would not allow sleeping together in his hotel. Nobody who was not married could get a room together. He warned Mario when he arrived never to make passes at the female guests, and Mario never did. When Dillon saw Mario coming out of my room he lost his temper.'

Hamilton considered this. 'Try and find some way to put this delicately, Miss Kryst. I'd like to be absolutely sure that Dillon was not a womanizer. Did she or Mario ever suspect him before with any of the other guests?'

When this was translated, the Italian woman responded at length.

'Never,' Bonnie Kryst said. 'She says her husband loved her. That is why she thinks it is all Miss Rundstedt's fault.'

Mrs Dillon interjected at the mention of Rundstedt's name. Bonnie Kryst looked puzzled and the two women worked on it for a few minutes, then Bonnie Kryst blushed.

'She says a woman like Miss Rundstedt has ways. That's more or less what she says.'

'Miss Kryst, even for a good man, Dillon's reaction was very violent. Had he ever shown any signs of such a temper before?'

Again the two women talked back and forth. 'She agrees,' Kryst said. 'It was strange and they were shocked by it. Mario thought he was a hypocrite, and he was not going to say anything but Dillon made him angry. Afterwards he told me he was sorry because it upset his sister.'

'He told you?'

'Yes. When he left. Frankly, Dillon sounds like a case of obsessional behaviour to me.'

'Yes? I never speculate about psychological forces, Miss Kryst. The theories behind them seem as crude as the theories of fifteenth-century medicine. However, you can see what I'm after. I'm trying to know something about this man, who he is, what he did for the thirty years for which we can find no trace of him, and what might have triggered him off lately, why his character suddenly changed, as they say. I'd like some concrete facts if I can get them. Were there any strangers around, any phone calls, letters, anything that he seemed to keep to himself? I have another question to ask and then I'll leave you to it. I don't want a final answer right now. Just talk to Mrs Dillon, would you, explain to her how important it is that we find some other possibility than her brother. I'll come back this afternoon for any trifles you've picked up. Now, here's my last question. Ask her to look over this register and see if it triggers her memory. Was there anything unusual about any of the guests?'

The girl translated, and Mrs Dillon hunched eagerly over the book. Almost immediately she put her finger on the entry from Valdottavo. She jumped up and went over to a drawer in the counter where she groped around at the back and came up with a picture postcard. It was a view of Lucca, in Tuscany. On the back was a message, 'Greetings from

Valdòttavo,' signed, 'Johnny'. It was postmarked 'Firenze'.

Bonnie Kryst said, 'This card came a month ago. Her husband threw it away, but later she found it in the back of this drawer. She asked her husband who Johnny was, but he said he didn't know. Then one day there was this entry in the register and no one knew how it had got there. It seemed to upset her husband, but it was soon forgotten. He said it must be a joke. Now she thinks her husband became strange from that time.'

'Let's not rush our fences, Miss Kryst. It probably was a joke that misfired. All right. Keep talking to her, would you, and I'll come back for any scraps you can gather.'

'Blackmail?' Salter asked, in the car.

'Possibly. Someone he didn't want to know turned up to tease him. But there was a meeting while the wife was at the theatre. A thousand pounds was made ready. Dillon's money? Now. You think there's anything to this gent from Italy?'

'If he exists he was in town a week ago. He didn't stay at Boomewood, but he might be listed in one of the other hotels.'

'We'll have a look, of course. Also—' Hamilton looked at the card in his pocket—'Valdottavo. Maybe the local *gendarmerie* can turn something up for us round about the date that he sent this card.

'*Carabinieri*,' Salter said.

'What?'

'*Carabinieri*. Not *gendarmerie*.'

'Really? What a lot you chaps know. Must come in very handy for doing crossword puzzles. Now I must get back to the office. Crime is breaking out all over. I'll send a message to Valdottavo, to the *Carabinieri*, and do the rounds of the hotels.' Hamilton pulled up outside the station. 'Well, Salter. I know you've been enjoying yourself, but I mustn't bugger up your holiday any more. Drop in tomorrow, if you like, and I'll tell you if anything has happened.' He nodded to the inspector to get out.

Just like that. Salter stood in the street feeling slightly foolish and cast adrift. At the same time he knew he had better take the opportunity to think about his vacation. The ever-soggy skies continued to leak or threaten, and their holiday had become stalled. On the whole, as Salter had pointed out, the Boomewood diversion had had its good side because he would not have remained cheerful on a steady diet of visiting abbeys in the rain, whereas Annie had found Maud (and occasionally Henry) ideal company for her kind of sightseeing. But it was time for him to make an effort.

The sergeant appeared at the station door as if summoned, and Salter put his problem to him. 'Stratford,' the sergeant suggested. 'It's a bit of a drive, but you should make it for the first race. Freddie Tinsdale's got one going in the third. He always gets one ready for Stratford.'

Salter sighed. 'Won't do, Sergeant,' he said. 'But you've given me an idea.'

He bought a newspaper and looked up the theatre advertisements and made a phone call, securing four tickets for an evening performance at the theatre. The play was *The Taming of the Shrew* about which Salter knew nothing, but that hardly mattered; Annie would be pleased. He drove back to the Plough and laid his gift in front of the other three over beer and tongue sandwiches.

'How lovely,' Maud said immediately. 'I know Stratford a bit, but it would be nice to see it again. Dinner is on us, isn't it, Henry.' The thick lenses flashed with joy.

The rain was no more than a heavy mist as they set off after lunch. There being no market in progress when they arrived, they found a parking spot in the square and began looking at the preserved remains of Shakespeare's birthplace.

Salter found it impossible to feel what he was supposed

to, and difficult to feel anything at first. As one of the hundreds of thousands of tourists who had trudged along this route, he was more conscious of the huge industry that Shakespeare had spawned than of any sense of reverence at the history that had soaked into these stones. He still retained a tiny but vivid awareness of bits of the one or two plays he had studied, but it was not enough to make this shrine speak to him immediately, and he felt untouched by the apparent religious awe of those around him. Missing any personal response, he determined to go without rather than simulate one.

They looked at Shakespeare's garden, his house, and several other significant buildings without any desire to linger on Salter's part. Then, in the church, which he had entered ahead of the others, he came unwarned to the famous inscription beginning, 'Good friend, for Jesus' sake forbear' and he felt the floor rock slightly as the voice of the man who had written those words spoke in his ear and made him slightly breathless. Then he wanted to go back and do the whole tour again, all by himself, but the others had caught up with him and he let the moment go.

When they came out of the church, Salter looked at his watch. He made a show of patting his pockets worriedly and announced that his wallet was missing, he was sure that it was back in the car, that the others needn't trouble themselves, that he would just nip back and look, and he disappeared in the direction of the square where he had noticed a Turf Accountant's office. It was two minutes' work to look up the trainers in the third race, find Freddy Tinsdale's horse—something called Montague Road, and put five pounds on the nose. He trotted back to find the others, waving his wallet.

They ate a not-bad dinner in a frenchified restaurant and strolled along the river bank to the theatre, where Salter settled himself for a light doze, but he was disturbed before the curtain went up by a drunk three rows ahead of him

who was terrorizing two nuns. The attendants seemed to be
having trouble handling him, and Salter rose in his seat to
help out, but Maud pulled him back and the drunk escaped
and reappeared on stage where he pulled down all the
scenery, at which everyone laughed, and Salter realized he
was one of the last in the audience to spot the drunk as a
leading character in the production. Sharply awake now, he
became engrossed in the play, and particularly enchanted
with the costumes, which were not the bloomers and panty-
hose he had been expecting, but the elegant suits and dark
glasses of modern Italy. They set him brooding about the
Italian connection in the Tokesbury Mallett murder.

At the end of the play, the transformation of Kate from
shrew to broken-spirited spouse was so shocking that it
silenced them all until they were in the car. Maud was the
first to speak. 'He doesn't give one much choice, does he?'

'Who?' Henry said.

'Shakespeare. Was that play, or that production, I suppose I should say, an attack on women, on women's libera-
tion, or what? I wish I could make up my mind.'

'That seems to give you a fair choice,' Henry said.

But no one else was inclined to talk about it yet. After a
while, Salter, who had been thinking about his experiences
in the church and the theatre, said, 'He's not dead, is he? I
mean he really is still alive.'

He had made the journey all by himself, and no one
pointed out to him that he was now one of all the other
travellers who had made the same journey.

Montague Road won at thirteen to two and all Salter had
to do the next morning was try to concoct an excuse to visit
Stratford again and pick up his forty quid. I could bet my
way round England, he thought.

They had to do some laundry, and Salter drove them in
to Tokesbury Mallett and dropped in to the station house
while Annie watched the machines spinning.

Churcher had his office back and was busily catching up on his work.

'There's nothing from the hotels,' he said, 'and we've heard nothing from Italy, either. No Englishman called Johnny has registered at a hotel near Valdottavo lately. That's a false lead. Superintendent Hamilton thinks it is probably a private joke between a couple of old buddies. At any rate it's a dead end, so we are concentrating on a blanket inquiry to see if we can find anything about Dillon's past. Long job, I'm afraid. I think the brother is probably our man, anyway. No sign of him yet and the longer he's missing, the more likely he's the one. I agree with the superintendent. He sends his regards, by the way, and best wishes for the rest of your holiday.'

Does he, indeed, thought Salter. Just like that? He could think of several things he would be doing himself, but he hesitated to make any suggestions. Hamilton knew his own business best. A more immediate concern was Churcher, who was being very cool, as who wouldn't be under the circumstances.

'I'm sorry we never took up that invitation to dinner, Charles,' he said. 'We'll be moving on almost immediately, I think, so I'll take a raincheck on it if I may.'

'You'll take a what?'

'I mean perhaps you'll invite me again if we come back.'

'Yes, of course. Now if you'll excuse me, I've got a lot on my plate this morning.'

Salter accepted the snub and left the station after a quick word of congratulation with the sergeant, and walked back to the laundromat. An idea was forming.

'Still raining,' he said to Annie.

'Let's push on, Charlie. The forecast for the Lake District is occasional showers. Even that would be a change.'

'How long will we be here?' Salter indicated the dryer which Annie was now stuffing with clothes.

'Three-quarters of an hour.'

'I'll be right back.'

The travel agent was a Tweedledum and spent half an hour showing Salter how he could do what he wanted, and he returned to the laundromat armed with brochures and schedules.

'How would you like three days in Florence?' he asked, without preamble. 'Three days of sunshine and wine, and when we get back it might be spring.'

Annie sat down on the bench and stared at Salter. 'Why Florence?' she asked.

'Because the weather is good there right now, because you would enjoy it, and because I've found a package that will fly us there and give us a hotel and a car, from Birmingham.'

'Wow! Is it expensive?'

'It seems dirt cheap to me.'

'When?'

'Tomorrow morning.'

'Let me think.' But the idea caught her quickly, and she agreed in the car on the way back to the Plough. At lunch they told the Beresfords, and suggested a little farewell dinner that night.

'I want to come,' Maud said.

'God Almighty,' Henry said. 'Look what you've done, Charlie. You've bewitched her. She thinks we're rich.'

The Salters were embarrassed. Money was not a major concern for them; Salter earned a huge salary by English standards, and Annie had her own trust fund, as well as her income from her job. They were aware, however, that the Beresfords might be on a tighter budget, and they were uncomfortable in the role of rich Americans.

Annie said, 'We can't drag you away from your holiday, just to keep us company. We'll be all right.'

Maud said, 'I want to come.'

'We can go if you want to,' Henry said. 'I'll sell the house when we get back.' Then, more gracefully, 'No, really, if

you'll have us, it's probably the ideal opportunity. Maud
has always wanted to go.'

Annie said, 'It would be nice to have you along, Maud.
Charlie won't go into an art gallery. Can you imagine being
in Florence and not seeing the Uffizi?'

'It's not that I don't like pictures,' Salter said. 'I'll come
with you to see the Mona Lisa . . .'

'That's in Paris.'

'Well, one picture of your choice, then. It's the bloody
galleries themselves. You are always viewing the remains in
a whisper. If you try to talk normally they kick you out.'

'If I'm going to spend my inheritance on going to Florence, I want to see some pictures,' Henry said.

'I'll be all right,' Salter said. 'I'll just have a mooch round,
looking at the beggars and whores.'

'Let's go, Henry,' Maud pleaded.

And so it was arranged. Salter and Annie conferred pri-
vately, and concocted a plan whereby he would buy two
packages, one for the Beresfords and one for themselves in
which they would bear the full cost of the car alone, and
Salter drove into Tokesbury Mallett to arrange it. The agent
enjoyed the little conspiracy and marked up the tickets so
that it would not be obvious to the Beresfords that they were
paying less, and Salter went off to the bank to get some lire.
When he returned to the agent, he bumped into a slightly
familiar figure on his way out. As the man went to step
away from him, Salter remembered who he was. Hamilton's
assistant. 'Sergeant Woodiwiss,' he said. 'How's it going?'

'Oh yes. Inspector Salter, isn't it?' He jerked his head at
the agency. 'Moving on, are you?'

'Just wanted to see what they have to offer,' Salter said.
'Sightseeing buses, that sort of thing. What about you?'

'Just thinking about my holidays, sir. Somewhere dry.'

'Made any progress?' Salter asked.

'How do you mean, sir?' Woodiwiss countered, his face
bland.

Cagey bastard, thought Salter. 'With your holiday plans,' he said. 'Give your superintendent my regards,' he added.

'I'll do that, sir,' Woodiwiss said and walked away.

Inside, Salter put his money on the counter, and collected his tickets. 'Everybody's travelling today, it seems,' he said. 'I just bumped into a friend of mine in the doorway. Where's he off to?'

'The gentleman in the raincoat?' the agent said. 'He was just inquiring.' He walked back to his desk behind the counter.

'Will the car be waiting for me at Pisa?' Salter asked.

'It's all on the ticket,' the agent said without looking up, turning into a Tweedledee in front of Salter's eyes.

Part Three

INTERLUDE IN FLORENCE

At Pisa they stepped out of the aircraft into the Italian spring. Underneath the smell of kerosene was a richer, older scent that told them they were no longer in England, the smell of a sun-soaked world compounded of unfamiliar flora, a fragrance sweeter and heavier than that of the English countryside. They picked up the car and turned on to the autostrada.

'It's all true,' Annie said.

'What?' asked Henry.

'Italy. Look at it.' She waved her hand at the golden landscape. 'I thought this light was an invention of Renaissance painters, something to do with the olive oil they mixed their paints with. I didn't think the world could really be that colour here. And look at those trees. I thought Italian painters had a passion for painting trees in rows, but it is like that. Look at those forests—are they forests? And those trees lining the roads—they look as if they were put in by a giant machine. What are they?'

'Cypresses, I think,' Maud said. 'That's what you always hear about, anyway.'

'There's no grass,' Annie said suddenly. 'All the houses are surrounded by gravel.'

'That's one of the things you can't smell,' Salter said authoritatively. 'Most people don't realize that grass smells. Not hay—grass. I spent six months in the Arctic once. When I came out, the smell of grass was the first thing that hit me in the Winnipeg airport.'

'Six months in the Arctic, Charlie? That's *very* impressive. Did you have to eat your dogs, that sort of thing?'

Before Salter could decide if Maud was making fun of him—had he told too many stories about life in the Canadian bush?—Annie interrupted. 'Look,' she said, pointing to a village on the top of a hill like a crown of brick. 'That *is* a painting, isn't it?'

'I think all the paintings have one of those,' Henry said.

Salter drove on at a hundred and twenty kilometres an hour, happy to be on the right side of the road again, undisturbed that everything on the highway passed him as if he were jogging.

They reached the outskirts of Florence in the afternoon and put aside Italy for an hour while they found a place to park. Salter offered the wheel to anyone who wanted to drive, and when his offer was refused, announced that he was going to enjoy himself. 'I'm going to drive round and round in circles,' he said. 'Without advice or help from anyone. We know the hotel is somewhere in the middle of Florence and we can walk from wherever I find a spot. I want no one to point out that we just missed a place. When *I* see a spot which *I* think I can get into, I'll take it. Now enjoy the sights.'

Annie poked her tongue out at him and Henry looked triumphantly at Maud, who sneered back, but everyone stayed gagged until Salter parked at the Piazza Indipendenza within two blocks of the hotel. Salter led the way into the lobby, where a young man sat behind the desk.

'*Deux camera matrimoniales pour Salter und Beresford,*' Salter said, getting four languages into the seven words.

'Could I see your passports, please?' the young man said after a few moments. Then: 'Ah yes, we have your reservations. This way, please.'

The tiled rooms were big and sunny with wooden shutters that opened on to balaconies overlooking the tiny street below. No one wanted to linger and they dumped their bags and wandered out, content to follow their noses into the crowds.

'The shops here are open until eight,' Maud sighed, as they shuffled happily along, pricing the clothes and looking for a restaurant. They had coffee at this café, followed by wine at that one.

'No wonder they came here,' Maud said.

'Who?' Henry asked.

'Byron, Shelley, Keats, Browning,' Maud said. 'Everybody.'

They ate dinner in a restaurant that looked affordable and where the food was nearly as good as that at Boomewood.

'Some people get to honeymoon here,' Maud said. 'We went to Yarmouth, didn't we, Henry?'

They drank two litres of wine with the food; then, overcome, they walked back to the hotel and to bed.

'What do you want to do here, Charlie?' Annie asked, after they had showered and were lying clean and cool on top of the bed.

For answer, Salter traced a route which began at her left ear, took in most of the country below, and ended at her other ear. Annie responded by turning on her stomach and running a smoothing hand over his chest. 'For three days, I mean,' she said.

This was a more delicate question. 'I'd like to see a bit of the country,' he said. 'We have a car.'

'Like where?'

'I thought I'd like to take a look at the village Dillon lived in during the war.'

'Once a copper, always a copper, eh?' She laid her head on his stomach and looked at him over his chest.

'All right,' he agreed. 'So I'm curious about this case. As far as I know, all Hamilton's done is phone to see if anyone called Johnny was around Valdottavo lately. A message like that gets in someone's IN-tray, he makes three phone calls, marks it NO TRACE and puts it in the OUT-tray. I'd like to look for myself. According to Churcher, the English are now betting on Mario, but there's too much other stuff. Apart from this Johnny, I mean. Who was looking at my passport? Who was playing at "wakey-wakey"? What was Dillon doing with a thousand pounds in an envelope? Last of all, why does a guy like Dillon suddenly spend a night with the Rundstedt woman? According to Gregory, all they did was talk and you can trust him on that.'

'You're assuming Mario didn't do it?'

'I'm not assuming anything. But the story Maud got out of Bonnie Kryst sounded pretty good to me. If I were Hamilton I'd be looking a lot harder in a lot of places.'

'Do you think this superintendent is a fool?'

'No, I don't. That's why I can't understand why there's not more activity.'

'What's the motive, Charlie?'

'How the hell do I know? Money, blackmail, something like that.'

'Not the killer's. Yours.'

'Me? I'm just curious.'

Annie tweaked a hair on his chest. 'You know what I think?' she said. 'I think you're just mad because he beat you so easily at squash.'

'What! That's ridiculous, for Christ's sake. I told you, I'm curious, that's all.'

'So what are you going to do?'

'I thought I'd drive out to this Valdottavo place and poke around until I found someone who knew Dillon during the war. And dig a little deeper for this Johnny. You'll be okay here with Maud, won't you?'

Annie rolled off him and stretched herself by his side. 'Why don't I come along?' she said.

'Oh no. Enjoy your holiday. Stay here and look at Florence.'

'I *am* enjoying my holiday. We are only going to get a

taste of the country in three days, anyway, so it doesn't matter what we do. We'll be back. But you need an interpreter. You just speak Canajun and ten words of French. At least I can understand some of what's being said to me by sorting through my French and Latin.'

Salter considered this. It was true that within half an hour of arriving Annie and Maud had created a technique for communicating with waiters by making the waiters speak very slowly and choosing items they recognized as they moved through the menu. The technique also worked in shops, but it required an elementary background in another language than English. On his own, Salter was dumb. 'You wouldn't mind?' he asked.

'It might be fun. I've never seen you on the job before.'

'Okay. But don't tell Maud what we are up to, will you? She'll want to come, too.'

'No problem. I'll tell her we'd like a day by ourselves.'

'Terrific,' Salter said. He turned on his elbow. 'Did I ever tell you thy belly was like an heap of wheat?' he asked.

'Yes, but not since we left Canada.'

'No? I guess you need a warm climate so you can see it.'

'Right,' Maud said, taking charge at breakfast next day. 'What are our priorities? We have three days.'

'I want to see some pictures,' Henry said.

'I wouldn't mind doing a bit of shopping,' Maud said. 'But that can wait. Charlie wants to see some beggars and whores. What about you, Annie?'

'I'd also like to see a bit of the country,' Salter said. 'We have a car.'

Annie's move.

'Maybe we should split up for the day,' she said. 'Charlie and I will go for a ride, then you two could go off tomorrow. If the four of us stay together all the time we'll get on each other's nerves.'

A tiny chill passed over the table while the Beresfords

considered the implications of this. Then Maud said, 'Very sensible, Annie. There speaks the experienced world traveller. But you'll have to come shopping with me at some point. After today I'll need a rest from Henry, too, won't I, dear? See you here for dinner, then. About six?'

After Maud and Henry had left, Salter pored over his map while they drank some more coffee. Their route lay first along the autostrada to Viareggio. From Lucca they would take the road to Ponte a Moriano, across a small bridge and on up to Valdottavo. With luck they should be able to do most of it in the morning and come back by a different route in the afternoon.

Leaving Florence was easy. They found the autostrada to Viareggio and forty-five minutes later were circling the walled town of Lucca. They circled Lucca three times before a policeman put them on the right road, and after that they began to see signs for Ponte a Moriano. Salter had little idea how he intended to proceed, and no idea at all of what he was looking for, but it was a superb day and all things considered he was just as happy to be driving around Italy in the sun as England in the rain. He pulled up at a café in Ponte a Moriano where Annie got some more directions by pointing at Valdottavo on the map, learning to her pleasure that in Italian the word for 'left' is '*sinistra*'.

As they approached Valdottavo, Salter saw a sign for '*Carabinieri*' and a problem occurred to him. 'If I check with the police,' he said, 'they might get curious, especially if Hamilton has already asked them to check.'

'Stop at that café,' Annie said. 'We'll just ask around. You see what a help I am? We look like a couple of Americans inquiring after an old friend. Much better than if you were on your own, reeking of the man from headquarters.'

Salter parked the car and they walked into the café. There were only three tables inside and at one of them four old men were playing cards. They ordered some *vino bianco*, for which they were charged twenty-three cents a glass, and sat considering how best to proceed. Then Annie wrote out the name 'Terry Dillon' on a scrap of paper and Salter signalled the owner for more wine. When he brought the bottle to their table, Annie showed him the name and said slowly, 'We are searching for this man, Terry Dillon.' She had thought about her words carefully, and chosen a verb that sounded similar in French as being likely to have an Italian cognate, but the barman shook his head and smiled.

'Looking for,' Annie said. 'Seeking, desiring,' and finally 'losing', adding the name Terry Dillon after each verb choice.

Still the man shook his head. '*Tedeschi?*' he asked.

Annie shook her head. '*Inglesi*,' she said. Was that Spanish? 'Canada,' she added.

It worked. The barman looked knowing, then walked over to the four old men and spoke briefly to one of them, who nodded and accompanied the barman to the Salter's table, where he sat down and waited for them to speak.

'We are looking for, searching, seeking, not finding, this man,' Annie said, not sure what the old man's role was.

The Italian smiled. 'I hope you find him,' he said.

'You speak English?' Salter asked in relief.

The man nodded. 'I was a prisoner of war for three years on a farm in Cheddar, in England,' he said. 'What do you want to know?'

At the other table the three remaining card-players were smiling and pointing, taking pleasure in the skill of the village linguist.

'I am trying to find someone who knew this man,' Salter said. 'He lived here a long time ago,' he added, instinctively slipping into the simple language of folk tales.

'My name is Franco,' the man said, and offered his hand, making Salter and Annie feel slightly discourteous for not having observed the formalities first. He looked at the name and shook his head, then walked over and showed it to the other players. The three men passed the paper around and shook their heads.

Salter tried another tack. 'This man, Terry Dillon, married a woman from Lucca a few years ago, maybe just two years. Maria Ponti. She went with him to England, and her brother Mario went with her this year.'

Franco translated this and the old men exploded in recognition. 'We know him,' Franco said. 'This man Terry Dillon was here in the war, yes? He came back and married the woman from Lucca.'

'That's right. Does anyone know anything about him?'

The men talked among themselves, then Franco stood up. 'Let's go to the trattoria. We think the owner knew him.'

They all left the café and walked about two hundred yards down the street, then turned off into the front yard of the trattoria. The owner was standing in the doorway and Franco spoke to him, telling him Salter's story. The man shook hands with the Salters and pointed to a large table under a tree where everybody sat down while he collected a huge flask of wine and some glasses from the bar. When he had filled their glasses he began to talk. Periodically one of the card-players would add something, and there would be an exchange among the group as the details of the story were confirmed. When the owner was finished, Franco started the translation.

'Here is the story,' he said. 'During the war there were these two Englishmen—Tommies—Terry Dillon and another one—who got lost behind the German lines. We found them—the people in Valdottavo—and a man named Giovanni Carosio hid them on his farm. They worked for him and he kept them away from the Germans. This was easy at first, but when the war went bad for us the Fascisti were looking for more young men for the army. They were looking for Italians hiding from the war. Some rich families in Rome and Florence paid farmers to keep their sons hidden from the war. The Fascisti were looking for these and

Giovanni knew he could not hide the Englishmen any more so he sent them away. No one saw them again, until, like you said, Terry Dillon came back about two years ago.'

'What happened to the other one?'

Franco directed the question to the owner and repeated it around the group, but no one responded except to shake their heads. 'They don't know. Nobody here knew the Englishmen—we were all in the army—but everyone knows this story.'

'What about Giovanni Carosio? Would he know?'

'Sure, but he's dead. But we can ask his daughter.' He stood up. 'She was only a child during the war but she will know the story.'

Salter's offer to pay for the wine was refused, and once more the group assembled in the road.

'You have a car?' Franco asked. 'Let's use that.'

They walked back to the café where Salter and Annie shook hands with the three other card-players, and Franco climbed into the front seat. He directed Salter through the village and up a winding road, then off to a gravel track which took them to the top of a hill overlooking the village. Whatever I find out, thought Salter, I'm certainly seeing the country.

The track ended at a two-storey brick-and-stone farm-house surrounded by fruit trees. In front, a fair-haired woman in her forties was seated at a wooden table under a vine-leaf arbour, sorting over a mound of beans. She greeted Franco, bantering with him briefly, and shook hands with the Salters as Franco introduced them. She invited everyone to sit down and produced some wine, and Franco told her Salter's story. Before he had gone very far, she was nodding and smiling in confirmation. Then she told Franco her version.

'Signor Dillon came back to see her father, to thank him for looking after him during the war,' Franco translated.

'After thirty-five years?' Salter asked.

Franco translated. The woman nodded and spoke. 'She says Signor Dillon told her that he was retired now and could afford to travel,' Franco said.

'Okay. What else?'

'She says Dillon told her that when the two Tommies had to leave the farm they hid in the woods up there.' Franco waved at the hills in the distance. 'Then they met some English paratroopers who gave them money and weapons and told them to make their way south. The armies were all mixed up and if they were careful they could slip through and get to their own soldiers. That's what Terry Dillon did.'

'And the other one?'

'Johnny?' the woman asked, and spoke a few words.

'Johnny is dead,' Franco translated.

'Dead?'

'Yes. Dillon said he was killed in the woods,' the translation continued.

'Was Dillon with him?'

The woman shrugged and spoke briefly.

'She doesn't know,' Franco said.

'So he might have escaped,' Salter said. He explained about the postcard from Valdottavo. 'It must be the same person,' he concluded.

Franco translated, and the woman shook her head decisively and spoke at length.

'No,' Franco said. 'If Johnny came back she would know. He used to play with her when she was a little girl. He would come to see her. Johnny never came back.'

The woman exclaimed and ran into the house. She returned with a photograph, an old snapshot of two Tommies with their arms around each other's shoulders. There was nothing distinctive about the two soldiers; the picture had been taken in England, and in the back garden of a small house: two eighteen-year-olds in battledress with cheerful grins that showed they had both lost some teeth to the army dentist. The real English disease.

'Which is which?' Salter asked.

The woman turned the picture over and showed him the back. An inscription read, 'Blighty, 1942. Johnny and Terry.' She turned the picture over again and pointed. 'Terry Dillon; Johnny Bessell.' She laughed and said something more. 'When Terry Dillon came back he was fat with a big grey beard,' Franco translated. 'She did not recognize him.'

'I know,' Salter said. 'I met him in England.' He decided not to spoil her day by telling her of Dillon's death. 'Thank her for me, please, Franco.'

They shook hands again all round, and Annie said, '*Arrivederci*,' to everyone's enormous pleasure, and Salter drove Franco back to the café where he had first found him. Once more they shook hands, but Franco made no move to get out of the car. Then he said, 'Signor Salter, everyone is asking me who you are, so now I will ask you. Why is a Canadian looking for an Englishman who lived in Italy in the war? Something bad?'

It was a question Salter had expected much earlier, but he still didn't have a reply. Annie filled the gap. 'It's about some money,' she said. 'A relative of Johnny Bessell died in Canada and left some money to him. But he has not claimed the money so my husband is trying to prove he is dead.'

Franco looked at Annie, then at Salter. 'You are a lawyer?' he asked.

'Sort of,' Salter said. 'I trace missing people.'

'You will spend all his money looking for him,' Franco said. Then he shrugged. 'There is one other place you can ask,' he said. 'The post office. The girl there speaks English, too. Good luck.'

They drove off in the direction Franco had indicated, and Salter pulled up outside the post office.

'Franco didn't believe me,' he said to Annie.

'No, he didn't,' she agreed. 'I'm not surprised. Why did you tell him you had met Dillon in England?'

'Oh Christ, I said that, didn't I? What do you think they'll make of us?'

'Nothing probably. They'll think this Johnny Bessell will be a millionaire if we find him, and talk about it for a few days. Come on, let's get this girl in the Post Office done with. I'm slightly drunk and famished.'

The girl who ran the post office knew all about Signor Dillon and confirmed the story that Salter already knew. She said that no one called Bessell had received any mail there; she was quite positive because it was still early in the season and there were very few foreigners yet. 'But why is everyone interested in Signor Dillon?' she added.

'Everyone? Who else?'

'Another man last month. He knew the story of the two Tommies in the war, too, and he was looking for Signor Dillon. He did not go into the village, after I told him that Signor Dillon was in England.'

'Do you remember what he looked like?'

'Not really. English, I think. Older than you. He was just in for a few minutes. I told him he could probably get Signor Dillon's English address from the trattoria in Lucca where his wife worked.'

Salter thanked her, watching to see if this was another time to shake hands, but she merely smiled and went back to work.

'So Bessell's been here,' he said to Annie on their way to Lucca. 'It had to be him. But why incognito? Why didn't he go up to the village and say hello?'

'Because he wanted to give Dillon a surprise,' Annie said.

'Catch him by surprise, you mean?'

Annie shrugged. 'What next?' she asked. 'Do you ever eat when you are on a case?'

They were approaching the walled town again. 'Let's see if they sell lunch in Lucca,' Salter said.

They parked by a gate in the wall and strolled into the town, coming quickly upon what they wanted, a restaurant at the corner of a large square with plenty of room at the tables outside. After an enormous meal that cost them twenty dollars, including, apparently, seventy-five cents for a bottle of wine that Salter calculated would have cost him nine times as much in an Ontario liquor store, and twenty times as much in the neighbourhood restaurant he and Annie favoured because it was cheap, Salter decided he had a problem.

'I need a siesta,' he said.

Annie laughed. 'You're drunk,' she said.

'Content,' Salter said. 'Just content. Anyway, when in Rome . . .'

They watched in silence as the shops began to close for the afternoon.

'Got any suggestions?' Annie asked. 'I could do with a nap, too.'

'If we were at home, now—travelling, I mean—we would find ourselves a bit of grass by the highway, but they don't seem to do that here. Maybe the risk of *banditti* is too great.'

Annie said, 'All the stories you hear about Rome and Naples, about how people are always getting robbed. No-body's even tried to short-change us yet.'

It was true. They had found restaurant bills impossible to read, which should have made them nervous, but the total was always so small that they couldn't believe anyone was cheating. The experience they had had so far was that it was impossible to eat badly in Italy and all meals cost ten dollars. Bread seemed to cost a dollar a head and wine seventy-five cents, and whatever else they ate cost six or seven dollars.

'Nobody cheats on bills at home, either,' Salter said loyally.

'Only the very expensive restaurants downtown,' Annie corrected, her eyes closed. The pauses between their remarks were becoming longer.

'You remember that first hotel in England?' Salter said, minutes later.

'Tweedledee,' Annie said.

They were very nearly asleep. They woke up to a mild squabble a few tables away between a waiter and a middle-aged English couple. They turned their chairs slightly, the better to listen and watch in comfort. The English couple were questioning an item on their bill, determined not to be robbed by foreigners. Salter admired their courage and predicted to himself that they were about to be embarrassed. Eventually the baffled waiter called the manager who spoke some English and pointed out that the item they had never ordered and were refusing to pay for was the date. The couple left, pink-faced, staring high over the heads of their audience.

Salter and Annie, slightly energized, resumed their conversation.

'In Florida once we rented a motel for a couple of hours, remember?'

'I remember. I felt like your secretary.'

'You think we might get a room here for the afternoon?'

'Sure, if you know what to ask for. Go ahead. I'll wait in the car.

'What's the Italian for "hours"?'

'I don't know. The Latin is "hora", I think.'

Salter tried out a sentence. '*Uno camera matrimoniale pour duo hora*,' he said.

'I'd check that if I were you,' Annie said. 'You might wind up in a room with me and two other ladies. Cost you a fortune.'

'For all I know we'll wind up in jail,' Salter said. 'Who knows what the local laws are. Maybe it's illegal not to stay overnight.'

'You aren't going to risk it, are you?' Annie said.

'No. All I want is a nap. If we got a room covered in red

velvet with a mirror on the ceiling it would keep me awake.'

By now they were alone at the tables outside the café. 'Let's go back to the car, Charlie, and take it from there,' Annie said.

They shambled, jelly-like, through the nearly empty streets of the town to the car parked outside the gate. Here Salter moved the car into the shade where it could be seen by a policeman on traffic duty twenty yards away. They rolled the windows down slightly, adjusted the seats back as far as they would go, and passed out.

When they woke up, thick-tongued and disoriented, they needed coffee before tackling the the autostrada to Florence, and they walked back into the town. Annie bought a guide-book, and they became tourists for an hour, paying a visit to the Roman amphitheatre where the first boutiques were peeping through the otherwise scruffy arena, the universal sign of urban renewal. When they got their coffee, the waiter told them they should stay until Sunday; an election was coming up and the local Communist candidate, a lady, had promised to campaign in the nude.

They drove back to the Piazza Indipendenza in plenty of time for dinner, and waited for the others to appear.

Maud and Henry had spent most of the day in the Uffizi Galleries, and like the Salters, they had found a siesta irresistible.

'What did you do?' Maud asked.

They told the Beresfords how they had driven around the Tuscan hills, had lunch at this wonderful town called Lucca, and poked about the streets in the afternoon. Annie suggested that Maud and Henry take a similar route the next day, but Henry declined. 'I don't trust myself on the wrong side of the road,' he said, 'so to avoid arguments I left my licence at home.'

Salter offered to chauffeur them, but Maud turned it down. 'We want some more culture,' she said. 'Henry is insatiable.' So they agreed that they would do the Pitti Palace, the Boboli Gardens, and take another look (at Henry's request) at the Uffizi Galleries.

The whole of the next day they looked and walked, with a two-hour break for a siesta. Salter, remembering his Stratford experience, went with the flow, prepared to be untouched unless something snagged him. He was indifferent to the Duomo and found the formality of the Boboli Gardens bleak after England. Although nothing spoke to him like Shakespeare's inscription, he nearly lost himself once at the sight of the restored original of a painting he knew as Venus on the Half-Shell, a poster of which Annie had owned when he married her. The hermit in him was struck, too, by the cells of the monks in the Museum of San Marco, especially that of Savonarola. Apart from all the praying, he thought, looking around the pleasant rooms, it wouldn't be a bad life—wine with every meal, a good dressing-gown to keep you warm, and all the time in this world to read and think. A life of total selfishness, apart from the praying.

During dinner they re-sorted their priorities for their last day.

'I've had enough culture,' Salter said. 'I want to see the rest of the town.'

'I haven't seen the Palazzo Vecchio yet,' Henry said.

'You've got to come shopping with me, Annie,' Maud said.

So they planned the morning. They would meet for lunch, and take the rest of the day from there, probably after a sleep.

In bed Annie said, 'Got an idea, have you, Charlie?'

'Nothing much,' Salter said. 'I just wondered if I could find out if Bessell was officially buried up in those hills. There must be some sort of War Graves Commission.'

'Then what?'

'Then nothing,' Salter said. 'Then I'll tell Churcher what

I've found out, and he can tell Hamilton. Give Churcher a bit of a boost.'

'A bit risky, isn't it? If Hamilton gets irritated because you've found out something he ought to have done, it will backfire on Churcher, won't it?'

Salter considered. 'Yeah, you're right. I'll leave him out of it. If I can find out that Johnny Bessell is still alive, or anyway not certainly dead, I'll tell Hamilton. Maybe it will upset him.' Salter smiled.

'Charlie,' Annie said, 'you aren't going to spend the rest of the holiday on this, are you?'

'Of course not. I'm not bothering anyone, am I?'

'No. Even better than that. I'm glad you found out about steeplechasing because you would have been a bloody misery otherwise. Maud and I have had a good time without you. And this murder has kept you cheerful the rest of the time. So I'm not complaining. And, too, I have to thank the policeman in you for Florence, which you might not have suggested all by yourself. So we've all had a good time where we might have been getting on each other's nerves by now. And I did enjoy the bit of sleuthing in Valdottavo. But when we go back, I want to carry on with the holiday as planned, especially if the sun has come out.'

'There's nothing else to do, anyway. Don't worry about it. But while we are on the subject, will you come with me to the races?'

'Sure. I'd love to. But not in the pouring rain.'

'I'll buy a one-day pass to the Members' Enclosure,' Salter said. 'We'll watch with the gentry. I'll buy one of those flat hats they all wear and a pair of those green boots.'

It took Salter most of the morning to find out what he wanted to know. He was tempted to identify himself properly, but while that might have produced quicker results, it was certain to lead to some polite questions that he didn't want to answer, and maybe an exchange of pleasantries between

the *carabinieri* and Hamilton. So he played the friend of a
friend, inquiring on his behalf about an old army buddy,
and after bumping around various police and army offices,
feeling more and more ashamed of his Anglo-Saxon mono-
lingualism (why the bloody hell didn't they at least teach
us some French in Ontario?—all these Italian coppers
seemed to speak at least one other language) he was referred
to the British Consul, where he was shown a list and found
no trace of Johnny Bessell.

As with the trip to Valdottavo, having an errand got him
into the city in a way that merely strolling around it as a
tourist would not have done. He saw no beggars, but a
beautiful girl spoke invitingly to him near the Pitti Palace
which could only mean one thing, and he had a nice encoun-
ter with an English-speaking waiter who was thrilled to
learn that Salter came from Toronto, where the waiter's
hero was now playing soccer for the Blizzard. A good
mooch round.

After lunch and a short nap, the four of them discussed
how to get the best out of their last few hours. Henry,
predictably, wanted to do two more museums and a church,
and when Maud refused, Annie offered to accompany him,
which left Maud and Salter.

'I wouldn't mind doing some shopping,' Salter said.
'When *she's* around trying to get me to buy stuff for myself,
I get Bolshie.'

'Don't I know it,' Annie said. 'Let's split up, then. What
about you, Maud?'

'I'll go with Charlie,' Maud said. 'I'll make him spend
his money.'

They started in the leather market, where Salter bought
a belt for himself and a purse for Annie which Maud said
Annie had admired but her Scottish ancestors thought too
expensive. Then they made their way to the Ponte Vecchio
to look at gold. Near the straw market they stopped at a
café where Salter had his first beer in three days, and Maud

ordered a huge glass, like a vase, of fruit and wine. The holiday was nearly over.

'How it infects the blood!' Maud said.

'What?' Salter asked.

For reply, Maud pointed to a young couple who had stopped in a doorway so that the boy could kiss the girl's eyes and neck and ears. 'Italy,' Maud said.

'What a great holiday,' Salter said. He meant what an agreeable companion Maud had turned out to be, what a difference from his first impression of her as a myopic busybody, and he tried to put all this into his voice. Maud, who was still watching the boy and girl, said, 'Have you ever had an affair, Charlie? Since you were married, I mean?'

Salter looked at her warily. She had taken off her glasses, and without them she had a slightly mad look.

'You want to know too much, Maud,' he said.

'Don't I, though.'

'Do your eyes hurt?' Salter asked.

'No. It's just easier to talk abnormally without my glasses on. Have you?'

Salter found himself caught among the desire to brag (I've had more affairs than you've had hot dinners), the desire to invent a virtuous persona (I respect Annie too much for that, Maud), and the truth. But any answer would involve, with Maud, a further discussion of why, or why not. He prevaricated.

'Are you making a pass at me, Maud?' he joked.

'No, I'm not. I just wondered about other people's life-styles, as you call it.'

Salter had the initiative now, and he tried to deflect attention from himself. 'What about you, Maud? Are you and Henry involved in a wife-swapping ring in Watford?'

'Don't be vulgar, Charlie. That's not what I meant.'

'Sorry. But have you, Maud? Ever been unfaithful?'

'Yes, I have,' Maud said promptly. 'Once. With an old

boyfriend I knew before I married Henry. I met him again years later and we went to bed. We never had before.'

'And?'

'It was bloody alarming. I kept expecting photographers to burst in.'

Salter laughed. 'Why did you do it, then?'

'I was curious. I wanted to know if I'd missed anything.'

'Not a *real* affair, then.'

'No. When I put my glasses back on he had a smug expression on his face, and I realized that he thought he had shown me what I had missed, or was doing me a favour because I was frustrated. Either way it wasn't very complimentary to Henry, was it, so we had words and that was the last I saw of him.'

'And that was it?'

'Yes, and it will probably stay that way. Sometimes, though, I feel out of joint with the times. There's that poem by Yeats that goes, "This is no country for old men/The young in one another's arms." I feel like that, sometimes. Everybody seems to know more about "life" than I do. Do they, Charlie? Am I missing something? Or is my condition a commonplace these days?'

'Don't ask me, Maud. I don't wander far from Annie because it's too much trouble. Not on principle, or because I don't want to. And because Annie would find out.'

'And she wouldn't like that?'

'No, she wouldn't.' Salter felt an odd sensation as if a silent vacuum had created itself on the back of his neck and he turned quickly to find yet another English middle-aged couple listening in to their conversation so hard that the man was in danger of falling off his chair. Salter turned back to Maud, who was laughing silently into her drink. 'Come on,' he said. 'Let's go back and eat.'

'You didn't really answer my question, Charlie.'

'No, and I'm not going to,' he said, pulling her to her feet and giving her a kiss for the benefit of their audience.

They found Annie and Henry in front of their hotel,
drinking wine, and Salter presented Annie with the purse,
happy that for once he had found a gift he was certain she
would like. They all exchanged accounts of the afternoon's
activities and went in search of one last, good, ten-dollar
meal. After dinner the level of contentment was so high that
they strolled about the town well into the small hours,
reluctant to end their interlude in Florence.

'The Land of Tweedledum,' Annie said later, as they lay
in bed listening to the city shutting up its doors.

Part Four

THE LAST FENCE

A light drizzle was falling on Tokesbury Mallett when they arrived the next day. The change from Florence created something of a culture shock, even after so short a trip, and they had to work hard to avoid feeling depressed. The holiday was nearly over for the Beresfords, and Annie and Maud planned a last outing together. Henry, after waiting for an invitation from Salter which never came, decided to join them.

Maud watched Salter dodge any involvement with the others and asked him what he was going to do.

'I have to spend some time with the local police,' Salter said. 'The inspector there wants to show me around, and I've been putting him off.'

'And catch up with the murder?' Maud asked. 'I wonder if they've got him yet?'

'I hope so,' Annie said, looking at Salter, to whom she had promised one more day on his own to satisfy his curiosity.

'We found the brother,' Churcher said at the station the next day. 'He telephoned Boomewood and when that American girl told him what had happened he came straight back to be with his sister.'

'And?'

'Oh, he's in the clear. On the night in question he was working as a part-time helper in an Italian restaurant in Reading. Eleven Italians are prepared to testify to that

and Superintendent Hamilton is inclined to believe them.'
Clearly Churcher had his doubts.

'Where is he now?'

'At the hotel with his sister and the Kryst girl. They are
going to reopen. The girl is going to give up the rest of her
vacation to help out.'

'Now what?'

'I have no idea. I'm not in charge.'

'Any other news from Italy?'

'None, as far as I know.'

'And Dillon. Anything turned up about his past?'

'Not as far as I know. We'll find out, though. Don't worry
about it.'

'I'm not. But *I* ran across something in Italy which you
probably ought to know about.'

'You ran across something? In Italy?' Churcher asked
unbelievingly.

'I happened to be passing through Valdottavo, the village
where the card came from.'

'What card?'

Salter sighed. They really were telling Churcher nothing.
He explained about the entry in the hotel register and the
postcard, and then what he had learned in Valdottavo.

Churcher listened sullenly. 'So you've found out that this
Dillon and Bessell were wartime chums, have you? Where
does that get us?'

'It might be worth checking up on Bessell,' he said.

'I'd better report this to the superintendent,' Churcher
said. 'I'll tell him you wanted to give him a message, shall
I? It doesn't sound like much to me.'

If you are going to sit and sulk, thought Salter, I'm
wasting my time. He made one more effort. 'Of course. But
maybe you could make a couple of phone calls while you
are waiting. If Bessell is alive, when he came out of the
army, he must have gone somewhere, to some address. It's
a long shot but just maybe he's still known there. The

chances are that he went back home—he was a kid when he joined the army—and someone might remember him, even if he's moved away from the district.'

'You mean follow this up on my own?'

'You could find out his address in 1945 and let Hamilton take it from there,' Salter said. It was risky, perhaps, but he still wanted to give Churcher a boost.

'I'd better check first. It's not my investigation.' He phoned his headquarters and asked to be put through to the superintendent. Hamilton was out so Churcher left a message. 'Some information about the Dillon case has turned up,' he said, and put the phone down.

'Now what do you suggest?'

'Okay. You've covered your ass, now phone the army records office. Get the address; start the inquiry. The local station can send a man round wherever the trail starts.'

Churcher looked nervous, but slightly excited. Then, with sudden resolution, he began to make calls. Eventually he got on to someone in London with access to old army records. He listened, made notes, and after an exchange of courtesies, replaced the receiver firmly in its cradle.

'Right,' he said briskly. 'Here it is, then. Johnny Bessell was demobilized in 1945, you're quite right. His address at that time was 78 Uppingham Road, Manor Park, E.12.'

'Where's that?' Salter asked, making a casual note.

'East London. Probably quite near Ilford. I'll call the Ilford police and ask them to give us a hand.' He made another call and explained what he wanted. He listened for a while, then said, 'Yes, yes, I understand. Right, Inspector, whenever you can.'

Once more Churcher took on the look of a chastened schoolboy. 'They haven't anyone to spare at the moment,' he said. 'He's putting your request on his list and will probably call back in three or four days. It seems they have a bit of a panic going on. He asked me if I ever read the fucking papers.' Churcher reached beside his chair and took the *Daily Telegraph* out of his briefcase, and looked over the front page. 'Here it is,' he said. 'I didn't get a chance to look at it this morning. Our charlady gave in her notice and my wife was very upset.' He read out, 'Two gang leaders found dead this morning behind a public house in Manor Park.'

The sergeant put his head round the door and spoke to Churcher. 'It's Mrs Bladgett, sir. She insists on talking to you about her burglar. Would you mind? She won't be satisfied with me.'

'Of course, Sergeant,' Churcher said, looking pleased. 'I'll be right along.' To Salter he said, 'She suffers from the delusion that she is being robbed nightly, but she has a little chat with me about it and that seems to do the trick.' He walked through to the outer office.

While Salter was alone, the telephone rang and he picked it up. 'Sergeant Woodiwiss here,' a voice said. 'Superintendent Hamilton's assistant. The Superintendent is away at the moment. What's this about information on the Dillon case?'

'Inspector Churcher just left, Sergeant,' Salter said, after identifying himself. 'I'm having a cup of coffee in his office.'

'When's he coming back?'

Through the partly open door Salter could see Churcher escorting Mrs Bladgett out of the station. Sergeant Robey was busily writing at the desk. Salter took a deēp breath and stepped gently out of line. 'I don't know. He left in a hurry and said goodbye to me, so it may be a while. He told me to finish my coffee.'

Woodiwiss grunted. 'Can't be very bloody important, then. Tell him to leave a message with someone here, will you?' He hung up.

Churcher returned in a few minutes, looking pleased. 'Sergeant Robey said I was wanted on the phone,' he said.

'I answered it. Just the London operator wanting to know

if you'd completed your call,' Salter said, giving the lie direct which would possibly mean his neck.

'Odd. Probably British Telecom getting their lines crossed again.' He smiled. 'I think Mrs Bladgett will be all right for a couple of days. Now, what about this Dillon thing?'

'Forget about it, Charles. When you speak to Hamilton, tell him you made some phone calls at my request. A courtesy, call it, and you are reporting the request to him in case he was not aware. Tell him everything. Don't get involved. It's not your case.'

'Right, right. I think that's reasonable. Now, Charles, my wife would like to meet Mrs Salter. She wants to invite her to lunch.' Churcher beamed.

'I'll check my wife's plans,' Salter said. 'If we decide to stay much longer in the area, I'll give you a call.'

He shook hands with Churcher and waited outside the station house for the sergeant to join him.

'Nice price,' the sergeant said, looking at his boots.

'I got thirteen to two,' Salter said. He looked at his watch. 'How long will it take me to drive to London,' he asked.

'About an hour and a quarter. Take the Oxford road, then turn off on to the M40. 'Course, it depends what part.'

'Ilford.'

'Ah. Allow another hour at least, p'raps more.'

'Thanks, Sergeant.'

'No gee-gees, today, sir?' Robey inquired politely.

'No. I've got to visit some relatives of my wife.'

'Ah. Pity. When you come back then, sir.'

Salter called in at the Plough and left a message with the host that he might be late for dinner and that Annie should go ahead without him. She and the others had gone to a sale of antiques that was taking place forty miles away.

The sergeant was right in his estimate of the time it would take him to get to London, and shortly before twelve Salter found himself in the Bayswater Road, heading for Marble

Arch. He turned along Park Lane with the stream of traffic and then turned left again and stopped in a side street somewhere in Mayfair to chart the rest of his route. He was now in Curzon Street. The road was obvious: he had to work his way back to Oxford Street and then go east to something called Aldgate. But why was Oxford Street marked in white? He asked a policeman. 'Because you are not allowed in it, sir,' the constable replied, saluting. 'Your best bet is to go along Piccadilly, round the Circus, up Shaftesbury Avenue to *New* Oxford Street, and then it's a straight road all the way.'

Salter thanked him and went back to his map. It looked easy enough. He went right at the next corner, then left at Piccadilly, noticing that pedestrians had no rights in this country when a car wanted to turn a corner. He went round the Circus twice, unable to see Shaftesbury Avenue as he clung grimly to a place in the flow of traffic which surrounded him on all sides. Eventually he edged to the left and chose a likely exit and found himself in no time at all in Trafalgar Square. A friendly cab driver gave him new directions and Salter turned north. Watch out for bridges, he told himself. If I cross the Thames, I've had it. At St Giles's Circus he saw the street he wanted out of the corner of his eye and continued glumly up the Tottenham Court Road to Euston Road, which looked important, and by making three left turns got himself on to it travelling east again. When he stopped to consult his map he saw that he could make it if he stayed on this road. 'Pentonville Road, City Road, Great Eastern Street,' he chanted to himself. Then he noticed signs for the A13 which he knew was his road, and after that it was easy. When he stopped for a rest, just past Stratford where the road had turned so sharply round a church that it had unnerved him, he found that he was only three miles from his destination. It was half past one.

78 Uppingham Road was the last in a row of small

attached dwellings that looked as though they dated from the First World War. Both sides of the street were packed with cars and Salter had trouble finding somewhere to stop, jamming himself finally into a space that was technically taken up with a motor-scooter. He walked back to 78 and knocked and rang, and heard someone begin chanting immediately, 'A . . . a . . . ll ri . . . i . . . ght, a . . . a . . . ll ri . . . i . . . ght,' the sound of shuffling feet, and a dog barking furiously. The door opened six inches, and a bald, egg-shaped head appeared, wearing slightly elliptical glasses which emphasized the face's egginess. 'Yes?' he asked.

The face was only three feet from the floor, but Salter was already familiar with this phenomenon, the result of trying to speak through the door without letting the dog out, which occurs in half the houses in England. 'Wojerwant?' the face said.

Salter showed his identification. 'Can I speak to you for a moment?'

'Waffor?'

'I'm looking for a Mr Johnny Bessell. Can you help me?'

'Why?' Underneath his hand, the dog was trying to tunnel through the floor to get at Salter.

'I'm trying to look him up. A pal of mine knew him during the war. Are you him?'

'No, I'm not. W'mminit. I'll just shut Jackie up in the scullery.'

The door closed and reopened a few minutes later and Salter was let into the tiny hallway. From the back of the house came the sounds of an enraged Jackie trying to chew his way out.

'Cuminere,' the man said. He led the way into the front room and Salter sat down in one of a pair of huge old armchairs.

'Wassertrouble?' the man asked.

'No trouble. I just want to talk to him.'

'You'll be lucky. He's been dead two years,' the little man said.

'Dead?' Salter asked, sucking air rapidly. 'Two years?'

''Ass right. Drowned in Lake Wossname.'

"Where?"

'Lake Toronto. In Canada.'

'There is no Lake Toronto. You mean Ontario?'

''Ass right.'

'You're sure?'

'I'm not sure of nothink, mate. That's what they told me, two years ago when they came round. The police, I mean. Now, what are you up to?'

'I was just asked to look him up by a friend who knew him during the war.'

''Ass a load of codswallop for a start,' the man said, belligerently. 'You wouldn't show me a bleedin' mountie's card if you was just asking after a friend, would you?'

'I'm not a mountie,' Salter said. 'But you're right. I'm looking for someone else and if I had found Johnny Bessell he might have given me a lead. But you can kick me out if you want.'

'I know,' the little man said, and sniggered.

Salter stood up. He had hoped to get a few quick facts on his thin excuse, but this was getting tricky. His host was obviously a man who was proud of knowing his 'rights'. Already he could see a complaint being laid at the local police station which would earn him a roasting from Hamilton and probably Orliff, too. It was time to go.

'Don't get aereated,' the man said. 'Sit down. I'm Johnny's brother. I havn't seen him for thirty years, though. Ever since he went to Canada.'

Salter sat down again. 'What happened to him when he came out of the army?'

'He lived here for a few years, didn't he? With me. I promised Mum that I'd give him a home, didn't I? Me and the wife—she's gone, now—took over the house when Mum died before Johnny came back. He was my only family then, see, and besides, this was his home. But we never got along. The wife couldn't abide him, could she?'

'So he went to Canada?'

'After he qualified, yes. He was a Public Accountant. Got qualified and then just slung his hook. Did he get into trouble?'

'No,' said Salter patiently. 'Whereabouts did he go?'

'I dunno. Last we heard he was in this place called Toronto.'

'Did you stay in touch?'

From the scullery, the dog was howling steadily.

'No,' Bessell said, 'He wrote us cards for a few years at Christmastime, then nothing. We was never close, and after he qualified he got too good for Manor Park.'

'When was the last time you heard from him?'

'Must be twenty years ago. Must be. I was thinking of selling the house—lot of coloureds were moving in—and the solicitor told me that legally Johnny still owned half of it, even though I'd done all the decorating and that, because Mum had left it to both of us. So I wrote to the last address I had and he wrote back saying he didn't want his half. Must have been doing all right, mustn't he?'

'And that's the last you heard of him?'

''Ass right. I sent him a couple of cards, but I never heard again.'

'He never came back for a visit?'

'No, he wouldn't do that. Vera hated him. Hated him, she did. Pity, really. She's gone too, now, and I'm all alone, and I can't get about much with my feet. I would have liked to see him again. Like a cup of tea?'

'No, thanks, Mr Bessell. I'm sorry I bothered you.'

Bessell looked at a loss. ''Ass all right,' he said. 'Tell you the truth, I don't think Vera was very nice to him. I let her drive him away. Still, you've got to stick up for your wife, haven't you? But it was nice of him to give up the house,

536

wasn't it? She couldn't see it. Oh well. Pity I never saw him.
But I don't want to be bothered if he was in any trouble,'
he ended warningly. 'Something's up or you wouldn't be
here, would you?'

He got up to let Salter out. As the door closed behind
him, Salter heard Bessell calling to his dog, assuring him
that release was on the way. There was the sound of a charging animal and a thump as Jackie hurled himself against
the front door. What a way to run a house, Salter thought.

He turned left at the end of the street and inserted himself
into the permanent traffic jam in the Romford Road. Beside
him a goggled youth waited on a throbbing motorcycle. On
an impulse, Salter rolled down the window and asked the
boy how he would get across London to the M40.

'Yank, eh?' the youth smiled. 'Bit of a poser, that one,
mate. Friend of mine always goes on the North Circular,
but I think you're best going straight through. A bit of a
gamble but I've always done it. Thing is, when you get to
the Bank, go along Cheapside to 'Olborn. When you get to
Tottenham Court Road, go straight down Oxford Street.
Bugger the signs. If they stop you, act daft.'

The lights changed and a car behind immediately began
honking. The youth turned slowly on his seat. 'Shut up, you
stupid git,' he snarled at the honking driver, 'or I'll come
back there and sort you out.' The driver rolled up his
window, and the youth turned back to Salter and smiled
warmly. 'All right, guv? Don't forget: Bank, 'Olborn, Oxford
Street. Got it?' The lights changed to yellow and he and
Salter ducked through, leaving the car behind to wait for
another change.

Tweedledum *and* Tweedledee, thought Salter.

In Tokesbury Mallet that evening, Salter explained to Annie
what was going on.

'Bessell drowned two years ago in Lake Ontario,' he
concluded.

'But that girl in Valdottavo said that Dillon told her that he died in Italy when they were trying to escape!'

'Right. Why? What happened in those hills?'

'Dillon might just have *assumed* he was dead. If he was listed as missing and Dillon never checked after the war, I mean.'

'They were buddies. He would have gone to see Bessell's family.'

'How could he? He went missing himself. He wouldn't have wanted to take any chances.'

Salter thought about this. 'Maybe,' he said. 'Maybe. But nothing else is explained, is it?'

'You mean the Rundstedt woman?'

'And Parrott. The guy who took me racing. He lived in Toronto for a while. There are too many connections to Toronto.'

'Dillon?'

'Maybe.'

'You think that Rundstedt and Dillon and Bessell and Parrott are all connected? It sounds a little wild, Charlie.'

'That's what Orliff would say. But it's a lot of coincidences, isn't it?'

'So are we.'

'What?'

'So are *we*. We're Canadian, from Toronto. On that basis Hamilton should have checked up on us right away.'

'Oh, he did.'

'*What?*'

'Listen, love. When you find a body in a hotel with half a dozen handy suspects you check up on all of them.'

'Me too?'

'Sure!'

'What's your guess, then? About this whole gang?'

'Something like this. Dillon and his wartime buddy knew about each other, maybe they met in Toronto, but for some reason, when Dillon visited Valdottavo he made up a story about Bessell having died in Tuscany. Maybe he knew that Bessell was now really dead. I'm sure that Rundstedt knew Dillon, and I'm guessing that Parrott and Rundstedt were more than just bedmates in the Swan for a night. I think they may have had something on Dillon, something to do with Bessell.'

'So what are you going to do about it?'

'Tell Hamilton in the morning. I think Hamilton has written off the postcard, and he's still trying to track down someone who had a grudge against Dillon.' Salter smiled. 'Combing the underworld, probably. It'll be fun telling him about Bessell.'

'Tomorrow morning, then? Then back to our holiday?'

'Of course.'

'I think you're playing with fire, Charlie. Hamilton's not going to be pleased, is he?'

'Probably not. That's the idea.'

'Okay. But I would like to be driving north the day after tomorrow.'

'You will be,' Salter said.

'Good. Because the forecast is for some cloudiness in the north-west. It might be breaking up. Anyway, I'm losing my chum. Maud and Henry are going home.'

'Tomorrow?'

'Yes. Maud paid us the nicest compliment this afternoon, by the way, while we were in Coutsbury. She said it has been the best holiday she has had since she and Henry got married.'

'She did? All because of us?'

'Mostly. She told me that before the holiday she and Henry had been having problems.'

'Why? Henry seems all right. And they seemed a good couple—she wants to know everything about everybody and Henry doesn't give a damn for anything except rats. What was the problem? Henry got a girlfriend? Or Maud a boy-friend?'

'Nothing like that. Just the opposite. Henry, apparently, can't get enough of her, and she still likes him, loves him, I think. That surprise you?'

'Nothing surprises me about other people's lives except the fact that they talk about them. But she couldn't stand him? In bed, I mean?'

'Not that, either. She just felt she was leading a very narrow life, and she is smart enough to believe that her curiosity about everybody is a bit old-maidish. Some stupid pal of Henry's told her this. He said she was substituting curiosity for experience, and it was an appetite that would grow, he said, by what it fed on. He suggested that she should fulfil herself, experience life, instead of living through other people. She even wondered if she and Henry should separate.'

'So what happened?' Salter asked. He had not told Annie about his conversation with Maud in Florence.

'That's where we came in. She talked to me a lot—there's nothing like someone you will never see again for having a good heart-to-heart. That's why she wanted to stay with us even to going to Florence. She saw us—*us*, Charlie—as people of the world and she pumped me—no, that's not fair —*asked* me to tell her just what was going on with our generation, theirs and ours, today.'

'You didn't tell her, I hope.'

'Sure, I did. She's certainly incredibly naive in her assumptions about other people's lives. Unless I am. No, she is. She put it well; she's always been a great reader and playgoer and when she was young the books and plays reflected life as she knew it. But lately, in the last ten years, nothing seems like anything she knows about. She began to feel as if she were like the Lady of Shallott. Life passing her by.'

'And now she doesn't. Just from talking to you?'

'I think she's taken comfort from living with us, Charlie. At any rate she's going back to Watford happy, feeling she's very lucky to have Henry, and looking forward to an interesting old age.'

'But a lot less nosey, eh?'

'I guess so. She says that she realized that under the tranquil surface of most people's lives lies a stagnant pond.'

Just from talking to me? Salter wondered.

'What about Henry? Is he aware of all this?' he asked.

'We didn't talk much about him, but he has his own anxieties, I think. He made a pass at me in Florence.'

'For Christ's sake!'

'Nothing serious. He put his arm around me in the Piazza del Duomo. I think he was just being gallant, in case that's what Canadians did.'

'The bastard,' Salter said. He laughed. 'Well, well, well, I'll challenge him to a duel, shall I?'

'You won't say a word. Now go and put a tie on for dinner. They'll be down soon.'

But before he went up to their room, Salter put a call in to Toronto, and spoke to his sergeant. The call was returned before he had finished dressing.

'What did you find out, Frank?' he asked. He was tying his tie with one hand, standing up at the front desk because the Plough did not run to telephones in the guests' bedrooms. Annie watched him from the bar.

Gatenby, Salter's cosy-voiced, white-haired assistant, began. 'I'll read you everything I've got,' he said. 'First. John Stanley Bessell is a missing person.' There was a long pause. 'That's helpful, isn't it, Charlie?'

'Read the bloody thing right through, Frank. We'll chat about it when I get home, not at ten dollars a minute.'

'Sorry. Well then, Johnny Bessell is, or was a missing person. He went sailing in Lake Ontario two years ago. His sailboat was found empty off Scarborough Bluffs but he never turned up. He's officially dead now. There was no sign he left the country and he's never turned up anywhere else. It was listed as accidental with a possibility of suicide, because he was a good sailor.'

'Why would he have committed suicide?'

'He was going to be in trouble with us. The Fraud Squad, that is. He was a partner in a small construction company with a fella named Cossitt, Michael Cossitt, and when we investigated the incident a few things turned up, then a lot more. You want me to read all this, Charlie? It's about twenty pages of summation of what they were up to.'

'What sort of things?'

'Skimming. Income tax evasion. Fraud. There were thirty-seven charges finally.'

'What happened?'

'Cossitt, the partner, went to jail. He denied everything. Said Bessell was entirely responsible for the books and he knew nothing about it. But his name was on the cheques, and he had more money than he should have according to the income tax declaration, so they got him on that.'

'And Bessell never turned up?'

'No. Why?'

'I'm curious. This guy came back to life once already. What about Dillon?'

'Nothing on him. He never immigrated here officially. The Immigration Department know nothing about him, nor does anyone else.'

'Shit. And Rundstedt?'

'We've already had an inquiry about her. From the bobbies over there. Nothing at all. She's just a nice Canadian lady on holiday.'

'Parrott?'

'Another blank. Nobody here has heard of him.'

'Okay. Thanks. I'll get back to you if I want anything else.' Salter rang off and joined Annie in the bar.

'Got an idea, Charlie?' she asked.

'I just thought I'd check them all out with Frank before I hand it over to Hamilton. I wish I hadn't now. Bessell *was* drowned in Lake Ontario. Rundstedt *is* what she seems to be, and they've never heard of Dillon or Parrott.'

'So much for the great Canadian conspiracy.'

'I guess so. But I dunno. There's still something screwy. Parrott told me he had worked for the Manitoba Government, and he knew about stuff like Greenwood racetrack. But Gatenby says there's no record of him anywhere.' He shrugged. 'I've run out of things to do, that's for sure.'

'Good,' Annie said. 'Here come Maud and Henry now.'

'You're leaving, I hear,' Salter said to Henry when they were seated in the dining-room.

'On our way tomorrow,' Henry said. 'It's been very nice knowing you, Charlie. You've saved us from a fate worse than death—three weeks in an English hotel in the pouring rain. What about you?'

'Oh yes. We enjoyed ourselves.'

'No, I meant, are you staying here much longer?'

'We are leaving almost immediately for the Lake District,' Annie said.

'In a day or so, anyway,' Salter said.

A bottle of unordered wine appeared on their table. 'What's this?' Henry asked.

'Found it in the stores,' their landlord said, over his shoulder, or rather, to the kitchen doorway. 'Not on inventory. Surplus to requirements. On the house.'

'How nice,' said Maud, who was the first to recover. 'We'll come back here.'

'That's the idea,' the host said to the notice-board.

The next morning Salter asked Churcher for half an hour to talk about an idea he had had. During the night he had worked out a theory which made sense of Gatenby's information, or lack of it.

'I see. I see,' Churcher said. 'So you think this man

Bessell, who died in Italy, then again in Canada, is still
alive?'

'I think he *may* be. If it sounds dumb to you, don't pass
it on.'

'It sounds like a bit of a fairy tale to me. Now, the second
point. You also think he was in the village on the night of
the murder. Calling himself Parrott?'

'I think Parrott *may* be Bessell, yes.'

'And you think Bessell somehow got hold of something
sleazy in Dillon's past and was blackmailing him?'

'Or the opposite. That Dillon knew something about
Bessell's disappearance and was blackmailing *him*.'

Salter watched Churcher trying to hold both possibilities
in his head at once.

'The first is more likely, isn't it?' Churcher said. 'There's
the card from Valdottavo, the entry in the hotel register—
both of them suggest that Bessell approached Dillon. And
Dillon, after all, was a deserter and might have been doing
anything for the last thirty years.'

Salter conceded the point. 'These two guys were together
in Italy,' he resumed. 'They got separated. Only one of
them returned, apparently, but the other one finally turned
up. Whatever was going on probably dated from then. One
of them—Dillon, say—let the other one down, and so long
as the other guy was dead anyway, that was the end of it.
Bessell survived, forgot about his pal, but maybe ran across
him—' Salter stopped. 'Of course,' he said. 'Dillon went
back to Valdottavo two years ago and met his wife in Lucca.
A sentimental journey. If Bessell had the same idea, a
coincidence, but possible, he would have found out about
Dillon, learned about his English address and come after
him. There was a guy asking after Dillon in Valdottavo a
month ago. Bessell. But why wasn't he showing himself?'

Churcher looked cunning. 'Because it wasn't a coincidence, Charles. Somehow he must have found out that this
Dillon who had let him down was still alive and started to

look for him in Valdottavo where he knew he might have visited.'

'Good. Let's not fuck around any more, Charles. Have you found out any more about Dillon?'

'Not much. He was an orphan, apparently. Went into the army as a boy in the Thirties. He might have met up with Bessell in North Africa, before the Italian front opened.'

'Why was he still a private?'

'He went up and down to corporal and back twice, but he was often in trouble. A bit of a maverick, apparently. Commended for resourcefulness several times, twice punished for being absent without leave and lost his stripes both times.'

'In fact just the sort of guy to finagle his way back to England and disappear into the streets rather than go back to the front. Only Bessell knew what really happened up there in Tuscany, and Dillon knew that Bessell wouldn't or couldn't testify that he was still alive.'

'He certainly sounds like a wide boy.'

'A what?'

'What we call his type. It means artful, on the fiddle, sticky-fingered. A kind of Duddy Kravitz.' Churcher looked proudly at Salter, waiting for him to catch the reference.

'I thought the only Canadian the English had ever heard of was Honest Ed,' Salter said, in acknowledgement of Churcher's learning.

'My wife reads a lot,' Churcher said. 'She recommends things to me. I have very little time for reading myself, but I do try and read one new book a month.'

'All right. You haven't found out anything about Dillon after the war?'

'Not as far as I know.'

'And the others, Parrott and Rundstedt—are they known to you?'

'I don't think so.' Churcher looked uncomfortable.

'I'm getting convinced that Parrott *is* Bessell, Charles. He *has* to be.'

'But it's just a wild guess, isn't it?'

'Not so wild. I know that he was pumping people about me. I am pretty sure either he or Dillon went through my clothes and found out I was a copper. It makes sense to me that Parrott and Dillon knew each other. It also makes sense that our Miss Rundstedt is involved. Parrott was her alibi, if she needed one, but no one bothered to notice that she was Parrott's alibi, too. Hamilton wasn't looking at Parrott. Do you know how far Hamilton checked him out?'

'We took a statement from him, of course, just to eliminate Rundstedt. As you know she was—what was your phrase? —shacked up with him on the night Dillon was killed. She has it off with anybody, it seems. A woman like that causes nothing but trouble, don't you think? I mean, according to Mario and Mrs Dillon, Dillon had never so much as looked at another woman since his marriage—certainly not at any of the guests—until she turned up, wiggling her rump at him. Bloody tart.'

'Bloody *Canadian* tart, you mean.' Salter wondered if he should give up on this man. Hadn't he been listening to anything? One more try. 'What I am suggesting, Charles, is that just maybe she wasn't screwing Dillon. She may have been in cahoots with Parrott. Some kind of go-between, known to both Parrott and Dillon. The conversation the Smarmy Boy overheard sounded to me like a long talk about something more serious than screwing.'

'Perhaps. I think I'd better call Superintendent Hamilton now and let him know what you think. I gave him your message about what you'd found out about Bessell.'

So that little trick didn't work. I might as well have told Woodiwiss myself. 'What did he say?' Salter asked.

'He called you a clever-dick and hung up.' Churcher blushed, but he looked slightly pleased, too.

'I'll tell you what,' Salter offered. 'Call him and tell him

I just dropped by to let you know I'd like to talk to him. And that I'll call him myself this afternoon.'

'All right. That makes sense. It's not my case anyway, is it?'

'Good. Now come and have a beer and a sandwich with me.' Salter was eager to keep Churcher away from the telephone.

'I usually eat a sandwich at my desk, Charles, to save time. The wife puts one in my briefcase.' He hauled out a paper-wrapped sandwich and held it up.

The war against crime in Tokesbury Mallett waged ceaselessly on, Salter thought, while the soldiers ate at their posts. 'Eat it tomorrow,' he said. 'This is on me.'

'Good-oh, then. The Swan?'

'No, not the Swan. The Eagle and Child.'

'The old Bird and Baby, eh. Right you are, Charles.'

Salter was glad to see some jauntiness creeping back into Churcher's manner. He would probably survive.

'I think after all I'd better let Superintendent Hamilton know about this idea of yours, Charles, in case there's anything in it,' Churcher said as soon as they were back in the office.

'I guess so. Cover your ass. Things might warm up. Let's just say I walked in and sprang this on you, shall we? Call Hamilton and relay my message.'

Churcher dialled Hamilton and told him what Salter had said. Then he listened for a few moments and put the phone down, looking frightened. 'He wants us both at headquarters immediately,' he said. 'He sounds in a bit of a temper.'

He can't do anything to me, thought Salter.

'Been doing a bit of sleuthing, have you, Salter?' Hamilton asked as soon as they walked into his office. 'Hands across the sea, is it? All right, tell me again what you have deduced. Leave us alone, will you, Churcher? I'm about to give this

man the bollocking of his life. You shouldn't have to watch
it.'

The door closed behind Churcher, and Hamilton nodded
for Salter to tell his tale. Once again Salter reminded himself
that Hamilton could only complain as far as he was concerned, and he told the story of how, while he was in Italy,
he had picked up a thread that wound through Toronto
back to Tokesbury Mallett.

'So what do we conclude then, *Inspector?*' Hamilton's
manner was jeering, but he did not seem very angry.

'I think it's a reasonable surmise that Johnny Bessell
came over here when he disappeared from Toronto, maybe
with some of the money he's accused of taking. He found
out that Dillon, his old wartime chum, was still alive, had
something on him and started blackmailing him. He went
too far and Dillon pulled a knife. There was a fight and
Dillon got killed. So Bessell took off.'

'Where to?'

Salter shrugged. 'You'll find him. Get a description from
Toronto.' Screw you, Bulstrode.

'Good, goo-ood,' Hamilton said. 'So now we know he's a
compatriot of yours. But otherwise we are back where we
came in, looking for the mysterious entry in the hotel register
who we *think* is Johnny Bessell?' Hamilton paused, and
added. 'A man there is no record of having passed through
Tuscany in the past three months, according to the
polizia.'

Salter shrugged. So the English are more awake than I
thought. If you hadn't played your cards so close to your
chest we wouldn't be sitting here now, waltzing round your
office, he thought, forgetting for the moment that he had no
right to know anything. 'You checked the Valdottavo end?'
he asked.

'Of course we bloody checked the sodding Valdottavo
end. Not, I may **say**, by poncing about with the local
peasants, but by calling our friends in Lucca who dug out

the Dillon/Bessell story in a couple of hours. We've been looking for him ever since.'

'When I was in Valdottavo, the locals said nothing about anyone else having inquired,' Salter said, his curiosity overcoming the desire to avoid humiliation.

Hamilton laughed with the sound of a paper bag bursting. 'You should have asked the *polizia* in Lucca. They asked the *carabinieri* in Valdottavo for us. The story's well-known. Mind you, the *polizia* wouldn't have told you anything. They were requested not to talk to Canadian coppers.'

'You knew I was going to Valdottavo?' Salter asked.

'Why else would you suddenly fly orf to Pisa? Not to see the sodding leaning tower. Perhaps just because it was raining in Tokesbury Mallett and it seemed like a good idea at the time?' Hamilton laughed again. He was having a wonderful time.

'Sergeant Woodiwiss,' Salter said, after a few moments. 'He saw me coming out of the travel agency. You've been keeping tabs on me.'

'You raised his curiosity, Salter. And mine. I wondered how far you'd go. And now you've caught up. We'd have heard what you were up to without Woodiwiss, by the way. One of the locals thought you were very suspicious—don't ever retire and go into business for yourself, Salter—and they told the *carabinieri* who phoned me yesterday, to tell me you'd been tiptoeing through the Tuscan hills. So we are back where we started, looking for the mysterious Johnny. Got any suggestions?'

'Not at the moment,' Salter said, feeling a keen sense of kinship with Churcher.

'If you do get any more ideas, let me know, will you? I might be able to save you some trouble. As you know, Johnny Bessell has not been seen around Manor Park lately.'

Salter stared at him. 'When I talked to his brother, he didn't say he had already been questioned by the cops. You people.'

He regretted it immediately. Hamilton bared his teeth. 'He hadn't, then. But when we heard that you had gone to see him, the Ilford boys popped round afterwards to see what you were up to. Thanks for the tip. We knew about Bessell's old home address, of course, but in view of other information in our hands we didn't think there was any point. Until you decided to have a chat with the brother yourself.'

'I didn't tell anyone where I was going,' Salter said.

Hamilton watched him until Salter found the answer to his own question. 'Sergeant Robey?' Salter asked.

'Well done, Salter, well done. Yes, yes. Robey heard you lying your head orf to Sergeant Woodiwiss on Churcher's phone, and he called Woodiwiss back after you left for London. The fact is, old boy, we've been watching you stumble across our screen from the beginning. You haven't done too badly.'

'Thank you,' Salter said. 'You still haven't got Bessell, have you?'

'We will. We will. And now I suggest that you lay orf. All right? We can manage on our own.'

Salter stood up, feeling slightly foolish. A thought, nearly impossible, struck him. 'Churcher,' he said. 'Is he in on your game?'

'No, Salter, he is not, as you say, in on my game, nor is he on yours, I gather. Let's leave him out, shall we? He's got his own problems.'

On that note Salter allowed Churcher to drive him back to the Plough in near silence. There he persuaded the landlady to make him a pot of tea which he took into the residents' lounge, hoping to be left alone.

Hamilton had left him feeling raw, and he had a strong need to score at least a couple of points before the Englishman found Parrott and wrapped it up, or not. Salter ruminated about the actors, or what he was assuming were the actors in the case. Parrott was Bessell and Parrott/Bessell was leaning on Dillon, he was guessing. So what was Rundstedt's role? An observation of Maud's came to mind and he wondered how far Hamilton had checked her out. One last call.

He finished his tea and phoned Gatenby, his assistant in Toronto.

'Frank, I want you to check up on Rundstedt, for me. I know, I know. You already did. She's just a nice lady on holiday. Now push it a bit harder. She may have changed her name in the last two or three years. So try everything you can think of. The passport office, maybe. But find out who she was and everything about her. Call me here when you know something. Tell Orliff what you are doing. Tell him the honour of the Force is at stake.'

The act of asking the question provided the answer and by the time Gatenby phoned back, after dinner, Salter had already guessed.

'Bingo, Charlie,' Gatenby said. 'I found her in the morgue at the *Globe and Mail*. Miss Rundstedt is the former Mrs Bessell. After her husband disappeared she changed back to her single name, to avoid people, I suppose. She appeared at the trial, too, I think. And she went back to work.'

'You didn't tell the English coppers any of this?'

'We didn't know it, did we? I just found all this out.'

'Good. That's it for now, Frank.'

'Oh, Charlie. I told Mr Orliff what you were up to and he said to warn you that Hamilton has probably got you on a bit of string in a glass tank. What does that mean, Charlie?'

'I'm finding out, Frank. But we'll see.' He hung up and dialled the Swan identifying himself as Churcher's assistant. 'Miss Rundstedt?' he asked.

'She left three days ago. I told the inspector already.'

'I know. I just want to get her forwarding address again.'

'Only her Canadian one. Would you like that?'

'No, thanks. All right.'

He had no resources which would help him find Rundstedt, and it was time for him to let Hamilton know about this latest call. First thing in the morning, he promised himself.

He went back to the bar and told Annie the story, or as much of it as she didn't already know.

'OK, Charlie,' she said. 'Phone Hamilton in the morning and let's get going.'

But he had one last problem. 'Mrs Churcher is calling on you in the morning,' he said. 'She wants to invite you to lunch before you go.'

'Oh, for God's sake. Was this your idea?'

'It's either that or dinner. I've put Churcher off three times now. We have a choice.'

'All right. And tomorrow night I want to go to the best restaurant in Stratford and I want front row seats for the play.'

'You're on,' Salter said. She was letting him off lightly, he thought, as he went in search of his host for advice on restaurants.

Before breakfast the next morning he put in a call to Hamilton who was not yet in the office, and left a message to be contacted at the Plough. The call was returned in half an hour.

'I'm in Tokesbury Mallett,' Hamilton said. 'What do you want.'

Salter considered. 'I'll come and talk to you there,' he said. He poked his head into the dining-room. 'I'll be an hour, dear,' he said, and ran off before she could reply.

'Still on the trail, Salter?' Hamilton jeered. 'Always get your man, do you?'

'That's the mounties, sir. They do it on horseback. I just wanted to tell you something I learned about the Rundstedt woman.'

'How did you learn it, Salter, and when? Don't give up easily, do you? I thought I'd told you to fuck orf.'

'I was talking to my sergeant last night about some other problems, and we got chatting about this case. He's been handling your inquiries, you see, and my name has cropped up.'

'Yes. I told Orliff you were buggering about.'

Bloody liar. The first thing you did was check up on a potentially bent copper with a taste for homicide. 'Anyway,' Salter said. 'He remembered something about Rundstedt after you called. Got a memory like an elephant, Gatenby has. It seems she recently changed her name.'

'Oh, really. What was her old name—Toronto Rose?'

'Mrs Bessell.'

Hamilton stuck a finger in his ear and rotated the side of his face while he considered this. 'Mrs Johnny Bessell?'

'Yes. The wife, or widow, of our missing person.'

'So they were operating together? A shake-down team?' Hamilton rotated the side of his head again. 'So Bessell faked his suicide to dodge the music? Later he ran across Dillon, probably picked up the trail in Italy, and together with his wife tried to get some money off him? It would explain why Dillon was in her room, and all the chat that wanker overheard. I've been trying to fit that in.'

'So have I. It fits now.'

'This means Bessell and his wife have been hand in glove all along? From the fake suicide right up to now? Somehow they have stayed in touch?'

'Maybe. They've been in touch lately, anyway, and now Bessell's wartime buddy is dead and some money was to change hands. She's involved, all right.'

'Isn't she, though? We shall have to have words with her.'

'You could trace her through the car rental company, like the American girl. It shouldn't take a couple of days.'

'It'll take an hour. She left here three days ago when her boyfriend left. Not with him, though. She is now in a hotel in Clodbury, about forty miles away. You don't think we waved her bye-bye, do you?' Hamilton smiled and went back to a piece of paper he was scribbling on. 'Let me finish this and we'll be off. If you want to come with me.'

All right, thought Salter. You win. You didn't know she was Mrs Bessell, though, did you?

While he waited for Hamilton, he pondered the possibility that Rundstedt herself was the killer. But she had an alibi, and even apart from the word of Parrott, now much in doubt, the hotel employees had confirmed that she had spent the night with him and been seen about the hotel at roughly the time of the death. Salter had another thought.

'Before we go, let's call in at the Swan,' he said.

'Why?'

'And bring that postcard from Valdottavo with you.'

'Why?'

'I'll tell you on the way. Ready?'

'Righto. Have your fun. The Swan it is.'

At the hotel Salter asked to see the register, and turned back to the entries of a week before.

'You won't find Bessell there, you silly sod,' Hamilton said. 'Churcher may not be bright, but he is efficient. He checked all these hotels when I took the case over.'

Salter ignored him. 'There,' he said. He put the message on the postcard underneath Parrott's name in the hotel register.

'Ah,' Hamilton said. 'It's the same writing all right. Don't lose this register,' he barked at the clerk. 'Put it in the safe. On second thoughts—' he reached over and tore the page out. 'You want a receipt?'

The clerk recovered himself. 'Only for police purposes,' he said.

'I *am* the police, laddie,' Hamilton snarled.

'So I gathered,' the clerk said, pointing to the mangled register. 'Who else?'

In the car on the way to Clodbury, Hamilton mused. 'So

Rundstedt and your pal Parrott are Bessell and Bessell. Blackmailing Dillon? Right?'

'It's not that certain yet. She might have been looking for Bessell herself. She probably knew the Bessell/Dillon story. Maybe she had a grudge against her husband, somehow turned up Dillon, and Dillon told her Bessell had appeared. Or better yet, when Bessell found Dillon, Dillon might have contacted Rundstedt.'

'If, if, if. Why would Dillon make contact with a woman he'd never met? Just to see if she had a grudge against her husband?'

'I don't know, do I? I'm just trying to adapt. This is an English murder. Where I come from we don't get too many of these clever cases. We deal mostly with mad trappers. But maybe Dillon did know her. In Canada. We don't know where he spent the last thirty years.'

'All right now, Salter. Shut up for a minute and let me think.'

A few minutes later, Hamilton pulled up in front of the Clodbury Arms and pointed across the street. 'That's our man, there,' he said contemptuously. A boy in a blond beard and sandals was standing outside a betting shop, reading the *Sporting Life*.

They walked over to him.

'Very clever, Simpson,' Hamilton said. 'Next time you go to the races, though, have a look and see how many of the punters are wearing open-toed sandals. You look like a Jesus freak. Where is she?'

'In the teashop, sir. She went in about twenty minutes ago. Should have finished by now.'

'Right. You know her by sight, Salter? Good. Okay, laddie. We'll take over now. Go and have your morning carrot juice and report back to Sergeant Woodiwiss.'

Five minutes later Rundstedt appeared in the doorway of the teashop, checked the sky for signs of rain and walked down the High Street to the Clodbury Arms. They waited until she was well inside, then followed her in. Hamilton identified himself. 'A little chat, Miss Rundstedt,' he said and steered her into the unopened bar. Salter had a word with the alarmed landlord, and shut the door.

'Now, Miss Rundstedt. Where shall we begin? At the end, I think. Where is Johnny Bessell?'

Rundstedt reacted satisfactorily. Her eyes widened, her face went white, and she started to walk backwards.

'Sit down,' Hamilton ordered. 'You too, Salter. So the name is familiar, is it? Johnny Bessell, your husband. Now, where is he?'

Rundstedt looked from one to the other without saying anything.

'You are Mrs Bessell?' Hamilton pressed her.

She nodded, jerking her head once.

'So where is husband Johnny?'

'He's dead. He drowned in Lake Ontario, two years ago.'

'No, he isn't. He's around here somewhere, calling himself Jeremy Parrott. That right, Salter? Now where?' Hamilton had become terrifying, a schoolmaster in a child's nightmare.

Rundstedt began to tremble, and Hamilton shook her hard. 'Landlord,' he bawled. 'Make some tea. Strong and sweet.'

The cure for everything, thought Salter irrelevantly.

Rundstedt's teeth began to chatter, and Hamilton shook her again. Slowly she recovered herself and when the tea came she drank it greedily.

'Now,' Hamilton resumed.

'I don't know,' she said. 'I don't know where he is.'

'But he's not dead, is he?'

She shook her head and stared at Hamilton. 'No,' she said in a little girl voice.

'Then where is he?'

'I don't have any arrangement with him, I told you. I don't want to see him. I just want him to leave me alone.'

Hamilton sat back in his chair. 'All right, Mrs Bessell. Mind if I call you that? Yes, I know you are Rundstedt now, legally, but my calling your Mrs Bessell means I can think more clearly about what you are up to. All right? Good. Mrs Bessell, tell us, would you, about the amazing series of coincidences that have brought you, your suicidal husband, and his once-dead army mate all to Tokesbury Mallett at the same time. And how, by chance, one of you got killed.'

'I don't know anything about that. Nor does Johnny. He was with me when it happened.'

'So you say. And all the hotel staff confirm that you spent the night in his room when Dillon was killed. Reliving old days, Mrs Bessell?'

Rundstedt was white-faced and beginning to tremble again. 'It's got nothing to do with you, has it?' she said. Then she found some defiance. 'I screw everybody. Haven't you heard?'

Hamilton reversed himself immediately and became avuncular. 'I'm sorry if I offended you,' he said. 'But I do want to know how you and Bessell and Dillon got here. And I don't think you do screw everybody. Nor do I care. Now tell me your story. What are you doing here? Eh?'

To Salter, Hamilton now looked like Wackford Squeers putting on a show for the parents of a new boy, but it seemed to work.

'Someone told me they'd seen Johnny,' she said. 'So I came over.' She was beginning to recover now, her defiance had given her some energy, and she collected herself in her chair and crossed her legs.

'Who?' Hamilton said coaxingly.

She shrugged. 'I don't know. I got a postcard from here. All it said was: "Johnny Bessell is alive and well and living in Tokesbury Mallett." '

'That sounds like a joke. Why did you take it seriously?'

'Because I never thought he was dead,' Rundstedt said immediately. 'I always knew he'd turn up. So I took my holidays and came over here.'

'And he was here? Where did you find him?'

'In the pub. On the first day.'

'And? Go on?'

'He told me he had found Dillon, his army buddy, and he had something on him.'

'What? What did he have on him?'

'I don't know. He said he'd been tracking him down for a long time and now he knew what Dillon had been doing when he was supposed to be dead, and Dillon was going to pay for deserting him during the war.'

'He was going to blackmail him?'

'So he said. And he tried to get me to go along with it.'

'Tried? You didn't go along?'

'No, I didn't. Bloody Johnny Bessell has ruined my life and I wasn't going to play his game. So I just pretended to, that's all.'

'What *did* you do?'

Now that Rundstedt was properly launched, Hamilton stopped his ingratiating pose and returned to the headmaster's role.

'I double-crossed him. I told Dillon everything.'

'While you pretended to go along with your husband?'

'Yes. My idea was that Dillon could pretend to be scared, then he could just as easily blackmail Johnny, who was still wanted by the Toronto police, something he thought Dillon wouldn't know.'

'And what would you get out of it?'

'Nothing. I just wanted to stop Johnny's little game. I planned to leave when Johnny realized that it was no go.'

'You're lying, Mrs Bessell, aren't you? You planned to have Bessell blackmail Dillon, then you would get the money as your price for not exposing Bessell. A dangerous game.'

Rundstedt looked confused at this. Then her eyes widened and she shrugged. 'Suit yourself,' she said. 'I don't want any part of it now, I'll tell you that, Mister.'

'So what went wrong?'

'I don't know. Dillon got killed, didn't he? By that waiter.'

'Now you're lying again, aren't you? Bessell killed Dillon and made you give him an alibi. You knew that, didn't you? Bessell killed Dillon.'

'No, he didn't. He was with me all night. But I got scared so I ran away and came here to wait for my plane. I'm on a charter flight and it doesn't leave until Sunday, so I came here to use up the rest of my holiday.'

'Bessell killed Dillon. You know that. Now, where is Bessell?'

Rundstedt burst into tears, but this time there was no hysteria behind them. 'I don't know,' she wailed. 'I didn't want any more to do with it. I told him to leave me alone.'

Hamilton went over the ground several times, but she would not be budged. All she wanted was to be left alone, she said.

'All right, Mrs Bessell,' Hamilton said suddenly. 'We'll find him. Before you leave, probably, and then we'll see, shall we? Enjoy your holiday.' He stood up and nodded to Salter.

Just like that? thought Salter. Then he remembered Hamilton's favourite technique of leaving people on a leash. He probably has my wife staked out, he thought.

The two policemen moved into the street and Hamilton led the way around the block to a truck which was parked behind the hotel. He opened the back door and motioned Salter in ahead of him. Inside, a young man in overalls sat listening to headphones. Hamilton nodded to him and sat down on a bench on one side, making room for Salter to sit beside him.

'Now,' Hamilton said. 'When was she lying?'

'She was covering for Bessell,' Salter offered. 'She ran away because she knew Bessell had killed Dillon.'

'Right. And the rest of it? This double blackmail rubbish?'

'Two things bother me. Why was Bessell blackmailing Dillon if they were such pals during the war?' He told Hamilton of the friendship between Dillon and Bessell he had learned about in Italy. 'And how did Bessell get her to cooperate with him in the first place.'

'We don't know what went on at the end in Tuscany in 1944, do we? Rundstedt says Dillon betrayed Bessell. We'll have to wait and see. As for the second, Bessell apparently persuaded her that there was money to be made out of Dillon. That was before she saw that she could make some money *and* get her revenge.' As he spoke each name Hamilton paused as if he had to constantly remind himself who he was talking about.

Salter remained doubtful. They were interrupted by the technician. 'Here she is, now sir,' he said. He flicked a switch and they heard the telephone voice of Rundstedt asking to speak to Arnold Burton. A male voice responded, 'Burton here.'

'They've been here,' Mrs Bessell said immediately. 'I told them the story, but I don't think they believed me. About knowing where you are, I mean. They are going to come back, I know it.'

'All right, calm down. Did you stick to the story? Every word?'

'Yes, I did. But they know you did it. If they come back, I'll make a slip, I know I will. I'm scared. I don't want any more to do with it. I'm going away. How did they know where I was?'

'I told you. They're looking for me. That whole village is crawling with coppers. All you have to do is shut up and keep telling them what I told you. They won't find me if you do what I told you. They don't even know who they are looking for. So don't worry.'

'I can't keep it up. If they come back I'll give in, I know I will. I'm going.'

There was a long pause. Then, 'You want me to meet you?'

'Yes, I do. Tell me what to do next. One of those policemen is really terrible. I'm an accessory now. It's not fair. All I wanted was to get my own back.'

'Where are you now?'

'In the hotel.'

'Fucking *hell*. Okay. Meet me by the fence like I told you. Don't say anything more on the phone.'

'When?'

'Leave now. They'll probably follow you, but don't panic. Do it like I told you.' He hung up.

'Well, well, well,' Hamilton said when they were in the street again. 'I thought *some* of it was true, didn't you? Never mind. She shall have bells on her wherever she goes. He was right about that. We'll catch him, sooner or later. I wonder where that fence is? The names are interesting—Bessell, Parrott, Burton, I suppose he changes names every time he moves. That *was* Parrott, I suppose? Your racing pal? The thing is, unless we get him now we might never get him. He's right; we don't know who we're looking for and it would be a hell of a job to track him down.'

'What are you talking about? You're looking for a guy named Johnny Bessell. You've got a description. Christ, you can get a photograph and fingerprints from Toronto. You might have to wait until he turns up at an airport, but you'll get him eventually.'

Hamilton, for the first time in Salter's experience, looked confused. If the idea were not absurd, he might have thought Hamilton was blushing.

'Right, right, right, right,' Hamilton said. 'Right, right. I'm despairing too soon. We'll get him. Let's set the wheels in motion.' He led Salter out of the truck to a car opposite the hotel parking lot where two young men were waiting. He leaned into the driver's window to give him instructions. The driver nodded, and Hamilton took Salter off for a stroll down the high street. 'Let's wait a few minutes, shall we?' he said. 'See if we get instant action.'

Almost immediately Rundstedt came out of the hotel and got into a car parked in the hotel lot. She drove off followed by the police car Hamilton had briefed.

'We'll follow in a few minutes. No rush. Once my men get Bessell in their sights they know what to do. Let's have a drink, shall we?' He pointed to the Clodbury Arms, and the two men walked into the bar where Hamilton ordered beer.

'You seem quiet, Salter,' Hamilton said. 'Thinking clever thoughts, are we?'

Hamilton's moment of embarrassment had exploded a tiny bomb in Salter's brain. Half way through the beer he saw how it had all been done. 'I was thinking I had better phone my wife,' he said. 'Do I have time?'

'Certainly. I think we can give them another ten minutes. There's a phone-box in the lobby.'

'The one you've got bugged?' Salter asked.

Hamilton laughed. 'I've sent that lad home,' he said. 'I have to watch every penny.'

It took Salter very little time to get through to Gatenby in Toronto, who gave him again the story of Bessell's suicide, as well as a full description of the man they were following. Then he phoned Tokesbury Mallett and asked the sergeant to read him some of the details of the pathologist's report. Hamilton, you bastard, he thought. How much of this do you already know? As he put the phone down, Hamilton rapped on the glass and signalled him to come out.

'What's the matter?' Salter asked.

'They've lost her already,' Hamilton snarled.

'How?'

'They are stuck behind a bloody great lorry in Cranstone, ·the next village. The lorry couldn't make the turn and *it's* stuck. She didn't even have to try to shake them. For Christ's sake! Hold on a minute.' He reached into his car and picked up the radio microphone. 'Yes, yes, yes,' he bawled. 'Hamilton here.'

'Suspect disappeared, sir. We have put out a search bulletin.'

'You arseholes,' Hamilton said, and put the microphone back. He turned to Salter. 'She's got a good enough start on them. God Almighty. Now we'll probably have to wait until she comes back and shake it out of her. Oh, those stupid sods. They are supposed to be our best men at this caper.'

Salter was looking through his diary. 'Hold on,' he said. 'While we're waiting, let's take a run into Harcourt Banbury. Not far from here, is it?'

'What for, for Christ's sake? Do some shopping?'

Salter explained. Hamilton listened carefully.

'Give me that diary.'

Salter handed over the racing diary and Hamilton studied it closely for a few moments. 'Right,' he said. 'It's the only steeplechasing meeting she could get to in less than three hours. It's about half an hour away. Worth a try, and a damn sight better than sitting here holding hands with you. We will go and park ourselves by the first fence and see if any plums fall. Hold on.' He spoke into the radio again, giving orders for the men he wanted and what he wanted them to do. 'Well done, Salter,' he said. 'If it works. Got any other bright ideas up your sleeve?'

'Yes,' Salter said. 'But let's do it one step at a time, shall we?'

A good crowd was expected that day, for the card contained a valuable race, the William Hunter Gold Cup Steeplechase, sponsored by the brewery favoured by the Plough. But a good crowd at Harcourt Banbury is no Derby Day and Hamilton's strategy seemed fairly foolproof. Half a dozen men were posted in the area where Salter suggested Rundstedt and Bessell would meet, inside the course by the first fence. At the entrance, two other men were watching the line of cars as they passed on to the course. A green mackintosh was enough identification to spot Rundstedt.

There is only one stand at Harcourt Banbury, but a small building some way past the finishing post, a building which houses a bar and a sandwich counter, has a flat roof where thirty or forty people are allowed to watch the races, and here Hamilton and Salter waited, armed with binoculars that Hamilton had commandeered from the clerk of the course. A dozen other men were posted around the course, all with their glasses trained on Hamilton.

The signal was flashed at fifteen minutes before the first race. Hamilton caught the white glove slowly circling the air. 'She's here,' he said. 'Wait a minute, I'll see if I can spot the car.'

In the distance the line of slowly moving cars broke into two streams; one line peeled off and parked by the turnstiles, the other continued to the gap in the course. 'There she is,' Hamilton said. 'Three cars back from the gate now.'

Salter picked up the car with his glasses as the driver paid the fee for crossing the track, and followed it as it curved out behind the ramshackle refreshment shed in the centre of the field, and reappeared by the first fence. They watched as Rundstedt sat in her car, making no effort to get out and join the crowd. There was no sign of Bessell.

Three races went by, including the big one. The two men on the roof ate cheese rolls and drank something called coffee out of paper cups, amusing themselves with small bets with each other on the early races.

Then Hamilton asked, 'That our man now?'

Salter trained his glasses on Rundstedt who was standing beside her car, talking to the man Salter knew as Parrott.

'That's him,' Salter said.

'Johnny Bessell, here we come,' Hamilton said, tucking his glasses away in one of his giant pockets.

'Not Bessell,' Salter said, still with his glasses on the

couple, feeling like Alec Guinness in Episode Four. 'Cossitt.'

Hamilton fished his glasses out and looked at the pair again. 'Not the laddie you went racing with?' he asked.

'Yes, that's him. But it isn't Johnny Bessell. His name is Cossitt, Michael Cossitt.'

'And who the hell is Michael Cossitt?' Hamilton asked in a friendly tone.

'He is Bessell's former partner in Toronto. He went to jail a couple of years ago. Bessell set him up.'

The loudspeakers announced the runners for the fourth race and Hamilton waited for the noise to stop, then asked, 'Why did Bessell's former partner kill Bessell's wartime chum? You know, don't you? This is Salter's finest hour.'

'He didn't kill Bessell's wartime chum. He killed Bessell. His partner.'

'Bessell. Not Dillon. Bessell.'

'Yes. Check the morgue. You'll find he has an old burn scar on his upper left arm.'

Hamilton nodded. 'Good, good, good,' he said. 'And what caused that?'

'I don't know. But that's how you can identify him.'

'And where is the mysterious Dillon?'

'I don't know. I haven't got that end figured out yet.'

'Good. I'm glad there's something left for me. Let's go.'

They climbed down from the roof and began to make their way towards the gap where they could cross the track and join Rundstedt and her companion on the inside of the course.

'*Will the riders please mount,*' the loudspeakers said, and a ripple of agitation passed through the crowd which now had only five minutes left to place a bet.

Hamilton and Salter crossed the track in the centre of a small group, and paused inside the rail.

'So what we have here is Mrs Bessell and someone called . . . ?' Hamilton resumed.

'Cossitt.'

'Cossitt it is, then. Getting their own back or blackmailing her husband who was living under the name of Dillon? Right? Bloody impersonator. Right?'

'I think so.'

'*Under starter's orders. They're off.*'

Salter was struck again with the casualness with which a steeplechase starts, with none of the excitement of a flat race. The first cavalry charge swept down the hill and jumped the fence in front of Rundstedt and her companion. The announcer kept up a steady quiet commentary as the horses disappeared round the bend into the country to begin the first circuit.

'But you don't know where Dillon is?' Hamilton resumed.

'No.'

'I do. He's in a grave up in the Tuscan hills where he died in 1944.'

'Where did you find this out?' Salter asked, after a very long pause. Bastard, he thought.

'I haven't confirmed it yet, so you can call it a guess. Ask me another.'

'All right. When did *you* know Dillon was Bessell?'

'Oh, *very* early in the game. We compared the pathologist's report with the army records. And Bessell's brother confirmed that he had been scalded as a child by his mother when she was straining some cabbage.'

'And you've been stringing this out, just to have some fun with me?'

'*There is a faller at the ditch.*'

'Don't exaggerate your own importance, old chap. I'd have closed this up a long time ago, but I didn't have Cossitt —didn't know who he was until you just told me. My guess was that he was some thug hired by Mrs B. And I didn't know where he was, so I had to wait for her to lead me to him. I filled in the time by watching you. Let's go.'

'*The horses are coming into the straight to begin the second and final circuit. Filthy Temper is in the lead, followed by Colonial Boy*

and Inside Story in that order. These are followed by . . .' and the
announcer listed the rest of the horses as they appeared at
the head of the stretch.

The ring of plain clothes men had their glasses trained
on Hamilton as he waved and moved along the rail. When
they were within ten yards of the couple, the leading horses
passed them and jumped the fence. Rundstedt looked
around at this point and saw Hamilton and Salter bearing
down, and shouted out in alarm and began to run away
down the rail. Cossitt looked around and saw the ring of
police and started to follow her as the police trotted forward.
Salter broke into a run but he was too late to prevent Cossitt
from ducking under the rail and running across the track in
front of the fence. The crowd screamed as a loose, riderless
horse, enjoying his freedom, jumped the fence in a graceful
arc and smashed into Cossitt with his front feet, then fell
across him, pounding his body into the turf.

The rest of the meeting was abandoned, 'owing to the
unfortunate accident'. Hamilton had taken charge, sending
his men home and helping the first aid attendants to put
Cossitt's body into an ambulance. One or two people in the
crowd smelled something more unusual than an accident,
but the scene quickly dissolved in the English anxiety to
beat the crowd home. Mrs Bessell had been caught and
taken into custody, and Hamilton and Salter went into the
bar, at the superintendent's suggestion, until the rest of the
crowd cleared.

'In some ways a bit messy. In other ways, not,' Hamilton
said. 'It'll save the Queen a few bob for the trial, anyway.'

'What about *her*?' Salter asked.

'I'm not sure yet. An accessory, of course, but she *might*
have been an unwilling one. If she cooperates fully it could
go easily with her. Let's go and have a little chat.' He led
the way to the office of the clerk of the course, where two
uniformed constables were watching Rundstedt in silence.

Hamilton began briskly, explaining to her how much the
police knew, and suggesting that providing the remaining
information would be helpful to her.

She confirmed that Hamilton and Salter were right in the
main, and that the story she had told them in the hotel had
been put together by Cossitt.

'He knew we were after him, did he?'

'Sooner or later. It was his big mistake. He knew you
would get on to Johnny Bessell, and you would soon have
an idea of who to look for. Then he knew that he would
stick out like a sore thumb. Especially to him.' She jerked
her head at Salter.

'*What* was his big mistake?'

'Using Johnny's name, in the register and on the postcard.
He thought it would be clever to soften Johnny up a bit in
advance. Kind of frighten him with his own name.'

'How did he know Bessell was alive, here?'

'We both figured it out. When Michael got out of prison
he came back to me and we worked it out. He knew the
story of Johnny and his pal, Terry Dillon . . .'

'Dillon died in Tuscany. Right?' Hamilton said, looking
at Salter.

'Yeah. Johnny buried him himself. He was his best friend
and Johnny decided to keep faith with him. He kept his tags
and his paybook in a drawer in his desk at home. He never
told the army what had happened because he wanted Terry
to stay in the grave he had put him in. When Michael came
out of jail we spent a lot of time trying to think where Johnny
might have gone. Neither of us believed that stuff about his
drowning. Then, when I told Michael that the tags and the
paybook had gone—they were the only things that *were*
missing—he figured out what Johnny was up to. So he went
to Italy and asked around and found out that someone
called Dillon had turned up alive, and after that it was easy.'

'You didn't tell the police about the tags and paybook?'

'No, I didn't even realize they were gone until Michael

kept questioning me to remember anything that might help us.'

'So you and Cossitt decided to blackmail your husband.'

'Call it what you like, Mister. Johnny screwed me and Michael, didn't he?'

'Why?'

Mrs Bessell blushed. 'Because he caught us. Three years ago.'

'In bed?'

Mrs Bessell shrugged. 'Johnny was the faithful type. He never looked at another woman, he told me, and he couldn't stand people screwing around.'

'So Cossitt sent for you, and you came over and acted as the go-between?'

'Yeah.'

'But Bessell wasn't playing, so Cossitt killed him?'

'I don't know about that. Michael said they got into an argument. Johnny said we could have a thousand pounds to give Michael a start. But if we tried any more he would go to the police, and take the consequences. Even if he went to jail, his wife would wait for him, he said, and she was more important to him now than anything. He would put everything in her name, he said. He said, too, he could still prove that he hadn't taken a penny of the money Michael went to jail for. I think Michael must have threatened him then and Johnny pulled a knife. But Johnny didn't know anything about fighting and Michael had learned a few tricks in prison. Oh, he killed Johnny all right, but I don't think he meant to.'

Hamilton sat back satisfied and raised his eyebrows at Salter.

Salter accepted the unspoken offer, and asked, 'When your husband caught you and Cossitt—three years ago?— did he decide then to do this disappearing act, and leave Cossitt holding the bag?'

'That's right. I didn't know about it then, of course. All

I knew was that the bastard wouldn't sleep with me again,
but he wouldn't leave me. Till death do us part, he said,
whenever I asked him. In the end I just lived with him and
did my own thing. He came over here first, right after he
caught us. For a holiday, he said. But he pretended to be
Dillon seeking an amnesty. Told the authorities he'd been
living underground for thirty-five years and now wanted to
go straight. He got his amnesty, and all the papers to be
Dillon, including a passport.

'He came back to Toronto and spent a year setting
Michael up. Then he disappeared, leaving me nearly broke.
He'd cancelled all his insurance and took out a big mortgage
on the house to put some money into the business, he told
them, but it never went into the business. He left just enough
in his bank to make his suicide story look good. They took
everything to pay the company's creditors.'

'When did he tell you all this?'

'In Boomewood. When he came to my room. He must
have already decided he wasn't going to go along with
Michael, and I said I'd tell the police. But he told me that
if I tried, he had tape-recordings which would prove we'd
been trying to blackmail him. Did you find them?'

Hamilton ignored the question. 'Finished, Salter?' he
asked.

The two men stood up. 'Take her into headquarters and
tell them to wait for me,' Hamilton said to the two policemen. 'You'll find my sergeant waiting downstairs. He'll go
with one of you.'

The two men walked silently out to the parking lot, digesting
Rundstedt's story. 'Shall I drop you at the Plough?' Hamilton asked when they reached the car.

Salter came back into the world of two people on holiday.
He said, 'What's the time? Stop at the nearest phone-box,
will you?'

Hamilton said, 'They'll be having lunch in Toronto now.

Better leave it until you get back to the hotel.' He laughed a short bark.

'I want to phone my wife. She's still on holiday somewhere around here.'

When he returned from the phone-box, he said, 'I have to be in Stratford by six. Can I make it?'

Hamilton considered. 'Just,' he said. 'I'll take you. What's the play?'

'Who cares?' Salter said. 'If it's not *Macbeth* it will be new to me.'

During the drive to Stratford, Hamilton started to snuffle. Salter looked at him in surprise. The superintendent was giggling.

'My game, I think,' Hamilton said.

Salter said, 'Bullshit. You wouldn't have got there today without me.'

'Right,' Hamilton conceded. 'Your point, all right.'

'And I got Rundstedt first, remember.'

'Right again. We'd have got to her soon enough, though. On the evidence of the wanker. It was fairly bloody obvious, except to Churcher, that she was involved somehow. And a short leap from there to wondering about her pal she was shacked up with at the Swan. My only problem was finding him, so I had to put some salt on her tail and wait. You saved us some time on that.'

'And you didn't know that Bessell was Cossitt, did you?'

'I didn't need to, old boy. I knew that Dillon was Bessell. The rest would all have come out in the wash. But I think you did well. Orliff should be proud of you.'

'Considering I was playing with my bare hands against ten guys with over-sized racquets . . .' Salter began.

Hamilton roared with laughter and cut him off. 'Don't get peevish, old chap. Now, where is this restaurant?'

Salter told him. 'You are not out of the woods, yet,' he added. 'If Rundstedt changes her story back to square one, and gives Cossitt an alibi, just to be awkward—what sort of lawyers do they have in Tokesbury Mallett?—you could spend a lot of time on this yet.' It was a dinky little shot but the best Salter could manage.

'We'll see,' Hamilton said. 'We'll see.'

Over dinner he gave Annie the final chapter of the story.

'Nice timing, Charlie,' she said.

'What?'

'Didn't you notice? The sun has come out.'

It was true. When they left the restaurant they walked out into a superb spring evening. Already the benches along the path by the river looked dry enough to sit on. The world had turned into a travelogue again.

That night, as he sorted out his money, Salter came across the winning betting slip for Montague Road which he would not now be able to cash.

'I have one more call to make on our way through the village tomorrow,' he said.

'The police station, I suppose. All right. Make it quick.' She stretched herself comfortably under the covers. 'Now come to bed,' she said.

The next morning the sun was still shining and they hurried to be off.

Salter found Sergeant Robey at the desk.

'Why, thank you very much, sir,' he said, when Salter handed over the betting slip. 'I'll put it in the entertainments fund, shall I? By the way, sir, there was a message for you from Superintendent Hamilton if you called.' He took a slip of paper and began reading. 'We found no tapes but we did find a commando knife in the dead man's car,' he read. 'It looks as though he had plans for Rundstedt. She agrees and is very cooperative.'

Salter laughed. 'Give him a message for me, will you, if he calls back? Tell him I've been picking up a little local

slang here. Tell him I think he's a jammy bastard, would
you?'

'Just in those words, sir?'

'Just like that, Sergeant.'

'Perhaps you'd care to write it yourself, sir,' Robey said.

Salter wrote the message on a piece of paper and watched
the sergeant carefully seal it in an envelope.

'I'll see he gets it, sir. By the way, sir, you do understand?
I was only doing my duty. Something the superintendent is
very keen on.'

'Oh, I understand, Sergeant. Without you, though, I
might have surprised your superintendent. Who knows, I
might even have won.'

'Oh, I don't think so, sir. Not against the superintendent.
He's very good at this game.'

'That was quick,' Annie said.

'I just wanted to give Churcher my regards. By the way,
how was lunch with Mrs Churcher?'

'Fine, Charlie. Just lovely. She's a wonderful cook.
Did Churcher tell you he's thinking of calling on you in
Toronto?'

For the first time since their arrival, Salter forgot where
he was and went round a curve on the right-hand side of
the road. He recovered himself and recrossed the line before
anything appeared in the opposite direction. 'What do you
mean?' he cried. 'Calling on me?'

'He's taking a week's leave, and his wife wants to visit
her mother, so he is thinking of taking a charter flight to
Toronto. I told her you'd be delighted to show him round
and explain your procedures. Hamilton has approved it,
apparently. I said he could stay with us.'

'When?' Salter asked. 'When? When?'

Annie giggled. 'Don't panic, Charlie. As Angus used to
say in kindergarten, "I'm just joking you." Now listen. I've
been looking up some guidebooks. There's a little village at

the end of the Lake District called Cartmel. Wordsworth mentioned the abbey in *The Prelude*. I'd like to see it.'

'Great. Maybe we'll meet the Ancient Mariner.' One place is as good as another so long as the sun is shining and the pubs are open, he thought.

Annie laughed.

'He's probably running in the fifth race,' she said.

'Huh?'

'They have races next Saturday and Monday. We'll just be in time. We can have a look at the abbey in the morning and go to the races in the afternoon.'

'Jesus,' Salter said. 'It sounds perfect. Now find us a Tweedledum to stay at.'